TWILIGHT OF HONOR

Books by Al Dewlen

THE NIGHT OF THE TIGER
THE BONE PICKERS
TWILIGHT OF HONOR

TWILIGHT
OF HONOR

AL DEWLEN

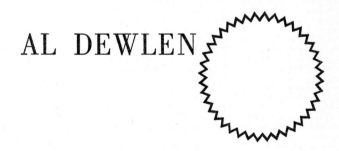

McGRAW-HILL BOOK COMPANY, INC.
New York   *Toronto*   *London*

TWILIGHT OF HONOR

Library of Congress Catalog Card Number: 61-13164

First Edition

16643

Third Printing

This book is for JEAN,
who doesn't suspect that
it's she who makes such
a   tender   world   of   it

PART ONE

I

It was a Wednesday forenoon and, as Jerry (bless her) might have put it, just half-past April. In amazement, Owen Paulk saw that it was spring. Here in the Texas Panhandle, nature knew no protocol; there was never a transition between seasons. One season snapped off, the next clicked on, and the spectacle was breathtaking, like the horticulture films Paulk remembered from Botany II where rosebuds unfurled themselves as if stretching and yawning and coming awake. Yesterday had been barren, cold, ending drearily in a downpour of frosty rain. Now, everything was virile and new. Just sprinkle a little night water over winter's final tantrum and, lo, you had instant spring.

Paulk left the Baldwin Building through a severe marble lobby which would resist for another month before letting itself be purged of stale winter air. Outside, the sequins implanted in a new sidewalk fired pellets of hot light at his eyes, and the suddenly expanded sky seemed to glitter as blindingly. He strolled along Main. At his thigh flopped the raunchy briefcase that, for thirty-odd years, had borne the crucial life or death documents of Old Jack Singer's historic—and, sometimes, histrionic—practice before the criminal courts of Texas. Since descending to Owen Paulk for projection into another era of law, the scuffed old case rarely had contained more than it did at the moment: a yellow legal pad, a few procrastinated Supplements and Pocket Parts waiting to be read, a dozen or so of the cheap ballpoint pens he couldn't refrain from buying, and the bottle of tomato catsup.

As he walked, he appreciated the morning. The sun felt good on his bare, butch-cut head. The small pulsing breeze aroused his sense of fitness. Paulk was, he knew, a bit too youthful for a man of thirty-eight. In the past, this had been a professional handicap. Clients observed his direct brown eyes and decided they were naive; they studied his wide eave of brow and found it boyish, still smooth with unruffled ideals. If they noticed his square jaw and heavy beard, they noted also the razor nick usually present in the cleft of his chin and they deduced that he was an apprentice at everything, even shaving. In several respects, Paulk thought, the appraisal was in error. But he had stopped worrying about it. Since he no longer worked before juries, he had less need to look hoary and ripe.

At Sixth he turned east and was halted by a traffic signal. The midweek milieu of Dollar Day shoppers eddied about him. Abrupt as it was, spring hadn't taken Dollar Day off guard. Specials on swim suits and charcoal braziers and those weird garments categorized as play clothes had appeared in the store windows overnight. The streets ran soft with women: pretty secretaries prowling for bargains on their coffee breaks, country women scurrying to finish before nightfall, city wives touring in pairs and sets and embracing labeled sacks to their stomachs while they smiled and chattered at each other. To Paulk there was something of wonder about them.

Beside him, a young woman said, "Hello."

She was a handsome, fragrant, upswept person he knew he'd never met. She wore mammoth earscrews of the sort once so irresistible to Jerry. He nodded and hurried on into the crossing, realizing the woman had spoken because he had been staring at her. He shook his head at himself. Last spring, too, he had stared at women. But if occasionally he did seem to search a little for Jerry, it was a nonsense he was conscious of, and he could chide himself about it.

He continued along Sixth, calculating as he referred to his watch. It was years since he'd been sent for by Judge Sharman, but he remembered not to be early. The Judge disapproved of impunctuality, just as he disapproved of almost everything. Sharman clucked his tongue over pool halls, liquor, gaming, wayward youth, bad ventilation, lawyers who didn't tip their hats to ladies, and, in the aggregate, all such sins as he could attribute to a lustful and ingracious twentieth-century society. It might have been argued that the old jurist rebuffed life, *per se,* except that he had already helped himself to some eighty years of it. At any rate, Paulk meant to meet him precisely at eleven.

Directly ahead, just a block off Main, was the Bonita County Courthouse. Facing toward Houston Street, it was an eight-story heap of gleaming terra cotta and sticking casement windows. It rose almost dramatically to a white belfrylike shaft that was the jail. Whether by intent or accident, the jail tower seemed to rule all of Civic Square. From masts mounted on the roof flew the flags of Texas and America, and this only intensified the illusion that Bonita County had wished to exalt its dungeon.

On a fore corner of the grounds, like a chunk broken off the main building, stood the one-time public library. The little blockhouse currently sheltered those half-wanted agencies dependent upon the county for office space, and it accommodated a pair of obsolete precinct constables whose existence seemed mythical except at election time, when they mushroomed everywhere as though sprouting up from the earth. North, across Fifth, was the Gothic bulk of the post office and Federal Building. Southward was the refurbished industrial building recently become home to the tax collectors. This, "The Annex," slumped badly, as if the county fiscal worries soon might shove it down into its own basement. East of the courthouse were the imposing buff wings and oriental spires of Shrine Temple and, beside it, the crumbling columns and verandas and ancient birds' nests of the Elks Club. Beyond these lay the huge, added-on-to eyesore that was City Hall.

Paulk liked the west side best. There, along Houston, ran a row of old-fashioned, two-story business buildings. At street level, these were taken up by office-supply stores, secondhand-furniture emporiums, pawnshops, liquor stores disguised as pharmacies, and several greasy-spoon cafés. Above were the walk-up hutches of attorneys, accountants, chiropractors, bondsmen, and those who specialized in fitting trusses or paring corns or administering electric massage.

Jack Singer had avowed that without walking a hundred yards you could try a lawsuit, hock your watch, pick up your mail, have a wart removed, buy a filing cabinet, win a pot at the Elks, eat a bowl of the world's richest chili, get drunk, pay your goddamned taxes, and inveigle the Masons into putting their mystic *it* upon you, all in the course of a day. He claimed he had done so. It was likely he had.

Paulk took a stained sidewalk angling across a dead bermuda lawn from which the sprinkler heads protruded like iron dandelions. Overhanging it were the stark, whitewashed elms populated, as ever, by noisy starlings still audaciously ignoring the aluminum owls posted by the Commissioners Court to frighten them away. He passed two old-age pensioners sitting on a stone bench to sun themselves while watching the comings and goings of the courthouse. At present they gazed at Billy Shepherd.

Shep wedged himself out one of the twin glass doors which, in lieu of any slogan about justice or inalienable rights, had been inscribed, "Air-Conditioned: Please Close the Door," and he advanced on Paulk, hailing and waving.

"Wen, boy! You litigating today?"

"No, are you?"

"I've got a DWI case hanging fire with Judge Grubbs. Right now the jury's out, so I thought I'd grab a bite to eat."

Round, pink-skinned, cherubic; rosy as though from a constant state of joy, The Shepherd made it difficult for you to look at him in the light of his rascally reputation. He had an angelic smile, a tidy effusive cheer. His shimmering silk suit, crisp white shirt, the radiant face, belied all the grime. It was said he scrubbed himself often.

"Good case?" Paulk said.

"I don't get those kind," Shep beamed. "They wrapped me up with a blood test. About all I could do for my pore devil was make the darkness a little more visible." He chuckled. "Hey, have you seen Judge Sharman?"

"Not recently, but I'm heading there now."

Shep lowered his head solicitously. A collar of fat flowed downward until it covered his small bow tie. "Well," he said, "after you've seen the old gent, I reckon you'll want to see me. I'll be in my office this afternoon. Or," his face lifted and brightened, "if you'd care to take lunch with me, I'll wait."

Every day Shep invited people to lunch. No one ever went.

"Do you know what the Judge wants with me?"

"Hell, Wen, I better let him tell you. I just hope you aren't going to get sore at me." He turned away as if not sure his invitation had been declined, then sighed. "Anyhow, I'll be looking for you. And I'll do what I can."

Watching him hustle off, Paulk frowned. He had thought it strange to be summoned by the criminal district judge when, for nearly five years, he had practiced no criminal law. Now the appointment alarmed him. If Billy Shepherd's hand was in a thing, it was wise to presume it tainted. Together with the rest of the Bar, Paulk knew the man as a jackleg of the highest water.

From his shysterish father, Shep had inherited a monopoly on representation of the city's ninety registered prostitutes. He tended the girls like a flock. Through a snug liaison with the police desk, The Shepherd posted bail for his sheep, entered their pleas, paid their vag fines, saw to it they stopped by the Health Department for checkups, made sure none ever lost a night's tricks from having to lay up in jail. When drinking, Shep would disclose that the business netted him fifty thousand a year, not counting the windfall of pandering and narcotics cases which, like fringe benefits, were channeled thereby to his office.

An even less savory fact well known to the Bar was that Shep didn't mind handling divorces for women who lacked the cash for his services. Sometimes before, sometimes after the decree, he would explain his willingness for the fee to be "taken out in trade." Paulk knew other lawyers might dabble in this, but Shep had made it a procedure. In his wake there bobbed up enough complaint to keep his name constantly before the Grievance Committee. Still, he had never really verged on disbarment. Lawyers, not unlike doctors and politicians, are slow to turn on their own. In a recent affidavit, a new divorcée had attested to the immediate settlement of her account in a courthouse broom closet located just outside the Court of Domestic Relations. The Committee's review had concerned itself chiefly with trying to fathom how Shep and a woman as ample as the complainant could have managed each other in such a restricted space.

Paulk climbed the interior stairway to the main-floor rotunda and saw he was two minutes early. He punched an elevator button. As he waited, his premonition increased. Before him, the elevator doors were green; about him was green plaster, a green drinking fountain, green tile. Green was somehow deathly. The night they had called him to the hospital about Jerry, he had seen that the emergency room was green. The color belonged to operating rooms and embalming rooms and the Death House at Huntsville. The courthouse, he thought, might better have been anything else. Tan, purple, even a flaming red.

"Four," he said as the car arrived.

The operator, a spare old man with that pleasantly dilatory look of county security about him, was a stranger. Formerly, in those years when he had been ablaze for an important criminal practice, one successive to Jack Singer's, Paulk could have chatted intimately with every clerk and janitor in the building. But the years of book-lawyering for Kelso, Lemons & Hurst had cloistered him; he'd lost touch. It didn't matter, except that in those earlier times the courthouse, like the law, had been fun.

He cut right off the elevator and went along a terrazzo corridor that clicked and echoed under his heels. The hall appeared to dead-end at the polished door of the courtroom, but did not. Opening off to the right was a low unlit cave which tunnelled back past the court reporter's office and led on to the Judge's chambers. The design inferred that the architect had believed a district judge should arrive and depart in the impartiality of darkness.

Paulk stopped at an oak door over which a small lamp burned, and fastened his coat. He heard the chimes of Main Street Methodist Church starting to ring eleven. Congratulating himself, he rapped lightly on the black lettering which identified James A. Sharman as Judge of the 191st Judicial District of Texas.

II

Judge Sharman's thirty years on the bench had taught the people of Bonita County to think of the law as snowy-haired and durable. Because of him, children grew up with a literal image of justice. To them legal equity was humorless and fussy, confused but sincere. It operated with a Mississippian drowsiness and mint-julep manners, and you would never catch it without its vest. Paulk thought it not a bad analogy.

The Judge was beautiful. He had an erect sprightly body, a dazzling mane of milk-white hair that would never turn yellow at the tips, and a magnificent face that seemed sainted by its lines of anxiety over the whole decaying state of mankind. The deepest trenches were etched downward from the ends of his mouth and, like moats, they appeared to hold in check much of the world's misery. Without them, the Judge might have been only handsome.

Among lawyers there ran a derisive undercurrent about Judge Sharman. If the testimony in a case was routine, he might lean back and doze, else sneak out his copy of *National Geographic* and, holding it beneath the bench, hunch down to devour the pictures. If the proceedings became lurid, the old gentleman couldn't help participating to a degree equaling his chagrin. His courtroom teemed with error, but somehow his record on reversals was not an unfavorable one.

Two years ago, Jack Singer had appealed a conviction solely on his exceptions to the Judge's trial behavior. But the Court of Criminal Appeals had held that Article 707, Code of Criminal Procedure, had not been violated as Singer claimed in his statement of facts. It ruled that "such grimaces, nods, scowls, shakes of the head, sighs and pursings of the lips as may have been perpetrated by the Trial Court cannot be considered to have prejudiced any legal right of the appellant, nor can the said manifestations be regarded as having exerted any undue influence on the jury, nor can such gestures and sounds be presumed to have constituted a commentary by the Court on the weight to be given the evidence or upon the credibility of the witnesses. The judgement is affirmed."

Thus, in a bit of case law the state's highest criminal court had granted the Judge full license to suffer as he would on his own bench. In effect, Sovereign Texas had seen fit to authorize Judge Sharman's personality.

Paulk accepted a chair in front of the Judge's great littered desk. The Judge, in haste and with the acidity of a harried and fruitless morning on his face, began plundering through his docket book. "Let's see, Mr. Paulk, I sent for you, didn't I?"

"Yes sir, for eleven."

Through five years, he thought, nothing about Sharman's office had changed. The sloping, copper-sheeted window sills still glowed from their daily buffing, the yellow oak furniture and woodwork sparkled with wax. The Judge's spare white collars, to be donned at set intervals through the day, lay curled in their usual place atop the bookshelves. A rickety screen still hid the Judge's lavatory, and at the windows were the same limp blue drapes, the ones redyed so often that it was said they had developed an immunity to Rit. Behind the Judge hung the old portraits of Louis Brandeis, Robert E. Lee, and Mrs. Sharman with a United Daughters' badge on her breast. Paulk smiled, remembering how Jerry used to dare him to donate the place a Confederate flag.

The docket pages flicked rapidly, snapping like cardboard.

"Mercy," the Judge muttered, "such slipshod attitudes as some of our elected officials seem to—oh, here we are." He bent his privileged scowl upon a partly filled page. "Cause number twelve-ought-sixty-two," he read, *"the State of Texas versus Raymond Elliot Priest and Patty Sue Priest.* That's the pair that murdered Jess Hutcherson, you know. Terrible thing," he shuddered, "ghastly, and so sad for Mrs. Hutcherson."

"Yes sir." Paulk waited, again preoccupied with the room, disinclined to any small talk about the notorious case which, it seemed, was becoming a conversation piece forever.

"To get right down to it, Mr. Paulk, I should say first that the District Attorney has asked a severance in this case, and I have granted it. The defendant Raymond Elliot Priest is to be tried first. We've called the venire, and the case is set for nine o'clock on Monday, May the eleventh."

Paulk stiffened, suddenly beginning to understand. He stared at the Judge's thin forefinger as it traced its way along the docket notes of proceedings.

"Let's see—the indictment for murder with malice, three counts, was returned February ten by the January-term grand jury. On Monday, April sixth—that would be something like a week ago—this man appeared for arraignment. He presented himself without counsel, and I entered a plea of not guilty for him. I advised him to make every effort, but he insists he hasn't the means to employ an attorney."

"Then, you appointed him someone at that time?"

"Of course," the Judge scowled. "However, that was prior to the motion for severance, and I designated counsel to act for both the defendants. The problem now—"

"Excuse me, sir," Paulk said quickly, "I don't practice criminal law."

"I believe I've seen you in my court."

"Yes sir, but not in the last four or five years."

The Judge was in a mood. "Don't be impatient, young man. It takes time to build a practice."

"That isn't exactly what I meant. Respectfully, I—"

"You mean, I take it, that you would prefer not to represent this man?"

"Well, that too." Priest and his wife, hitchhikers, had killed their benefactor. Mr. Hutcherson, the victim, had been hero, idol, reference point for half of Texas—the only Panhandle personality ever profiled in *The Saturday Evening Post*. The manhunt had been a stampede of shock and energy and passion. If ever a prisoner was ticketed to "ride Old Sparky," as the jailhouse argot put it, Priest was he. "I was trying to say Priest needs the best representation, by someone more experienced than myself, and to explain that I'm with the Kelso firm. As you know, Mr. Kelso restricts us to civil practice. It's his policy to avoid any criminal matter whatsoever."

"Mr. Kelso does not superintend this court."

Paulk tried again. "Sir, since I couldn't work up a defense on just the appointive fee, I think it's important to tell you that I couldn't rely on much help from the firm."

Dryly, "I'm appointing you, not your firm."

The old mirages were stirring, the tiny fists of panic had begun to pound. "But if there's only three weeks before you go to trial, when all I know about this case is what I've seen in the newspapers—"

"Sit down, Mr. Paulk; when you pop up that way, you crane my neck." Sharman's scowl had darkened. It was settled, then—done.

"This being a capital case, you understand, your fee will be twenty-five dollars rather than ten. I should think that can be stretched to cover any filing costs you might have. Secondly, I see no reason why three weeks for preparation isn't enough. The statute says one day is sufficient. . . ."

Paulk dried the palms of his hands; he forced back the recollection of his last criminal defense as it threatened to form against a backdrop that was his last mental picture of Jerry. He stared at the old puritan and yearned to swear. Because cats hate water, there is always someone to chuck them into the pond.

"Before we get on, Mr. Paulk, let me say that I haven't any patience for the attorney who would shirk his turn at serving an indigent offender. In the past I have been too lax with many of you who claim special excuses. Surely you know enough of this case to realize it can do you no harm. Losing it couldn't possibly affect your standing, regardless of the volume of publicity, and I believe you realize that."

Nuts, Paulk thought, and he reviewed his chance conversation with The Shepherd. It wasn't like Shep, knowing so much, to have revealed so little.

"May I ask if anyone suggested my appointment?"

"Someone may have," the Judge sighed. "Offhand, I can't say."

"Could it have been Billy Shepherd?"

"Perhaps." The finicky old eyes glowered up at the clock. "At the arraignment I appointed Mr. Shepherd for both these defendants, naturally. With the severance, he elected to continue with the girl. Otherwise, I assure you, I'd have given you earlier notice."

Involuntarily Paulk smiled. Shep always landed on his feet. Patty Sue Priest had surrendered somewhere in the East, giving a detailed statement of the crime at a moment when the last clues were petering out, and she had directed officers to the arrest of her husband. Then, in astounding eighteen-year-old aplomb, she had claimed the *Evening Tribune*'s $5,000 reward. Although embarrassed and furious, the publishers had been forced to concede her claim was good provided Raymond Priest was convicted. It meant Patty Sue could afford a capable defense of her case; it suggested that, in his way, Shep was slightly marvelous. Tagged for a charity defense, he had maneuvered a bit and emerged with a pretty, moneyed client. One who, if the press insinuations were reliable, might pay off both in cash and in trade.

Paulk said, "Isn't there to be a special prosecutor?"

The Judge nodded. "Mr. Tigart, I'm told."

Ike Tigart, of course. Big, nimble, wise, and truculent—the Hutcherson family could afford the best. Besides, Ike had the super-incentive of a long friendship with Jess Hutcherson. Ike's participation made certain a prosecution that was competent as well as fierce. Thinking upon it, Paulk calmed, perhaps from sudden relief. He'd gotten his fill of winning for the guilty.

"If you've no questions, Mr. Paulk—?"

"I wonder what you'd think of a motion for continuance, to give me a little more time?"

"I'd refuse it. I'm sure you know there's no basis in law for it, not on the ground you've just stated."

"Then, what of a change of venue? Considering all the anger and furore, we couldn't count on getting a jury here." He proposed it in sincerity. The old, long-rested instincts were marching forth. Strange how, at the instant a man became a client, he seemed maligned. You bristled with jealousy for his rights, you even cared whether he was sleeping well. "Sir, in fairness, I think we ought to move this case as far from Bonita County as we can, to some place where Mr. Hutcherson wasn't so well known."

"That won't be necessary. I've ordered a special venire of five hundred people." The Judge still glared at the clock. "Out of that number, we'll get a jury."

"Well—"

Judge Sharman said, "Good day, young man," and brought from beneath his desk the small black lunch pail Mrs. Sharman sent to the courthouse with him each day.

Paulk hesitated at the door, looking back from the dark maw of the corridor. "I should have my copy of the indictment, the jury list—"

"Mr. Shepherd can give them to you."

"Judge, did Mr. Shepherd happen to say if he found any sort of legal defense for my man?"

My man, yet.

The Judge didn't trouble to look up. Paulk left, thinking that even with a drooping jelly sandwich in his hand, James A. Sharman was beautiful.

III

He was out of the building, pausing to adjust to a white noon sun, when his hands began to tremble.

Not so long ago, such an appointment might have enraptured him. Every young lawyer dreams of ascending to fame overnight through victory in one sensational, supposedly indefensible case. Originally, Paulk had been no exception. He had dreamed it once, with Jerry. And for them, he still believed, it had been more than just a youthful longing for the torch of glory.

As far back as high school, he had known he would become a criminal lawyer. Even then, Jerry had wanted it for him. She had almost not married him after graduation, for fear the grocery bill or a baby might worry him out of the University. When she did consent, it was upon condition of his degree in law, come what might. She moved downstate with him, shared his garage room, clerked in the registrar's office to supplement his GI check, and she devised all manner of schemes to make his study of law agreeable.

Jerry had been his reason, the spark. Small, warm-eyed, chronically gay, she could exclaim, "Well, I should smile and kiss a pig!" over almost anything. In those early years she invented endless charades to expostulate his future: the Honorable Owen Paulk, reducing an icy-eyed jury to tears; the fabulous Wen Paulk, bartering off his services in terms of his weight in gold; the same said, distinguished Mr. Paulk, pleading in sophisticated eloquence before a mesmerized Supreme Court. She drove him to his books, crammed him for his exams, kissed him out of his frustrations. Holidays, when other students were dispersing to hometowns, Jerry guided him to the nearest session of court.

Together they sat at the rim of the pit, compiling huge notebooks on tactics and errors, sifting the succinct from the twaddle, locating the chasms that separated law-school law from the more vaporous law of the practitioner. Later, when Jack Singer lent them a basic library for their low-rent cubbyhole above Houston Street, Jerry installed herself as receptionist, bookkeeper, charwoman, and stenographer. At times she authored his petitions; occasionally she wrote one of his briefs. Old Jack also helped.

Declaring his motive was to keep the dust off his books, he refracted them a steady stream of minor thugs. These Jerry sorted out for him. She had an uncanny intuition about clients; at a glance, she could tell which ones to accept, which to send away. Her talent for selective barratry was, as he told her, another proof that she was the damnedest unlicensed lawyer in town. To which, he remembered, Jerry had only smiled and kissed a pig.

When Singer began sending him a few of the lesser murder defenses, he was ready. The fees were small, if paid at all, but he handled them well. Several resulted in suspended sentences, a few resolved in outright acquittals. Most of the clients were Negroes brought in from the Saturday-night knife duels in The Flats. Since Texas juries, when sitting on "just another nigger killing," punish indifferently if they punish at all, Paulk couldn't be sure how good he was. Nevertheless, he began to feel very capable, and he took pains to preserve a decent humility about it.

He was thirty-two when he bought a house and Jerry quit the office. That same year, his first big client wandered in off Houston Street. John Gleason wasn't the ordinary police character. His record retroacted over thirty years of peeled safes and jimmied windows. The District Attorney's office, which happened to be receiving its usual election-year jogging from the press, had promised that this time Gleason would be put away. The case excited Paulk from the start. The charge was armed robbery, the political overtone was considerable. There would be a full courtroom, a significant press. Further, he discovered, the case file was acrawl with investigative errors. Gleason, he decided, was patently guilty but could not be convicted legally.

The trial was short. Paulk blocked a confession as obtained on a promise of leniency, proved up an illegal search and seizure, then argued the doctrine of reasonable doubt, and won. He relished Judge Sharman's stricken expression as the verdict was read; he had, perhaps with a flourish, picked up Gleason's revolver from the reporter's table and passed it back to him with the exhibit tag still dangling from it. That night he talked his throat dry, so that Jerry might share every detail of it. Then, exhausted, he persuaded her to go to Jack Singer's party without him. He was lying on the divan, adding up like a miser all the pretty points of law, the lovely impeachments, when the telephone rang.

The voice belonged to an assistant prosecutor. The District Attorney, it said, wished Mr. Paulk to know that John Gleason had just hijacked a gas station; that the elderly night attendant, a cripple, had been shot to death while resisting.

Paulk wanted to summon Jerry home, but put it off. He needn't let this get him down. Such misfires were bound to occur once or twice in a career. He thought of the resented lay idea that the term "criminal lawyer" meant "criminal *and* lawyer," and he strained to refute it. The statutes, the Canon of Ethics, supported him. These spelled out no excuse for the attorney who rejected a client solely for the reason of guilt; indeed, they underscored the guilty defendant's right to counsel, to due process, to a good run for his money. Didn't process transcend any single injustice, any fluke? One reaffirmed principle, said Jack Singer, outweighed ten thousand tragedies. You accepted a defense, set yourself aside, catered to the law, made a fair fight of it. Only the law acquitted or convicted; thus, only the law might err. "The law itself is mission enough for the lawyer," Singer preached. "The Democratic party and the Community Chest are attending to social welfare, and the Church will pass upon matters of morality and reformation."

Still, he wasn't comforted. In sudden little flashes he saw himself smugly thanking the jury, he saw a faceless invalid lying dead on a greasy floor. He perspired from the dreadful suspicion that the crime might have been conceived to raise the remainder of his fee. Perhaps he had a critical defect in his legal temperament, but the Penal Code had not become his whole conscience. He was pacing, hating his ambition although it belonged as much to Jerry, when the second call came. He could remember little more of that evening.

He had sped to the hospital, wearing a robe and house slippers. A nervous JP, the acting coroner, had beckoned him into the emergency room. "I don't like doing this, Wen," the JP said. He drew back a sheet. "Ain't this your wife?"

Paulk had looked once. "Yes," he had said, "that's Jerry."

The grief, the loneliness, engulfed everything. There were blanks and voids in his understanding of the accident, but in the doldrum years that followed, he made no effort to fill them in. Sometimes, when he could recall that night emotionlessly, the vagueness bothered him. But, whatever the facts, he knew it was ridiculous and unhealthy to imagine that he had forfeited Jerry's life by way of restitution. In logic, the two calls had been linked only by a common date on the calendar. Knowing this, he could be certain he had revised his aims, changed to civil law, strictly because he had wanted to.

Gradually (and even the Bar's skeptical oldheads were noticing it) he was becoming a journeyman at office law. On last count, the *South West Reporter* was carrying fourteen opinions extracted verbatim, or nearly so, from the briefs he had drafted for Kelso, *et al*. He had distilled a great deal of satisfaction from it; there was a calm, scholarly elation in having written some law. Obviously, his life didn't need a Ray Priest.

Just where did old Judge Sharman get off?

IV

On the courthouse steps, under the high Gothic arch that seemed more ecclesiastical than governmental, he hesitated over a cigarette. He considered turning back, making a call on the District Attorney. But Herb Cameron would be out of pocket by now. The courthouse people were flowing from the building, splitting off along the walks toward the Houston Street eateries. Since the organization of Bonita County seventy years before, the courthouse "family," as it called itself, had observed a conjugal lunch hour. At twelve o'clock the offices, except the sheriff's, were closed and locked; law and order were suspended until one-thirty.

Paulk fell in with the flow, angling across the grounds toward the cheap tin sign of the Little Star Café. As he walked, his addlement gave way to recognition of the irony of his position and to a surge of questions. Back in January when they found Jess Hutcherson's body, he had been as shocked as anyone; he had even thought he might welcome one more fling at criminal law if he could have it as the special prosecutor of Hutch's killers. Well—if he had coveted Ike Tigart's place then, he lusted for it now. As for the questions, a horde of them hovered about, half formed, not yet in reach; others hit him point-blank. How did you prepare a murder defense on twenty-five dollars? Was the Judge honestly unaware of his switch to civil practice? Who, really, had advocated his appointment?

In theory, the defense of the destitute was a Bar obligation to be rotated impartially among its members. But it had never worked that way. The prosperous lawyers, the elders, the risen cream, escaped appointment through the press of other cases. In league with the judges, these had made the duty a specie of handout, a crumb to be thrown to the Association's needy.

Among the city's two hundred barristers were scores ready to compete for appointments. Some were barely recuperated from their bar exams, starved for business, seeking the advertisement usually bound up in the capital case. Although they could least afford to work free, these young lawyers were enthusiastic and turned in credible performances. The fault of the system lay elsewhere, in the majority of charity defenses which landed with the opposite segment of the Bar. Mexicans, Negroes, and the other glamorless felons went to trial represented by the senile ex-judges, the night-school lawyers, the pathetic old drunks long since cashed in except for their black string ties and unpawnable diplomas. The "sundown lawyers," as Jack Singer referred to them, would queue up and quarrel over any appointment. To net something from the state's microscopic fee, they had to forego all save an appearance in court on trial day.

There under the bench, planted staunchly beside the defendant, they would shake their heads sadly and pat the poor devil gently on the back and waive away his rights while sentence came crashing down upon him. The horror was compounded, Paulk thought, by such senior attorneys as Kelso who, without saying so, preferred the tottering has-beens to the young. After all, an alert young defender might win too often, might attain a reputation faster than was good for him; he might, by zeal, parlay his appointments into a reputation threatening the nice, existing apportionment of the available practice. The deaf, boozed-up, or inept oldtimer presented no such menace. Further, when the old fellow had cases on the docket, he didn't show up so often to plague his colleagues with hard-luck stories and an extended palm.

That justice discriminates because lawyers do, that the pauper in trouble bears a greater jeopardy, had been among Paulk's earliest disillusionments with the law. Still, this was no explanation for what had happened to him. The Priest appointment was outside the pattern, for he was neither novice nor humbled wash-out and, insofar as he knew, his name was on no one's benevolence list.

He reached the Little Star in time to claim the front booth. That first office, his and Jerry's, had been directly above this grimy tin ceiling. Used to, they would have lunch in this booth so they could keep their eyes on the street, on guard lest a client who had found their door locked should slink away and be lost.

A smudged waitress with dyed red hair, one of those *prima-facie* slatterns who prompt a man to rue every libido of his life, arrived at his table and laid her belly on the edge of it. The jukebox was whanging out a hillbilly lament, one of those bald prairie pieces exactly right to eat chili by.

"Chili," he said, "without beans."

The woman bleated at the kitchen, "Bowl of red, and hold the shrapnel," and she passed on to the courthouse foursomes who were jamming into other dingy stalls.

Paulk unlatched his briefcase and took out the bottle of catsup. The Little Star, like the Lone Wolf Café next door, served devastating chili, but both places diluted their catsup. It was Jerry who had double-dared him to bring his own, had gotten him into the habit. Remembering this, he recalled also her laughter when, during the trial of a burglary case, he had absentmindedly set out his catsup on the counsel table and thus, unintentionally, had awakened a bored summer jury.

He smiled, and glanced about to see if the Little Star had changed. The place had begun as a façade to cover other enterprises. The owner, an Oklahoma ex-con, had hired accidentally an excellent Mexican chef. The cook stayed because it kept him near the jail, from which his sons could wave to him, and his craftsmanship attracted the clientele.

The place would have flourished off the courthouse people alone, despite its shabbiness. It used the front thirty feet of a building five times as long. A cheap partition festooned with beer signs, wrestling posters, and electric fly traps cut off the kitchen from the dining room. On back, there were backrooms behind backrooms. In these the pros gathered periodically to entertain the amateurs at dice. Once in a while, a squad of big-hatted Texas Rangers slipped into town and undertook a raid. But after pounding their way through a catacomb of sturdy doors, they would apprehend only a roomful of smoke.

Jerry had delighted in the raids. She prayed that The Hats would someday rout out a great covey of gamblers. "Then," she said, "you could run down there and pass out your cards and wind up representing every last one of them!"

As Paulk finished his meal, he saw Hollis Anglin steering toward him through the maze of deputy assessors and oilclothed tables. The tall, sandy-blond assistant district attorney always had the look of recent sleep, the manner of one just kicked bodily out of bed. He approached in the slack lazy gait that mirrored a rural boyhood.

"Hello, Wen," he slid into the booth. "Off your beat, aren't you?"

"Some. Nor can you guess why."

Anglin smiled. He had a sulky, full-lipped face capable of sudden, disarming friendliness, and a cool laconic air that seemed to cover a ready silken power. Herb Cameron boasted openly of his brilliant protégé. At twenty-eight, Anglin had a wife, five daughters, and a legal finesse that recently had won a life sentence off Ike Tigart. Herb ought to watch out, Paulk thought. This was an opossuming young lion.

"I heard about it," Anglin broke a toothpick between his hands. "Too bad."

"Your case is that good?"

"A 'savage, malodorous and horrible murder,' just like the newspapers say. So Priest has to burn. But," Anglin shrugged, "that makes it easier for you. All you've got to do is show up, submit a couple of motions, and hold his hand. We'll attend to the rest."

It was offhand, yet meaningful. Anglin was reminding him that the verdict was already in, that the press and public had convicted Ray Priest, that the trial need but formalize it. The prosecutor was asking whether he would be foolish enough to stir up a battle.

"About that severance," Paulk said, "how come? Why not try them together?"

"Because Priest did the killing. Patty Sue didn't even hold his coat. Besides, she's cooperating. Of course, as the guy's wife, she can't testify for us—nor for you, since she's under indictment as a principal—but like I say, she is doing her bit."

"Then you have a good statement from her?"

"A dilly," Anglin said. "I'll send you a copy, right after we sentence him."

They sat a moment in consideration of each other. It seemed to Paulk the prosecutor must grin or fall sullen; he appeared incapable of any pose in between.

"Here," Anglin held out a mashed package, "have a cough drop. Or, have you already had your flu? Mine hangs on, fags me out about this time every day."

"No thanks," Paulk said. "Look; ordinarily, the Judge would appoint two men to defend a case like this. How do you account for my getting it alone?"

"Ask the Judge. But one, two, a dozen—what difference would it make?"

"I can't say right now. I haven't seen Priest. But, surmising it's all as you say, how do you think Herb Cameron might react if I offered to plead him guilty?"

Anglin shook his head. "It would still be the Chair. This one goes whole hog, Wen."

"Does Hutch's widow want it that way?"

"I don't know; she's Ike Tigart's province. But whatever she wants, Ike and Herb and I see it alike. If you don't go for the death penalty in this kind of a case, just when do you? An Okie hobo murders and robs the biggest man in town, runs all over the country trying to get away with it, drags a teen-age girl through the whole mess with him, then admits everything when he's caught." Anglin broke into a quick, half-awake grin. "No right to live, this boy. He has swapped out, poof. The jury ought to kill him, but if they chicken out, what the hell; I'd be glad to do it myself."

"You do that," Paulk said, "and maybe I'll consent to defend you."

Anglin laughed as he got up. "I guess we can be expecting you to visit?"

"I suppose. I'll be the fellow in the sackcloth."

"One thing, Wen. I'm glad you're in, instead of that sonofabitch Shepherd."

Watching him depart, Paulk reflected on how, in the past, he had accused himself of misgivings about Anglin because of a disturbed ego. His vanity could kick up whenever he beheld a younger man he knew to be his professional equal and this, he had thought, accounted for his aversion to Herb's assistant. Now, he decided it was something else. Anglin was always one with whatever prevailed; he seemed connected to popular expediency by a short umbilical cord. Still, what he'd seen in the sleepy eyes was more than this. It was as though Anglin had absorbed triple portions of the community hatred for Ray Priest, had let it become personal.

Paulk restored his catsup to the briefcase, paid his check and set out for the Baldwin Building. Along Main the Dollar Day crush had swollen. He saw again all the silly pretty women who, now, did not divert him. After a wait beside an enormous bas-relief stone carving of an amazed Coronado gazing with upswept arm at the new-found Texas tablelands (a piece that might one day pull down the lobby wall), he took the elevator to the seventh floor. He passed Billy Shepherd's office without an inward look and went on to the sedate, comparatively modest suite of Kelso, Lemons & Hurst.

Mrs. Reddock, the plump dark receptionist, met him. She was a sweet woman, typical of those unhappy females who become enamored with the law or their lawyers during their divorce suits and afterwards make legal secretaries of themselves. Mrs. Reddock yearned, unaggressively, for Terry Hurst. Ten years in the office had taught her that Hurst wasn't the sort to put aside his aging wife. The hopelessness, Paulk thought, had only made Mrs. Reddock sweeter.

She said, "Mr. Kelso will be in shortly, and he says he will want to see you."

"Thanks; I want to see him."

"There's a Mrs. Johnson to see you," she indicated a woman seated in the farthest corner. "She's waited all through the noon hour."

Paulk led the woman into the crowded office that had been made for him out of a storeroom. He switched on the lights—Kelso himself must have turned them off, as he did whenever he found an office not in use—and smiled at his visitor.

She was a massive, unsymmetric person in flat-heeled shoes and grayish cotton hose that sagged in swirls about her legs, and she entered ploddingly on enlarged ankles. He held a chair for her, thinking how obliged he'd be if she could dispel his brooding over the Priest affair.

"How can I help you?"

"Are you a lawyer?" she said. "Looks like you're kindly young, if you don't mind my saying."

"I'll do my best for you."

As she talked, Paulk slipped into conjecture on Ray and Patty Sue Priest. He had seen the newspaper pictures of them both: the pretty doll face of the girl, the blank wide-eyed stare of the man.

"Which," the woman was concluding, "is how come I decided I've done took all I aim to take of it."

"I'm sorry," Paulk said. "Would you mind explaining it again?"

Mrs. Johnson seemed to view his lapse as an indication of thoroughness, and she smiled.

"Well, my husband, although he's my ex-husband when you get right down to it, done just what I said. Soon as our oldest son got kilt— I guess you heard about it, that wreck out on the expressway last winter —well, a month or two after that, my husband upped and married my son's wife. They didn't nobody have to tell me it was nasty, but I said, 'Well, that's between him and her, it's them that's got to put up with each other.' That was before I knowed it was going to cause all the trouble. If people just make fun of them, all right, they got it coming, the way it looks and all. But I ain't going to stand for 'em starting in on me. They say Fred, that's my husband's name, being married now to his own daughter-in-law, makes him the stepdaddy of his own grandchildren, and they've got it all twisted around until they say he's a son-in-law of mine. I've been told up at Sunday School that I ought to call the law about it, get something done before any poor little babies comes along and don't know who they are."

"Did you call the police?"

"Well, what I did, I seen the high sheriff, and he taken it I ought to see a lawyer."

"You do have a divorce from Fred?"

"Yes, sir, I do."

"Is there any property in dispute between you?"

"None I know of. Except he has got a pretty fair old car up there I'd mighty like to have, now that I got my job at the motel. From where I live, it's a far piece to walk."

"Which motel?" he said, feeling he already knew the answer. It was not clairvoyance; rather, there had been so many coincidences in his life, so many things which overlapped, that he had come to anticipate them.

"It's that Ranch Inn, out on 66, where the rich man got murdered a while back."

"Were you working there back in January?"

"No, not when them two hoodlums butchered Mr. Hutcherson, if that's what you mean. The way it was, all the big shots was mad about what happened out there so the manager got fired and everybody else along with him, which is how I got my job myself. I'm the one that scours out the rooms of a morning. That room where it was, right where they first seen the body, I've been in there lots of times."

"About your problem," Paulk said gently, "what remedy do you feel you need?"

"Well, it's a pretty trashy thing, and if they ain't any law against a man doing what Fred done, then a woman don't have any rights anymore."

He took her telephone number, promised to call if he found anything he could do for her. It was after two before he started to Mr. Kelso's office. At Mrs. Reddock's desk he asked, "Does he know about this Priest thing?"

"Yes, sir," she said gravely.

E. C. Kelso had broad access; he knew of every calamity the instant it occurred.

E. C., a big man, did not seem so in the vastness of the carpeted, leather-upholstered chamber which was the principal luxury of his life. He waved for Paulk to close the door.

"Sit down, Wen, put your feet up. Maybe you can help me be less ashamed of what I fear I'm going to say."

He had expected Kelso to be upset. Nevertheless, Paulk was annoyed by the stricken visage, the reproachful way the stubby fingers were spreading apart and pairing off, tip to tip before his chest, in what was designated as E. C.'s alas gesture.

For a time they gazed out the large tapestried window at the city. It was an august view, appropriate to the man who had founded the firm, powered it up to a peak of prestige. He was astute, and he had an integrity rarely found behind a reputation as prim as was his. Twenty years ago he had served in the State Senate, and Paulk suspected it pained him that few persons still addressed him as Senator. Kelso might regret, also, that he once had declined a federal judgeship. But he was not unsettled; his mark was on his era, and he knew it.

"Hutch," he began abruptly, "was a dear friend of mine. I wonder if you knew him?"

"No, sir, except on sight."

"I drew the charter that incorporated him, handled the trusts for his youngsters. I drafted some of his contracts—not all, because he liked to spread his business around among his friends. Hutch and I had our hands in a lot of civic promotions together, and I've used his fishing cabin in Colorado."

Paulk wondered if E. C. expected an apology.

The senior partner cleared his throat. "A terrible blow, his death; a great personal shock to me. Especially at the way it happened. This isn't to say I would dump my forty years with the law to see these murderers drawn and quartered. But, to be fair, I do want to say my friendship with Hutch may have colored the position I'm going to take."

He searched a cigar out of a box, as if no two of them were alike, slipped off the wrapper, and began twisting the cellophane into a rope.

"I called Judge Sharman as soon as I heard." A dour smile crossed his face, the smile the good lawyer can't hold back when he is mentioning the name of a lesser one. "The upshot is, he stands fast. You are going to have to represent this man.

"From here on, then, I'll be thinking of the firm, as you know I must. It occurs to me a number of our clients were close to Hutch and his family. Some put up money for the investigation, the same as I."

"Reward money, you mean."

"No, money to track those people down. There were matters not provided for in the District Attorney's budget. We created a special bank account—but, this isn't the issue.

"I'm trying to say it's undesirable to have the firm name connected with this defense. Understand, I am not pleased to say this. But I honestly believe this would be my position, even if Hutch had not been my friend. You might save this boy's life, and you should try. But to stand a chance, you'll have to fight for one of these riffraff juries, you'll have to offend the best people in Bonita County. God knows what the repercussions will be, no matter how it turns out."

Paulk's face was stinging.

"Right now," Kelso smiled, "you hate my guts. I'm glad you do. Anyway, I have talked it over with Lemons and Hurst. The firm wants to put you on leave, with salary, of course."

Paulk got to his feet, as stunned as he was angry. They'd turned him out. He had no library, no stenographer, not even a phone number.

"When it's over," Kelso said, "come in, and we'll see where we are."

He could as well have said, your job depends on whether you embarrass
us. Paulk watched a cigar ash drop to E. C.'s lap.

"Go ahead, Wen, swear if you like. I feel this is the shoddiest, and
the shrewdest, stunt of my life. I'm very damned sorry, but I think I'm
very damned right."

Paulk strode out across the reception room, and as he passed Mrs.
Reddock he said, "Why the blazes do *you* work here?"—and he banged
the door of his office. He stood at his one window, glaring down on his
own august view, that of the alley, of its utility poles and garbage heaps
and delivery wagons. As he calmed, he purged himself of martyrdom.
Then, if it was fear he felt, he felt it keenly, and it was like revival from
a useless slumber.

V

Three new office buildings had risen downtown since the war. Sheer,
modular, airy, they finished the antiquation of the Baldwin tower. Doctors and lawyers who had begun their practices in the old landmark
looked out at the new aluminum and glass and were packing to
move before the Baldwin stockholders consented to a renovation. Air-
conditioning, plush carpets, mahogany paneling and lowered ceilings
were contrived to supplant the old atmosphere of greasy floorsweep
and naked steampipes. When the trembling and pounding ended, only
the lobby and three office suites remained as before. The latter were
under lease to unappreciated tenants. One was a society bookmaker
fronting as a broker; another, a partnership of osteopaths; the third
was Billy Shepherd.

When Paulk entered, the reception room lay hollow, dead except
for the fresh rose standing in a vase on the deserted desk of the secretary. As he hesitated, a voice from a deeper room cried, "Come on
in, son!"

The inner office overlooked an air shaft. There was a desk interred
in paper and flanked by tables laden with files and *Standard Forms;*
there was a horseshoe of glass-fronted bookcases standing suffocatingly
close to everything. There were chairs, a corrugated leather couch, a
wall of diplomas rippled up by the primitive glue mounting them in

their black frames. A sign read, "A Lawyer's Time Is His Stock In Trade." There was a set of the "see no, hear no, speak no evil" monkeys and, behind them, The Shepherd himself.

"Take a chair, boy!" Shep hastened to a rack and drew on his coat. He plumped back down, panting and radiant. "Did old Sharman give you Ray Priest?"

"You know he did."

Shep opened a drawer, fetched out a bottle and glasses. "Good time for a drink," he said heartily. "Especially while my girl is out of the office. She's got a Baptist soul, that kid. No hootch, no squat, no nothing. Don't know why I keep her around."

Paulk grimaced at the whiskey, wondering if he was ruffled enough to drink it.

"I hope you ain't peeved at me," Shep beamed. "It's a rugged deal."

"For Priest it's worse than that."

Shep inclined his head as if careful not to dislodge a halo. "I hated to pull out on the pore bastard, believe it or not. But, two clients with a conflict of interests—you know how that goes."

"How does it go?" Paulk said. "I'd like to know what has happened between these people, why the girl wants to help them execute her husband."

"Kids her age do queer things, Wen. Once she turned him in, she was committed."

"Did she tell you why she blew the whistle?"

Shep shrugged. "I'm not clear on it, son, that's the truth. I gather Ray treated her pretty rough. Then, when they woke up with this killing between them, they were afraid to stay together and afraid to separate. She ran away from him a good while before she turned him in. She was living scared. Now, of course, she wants to come out of this thing the best she can."

"With the *Tribune*'s reward money."

Shep chuckled. "Half the country is claiming a slice of that. But Patty's got the inside track. They worded the offer, 'for the arrest and conviction of.' She's come through with the arrest. So, if Ray's convicted, we've got it made."

"Which makes you a prosecutor."

"Strange bedfellows, hey?"

Paulk counted up. Shep hiked the State's array to four. Or, more realistically, to five. Sharman would prosecute to one extent or another,

as district judges always do, out of their knowledge that most defendants are guilty.

"Some odds," he said.

"I hate to be lined up with any of them, especially that Anglin. But,
I've got to look out for Patty Sue."

"And, for your fee."

"Oh, hell yes," Shep accepted the dig happily, leaving Paulk uncertain as to whether this untouchable genuinely liked him or was
merely desolate for companionship. "If I've got to have me a mole,
then I want me a nice long hair right in the middle of it."

"Judge Sharman tells me you have Priest's papers."

"Right here, Wen. Let me see, I ain't got much. Here's a copy of the
indictment, the jury list. I've rounded up the newspaper clippings,
and here is the boy's rap sheet—have a look, he's been vagged seventeen times in nine states. Now, these," he waved a few dog-eared sheets
of yellow paper, "these are the notes I made when I talked to the boy,
and to a couple of the witnesses, if you can read them. I guess that's
all of it, since I never really got started. This other stuff here is Patty
Sue's."

"Including her statement?"

The Shepherd grunted. "Well, I do have a statement from her. Not
the original one, though. Krist, I think she's made a dozen. One to the
Baltimore cops, one to the grand jury, two or three for Herb and Hollis
Anglin. All I have is the deposition I took for myself."

Paulk frowned. Why so many statements from Patty Sue? Had
some editing been required, to recast her story into a form satisfactory
to the State?

"I'd hand it over to you, Wen, if I could. But, until things jell, I can't
be flashing Patty's hole card, can I?"

Paulk finished his drink and picked up the sheaf of papers. "What
kind of a man is Ray Priest?"

"I saw him only once. He didn't talk much, didn't impress me as a
guy who would be worth much at helping himself. By the way, here's
a letter that came from his sister today. She lives at Peoria, Illinois.
Priest was at her house when they caught up with him. She says she
can't raise any money, but she means to make it down here for the
trial. She calls him 'Baby.' 'Poor Baby' this, 'poor Baby' that."

"Did you talk to him about any particular defense?"

"Oh, I prodded around a little, but the fact is, I don't think I ever got his attention. It looks to me like he had a few drinks, saw Hutch's money, and that was it."

"You think he had to kill Hutch in order to rob him?"

"No," Shep grasped the bottle in a soft, manicured hand, "but he did. Another little snort?"

"Not me." Paulk was realizing how much he wanted help, sensing how little he was apt to get. "Shep, how would you present this boy?"

"I think I'd just lead him into court, then jump back out of the way. To see what I mean, have a look at that jury list."

Paulk unfolded the onionskin sheets. The first name was that of Stanton Jones, ex-mayor. A few lines down was Thomas Ireland, cattleman, oilman, customer of the late Jess Hutcherson. Venireman Number Thirty was Donald Mikesell, retired chief of police. It was brazen, absurd.

"You always hear about 'blue-ribbon' juries," Shep sighed, "but me, I never expected to see one. Don't ask me how they spun the jury wheel and drew out a Who's Who. Maybe no one except Hutch's buddies paid their poll tax this year. Anyway, there it is."

Paulk spotted names suggesting the Chamber of Commerce, Hutch's horse club, the Fair Association. One of the veniremen, he thought, had been among Hutch's pallbearers. Strewn through were names he did not recognize, these the average people called to lend the list a discreet pretext of normalcy.

A riffraff jury, Kelso had said. Paulk snorted. Somehow it was arranged to deny Ray Priest a jury of his peers, to try him before the local peerage to which Hutcherson himself had belonged. *And wretches hang,* Paulk thought, *that jurymen may dine.*

"No use staring at it," Shep said.

"I'm looking to see if the Widow Hutcherson is on the panel."

"Hey, might be!" Shep's jowls bounced with laughter.

Feeling manipulated, Paulk prepared to leave. The Shepherd rose with him. "Stick around, Wen. By the bye, how did old Kelso take all this?"

Paulk saw no harm in telling him. "I'm off on a sabbatical."

For an instant Shep's eyes glowed, as if this evidence that the mighty were fickle somehow gave him succor from his own ruses and deceits. He said, "What will you do for money?"

"I haven't thought about it."

"I could lend you some."

"No thanks." He felt Shep following him, being clumsy and transparent in his frenzy to prolong the interview.

"If I can help you, son—"

"You could have, by keeping my name away from Sharman."

The Shepherd was scratching his head, peculiarly not smiling. "Hell, it ain't gonna kill you. Hutch and his buddies, they put their pants on like anybody else." Without the aura of chubby mirth, the man seemed to mutate; the soiled cherub became a fat and pallid Buddha, somber yet somehow aghast at himself as if seeing, as did others, that he was a creature of tendrils and secrets.

Paulk said, "I'll mention that to Priest's jury."

"Yes, son, do that. You do exactly that."

Paulk turned, puzzled, questioning. The Shepherd retreated. "So long," he said, and he pushed him out the door.

VI

The preparation of a major criminal defense is an appalling job of work. Before him Paulk saw the long, disappointing talks with an evasive, self-justifying defendant; the wheedling, fruitless interviews with State's witnesses who, without exception, would believe only the prosecutor was entitled to the facts; the exhausting hunt for defense witnesses who, once found, were apt to lie out of the common phobic resolve "not to get mixed up in anything."

He had to commit his client to a specific defense, must worry thereafter that his choice might prove a fatal miscalculation. He must spend his nights with the law, reviewing statutes, digging out authorities. He had to draft his motions, the suspended-sentence application, his request for special charges. He ought to brief his key objections, and there would be subpoenas to get out and a score of filings. He needed to design the State's case just as though he meant to prosecute it, then locate the gaps that might be filled with mitigation and the reasonable doubt. Each State's witness was to be researched with view to cross-examination. Then he must check on five hundred prospective jurors. These you sorted out like peas: this man is theirs, that one is mine, and as for the next one, God only knows. . . .

With it all, a hundred other chores would appear, each urgent and fraught with risk. As he beheld the prospect, Paulk was beset with pessimism. He slowed the car, wishing he could enjoy this first spring night. A low moon flirted with a harem of filmy clouds, and along the parkways the locusts and elms rasped with early crickets. The breeze was languid, cool, scented with damp earth.

He turned on to a southbound boulevard, not quite colliding with the esplanade, and considered how he might have passed the evening if Jack Singer hadn't phoned. Probably, he thought, he'd have bought a six-pack of beer, holed up in his apartment and pored over the clippings of the crime. It would be a way to begin, although he didn't expect to hit upon anything encouraging. Thus far, Shep's miserable little file had yielded only bad news. The indictment was a prime example.

Flawlessly drawn, it charged murder with malice. Since Mrs. Hutcherson had prevailed against an autopsy, the grand jury had voted three separate counts, these varied only as to the alleged mode of the killing. Taken together, they covered all the possibilities. To Paulk, the document was more disheartening for what it did not allege. Absent were counts on the lower grade offenses, the "lesser-includeds" customary in a Texas indictment.

Frequently a murder bill alleged most of the Penal Code. Opening on murder with malice aforethought, it might proceed through counts charging murder without malice, assault with intent to murder, assault with a deadly weapon and continue on down to the misdemeanor offense of aggravated assault. Sometimes negligent homicide, simple assault, or the other Offenses-Against-The-Person could be wrapped in. The Texas juror dearly loved to make his selection from a tempting assortment.

But the Priest jury would be offered no such alternates. Paulk imagined he saw the touch of Hollis Anglin or Ike Tigart, rather than the gentler hand of Herb Cameron, in the document. Herb would never have used an indictment to boast of a perfected case, or to proclaim an all-or-none prosecution.

He had been studying it, together with the star-spangled jury list, when Singer's call came. Despite his mood, the sound of Jack's drawling good humor had delighted him.

"Wen, come out to dinner tonight, hear?"

"Hello, Jack. Oh, man, hello."

"Laura is back in town, eager to scorch us up a meal. I'll mix a drink

—I'm might near an alcoholic by trade, these days—and we'll have us a session."

"Or," Paulk said, "a good cry."

"Suit yourself. How about eight o'clock?"

"Fine." He thought how he had missed these Singers, how badly he needed them. In former years, with Jerry, he had known the Singer house as intimately as his own. Since her death, he had stayed away. Not all the old associations were pleasant. A few times, he and Jerry had fought there. Besides, he'd not been insensible to Jack's crashing disappointment when he broke with criminal law.

The house stood at the end of a turtle-backed brick street in a good, obsolete neighborhood. It was tall, girded with porches, capped by cupolas and lightning rods. Old Jack owned irrigated farms, grassland underlaid with natural gas, a herd of purebred Herefords and a hundred weedy town lots scattered through the poor, dying little villages which dotted the plains. Much of the property had come to him in fees during the Dust Bowl thirties when an attorney would sell his services for anything, even a milk cow or a junked automobile. Singer had never felt obliged to move into one of the gilded new developments reserved for the wealthy. Still, unlike most lawyers, who live well but die penniless, he would leave his daughter an estate.

Paulk parked at the curb, since there was no driveway, and started up the broken sidewalk. Jack Singer was awaiting him on the porch. Bald, gray-browed, pale from his two years as a shut-in since his coronary, the old man looked thinner than Paulk remembered. The left shoulder stood inches higher than the right, the fingers of the left hand had drawn down against the palm and were useless. But the massive spectacles were in place, the eyes alight, the off-center grin exposed the same bad dentures he used to stick out at juries while clowning to expiate a bit of damaging testimony.

"You outlaw!" Jack cried, and embraced him. "Come in, get a drink."

"Don't tell me you're allowed liquor."

"Aw, I'm drinking vicariously. I get someone in, pour for him until he's plastered, then I stagger upstairs to bed."

"Are you sick the morning after?"

"Every time," Singer laughed. "So I don't get up until noon."

Laura Singer met them in the flowered, outdated sitting room. "Wen," she said. She took both his hands. He looked into the quiet gray eyes, the smooth tanned face, and he understood that they reminded each other of Jerry. It seemed a short while since he and Jerry had baby-sat with this girl, since Laura's gawky, solemn little person had been the repository of every tall tale he could manufacture for her. The child seriousness remained, but the prettiness, the hint of grown-up realism, startled him. It was difficult to account for how she had become a woman of twenty-five.

"You're shocked, Wen."

"Yes, you're supposed to be a freckled little brat. How, and where, have you been?"

"Good," she smiled, "and in Mexico, wasting Pop's money. Oh, I'm glad to see you. Since I've been home, the tyrant of this household has done nothing but fret over you. You look grand."

"You too. Didn't I read somewhere, in a list of the ten best-dressed women—?"

"Sure," she laughed, "but I'm a fraud. I did it on two Dollar Day suits and a trench coat. Here, give me your hat, and if you want a drink, you better hop to it. The dinner has run away with me since I burned my finger."

Paulk knew little of her dismaying early marriage. After it ended, Laura had traveled a great deal, darted in and out of colleges, skied and painted, and, when at home, pampered her father. As she vanished, Paulk glanced about the house.

Only the parlor, beyond a set of high French doors, looked different. It had been cleared of its furniture and converted into a library. Singer would never try another lawsuit, but all his books were there. On the floor was a stack of steel-strapped boxes recently arrived from Vernon's and Martindale's, waiting to be unpacked. The old firehorse still subscribed to everything. The law, his lifelong mistress, appeared to have become his hobby.

Singer opened a bar cabinet. He mixed the drink slowly, apportioning ingredients with painstaking care. As he strained out the ice his lips pursed, relaxed, then pursed again. He brought the drink and delivered it up with such an entreaty that Paulk was sorry he hadn't declined.

"You've got the Priest case."

"Yes."

"Wait," Laura called from the dining room. "Don't say a word about it until I can listen."

Through the meal, he talked about it. Singer smiled at Shep's neat escape, tittered over the withdrawal of E. C. Kelso, then grew stern over the top-heavy venire and the unequivocal indictment. Now and then, Paulk thought, they exchanged glances over him. The appointment, the references of these surroundings, depressed him, and if Jack's eyes shadowed, if Laura didn't smile, he couldn't help it. When he had finished, they remained at the antique round table while Laura cleared it. She moved silently, having kicked off her shoes without apology. She brought coffee. They sat over the cups like a family, not bound to conversation until they wanted it.

At last Singer said, "The law presumes this boy's innocence, Wen, no matter who does not."

"The law holds a lot of innocuous presumptions." Paulk meant it. The statutes presumed officeholders did their duty, that every citizen knew his rights, that every man intended the consequences of his act. Law presumed universal sanity; it even presumed every woman to be chaste. But human presumption was something else. "Jack, you know the people on this jury will presume only what they already know, or think they know; that Ray Priest murdered Jess Hutcherson."

"They will, if you let them."

"A robbery killing *is* murder."

"Indeed. But you haven't yet heard from Priest. Why not put off any opinion until you do?"

"He'll tell me he was drunk, and when I show him that is no excuse, he will say 'everything went black'—he's been in jail long enough to have learned that one."

"If that's all you get," Singer said, "use it. I've won on less. The point is, make sure you don't go in there with no legal position at all. Don't take your man to trial hoping for error or relying on oratory. Mercy does not droppeth as the gentle rain, not at the courthouse. And, if you'll forgive me, I'd like to see you feel some real pity for this boy."

"Do you?"

"I don't know. I loved Hutch. Still, these Priests are little people, the kind that get trod upon."

Laura said, "Dad, take your pill."

They watched him swallow the tablet that had lain beside his plate through dinner. "Strychnine," Laura's lips confided.

"Wen, nobody would jump for joy over this appointment. But with you, I think, it's not just the nature of the case." He shrugged off Laura's warning frown. "Why shouldn't we talk about it? I know what happened *when* you quit criminal practice, but not *why* you quit. Were you demanding that the law function as precisely as mathematics, when, as yet, it's less perfect than philosophy? Were you thinking you ought to have prejudged that Gleason fellow, the way you're prejudging this Priest? Man, settle on an attitude!"

It was blunt, hurried. Perhaps, Paulk thought, Old Jack had entered upon his dotage, was saying more than he intended.

"In my time, I've known every variety of lawyer. Billy Shepherd's kind, after the dollar, but never fastidious in the name of honor, so that I can almost respect him. Anglin's sort, climbing by the shortest route. And worse, the fools who want to delude themselves that all their clients are innocent, who think they wear a cross on their breasts, who are surprised and beaten in court because it's impossible for them to go there prepared.

"I've seen a few legal anarchists, rigging testimony, suppressing facts, subordinating perjury and calling it defense. They've boned up on heredity and environment and neurosis, convinced themselves that no man is accountable, that punishment is only a second crime because there is no guilt. They say, rescue the unjust man from the unjust law by any means, and if it poisons justice, what does it matter since the law is stupid and archaic.

"Then, thank God, there's the real lawyer. His religion is due process. He won't lose sleep over the guilty who may go at large because of him; instead, he is grateful for having helped keep the law's fallibilities banked up on the side of redeemable error, and he'll go on wrapping his man in every protection the statutes afford. This is the sort of lawyer the poor devils like Ray Priest ought to have."

"You would do," Paulk smiled.

"Truth is, it seems I wouldn't."

"I beg your pardon?"

Laura said, "He's been bursting to tell you he offered to represent Priest."

"You're kidding."

Singer ducked, grinning meekly. "I phoned around, dropped a few hints while Laura wasn't riding shotgun on me. Finally I called Jimmy Sharman. No soap, he said; he wouldn't care to imperil my health. He also pointed out the mess they'd have if I happened to fold during the trial."

Paulk shook his head. It troubled him. Another oddity? Or was this one more piece of an expert pattern, a well-wrought collusion? Ray Priest might have had the most successful of defenders, and probably didn't even know it.

He said, "While talking to the Judge, did you happen to mention my name?"

Singer laughed and got to his feet. "You'll have to excuse me, it's time I got busy on my alcoholic dreams. Wen, if you'll let me smell your breath once more—"

They walked with him to the stairs. Jack paused, head bent, arms folded across his back. Paulk recognized it as the posture the old man often had affected to mock opposing lawyers he regarded as overly dramatic.

"As I recall, Wen, you never did approve of our quaint way of trying the deceased in a murder case."

Paulk waited. The method was becoming almost standard. You forced the victim's reputation into issue. Then you tried to show that the deceased had deserved killing. Finally, if you could, you showed he deserved it at the hands of the defendant. Since Singer's retirement, Ike Tigart had risen as the reigning master of the technique. Only recently, in defending a father who had beaten his five-year-old son to death, Ike had put on testimony proving that the child was unruly, not housebroken to the degree normal for his years, and might once have inflicted a deliberate injury upon himself. Although none of the jurors had ever seen or heard of a five-year-old masochist, they convicted the dead baby and the killer was discharged.

"It's not fun," Jack said, "but in some cases, it's the only approach. I'm thinking, really, about that peculiar jury. If I were going before a jury of Hutch's peers, then I'd hope it was Hutch I was trying."

"You hardly sound like Hutch's friend."

"You're right," Singer yawned, "but I was. Well, good night. Thanks for coming; I've had a ball."

They watched his cautious ascent of the stars. A door closed and Laura said, "More coffee?"

"I must go, get started on my homework." At the front door, a museum piece framed by an arched transom and side windows of stained glass, he asked her, "Why did Jack want this case?"

"Oh, he claims to have a hunch about it, but probably doesn't. It's big, that's all, and he can't bear being left out."

"The work could have killed him."

"Yes," she said. "He knows that."

He complimented her on the dinner, touched her hand, and went out into bright moonlight. He had entered his car when she came running after him, skirt blazing back, her shoeless feet silent on the walk. For an instant, she seemed a fantasy.

"We forgot something. You'll need a place to work, and Dad says you must use our library. It would please him, Wen. And me, too. Maybe I can help. I can type, and there's a dictaphone left over from the office."

"Thank you. But, until I get organized—"

"Then take the parlor without me."

"I didn't mean that."

"I know," she said. "May I sit with you, long enough for a cigarette?"

"Sure." He got out, held the door while she slid across under the wheel. She shuddered from the late chill, drew her feet beneath her. He lit her cigarette and sat gazing ahead through the windshield. For a moment he resented her for how her presence prompted his memories of Jerry.

"I feel like a heel when I smoke around Dad. He misses smoking more than anything."

"He's missed you, I imagine."

"This time I'm home to stay. Or at least, I want to be." She smiled. "It's a stage, not an illness. I'm not lost without my husband. But not being married—yes, that does lose me a little."

"I thought it had been years—"

"Which makes hardly any difference; you must know that. Hasn't it been five years, since Jerry?"

He nodded curtly. His sudden expulsion from the world of wills and leases and torts seemed to keep on propelling him backwards toward musty, forgotten things.

"Forgive us, Wen. Dad rails at you about the law, and I—well, this evening was so much like old times, I get reminiscent and pick at you, too. We Singers pry, and we've never learned to be subtle."

"Seems to me I got acquainted with your straightforwardness when you were about twelve years old."

"No," she laughed, "thirteen, if you're thinking of the day I insisted you leave Jerry and elope with me."

"Anyway, you confronted her with it."

"Oh, I did, didn't I? I was feeling like Lana Turner, and Jerry was Joan Crawford. I remember she swatted me on the rear and said, 'Sic 'em, honey, you'll go far.' Then, when you had finished with me, I was ready for a convent."

"Was it that critical?"

"Perhaps. But nothing ever is as you remember it." She crushed out her cigarette. "Whatever, I'm not very predatory anymore. You'd be safe in our parlor."

"All right," he smiled, "I'll use it."

She left the car. He watched her into the house, then drove home through streets idle except for prowling dogs and lonely-looking sweeping machines. As he parked on the circle in front of the apartments, he heard a stereo party at full spasm in the rooms below his. He supposed he had been invited, and had let it slip his mind. He switched off the headlamps and sat, tired but unsleepy, in an inventory of this astounding day.

He thought of Shep's parting remark, which he supposed he was to regard as cryptically significant; of the Judge's sandwich, of Kelso, of Jack Singer soliciting this case, of Laura looking so serious while she feigned to be gay. He constructed a tentative likeness of Ray Priest and wondered if the man was lying awake in the dismal gaminess of a jail bed; if, just now, he was anticipating how it would feel when they put the hood over his head.

Mixed with his thoughts was the ABA Canon of Defense. "It is the right of the lawyer to undertake the defense of a person accused of crime, regardless of his personal opinion as to the guilt of the accused . . . having undertaken such defense, the lawyer is bound by all fair and honorable means to present every defense that the law of the land permits, to the end that no person may be deprived of life or liberty but by due process of law."

Old Jack, he decided wryly, would have written it no differently.

He locked the car and went upstairs to Shep's clippings.

VII

The capital of the Panhandle is a temporization; old, new, and preposterous for having occurred on a flat dry land intended for little more than the wailing drag races of the winds. Mostly, Paulk excused the adolescence, the precociousness, and dissonance of his town. But on certain days it exasperated him.

Begun as a tent town for hide hunters, the city had been fizzling out with the buffalo when the railroads and English capital arrived. It burgeoned into a cow town, the heart of a short-grass civilization which soon underwent a series of swift, jarring modifications. Wheat came, followed by broad territorial wholesaling. Ultimately there came the oil and gas strikes which established that this was, after all, God's country. The wealth was sudden, and so great it was boasted of even by those who failed to share in it. Along with pride, the money ignited haste and compression. The boom caught Bonita County short on history and without an aristocracy, so that by general consent, the right to rule was handed over to the new rich. To cover the rural roots, the freshman lords bought up sophistication by the gobs, and before long the Panhandle Texan could hold up his head in Dallas.

The resulting incongruity became spectacular. On Main the Brooks Bros. suit wore well with the ten-gallon hat. The denimed old cowboy pushing along Fourth, hunting one of The Shepherd's flock, ready to stand her to a belt of Hot Lucy, might be equipped with contact lenses and a hearing aid. Van Cliburn at the concert hall and Jim Shoulders at the rodeo arena played to the same people and rated equal press notice. Oilmen who had quit education upon learning to write sent their children East to the fancy boarding schools.

At the symphony the drowsy gentleman in white tie and tails might lean back and prop his foot on the rail of his box and startle no one with his boots or the trace of manure on the heel. Later he might drive his minked wife out to a country club built by Frank Lloyd Wright but encircled by a barbed-wire fence on the posts of which hung the head-down carcasses of cyanided coyotes, strung up by their hindfeet.

Paulk enjoyed the exterior contradictions. But the deeper ones disturbed him, seemed to limit him personally. In politics, for instance, nobody could find clear lines. The rancher was likewise the oilman; the banker was also the farmer. At home in the country, such men were socialist Democrats. But in their downtown offices, they became capitalist and Republican.

Last year Mr. Kelso, while urging Paulk to run for Congress, had explained these matters as consistent for being so reliably inconsistent.

Praise be, E. C. said, that in the Panhandle there lived a breed of men not identifiable by any phrase or statistic.

Such a man was Jess Hutcherson.

Whether the country had produced Hutch, or whether Hutch had produced the country as a suitable background for himself, could have been argued. He grew up a lusty, reckless ranch boy unintimidated by sandstorms or blizzards and miffed because the time of rustlers and Indians had passed. His "roisterous, unfettered spirit," as it was described in his eulogy, expressed itself through an affection for danger.

Years before the Panhandle's own oil strike, Hutch was shooting wells and fighting fires in the East Texas fields. With canisters of TNT, which he handled as casually as milk buckets, he blew in new wells or snuffed out burning ones and rumbled with joy while doing it. He would fly to Venezuela, Arabia, or wherever, to take on a fire that had stymied others and between calls, he wildcatted, traded leases, manufactured explosives, ran cattle in four states and Brazil. He married a serene, cultured schoolmarm and they reared brilliant children. But wealth, fame, and Martha caused no change in Hutch. He loved explosives.

On his fifty-ninth birthday Hutch flew in from Iran with his eyebrows singed off and an arm patched with fresh skin grafts, and, doubling with laughter, he told how those kimono-wearing *A*-rabs didn't know beans about oil fires but sure knew about being polite, as shown by the huge diamond that the head man, the Big Cloak himself, had sent along as a courtesy gift to Mrs. Hutcherson.

Heavy, bowlegged, ruddy faced, and uncombed, Hutch dressed in boots, fancy western shirts, a greasy Stetson, and those tan, flap-pocketed trousers generally seen on the drugstore cowboy. He rarely carried less than three thousand dollars, this stuffed here and there on his person. He would hail you down, propose a pointless wager, offer you either side of it, and bet you any amount you could stand. If you were broke, he might give you the money to call him. You could borrow his watch, his bird dogs, his employes or his favorite car, a black Cadillac with steer horns mounted on the front.

In Bonita County, Hutch's name meant something. Once it was attached to a project, success was certain. People rallied to him. It seemed they saw in him the imagination, the forthrightness they did not dare for themselves. He built a hospital, rebuilt his wife's church.

In charity drives he browbeat the other rich when he thought they needed it and they fell, whipped, into line. During the black dusters of the thirties, Hutch spent a fortune sending up balloons loaded with nitro to explode the clouds into rain. He moved a lake with dynamite so that a highway might go through. Another time, to revive a collapsing automobile show, he sold tickets on the promise he would wreck a car without touching it. He rigged a Reo Flying Cloud with small charges. Then, by pressing buttons, he dismantled the car piece by piece, laying the parts out neatly, as if for a diagram.

People expected a unique death for Jess Hutcherson. He would die saving a roughneck's life, or trapped in gas flames; he might even miscalculate a bottle of nitro someday. This scarcely prepared them for what did happen.

It was January 14, 1959, a sunny Wednesday. Hutch was driving home alone, tired from three days of field work in New Mexico, when he picked up the hitchhikers. One was a man who left no clear impression on anyone, the other an eye-arresting girl later described on the wanted posters as "vivacious." The three of them were seen first at a crossroads bar a quarter-mile short of the Texas state line. The bar operator, a quarter-horse fancier who had aspired for years to trade Hutch out of one of his sleek appaloosa mares, served them. The young people ordered beer, Hutch took his usual whiskey sour.

As they drank, the bar owner recalled, they talked intently in tones below his hearing. Soon the girl left their booth to play the rock and roll tunes on the jukebox. Eating peanuts, swirling a full skirt, she danced through four or five records. The host, named Browning, and his patrons watched her. They remembered that she had long jouncing brown hair; that she kept time to the music with her lips, making a rhythmic sound "sort of like a bunch of little kisses." Later, when the young man called her back to her seat, she appeared to pout, and she pulled the petals off a flower decorating the table.

When they were ready to leave, they ordered a fifth of Seagram's, a package of beer, and more peanuts. Hutch paid the bill. Said Browning, "He just flopped a big wad on the bar and told me, 'Take out what you want, Brownie, so long as you leave me a couple of bucks to get home on.'" There may have been a thousand dollars in the roll, Brownie estimated. Maybe more.

The party next appeared at a ramshackle gas station beside a grain elevator, some fifty miles from the Bonita County line. Two boys tending the station remembered the Cadillac for its steer horns, and one of them recognized Mr. Hutcherson. A young man was driving, they said. Hutch rode on the right side, and between them sat a good-looking girl, who was laughing.

The boys filled the gas tank, washed the windshield, checked the tires. They did not raise the hood because the motor was running. Hutch, as he passed out his credit card, explained that something was amiss with the car. If it was shut off, he said, it might not start again. He tipped them, inquired as to the depth of the moisture from the winter snows and when the new wheat might be fit for grazing. The stop must have come about supper time, the boys agreed; they had seen the big sedan's lights come on as it dug out, "pretty hot," from the driveway.

The next morning a maid named Rose tapped on the door of Cabin 4 at the Ranch Inn Motel. Hearing no response, she used her passkey. Rose deposited her armload of linens on the front-room bed. Carrying fresh towels, she started back through the hall to the bathroom. The door of the rear bedroom stood open. She glimpsed someone in bed, head covered, only a bare foot exposed. Then she saw the blood. Still hugging the towels to her breast, she dashed out to the office.

Officially, Hutch's body was discovered at 8:47 A.M. Five minutes later Andy Grosscup, the giant hawk-nosed sheriff who was beginning his twelfth day in office, sped into the drive in a dead heat with a car of city detectives.

Andy Grosscup had sold fire and casualty insurance until drafted for sheriff because he looked like one. Andy wore great white hats, an engraved belt with a steer's head buckle, and expensive shop-made boots. He stood six-feet-six. He had to stoop as he strode into the cabin. He jerked back the bedspread and, instantly sick, went stilting off to the bathroom. When he returned, gray and reeling, the police detectives told him there wasn't a doubt of it, this was Jess Hutcherson.

The sheriff raised the bedspread again. "Oh, my God," he groaned, "this is awful! I've knowed Hutch all my life!" As if stricken blind, the sheriff stamped about the room, banging into the furniture, saying over and over, "Poor Martha," and vowing he'd see that somebody paid.

By nine, the Ranch Inn was overrun. Shaggy, mad-eyed newspapermen raced in. Business neighbors came in a flood from along tourist row. An ambulance, then more screaming police and sheriffs' cars, shot in through the arched gateway. Hutch's friends began to arrive in a procession of luxurious automobiles. They shook their heads at each other. It wasn't so, it couldn't be Hutch. They wedged inside to see, then emerged, pale and incredulous. Members of the Bonita County Posse, Incorporated, assembled around the door.

The Posse was Hutch's, he had founded it for wealthy men who enjoyed stag society and still admired good horseflesh. Behind a splendid adobe clubhouse the Posse kept a stable of palomino quarter horses. The club sponsored an annual rodeo; it mounted up and bore "the flags of all nations" during the Grand Entry. For the Fourth of July and the Fair opening, Possemen donned gold satin shirts, forked their inlaid silver saddles, and rode their fat blond horses four abreast down Main Street. On occasion the Posse had mounted up to aid in the search for a child lost in state park. Once a year, in what was named The Trail Drive, the Possemen undertook a week's ride along the river breaks, living out of a chuck wagon and sleeping on the ground. If the outing chaffed and sunburned and sometimes prostrated them, it did jolt off an inch or two of paunch. Now, with Hutch's dead stare branded on their minds, they milled and swore and talked of gassing up their Imperials and giving pursuit.

"No," Sheriff Grosscup shook his head. "Right now, they ain't much to be done."

Hutch's body was unclothed. It lay at an angle. His blood had spurted out through two deep holes bludgeoned through his skull. The blood had soaked through the mattress, it spattered the wall, dried in the lines of his face; it had saturated his western shirt, which was tied in a granny knot around his neck. His broken denture was under his back. His trousers hung over a chair back, his watch was ticking on the dresser. His money and the Cadillac were missing.

As policemen tried to shoo influential people from the cabin, Sheriff Grosscup stood at the door greeting latecomers, directing them back to see for themselves. A Ranger arrived, demanding to know why no pick-up order had been broadcast on Hutch's car. Before responsibility could be placed and the alert put on the air, it was almost noon, and the *Tribune*'s extra edition was being hawked outside.

Ranger Captain A. B. C. Smith, suddenly tired of tugging at Andy Grosscup's sleeve, grabbed a prominent department-store president and heaved him outside. He locked the door, excluding even the Posse's guide-on riders. The officers began to think.

There had been little struggle, if any. A whiskey bottle was on the floor, but the two water tumblers with traces of drinks still in them had not fallen from the bedstand. (As Sheriff Grosscup hastened to point out to the reporters, the glassware indicated only light drinking; Hutch wasn't a man to get off on bouts with the stuff.) A Lucky Strike package had been found on the floor, along with a man's handkerchief monogrammed *TR*. The Ranger discovered beads of bloody water in the lavatory bowl. He disconnected the drain trap and bottled a sample of its contents. Also in the bathroom, detectives picked up a pair of bloody trousers. Brown tweeds, size thirty-two, they bore a distinct cleaner's mark inside the waistband. It identified the killer as a K. F. Stanfield.

The motel manager brought in the registration card. The girl, he said, had filled it out: R. E. Priest, Chicago, Illinois. Of course, bandits preparing to do murder wouldn't have signed their correct name. Still, the handwriting sample might prove useful, later, as an item of corroboration.

Fingerprints lifted nicely. While the ID men worked, the key officers gathered in the front bedroom to brainstorm the crime. They compounded a theory. When the meeting broke up, Sheriff Grosscup summarized it for the press.

"Hutch gave a lift to a K. F. Stanfield and his girlfriend. They decided to rob him, or maybe to get him into a place where they could roll him. Now, a man built like Hutch wasn't overpowered by a guy who wears size thirty-two pants, so we figure the killers got him into the cabin on some cock-and-bull story. Or, they might have doped him; we're checking on that. Anyway, when they got him inside, they beat and strangled and robbed him—I reckon they taken him by surprise.

"This Stanfield got blood on hisself. So he washed up in the bathroom and left his bloody pants there. Then they covered Hutch's body, got in the car and took off. Since we ain't found any murder weapon, we figure they carried it off with them. From the wounds it made, sort of three-cornered punctures, we think it might have been a piece of angle iron. Myself, I got a hunch it was one of those war-surplus trench knives, the kind that has them three-sided teeth on the hand guard. It don't matter, they left us enough to go on. I reckon I can say we'll have them in custody in about forty-eight hours."

They held Hutch's funeral on a windy, frozen afternoon. The Main Street Church was jammed. Hundreds more stood mute and bare-headed and shivering outside. Straight, tall Martha Hutcherson arrived with her sons, one a Marine Corps major, the other a Shell Oil executive, and her young daughter, Valle, the baby, the child of Hutch's middle age. The widow held her head high; for her, there was no impropriety in disdaining a veil. She was a lady, and looked it; people remarked that she had looked it even back in the early days when she drew on coveralls, and hauled nitroglycerine out to her husband.

The service ran long. Policemen stood at either end of the casket, for Hutch had put through the department pension plan. Along the church walk, a guard from Hutch's squadron in the Posse was posted at parade rest. The eulogy was elaborate. Letters praising Hutch's valor, candor, and kindness had been received from throughout the state, and the pastor sought to include excerpts from them all. At last, at the cemetery, the Masons assumed control. Hutch was buried as a potentate.

The same day a woman at El Reno, Oklahoma, informed police that a black car with horns on the front had been standing in sight of her home for two days with no one coming near it. Patrolmen found Hutch's wallet on the floor. In the rear seat was his luggage, a pair of hand-tooled boots bearing his initials, and a bundle of laundry tied up in a shirt. Since the keys were missing, the officers pried open the trunk. There they discovered Hutch's silver-skirted saddle, his gold-inlaid bridle, a case of dynamite caps, the concho-studded white chaps he wore for the Posse's parades, and his tattered work gloves.

Sheriff Grosscup and Ranger Emmitt Turnbow drove to El Reno to take charge. Enroute home they located an all-night café where the killers had stopped to eat. The girl had asked only for a Coke, but the man had consumed five hamburgers. While sitting in Hutch's car to talk about it, the officers happened on to a dime-store lipstick wedged between the seat cushions. These developments moved the sheriff to promise, once more, an impending arrest. Thereafter, as if the gods conspire against new sheriffs, the leads began to fade.

The prints raised on the Cadillac proved to be those of the El Reno housewife, the night watchman who responded to her call, and Sheriff Grosscup. Those copied from Cabin 4 traced out to Detective Lieutenant Mitchell Wiley, Hutch, various spectators and, again, to Sheriff Grosscup. The cigarette package belonged to the motel manager. The blood from the plumbing matched Hutch's. The handkerchief em-

broidered *TR* was eliminated when Thomas Rawlinson, a bank director and Posseman came forward red-facedly to claim it. Within the
week, there arose a suspicion, a horror, that the hitchhikers were going
to get away with it.

The *Tribune,* in its Sunday edition of February 8, posted a reward.
Daily, during the next weeks, it bore a Page One ear asking, "Do You
Know Who Killed Jess Hutcherson?," and underneath it repeated the
terms of the bounty. The Bonita County grand jury voted murder in-
dictments against John Doe and Jane Doe. A federal charge of unlawful flight to avoid prosecution was filed under the same ambiguous
identifications.

Rangers set out west on Highway 66, showing K. F. Stanfield's
trousers to dry cleaners along the whole route to California. Sheriff's
deputies and volunteers from the Posse, equipped with enlarged photos
of the trousers, trekked eastward on 66. Another squad invaded El
Reno and from there jumped off on inquiries along traffic arteries
leading out in all directions. An artist's sketches of the suspects, com-
posed from the descriptions supplied by witnesses, were flashed everywhere. Handbills reprinting the sketches and photograph were prepared. The Posse got busy mailing these out to every cleaning shop in
the nation.

Once, word was leaked that the case was solved. At El Reno, an
itinerant farm laborer surrendered a pistol he said he had recovered
from a ditch. The nickel-plated .45 was Hutch's; he had often carried
it in his car while traveling. Officers interrogated the finder three days
before releasing him. The "break" had established only that Hutch
had been beaten with his own gun.

Late in February the mayor, assuming the problem to be a lack of
organization, called a meeting. It was decided to rent the mezzanine of
a downtown hotel. There an administration, a clearing house, would
be set up. With Police Chief Max Hardeman presiding, information
would be evaluated and filed; an orderly new start would be made.
Surely centralization would succeed.

Friends of the Hutcherson family contributed an expert criminol-
ogist to the new bureau. From the University of Texas came a hypnotist, assigned to deal with the harassed witnesses. Wasn't it possible each of them had seen more, could remember more, than he
realized? The owner of a private airport donated three planes and

pilots. Whenever a hitchhiking couple was picked up anywhere, the planes scrambled, transporting the eyewitnesses for a look. Still, nothing availed.

By March the manhunt was heeding crank letters, threshing out bits of gossip. The newspapers lost patience. They began to assess the failure in light of the original mistakes, which led to censure of the police, faint applause for the FBI and Rangers, and a demand that Andy Grosscup resign. Inside the investigation, the result was a frenzy. An oilman from the Posse was jailed in a Michigan hamlet for impersonating an officer. A deputy sheriff got into a fist fight with an Arizona dry cleaner. In Kansas, a pair of Rangers ran down and maimed a hitchhiker. The sheriff lost weight and spent his days aloft in one of the airplanes, which, commented the *Tribune,* was wise since he was safer there than on the ground.

Then, on March 25th, Patty Sue Priest idled into a Baltimore police station and, to a patrolman distracted by the hoydenish twitch of her skirts, said, "I want to tell you about a murder." As the news spread, Illinois troopers and FBI agents rousted Raymond Elliot Priest out of his sister's home in Peoria. On the second day, Ray confessed.

Sheriff Grosscup flew the prisoner in. The plane's ETA was broadcast hourly. Listeners were told Hutch's killer appeared calm, that he had eaten two oranges enroute. Through an enterprising radio relay, the sheriff was able to address the voters from the air. He announced he was enjoying the flight, that the Cessna was performing beautifully, the pilot was witty and skillful, that Priest had given him no trouble, and he thanked the Posse for having put a thermos of coffee aboard. Asked to explain the trousers marked K. F. Stanfield, Andy said, "Oh, Ray tells me he got them britches at the Salvation Army up in Salt Lake City. That's how come the joke was on us. . . ."

The plane put in just at dusk. Three thousand persons met it, elbowing for position, but silent and grim in their reverie of Jess Hutcherson.

The sheriff climbed out first. From the wing, he saluted the crowd before turning back to help Priest alight. To make sure the gesture was not misconstrued, Grosscup spoke harshly to the prisoner and yanked hard on the leash chain. Then, to accommodate the cameramen, he posed Ray Priest and stood beside him, his fingers raised in a V for victory.

VIII

Paulk had read through the clippings in order. Now he sat over the picture. From the plane, Priest had stared down at his audience, his face bewildered, his ankles and wrists shackled, an iron collar around his neck.

The man's look, Paulk thought, wasn't of fear. Rather, it was that of someone who had anticipated peril always and was not surprised that it had come. The wide dumbfounded gaze seemed only to question why this, the inevitable, should have stirred up so great a fuss.

The party downstairs had ended hours ago. Paulk blinked at his watch. It was nearing 4:00 A.M. Perhaps the fatigue had something to do with how his abstraction of Ray Priest was coming to life, with how the man was materializing in the periphery of his mind as one of Jack Singer's pitiable "little people," the kind predestined to be trod upon.

He limped from the kitchen and fell on to his bed without tossing back the covers. "Jerry," he whispered, "I think this is one you wouldn't have sent away."

IX

Wounded from but three hours' sleep, Paulk stumbled into the shower. He throbbed with a headache, felt the clamor of an inner alarm. He was conscious of his dreams; they had been unbroken and realistic, projecting the trial, imbued with the tensions of the pit. He knew the symptoms, they belonged to that genus of borrowed trouble peculiar to the criminal lawyer. He shaved, dressed, and cooked his breakfast, then passed another hour over the clippings.

It was nine-thirty when he parked, illegally, on the drive reserved for sheriffs' cars. He entered the north door. Andy Grosscup's head-quarters, chopped into small rooms and stalls and stations to suit the departmentalization Andy had advocated during his campaign, was just inside and to the left. Paulk walked on past, to stand before the sheriff's bulletin board while he inhaled deeply and tried to expel the lingering clouds of last night's cigarettes.

From habit he scanned the purple-bordered forms with their affixed county seals. Postings were tacked up atop other postings: the Citations in Guardianship, the Applications To Probate Will And For Letters Testamentary, the Notices of Sale and Trustees Sale, the Notices On Petition For Beer License Or Wine And Beer Retailer's Permit: Greetings, To All Persons Interested, Know All Men By These Presents. . . .

"Hello, Wen."

He turned to Herb Cameron's offered hand. He took it gladly.

Not so many years ago, during Bonita County's six-shooter era, a disgusted editor had written that as an initial move toward law and order "we ought to hang all the lawyers." This hadn't contemplated men like Cameron. Herb restored one's faith that some of the seats of justice were occupied by good men, men *not so absolute in goodness as to forget what human frailty is.*

True, the prosecutor was no fireball. While voters demanded dash, prejudice, and a supercharge of wrath in their district attorney, Herb gave them courtesy and fair play and a scrupulousness sprung out of his own large compassion for people in trouble. Short, curly-haired, and at forty-five still not gray, Herb had, as Jerry used to say, "a kind of an unborn look," an embryonic air that inspired gentleness. He wore his ill-fitting dark-blue suits summer and winter, and let the seat of his pants shine like a badge of honesty. It was said Herb had too much integrity, that he was miscast, that he continued in office only because the city's defense attorneys saw to his reelection. Recently, however, Cameron's record had improved. Since the addition of Hollis Anglin to his staff, State's verdicts and stiffer penalties had come more frequently.

"Well," Herb said heartily, "we haven't seen you around in a long time. Calling on your client?"

"Any minute. How is he getting on in jail?"

"All right, I'm told, considering that it's pretty confining." This was Herb, disinterring the oldest courthouse joke, chuckling over it in genuine appreciation.

"Look," Paulk said, "have you subpoenaed your witnesses?"

"We've got return of service on most of them. There's a copy for you upstairs, any time it's convenient for you to pick it up."

"How many, and who?"

"We've called about nineteen people. You know, officers, that bartender, the motel folks—the ones you've read about in the papers."

Paulk said, "And who are the witnesses you have *not* subpoenaed?"

Herb laughed. "Wen, how long has it been since you and I shadow-boxed over a case?"

"Long enough so I'm out of practice. Why don't I just ask you things, straight out?"

"Sure, although I'd rather we got together with Mr. Tigart and Anglin."

Paulk noted Herb's flush. It occurred to him the District Attorney might be hurt that Hutch's family and important friends had not trusted him to prosecute Priest unaided. Actually, despite his penchant for humility, Herb probably was resenting Ike Tigart. The special prosecutor would have taken full charge; everyone knew Ike would work no other way.

"Herb, tell me why I didn't draw co-counsel for this case."

"Gee, I don't know. But the Judge was paying you a compliment. We all wanted somebody who wouldn't make a circus of things."

Cameron was gazing down at his toes; it was as if some sort of a slip had been averted. Paulk chose to overlook it.

"Would I get anywhere on a continuance? I couldn't argue a sick or missing witness, because at the moment I've got no witness. But if you joined me in the motion—?"

Herb bit his lip. "I wish we could do that, Wen. But we could announce ready five minutes from now, if need be. Besides, the Judge is set against it."

"Just fishing," Paulk said. "What about a hearing on a change of venue? Who knows, maybe I could show a dangerous conspiracy. But the easiest thing would be for you to agree we can't get a fair trial in Bonita County."

"That's up to you. And you know the Judge."

Sheriff Grosscup passed, leading a pair of his uniformed office girls to their coffee break. He spoke, tried to nod, and emitted a moan. Andy had a carbuncle on the back of his neck, and he walked so rigidly that his towering hat seemed to be carried on a pike. One thing and another plagued Grosscup, and it had been so from the day he took office.

"Wen," Herb rocked back on his heels, "are you afraid, seriously, that we can't get a jury?"

"My thought is that we can get *you* a jury. I'll exhaust my challenges, then you'll pour it on. I figure you've beaten me with a lopsided jury wheel."

The District Attorney grinned. He had taken no part in the chicanery, but it flattered him to be suspect. He said, "I do what I can."

"What have you got on tap for Patty Sue?"

"We'll see when we've finished with Ray."

"A big help, isn't she?"

Herb shrugged.

"Is she as attractive as they say?"

"I guess so. The sheriff says she's been getting bouquets, candy, and fan letters since her pictures started running in the newspapers. As for me, I've scarcely seen her; Anglin is handling her end. He thinks it's a shame the jury won't have a chance to see and hear her."

"Too bad," Paulk smiled and stretched. "Now I better go on up and find out how abusive you've been to my boy."

As they shook hands, Herb said, "You can pick up your copy of our subpoenas any time you want. And I wish you luck, Wen. I mean that."

The ritual, if somewhat curtailed, was complete. The prosecutor and the defender had met and talked, not because it accomplished anything, but because it was prescribed. Starting for the sheriff's office, Paulk speculated on the relief he would feel if he and Cameron were trying this case on its merits, with Anglin and Tigart excluded. It was easy to visualize Herb and himself in a clean, unimpassioned duel, planting neat points in a record that might be perpetuated as a new model of criminal procedure. Too bad, he thought, that Priest couldn't have such a trial. As matters stood, Ray would be fortunate if even his lawyer came out alive.

Several of Andy Grosscup's deputies, huge men who lounged about with their umbrella hats shoved back and their booted feet stashed in desk drawers, watched him as he identified himself to the head jailor and drew a pass.

X

The courthouse elevators were extravagant in comparison to most tax-bought equipment. Carpeted, fitted with buffed brass handrails, they were rimmed, high up, with ornamental stained-glass portals inlaid with the legendary cattle brands of the region: the XIT, the Rocking Chair, the JA, the T-Anchor and XL, the K-Bar and Lazy J, the Circle Cross. Only the jail elevator was appropriately austere.

It crept upward from the sheriff's office to the jail tower with no stopping-off place in between. Oblong, heavy with gray steel, it bumped and rang as it climbed. The duty jailor, a wrinkled, concave former constable named O'Brien, operated the car with a switch tripped by a huge flat key. Paulk remembered him from earlier years. O'Brien was prone to long recitals which usually began with "I was saying to the wife" and progressed eventually to the clincher, "So, the wife says to me, 'Charlie, that's how it goes, and all folks can do is just hang loose and hope to God.' " Paulk thought him a bore, but not quite a pest. At least O'Brien reminded you that people hoped when there was no hope, kept faith when it brought nothing, and would pray even if it could be shown them that God had no ears.

They alighted at the jail office and went on through, into a long concrete galley where the odors of Sani-Flush, bedbug eradicator and burnt sowbelly mingled with the scent of the sweating trusties wiping away the breakfast debris. In relief of the iron and melancholy, the jail had a view. Through the windows above the dish-washing vats you could see to the city's farthest outskirts, or you could gaze down on the whitewashed trees and the green benches on which old railroad men would sit out the summer, or, if you tiptoed, you could watch the pigeons making love on the fifth-floor roof. The only better view, it was said, could be had from the men's restroom which neighbored the 191st District courtroom.

"Now, who was it you wanted, Mr. Paulk?"

"Priest."

The jailor nodded. "Take a chair. I think we've got some leftover coffee, if you'd care for it."

Paulk waited in a concrete cubicle built for solitary but converted by Andy Grosscup into an interview room. Formerly, an attorney had to talk to his clients in a cell with the rest of the jail attuned to every

49

word. Here there were three cane-bottom chairs, a rough pine table and a Gideon Bible. Not enough light entered through the one high window, but there was privacy.

A husky Negro trusty wearing a flour-sack apron over his white ducks like a loincloth hesitated at the door, then came in to place a crock saucer on the table. "Ash tray," he said. "We done mopped out, and we got to stay clean until the sheriff comes for inspection."

"Hey," Paulk detained him, "do you know Ray Priest?"

"The man that's goin' ride Ole Sparky? Yes, sir, I know which one he is."

"Ever talk with him?"

"Not to speak of. He's in the white men's tank."

"What do you hear about him? Does he cause any trouble?"

"No, sir, none I know of. Some says he gets sore on account of they won't let him visit his wife."

"What's the general feeling about him?"

The prisoner fidgeted. "Like I say, sir, he don't talk to me none, 'cepting maybe when he's after some extra coffee."

"All right," Paulk said, "I'll be careful of your floor."

Five minutes passed. He was wondering if O'Brien had forgotten him, or if Priest was refusing a lawyer, when he heard a step. He turned to see a girl standing in the doorway. Her hand was on the frame, her head tilted, as she studied him. She had dark hair shored back with rhinestone combs and a petulant teen-age face obviously made up a moment ago, its excess lipstick not yet blotted off. Her brown eyes were insolent and amused.

"Oh," she said, "I thought you were Mr. Shepherd."

He smiled, exulting at O'Brien's error and rallying himself to make the most of it. "You flatter me," he said. "Come on in, if you will."

The girl's white blouse was fresh, its uppermost buttons left open. She wore a broad red belt pulled taut around her amazingly small middle, a full black skirt of the high-school sort, and sandals. Her legs were slim, bare and marked by the minor wounds of a recent shave; her toenails had been enameled a bright red. As she entered, uncertainly, he saw that she was a busty, rumpy little creature who moved with the energy and grace typical of her vitamin-fed generation, and he understood why the press had softened toward her.

"Are you the doctor?"

"No, my name is Paulk. Are you supposed to have a doctor?"

She nodded.

"Have you been ill?"

She shook her head. "You're a policeman?"

"A lawyer. Please sit down, I'd like to talk to you for a while."

"I don't know," she said doubtfully, still examining him. "Mr. Anglin and Mr. Shepherd—they said I wasn't to talk with anyone, unless they told me it was all right."

"I'm surprised," he said, and wasn't. "When did they tell you this?"

"Well, Mr. Anglin told me again last Sunday."

"I didn't know he worked Sundays."

Her gaze had fallen to the table, where his cigarettes lay. Although the sensation was of contributing to the delinquency of a minor, he offered her one. She sat down, holding the cigarette expertly, forcing him to circle the table to light it for her. She smelled of soap and cologne, to a degree discernible above the jail's stinging germicides. She inhaled deeply with an apprehensive glance at the door, as if she expected the jail regulations to enter and forbid this luxury. It provided Paulk a reason to close it.

He said, "Patty Sue, are you getting along all right?"

"Jail is jail."

"—is jail," he added, but the meagre witticism foundered. "You look as though they're treating you well."

"Oh, I have some things the others aren't getting."

"Like—?"

"Lipstick and stuff."

"And new clothes?" Now was the time for the blind shots. In court it would be too late. There you dared no question unless you already knew the answer. Except, he remembered, Patty Sue couldn't appear.

"My lawyer brought me this dress."

"Very pretty. Good for your morale, isn't it?"

She crinkled her nose. "My morale does okay. There's plenty worse jails than this. I wouldn't mind it much, if they'd hurry up and turn loose some of those old bitches up there."

He lowered his head, covering his shock at a word so inharmonious with the child face. "We seldom have many women in our jail."

"Well, there's five or six now. Dirty old hags, screeching so you can't read, always wanting to see you naked."

The vehemence was normal; all jails maintained their class lines. Inmates needed to feel superior to some others, thus the armed robber disdained the sneak thief, the thief looked down on the forger, and all of them despised the pimp. But even a pimp held to a standard, one that enabled him to scorn as unspeakable the pusher of narcotics. Paulk realized that this girl, indicted for the highest crime, was upon a pinnacle. Naturally she was disgusted by wretched crones serving thirty days for drunkenness or soliciting. And, he suspected, she condemned them also for being old when she was young.

"Reading?" he said. "What do you read?"

"Oh, about everything—*Private Eye, Wonder, Golden Space, Famous Funnies.*"

Comic books. He smiled, dissuaded a little from the feeling he'd had, that she knew more of life than he. "Where do you get your books?"

"He brings them—Mr. Anglin. Look, you are Ray's lawyer, aren't you?"

"Yes."

"Then I've got nothing else to say."

"Wait, please. I'm sure you know you cannot testify. But, you are still an eyewitness. That makes you important to both sides. I want you to help me get the truth, that's all."

"I've already made my statement."

"To the prosecution. But they aren't required to show it to me. I am entitled to ask you some questions."

She appeared more bored than alarmed. "I don't have to answer you, do I?"

Paulk frowned. "Your husband is in terrible trouble, Mrs. Priest."

"Will they electrocute him, really?"

"As it stands, they will. Is that what you want?"

She gazed up at the small window. Her lips parted, and she moistened them with her tongue. There was a wistful, hazy instant, as if she were striving to reexperience love through some marvel of memory and thought.

"Do you want Ray to go to the Chair?" he repeated.

"Yes, damn him, I hope he fries."

It took Paulk aback. As he recoiled, she smiled and stood up.

"All right," he said, "I'll call O'Brien to take you to the jail office. You telephone Hollis Anglin, and if he tells you that you should talk to me, will you come back?"

"I don't care," she answered indifferently, "I've nothing else to do."

Alone, waiting, he considered how handily she had baited him, how pleased she was with it. Malice, sport—whichever it was, he would have enjoyed spanking her. But he knew he would crawl to get her story if she wished it. The consolation was that he'd kept his wits, had sent her to call Anglin instead of Shep. The prosecutor's best move would be to advise her to answer his questions, now that the accidental interview had begun. Anglin wouldn't want the State castigated later, before a jury, as having impeded the development of a fair defense, while Shepherd, correctly, would have urged her to disclose nothing.

He avoided any I-told-you-so air as she returned. "What does Anglin say?"

"He says you can ask all you want. And he says I should tell you Mr. O'Brien didn't goof, whatever that means."

The sharp, smug little bastard, Paulk thought; he wanted it known his finger was on things, that anything gotten from Patty Sue came out of the largess of a magnanimous prosecution. O'Brien had followed instructions; probably had tipped Anglin as soon as Paulk was out of hearing.

Brusquely he said, "How old are you, Mrs. Priest?"

She was eighteen; her parents lived in Glendale, California. Her father was a factory worker usually embroiled in union politics. Occasionally, she said, he turned his spleen on her, and upon her mother for defending her truancies. Patty was dating almost nightly at thirteen—"Oh, I matured early, Mother says"—and at fifteen she had been married.

"I see. Where did you meet Ray?"

"In a place. A sort of a dance hall in Los Angeles; I don't remember the name."

"Had you known him very long before you were married?"

"Two or three months, I guess. But we'd been together a lot, since I wasn't living at home."

"Why weren't you?"

"Daddy and I had a fight. Mother thought I ought to get away from the house for a while."

"Where did you live?"

"In L. A., with Ray."

"I mean, before you married."

Without a blink she said, "I moved to Ray's place the night I met him."

"What was Ray doing in Los Angeles?"

"Well, he just sort of fooled around. We didn't stay very long. We didn't have enough money to stay in L. A."

"Where did you go?"

"Lots of places. We went around the country, doing different things. Sometimes Ray worked a while, and we'd stay until the job was over. Mostly, we just bummed around."

"Hitchhiking?"

"Some. When we had some money, we rode the bus."

"When did you decide to get married?"

She frowned. "I told you, in February of fifty-six."

"Why? I mean, after waiting so long?"

"Ray made me. I met boys in some of the towns we stopped in, and I had some dates. Ray didn't care sometimes, and other times he would get real mad about it. We were in Kentucky that winter, and Ray picked a fight with a fella I knew. They put us in jail. When we got out, Ray took me around to the alley behind the police station and beat me up. Then he said we were going to get married, and we did."

"How soon?"

"Right then, that day; before my eye turned black."

Paulk said, "Were you getting even for this when you went to the police in Baltimore?"

The girl lifted and dropped her shoulders theatrically. "That wasn't so much. He whipped me lots of times."

Paulk reached for a cigarette, pushed the pack toward Patty Sue. This was State's ammunition, the sort fearfully effective with a jury. Priest, aside from his record as a vagrant and loafer, was a habitual wife-beater; his bride had worn a black eye to her wedding. Such remote facts were no part of the *res gestae;* they were not admissible as bearing upon the crime. Still, he could not keep them out if his defense necessitated Priest's own testimony. Once Ray took the stand, these unsavory bits of his past became the proper basis for an attack aimed at impeachment. Such proofs eased a jury's conscience, they reduced a defendant's chances by depriving him of sympathy. The odds on mitigating regular wife-beating were almost nil.

"Why did Ray whip you?"

"Over one thing and another. He's always getting mad."

Bad temper. Or, Paulk thought, madness; wasn't that Patty Sue's own word? He tucked it away for safekeeping.

"You still haven't told me why you decided to prosecute your husband."

She was sitting less at ease, her manner less forbearing, and he congratulated himself. He watched her recross her legs, rake her fingers through bulky hair that crackled electrically.

"I don't see how that is important."

"Maybe it isn't," he said. "But you've told Anglin, haven't you?"

"Well—Ray and I broke up after the—after what happened out at the motel that night. He went to his sister's, and I went to stay with a girlfriend in Florida. He started writing letters, saying what he'd do if I told anybody. I got scared."

"Had you heard about the reward at that time?"

"Sure, I read the papers." She brightened while making an effort not to. "Mr. Shepherd thinks I'll get it. I never had three thousand dollars before."

"Three thousand?" Paulk said, then checked himself. "What will you do with it?"

"Pay lawyers," she winced. "Mr. Shepherd says I'll have about a thousand dollars when it's over."

Ah, The Shepherd. Knocking down two thousand by convincing her the reward was only three, creaming off another two thousand as his fee.

"First," she was cheerier, less worldly now, "I'll have to pay for my divorce, if Ray only goes to the pen. Then I want some new clothes. My mother thinks I ought to save the rest, maybe for business college when I get out of this mess. Daddy wants me to come back home, but if I do, he'll pay the money down on a new car. . . ."

Ethics, privileged communications be damned. Paulk said, "What is Mr. Shepherd charging you for the divorce?"

"It's not him. Mr. Anglin says he can get it for a hundred dollars."

"I thought you'd hired Shepherd."

"I have, but I talked to Mr. Anglin about the divorce, before I met Mr. Shepherd."

Paulk felt like beating his fists on the wall over the state of his profession. He had known that Herb Cameron permitted Anglin to practice civil law on the side to pad out the skimpy assistant's salary; it was no secret Anglin handled a number of divorces for women who appeared at the district attorney's office intending, instead, to file criminal complaints against their husbands. The dockets were always cluttered with hit-and-run domestic cases which fell through when the prosecuting wife made up with the defendant husband. Anglin made fees, and saved the court's time and money, by steering assaulted wives toward divorce suits in place of criminal action. It was a mild barratry, outrageous to no one. But with Patty Priest, the situation was different. Anglin was compounding his prosecutor's relationship; he accepted the girl as a client in one cause and was committed to prosecute her in another. Paulk sighed.

"Mrs. Priest, tell me what happened the day Mr. Hutcherson picked you up on the highway."

She described sketchily their stop at the New Mexico bar, skimmed on through the gas-station stop, the arrival in town, the registration at the Ranch Inn.

"When Mr. Hutcherson first picked you up, where were you?"

"I don't know, just out in the open, where a fellow had put us out because he wasn't going any farther."

"Did Mr. Hutcherson simply pull up and offer you a ride?"

"Well, he was running real fast. He went on past, then turned around and came back for us."

"All three of you rode in the front seat?"

"Yes. Only we changed around; Mr. Hutcherson said he was tired, and he wanted Ray to drive."

"Who suggested stopping for drinks?"

"Mr. Hutcherson did. He said a friend of his ran the place, that he always stopped there."

"While you were driving, what did you talk about?"

"Different things. We talked all afternoon, I guess."

"What were some of these things?"

"Well, Mr. Hutcherson wanted to know where we were going."

"What did you tell him?"

"Florida. Ray had heard about a job there."

"All right, then what?"

"Well, Mr. Hutcherson found out we didn't have any money, and he said he'd help us out. He said he could get Ray a job here, and that he would get us a place to stay overnight. He talked some about wheat and oil, and about how much snow there'd been, and how he was worn out and in a hurry to get home."

"Did he drink any during the trip?"

"Some."

"Did Ray?"

"No, he was driving."

"What about you?"

"I had a little beer. Not much, I don't like it."

"Was there any trouble, any arguments over anything at all?"

"No. Mr. Hutcherson was nice to us. He said he knew a lot of people here in town, and if he couldn't find Ray a good job, he would hire him himself."

"What else?"

"He talked about some trips he'd had to foreign countries—I don't remember all that."

"What happened when you got to town?"

"We drove on through, out to the other side, looking for a place to stay. It was after dark, and a lot of the places were full."

"When you found a place, then what?"

"Mr. Hutcherson gave me some money and told me to go in and register. Then we drove on back to the cabin, and a porter let us in."

"Mr. Hutcherson went inside with you?"

"Yes."

Paulk said, "Why?"

"He didn't say, but I think he wanted to use the bathroom. We all went in, and there was some boxing on TV. Ray and Mr. Hutcherson got to looking at it."

"What did you do?"

"Nothing, just sat around."

"Then what happened?"

"Ray and Mr. Hutcherson had the rest of the drinks, and then Ray told me to go out to the car and get our suitcase. I did, and when I came back, Mr. Hutcherson and Ray had gone back into the other room. I sat down and watched television some more."

The girl's hands were steady as she took up another cigarette. He smiled at her as he leaned across to light it.

"What happened next?"

"Ray came back up to the front room. He had a gun in his hand. I got up, and he started back into the back room, and I followed him."

"Did he say anything?"

"No."

"Are you positive? Not a word?"

"No. He just pulled Mr. Hutcherson over—"

"Wait, just where was Mr. Hutcherson?"

"On the bed, in the back room. He was lying on his side, and Ray grabbed him and pulled him over on his back and started hitting him in the head with the gun."

"You saw this?"

"Yes."

"How many times did he hit him?"

"I don't know, three or four times."

"Did either of them say anything?"

She shook her head. "He just hit him, and it sounded like when you stomp on mud, and blood splattered everywhere. I ran back up to the front room. I didn't go back there anymore."

"What did Ray do?"

"He changed his clothes. He wiped the gun off on his shirt and stuck it down into his pants. He told me to get our stuff and come on. I did, and we left."

"In Mr. Hutcherson's car?"

"Yes."

"Where did you go?"

"On out the highway, on into Oklahoma. Ray drove real fast, he showed me once we were going a hundred and ten. He said we had better get as far as we could before morning."

"What time did you leave?"

"About ten o'clock, I think."

"Did you stop anywhere?"

"Once, to get something to eat."

"Then what happened?"

"Nothing. We kept going, and we got on the wrong road once and had to cut back. It was about daylight when we got to El Reno. Ray said the car would be easy to spot, because it had those horns on the front and he couldn't get them off. He said we better leave it and split up. He gave me some money and said he'd meet me in Atlanta in two days."

"Where in Atlanta?"

"A place we know, sort of a rooming house."

"You say Ray had some money?"

"A great big wad of it. He give me a big handful."

"How much did he give you?"

"I didn't count it. I guess it must have been three or four hundred dollars."

"Did he tell you where he got it?"

"No, I already knew. He got it from Mr. Hutcherson."

Paulk leaned back, worried that he had no instinct about her. There were gaps, thin points in her story, but his feeling was neuter; he seemed to be matching her own extraordinary detachment.

He said, "Was Mr. Hutcherson asleep when you followed Ray into the back room?"

"I don't know."

"Was he undressed?"

"Yes."

"Why had he gone to bed in the motel, instead of going on home?"

"All I know is what he said. He wasn't feeling good, and there was trouble with the car. I think he was going to call someone to come fix the car, so he could drive it home."

"But Ray had no trouble with the car."

"Oh, he did, too. When we left, it wouldn't start. So we pushed it out the drive, on to the highway, and Ray waved a man down and he gave us a shove to get it started."

"It ran all right, once it was started?"

"Yes."

Paulk thought back through his questions and the answers. As a whole, it was as the newspapers recounted it, the robbery murder of a Good Samaritan.

"This is what you put in your written statement, isn't it?"

"Yes. Not word for word; I don't know why people expect me to tell it exactly the same every time."

"You've had to tell it a number of times, haven't you?"

"Enough that I'm tired of it."

He stood. "Then I won't go into it any deeper today."

"There isn't any deeper to go." She left her chair, frowned thoughtfully, and rested her hip on the table.

"Is there something else?" he said.

"Well—how is Ray? Is he getting chicken, or anything?"

"I haven't seen him."

"He'll lie about what happened."

"Why are you telling me that?"

"I don't know," she giggled. "I guess because you look kind of damp behind the ears to be a lawyer."

"I am," he tried exploiting it. "I'll need all the help I can get."

"I've helped you, haven't I? If I could have another smoke—?"

"Take the package. Shep must be slipping; he ought to bring you cigarettes."

"He does." She folded the empty half of the pack around the rest and pushed it down between her breasts. "Mr. Anglin gives me some, too. I'd have plenty, if those creepy old sluts up there didn't steal everything."

He walked behind her, out through the galley where two tubs of pinto beans simmered, toward supper, since in Bonita County jail noon meals never came. At the office, Charlie O'Brien met them, wagging his head and grinning.

"All finished, Mr. Paulk? Sorry I got yu' the wrong Priest, but since this 'un usually gets all the visitors, I figured right off—"

Yes, you crusty old liar, Paulk thought; hang loose and hope to God. He said, "Never mind. Now, I'd like to see my client."

"Sure thing, except I've got to lock this one up first; can't have too many of 'em out in the run-around at the same time. You make yourself to home."

Paulk nodded to the girl. "Thank you."

"You're welcome," she smiled coyly, confident of having intrigued him, "and I didn't mean what I said about you being wet behind the ears."

He watched O'Brien lead her up a spiraling stair, then went back to the galley and asked a trusty for a cup of coffee. He sat down, draping his arm over the meat block, and wished he had known enough of his case to question Patty Sue more pointedly. And, why was she expecting a doctor?

XI

From the interview room, listening, Paulk could trace Ray Priest's approach. A door clanged, there was a tread on an iron ramp, another door rumbled on its steel rollers. The cell-block voices quieted; then, as they resumed, the clatter of the kitchen abruptly stilled. Along the route with Priest came a wave of silence, and, Paulk supposed, stares. It wasn't likely that the vags and brawlers and authors of bad checks regarded the killer of Jess Hutcherson as a celebrity among them.

Rather, Priest's was the fascinating presence of a man already dead. Other prisoners counted off jail days, else looked ahead to time at Sugarland in Uncle Bud's pea patch. But this man saw the spectre of Old Sparky. If you watched him through a squinted eye, you saw him shaved, dressed in the State's white shirt, wearing the electrode around his ankle. He was near the last secret, and other men wondered if he had begun, already, to unravel it.

Paulk was surprised. The man was no more than five-feet-six, compactly made, and it was obvious he recently had lost weight. Good, he thought, good. On the stand Ray would look slight and miserable. Priest gripped Paulk's hand awkwardly, then took the chair his wife had used. He leaned forward, forearms resting on his knees. The attitude was of cowed resignation. This Paulk did not like.

Priest's khakis were unironed. He wore bulging clodhopper shoes. The sandy hair was wild. It swirled in a whirlpool cowlick at the crown, was piled in a high foretop over his brow, shaggy on his neck, and it grew in thick sideburns reaching down to the lobes of his ears. His jaw protruded at the hinges, his mouth was set half open by an underbite. He had a flat nose, small flat ears. Under heavy white lashes, the pale blue eyes looked blank, immobile, as though belonging to a mounted animal. Paulk hoped his man wasn't as vapid as he seemed.

"Ray, I'm sorry you couldn't choose your own counsel. But the Judge has appointed me to your case, and we'll have to do the best we can by each other." As he spoke, he caught a glint of gray in the sideburns and, perhaps, a hint of interest in the shallow eyes. "We've a lot to do, and no time to beat around the bush on anything. So, first off, I'll advise you to get rid of those sideburns. In this town, those things identify the crumbs. All right with you?"

"Yes, sir."

"I'll send a barber up here. I'll tell him what you need, and you let him do it. Now, do you have a good suit of clothes?"

"No, sir."

"We'll have to get you one, and some dress shirts. Do you know your sizes?"

Priest rustled a slip of paper out of his breast pocket. "My other lawyer told me that, so I wrote it down."

"You've been told, haven't you, that Mr. Shepherd has no connection with your case now?"

He nodded. "Sir, can I say something?"

"Of course."

"Well, I ain't heard why that Shepherd quit me, and nobody told me you was coming. This ain't a trick, is it?"

"No." Paulk explained the severance. "As it comes out, Mr. Shepherd will be acting for your wife."

Priest sat a moment, absorbing it.

"Actually, you've got the right to waive counsel and represent yourself. But, I doubt the Judge would allow it, considering the seriousness of this case."

"I'm satisfied," Priest said slowly. "To tell you the truth, I sure wanted Patty to get a good lawyer."

Paulk was unable to mask his annoyance. "Shepherd is her man."

"Yes, sir, him and me only talked a little while and we got my defense all fixed up."

"I'll bet you did," Paulk said. "You'll find I work a little differently. To start with, we've got to talk about money."

"That ain't so different."

Paulk grinned; this was better. "I'm speaking of money for your clothes and to prepare your defense."

"I ain't got any."

The oddity about the man's eyes, Paulk decided, was that they seldom blinked.

"How about friends or relatives? Is there anyone who'd want to help you?"

"My sister is the only one, I reckon."

"What is she willing to do?"

"She says she might send some money later on, provided her husband gets any back on his income taxes. She aims to come down here for my trial."

"This is Mrs. Callahan you're speaking of?"

"Yes, sir, Angie. My brother-in-law is named Frank, he works at the foundry. He ain't coming, but Angie will if she can get anybody to stay with the kids."

"She's the sister that raised you, isn't she?"

Priest nodded. "Only one I got."

"Have you a picture of her?"

"No, sir."

"What does she look like?" Once more, Paulk was concerned with appearances, with the business Jack Singer spoke of as "setting an

atmosphere." You presented a man looking his best, you surrounded
him with handsome—or, at least, stolid—friends and kin clearly parti-
san in sight of the jury. This was visual character testimony, the sort
not reflected in the transcript but constant and accumulative through
the long run of a trial. A respectable sister showing faith in Ray might,
as Shep put it, make the darkness more visible.

"Like a housewife, I reckon."

"All right. Can you think of anyone else who might want to help
you?"

"To tell you the truth, Mr. Polk—"

"My name is Paulk."

"Yes, sir. Anyway, I ain't bothered myself much about money. The
Judge told me the State would pay my lawyer."

"I'll be given a warrant for twenty-five dollars. That won't make the
down payment on your clothes. Do you own any property, have an
interest in an estate—anything that could be turned into cash?"

He shook his head. "The last money I seen—"

"Go on."

"To tell you the truth, the last money I seen was Mr. Hutcherson's,
and Patty blowed through that pretty quick."

The tidbit begged amplification. But, for the moment, he let it pass.
He said, "Ray, do you always begin what you are saying with 'To tell
the truth'?"

"Well, I guess I do."

"Starting now, don't. A jury could take it to mean you are accustomed to lying. Or they might think you *are* lying because you're
telling them you are not."

Priest shrugged.

"Do you understand?"

"Yes, sir, I reckon. But Mr. Shepherd didn't say nothing about
that."

"Let's dispose of Mr. Shepherd right now," Paulk spoke sharply.
"His job is to protect Patty Sue. He'll be working with the District
Attorney, trying to put the responsibility of this killing entirely on you.
You'd better forget about him. Any chance you have is with me."

Priest's stuffed, soulless look did not alter.

"Ray, how long since you've seen your wife?"

"Quite a spell, I guess."

"I want to know if you think she could be pregnant."

Priest blinked and his eyes suddenly seemed not so utterly vacant. "You heard something like that?"

"No, it's just that she's expecting a doctor. Could that be the reason?"

"I dunno, I reckon it could."

"How far along would she be?"

"Two or three months, maybe, if it's mine."

Now it was Paulk who was startled. "You mean you think your wife might be having someone else's child?"

"No, sir, that ain't what I said. All I said was I ain't seen her since we was in Florida."

Seeking another tack, he said, "Why is she racking you up, Ray?"

"They won't let me see her, so I don't know nothing. But I ain't mad at her about it."

"Do you believe she would turn you in just for the reward?"

Priest's brow had wrinkled. The blankness, Paulk was learning, could be dissipated by every mention of the girl.

"Well, maybe," Priest answered reluctantly. "To tell you the truth— I mean, she might aim to get even with me."

"For beating her up once in a while?"

He saw the flicker of rage, then the nothingness he was beginning to hypothesize as an armor, a guile.

"I always treated my wife good."

Paulk leaned on the table, massaging his temples. It irritated him to find the man less frightened than he ought to be. Terror, while not desirable, would be preferable to this. He drew a long breath.

"Before we go any further, Ray, you ought to know your prognosis. You're under indictment for a capital offense, and the FBI has charged you with unlawful flight and Dyer Act, which is transporting a stolen automobile across a state line. The only eyewitness is lined up with the State to save her own neck. Add to this the fact that you haven't got a dime, and your rap sheet is as long as my arm.

"You killed the man who was the backbone of this town, and his family has hired the best special prosecutor money can buy. Then, even if we get all the breaks, there'll be some of Jess Hutcherson's friends sitting on your jury. On top of all this, I'm a civil lawyer, a bookworm."

He paused, hoping to perceive some sort of dawning on the crude, taciturn face.

"Legally, the State is supposed to grant you full innocence, then set out to strip it off of you with evidence. If Hutch had killed you and was going on trial, he would have the benefit of that. But you won't. Not in law, but in fact, you stand convicted right now. In a run-of-the-mill case, a reasonable doubt on a material point would save you. But you've had a big press; it'll take solid proof just to give you a prayer. Do you understand this?"

Priest nodded, his plain vanilla expression not perceptibly changed.

"All right." It occurred to him he was approximating what Jack Singer would have said; that he was an unwilling prodigal plodding glumly home. "Another thing, you must realize that the prosecution knows everything your wife could tell them. Whatever that is, I've got to know, too. I don't have to think you're innocent; indeed, if you're guilty, I want to know it. The point is, you can't afford to tell me only what is favorable to you. I must have the whole tale, regardless of how rotten it may make you appear. If I know, I can defend you.

"It'll be a calamity for you if you let me be surprised, let me hear something from the witness stand that I don't already know and am not prepared to handle. The State will hit me with anything you leave out. Get it straight, I'm not worrying about being embarrassed before that jury. I'm simply telling you that if you hold out on me, you may be committing suicide."

Still there was no sign the speech was taking effect. Priest sat motionless, brimming with stupidity or indifference.

"I assure you," Paulk challenged him, "that you can't reveal anything that would shock me. The reason is that, as we stand, I suppose you to be a murderer of the sorriest kind. I've started out assuming the worst, because any lawyer is a fool not to. When I've heard it all, good and bad, I'll try to hunt out a plausible reason to tone down my opinion. If I find it, I'll know how to present you to your jury. No lies, no distortions, Ray. Clear?"

"Sir, I ain't a liar."

"We can talk a little law, then. In Texas there are four possible pleas. One is the motion to quash, to set aside the indictment as faulty, or discriminatory, or voted by a conspiring grand jury, or by showing the matter alleged is not a criminal offense. Another is the special plea. If you had a perfect alibi, if you had been charged on mistaken identity, if you were so insane you couldn't aid your own cause, or if you had dropped dead and therefore couldn't appear in court, I could put a special-fact issue before a petit jury, ahead of the murder case. For you, I think, these are out.

"Then there's the plea of guilty. In this state, a guilty plea in a capital case is heard by a jury, and the State puts on its evidence just the same. You could plead guilty and still get the death penalty, which means there's no advantage unless you can make a bargain in advance. I've checked, and you can't.

"That leaves just one, the plea of not guilty. Which means we go in there, square off, and fight like hell."

Priest acknowledged him with a brief, grubby smile. "That's what I want," he said. "Unless it would mess up Patty Sue."

Who, Paulk felt inclined to ask, was messing up whom? Instead, he said, "How could it?"

"Well, I wouldn't care to make no trouble for her."

Paulk opened his briefcase, took out a pad and a handful of pens. As he sought one that would write, he marveled a little at Ray's recurring concern for Patty Sue. Was it forgiveness, love, or but a paroxysm of the yearning which gnawed at a man shut away from his wife?

"A while back," he said, "you mentioned that Mr. Shepherd had worked out your defense. What was it?"

"To tell you the truth—"

"Ray, I'll interrupt every time you say that."

"Yes, sir. Well, I ain't real clear on all of it, but he told me if Mr. Hutcherson commenced to attack me I had the right to stand my ground and fight back. And he said we'd talk some more, later on, about the headaches I get and that business about blacking out."

Paulk shrank from it. Here they were, the stand-bys: self-defense and temporary insanity. It sickened him to think he might be saddled with these tired clichés of defense, these expectable excuses claimed by every killer otherwise caught without a legal defense. If Shep had schooled too much, interposed a few details, Priest might be unable to let them go. For the present, Paulk did not want to find out.

"Another thing," Priest said, "we was doing some drinking that night."

It was the man's first volunteered statement, and Paulk ignored it. He said, "According to the newspapers, you are twenty-eight."

"Yes, sir."

"Where were you born?"

"Over in Oklahoma, at Sand Springs."

Priest had lived with his grandparents until he was ten, when he went to Peoria as the ward of his sister Angie Callahan. After a sequence of failures in school, he quit to go to work. He began and abandoned eight jobs in Peoria and Chicago and was, most of the time, at large under juvenile probation. For more than a year he drifted over the country, sleeping in parks and auto hulls in wrecking yards. Occasionally he drew unemployment checks, hired out as a swamper in a bar, or served a jail term for vagrancy.

"Have you ever been convicted of a felony?"

"If I knowed what you mean—?"

"Were you ever convicted of an offense in which the penalty was penitentiary time, rather than jail time?"

"No."

"Then I can file you an application for suspended sentence. You'd have to get five years or less to be eligible, and you won't. But, it'll help me disqualify some jurors, since a lot of people disagree with the suspended sentence law. Incidentally, you should have been informed of your right to file when you were arraigned. Were you?"

"I guess. I don't remember all they said."

"All right. Now, there are twenty varieties of vagrancy. What sort do you have in your vag record?"

"They was different ones, different times. Not having a job, getting drunk, sleeping in the bus station—mostly things like that."

"You say mostly?"

"Well, a couple of times I was picked up for riding boxcars, or being with girls."

"Being with girls? What does that mean?"

"Out in California, I used to know some girls. Friends I got dates for, once in a while."

Paulk ground his teeth. "Are you saying you have been arrested as a procurer?"

Priest nodded, "I reckon they called it that."

"If they didn't," Paulk gruffened with disgust, "Ike Tigart will. Have you told anyone this?"

"No, sir."

Revolted, shaken out of the righteousness he had compelled himself to feel, beginning to lose the concept of himself as the last refuge of a small and persecuted man, Paulk glared across the table. Priest stared back dully.

He rummaged out the FBI sheet. None of the arrests in Priest's monotonous jail history had been recorded as for pimping. Nevertheless, the prosecution would have checked, would know the full nature of each offense. Another debit. Already it appeared this man would have to be kept off the witness stand.

"What type of discharge did the Air Force give you?"

"To tell you the—I mean, I got one of each."

"Two discharges?"

Ray explained emotionlessly. At the close of his first hitch, after Korea, he had been discharged honorably. Later he had reenlisted and the Air Force had expelled him.

"Your second discharge was dishonorable?"

"No, sir, it's what they call a blue one. I went AWOL a few times, so I could see Patty Sue."

"Why couldn't you see her on your regular off-time?"

"I did, some. Then she up and ran off with a guy, and they went somewheres back East. Me, I couldn't get no leave. Wasn't no way I could go looking for her, except just to go."

Paulk's interest rose; this, at least, might have been worse. Perhaps he should attempt to place a few women on Priest's jury. He hadn't tried a case since the Legislature's decision to qualify women for jury service; neither he nor any other Texas lawyer knew, as yet, how to predict them. Still, theories circulated. One was that women jurors were extremely sympathetic to a man whose troubles centered around an unfaithful woman. It was a part of the broader supposition that women are harsh in judgement of their own. He must remember to ask Jack Singer about it.

"What were you doing when you were arrested for murder?"

"Nothing. Sleeping."

"Was it at night?"

"No, it was daytime. I was at Angie's, up in Peoria, laying on the divan, and them three laws walked in on me."

"Who were they?"

"It was two state troopers and an FBI guy. They didn't knock, they just came in and told me to put my shoes on. They looked at the papers in my wallet and put the cuffs on me and taken me right on, before I could holler to Angie. She was out back, hanging up clothes."

"This was on the twenty-fifth of last month?"

"I reckon. Anyway, it was Wednesday, about nine o'clock in the morning."

"What happened next?"

"Well, they carried me to the station and commenced talking to me. They said Patty Sue had told about Mr. Hutcherson."

"Did you admit killing him?"

"No sir, not then I didn't."

"But later you did give them a confession?"

"I didn't aim to. There was a lot of laws around there. They asked me questions all day, except when they went off to eat."

"Were you fed?"

"No, sir, I didn't get any dinner, or any supper either. This one law told me we'd eat when we got our work done."

"You understood that to mean, when you gave him a statement?" Priest nodded.

"Did you tell them you didn't want to make a statement?"

"Well, I told them I didn't see how it would do me any good."

"How long did they question you?"

"That day, and then this FBI man stayed with me during the night. He wasn't so bad. He said I could sleep when we got finished, and he gave me coffee and some cigarettes."

"Did he take your statement?"

"In a way, I guess. He said I wasn't going to have to write it down unless I wanted to, but if I'd just tell him about it things would be easier for everybody. So I told him yes, I done it, and he asked me how I done it, and I told him. Then he left, and I didn't notice him around there anymore."

The slick sonofabitch, Paulk thought. "What time was this?"

"I don't know. Wasn't very long before daylight."

"Now, Ray—when did you put your statement in writing?"

"That was the next day. These two laws came in and said why didn't I put it in writing, so I could get some breakfast and go to bed, and I told them I better not. Later on, they brought me some papers. They said it was exactly what I had told the FBI man, and I might as well sign it."

"Did you?"

"Not right then; not till this other officer came in there, after the rest of them left."

"Who was he?"

"I dunno, a big cowboy-looking fella—"

"The sheriff, Andy Grosscup?"

"No, it wasn't him. Anyway, he got me to sign it."

"Why, if you had refused all the others?"

"Well, if you'd of seen him—he said, 'Son, I'm a Texas stranger and I've drove a long ways for what I want.' He said, 'You'll sign, or I'm going to stomp your guts out.' "

Paulk swore. This was truth, not the invention of a half-literate defendant. It would sound as convincing in court, if he could see to it Priest spoke as directly.

"What was next?"

"This feller put me down in a chair and stood on my toes and commenced grinding them. So I seen he meant what he said, and I signed the paper."

"Were you alone with him?"

"Yes, sir; they was just him and me."

Paulk shook his head. Procurers and wife-beaters didn't win many swearing matches against lawmen. "How did you say this officer was dressed?"

"Boots, big hat, a star on his shirt."

"Are you positive he said he was a 'Texas stranger'? Couldn't he have said, 'I'm a Texas *Ranger*'?"

"To tell you the truth, I was getting pretty sleepy by that time."

"But, you were told that since you had admitted the killing orally, you might as well do so in writing, is that correct?"

"Yes, sir, they told me that."

"All right. Was this the only statement you gave?"

"No, there was one more."

Paulk's projection of a tooth-and-fang battle, climaxed by a ruling declaring the confession inadmissible as had by duress, began to fade. "Tell me about it, Ray."

"It was right after I came here on the airplane. They talked to me here, in this room."

"Who were *they?*"

"Well, it was Mr. Anglin and the sheriff and a redheaded man I forget—"

"Tigart?"

"I reckon that's him."

"Did you tell them the same story you told up in Peoria?"

"I guess. They asked me questions, and I answered them. Mr. Anglin had a typewriter, and he put down most of it."

"But not all?"

"Some was left out, they said it was getting too long."

"How do you know they left out anything?"

"Because when it was done, Mr. Anglin read it to me."

"Did you tell him it wasn't all there?"

Priest shook his head.

"Why didn't you?"

"Well, them being lawyers and all, I figured they knowed what they was doing."

Paulk was tingling. You poor ass, he thought; they did know what they were doing, them being lawyers and all! If one piece, one fragment of the omission, happened to be material—

"Exactly what did they leave out?"

"I don't remember everything, but they didn't put in what I did in the Air Force, or all the jobs I had."

"What else?"

"Well, one thing I noticed looked sort of funny to me. They stuck in about when me and Patty and Mr. Hutcherson stopped at the bar and the gas station, but they left out about when we stopped at the post office."

"Tell me about that," Paulk said, his expectancy up, his mental fingers crossed.

The vacant eyes held steady. "It was after we got to town. We parked at the post office, and Mr. Hutcherson told me to go in and get his mail for him."

"Did you?"

"No, sir, I didn't aim to let him get shut of me that easy. He was planning to drive off without me, quick as I got inside."

"How do you know this?"

"What happened was, he told me the number of his box. The key to it was on the ring with the car keys. He told me to take it off, without turning off the motor. I done that, but I got to thinking about it, and I decided he was meaning to ditch me, so I wouldn't go."

"Didn't he want the keys left in the car because there was some trouble, the car was hard to start?"

"I thought maybe he did, but I didn't like how it looked, so I told Patty Sue to get out and go inside with me. That's when Mr. Hutcherson said, 'No, she's tired; let her sit here with me.' "

"Is that all that happened?"

"Well, we argued about it a little bit, and then I got back in, and we left without getting his mail."

Paulk rubbed his forehead. "You are saying, then, that you didn't intend to let Hutcherson put you out of his car?"

"No, sir, it wasn't that. I didn't care none where he put us out. But I didn't want to leave my wife out there while I went for his mail."

"In other words," Paulk said, disappointed, "you don't trust your wife out of your sight, not even with a man like Jess Hutcherson."

"Well, I didn't want to leave, that's all. Not when I'd seen how he goobled around on Patty all afternoon."

"*What?*"

"You know," Priest said, "grabbing at her, feeling her tits, all the time getting her dress pulled up."

Paulk's chair upset, the crash echoing, as he shot out of it. He stared at the blank face. "Gosh," it was saying, "I sure wish we had something to smoke."

XII

A fraction of Texas law is Constitutional, much more is statutory. But the main body of it is precedent, the rules reposing in the countless parables of an enormous jurisprudence, almost lost in a great "wilderness of single instances" that can never quit growing. Paulk had decided that most Texans cherished this staggering volume and complexity.

Even the lawyers, their intellects confounded by it daily, regarded the law's mass and illogic with a tolerance so emphatic it was like a pride. After all, with so much precedent at hand, you could find law to justify every man in every fix. Besides, it was unthinkable that a code as seasoned and cured, as earthy and antique, could ever be discarded. Although there was always a State Bar committee for the revision of everything, it was lonely in its zeal to erase and start afresh. A lot of unique Texas precedent dated back to the Republic, and where was there another state that first had been its own nation; where was the native son who could think seriously of mutilating such a legal tradition?

Some of the dominant opinions were astonishingly merciful, seemingly authored by some this-or-that Justice on a day of benevolence celebrating the birth of a grandchild. Others were fierce, sour, as if written on a cranky day by an old jurist suffering from an inflamed prostate. Stranger yet was the law arisen out of the offhand "horseback decisions" of the last century. Circuit-riding judges had been too weary, too dried by trail dust, to ponder all the everlasting consequences of a ruling issued across a watering trough.

There was a base of English common law, a spicing of old Spanish codes, and an unpredictability that was pure Texan. A robber might pay with his life while a murderer could go free under a two-year suspended sentence. It had always amazed Paulk that few saw this as any inconsistency. People liked knowing that every case went to court to stand on its own bottom.

Except, Paulk thought, in a precedent and case-law state, how could you decide what a man's defense ought to be? Who knew what would succeed for Ray Priest when Ray had never killed Jess Hutcherson before?

Singer laughed, conceding the point. "If you knew for sure, Wen, you'd miss all the fun. Let the law be a little foolish, to fit the people who plead before it."

Sighing, Paulk looked down to read, for the tenth time, Article 1220 of the Penal Code. He couldn't have said whether he was pleased or sorry that Texas had written the "unwritten law."

> *Homicide is justifiable when committed by the husband upon one taken in the act of adultery with his wife, provided the killing take place before the parties to the act have separated. Such circumstance cannot justify a homicide where it appears that there has been, on the part of the husband, any connivance in or assent to the adulterous connection.*

They had spent the evening over the statute and in study of Ray Priest's account of the killing as gleaned by Paulk during three difficult days of conversations at the county jail. They had attempted to gauge every fact of the tale, every critical probability, against the provisions of the law. And, such precedent as could be pulled down readily from Jack's bookshelves, they agreed, offered a glimmer of hope. That is, if Priest had told him only the truth.

Like all criminal lawyers, Paulk held the assumption that every accused person lies to save himself. Even the Gatekeeper of Heaven had been no exception. But this defendant, a near moron, ignorant of everything—could he have devised so whopping a falsehood, one that almost dovetailed with the whole digest of 1220's appellant decisions?

The opinions said, "The husband need not be an eyewitness to the act of coition . . . it is sufficient if he sees them in bed together, or leaving it, or in such a position as to reasonably indicate with reasonable certainty that they have committed adultery, or are about to . . . even though a mistake as to the fact of it may exist, the homicide is not punishable if the defendant took reasonable care to verify . . . a person may always act upon reasonable appearances, these appearances judged of from his own standpoint . . . the words 'before the parties to the act have separated' do not mean still united in copulation but, rather, only that the parties are still in company with each other . . . adultery as used in the Article is ecclesiastical, not statutory adultery . . . to avail himself of the Article, the defendant need not show adultery as defined by Article 449 of this Code . . . it is sufficient if he show a single defilement of his marriage bed, and the Court should so instruct the jury. . . ."

From the outset Paulk had sought the law and facts for mitigation. But this wasn't the weak stuff for reduction of a penalty. This granted excuse; it was acquittal law. As he realized it, his hands slickened.

"Assent to, and connivance," Singer mused, "these would be the big obstacles."

Paulk nodded. There was Ray's record as a panderer, and he had been present when the adultery took place, if it did. Wasn't his connivance in, and assent to, powerfully implied?

"Something else, Jack. How would a jury of Hutch's lifelong friends react if we threw this into their faces, especially with the great man dead and unable to answer? They might clap Ray into the Chair so fast he'd miss meeting the chaplain."

"That's so. But what has he got to lose?"

They watched Laura enter, drop her wrap here, her purse and gloves there. She spoke, shrugged at the absent nods they gave her, and moved a chair up to the crazed old library table. Returned from an Art Guild meeting, probably tired, she reclined with her hands behind her head, her knees extended, and she gazed at the ceiling in a silence honoring the preoccupation of Paulk and her father as the sign of legal minds hard at work. At the foot of the table, Old Jack massaged his crippled fingers and sank lower in a wicker wheelchair. He no longer needed the contraption, but it served to excuse him from getting up and down. When he wanted a book, he had only to sit and grumble and Laura would haul it down for him, then they would quarrel as to whether he was invalided or just lazy.

Paulk's brain seemed to tick, falter, then tick again toward a struc-

ture of defense. Whenever he paused to reexamine his handiwork, it
crumbled, and he had to begin again. He yawned, got out a cigarette;
then, remembering Singer's frustrated appetites, put it down unlit. He
noticed that one of Laura's small blue pumps had appeared on the
table. Among the scattered volumes of the *South West Reporter,* it
struck him as symbolic. Legal purpose was to reconcile man to the
law, but since this had to fail, lawyers tried to flex the law into com-
patibility with men. Neither was ever quite accomplished because—
well, alongside the provocative little slipper, didn't the lawbooks look
stern and pompous and ridiculous?

Singer said, "Why would Billy Shepherd offer to lend you money?"

"Maybe he was having a twinge of conscience."

"Not Shep, he wasn't suckled at virtue's paps. And I doubt he'd let
his grudge against Hollis Anglin, whatever it is, confuse him as to his
own interests. My surmise is that he happens to like you."

"I wish he cared enough to explain Patty's string of statements."

"It's possible," Singer said, "that he has explained. He tells you
there have been several redrafts. Now, why would the State discard the
original statement, unless there was something in it they didn't like?
Doesn't it occur to you that Patty's first account of it might have confirmed what Ray told you? I think Ike Tigart knows robbery wasn't
the primary cause of the killing. But, since Hutch was robbed, since
you will have to concede that he was, Ike intends to ram the case
through as a straight hijacking murder. That will be more palatable
to all concerned, particularly to Hutch's survivors. And Ike is betting
you'll let him handle it his way."

"Are you saying they'd fabricate evidence?"

"Not at all. The testimony they'll put on will be factual, it's simply
that they needn't offer all of it. Oh, they're sincere in thinking Priest
ought to die; it's all a question of means. Remember, Hutch's family is
paying Tigart, and he'll do all he can to spare them any humiliation."

"Herb Cameron would never try to bury the adultery angle, not to
please anybody—"

"Which," Singer said, "enlightens us still more. It tells us Herb isn't
running this show."

Under all the careful indirection, Paulk knew, they were talking
about the blackest of trial crimes, the deliberate suppression of facts.
They were anticipating a tangental prosecution, one aimed at mercy
for Jess Hutcherson instead of justice for the helpless nobody who

had killed him. At the implications, he shuddered, repelled by the alternative left to him. He didn't want to try a dead man's morality in a court of law, he hadn't the stomach to bring down a giant over what may have been the one serious lapse of a magnificent life. On the other hand, how could he stand off and let them ignore Ray Priest's only extenuation, the sliver of truth that might keep him alive?

Singer was smiling crookedly. "They've given you some interesting ground rules. You'll have to consider that bit of Shakespeare, 'To do a great right, do a little wrong.' "

"Nuts," Paulk frowned. "With that, Tigart and Anglin could whitewash themselves just as nicely as I could excuse me."

"Precisely," the old man twinkled. "Both sides are right. Which ought to guarantee one helluva fight."

Paulk thought back to his appointment. Had the prosecutors rated him gullible enough, or frightened or expedient enough, to wink at such savagery? If they had, were they wrong? Here, in a room where he had known gala evenings with Jerry, where he had borrowed advice for the defense of John Gleason, he was certain only of his dread.

Laura said, "Dad, please go to bed. It's nearly two o'clock."

Fibbing elaborately that he would never have guessed it, the old fox heaved himself to his feet. Then, as if something in the clutter of note pads and books had commanded his eye, he stood squinting at the table, his arms folded across his back.

"A shame," he said, "to think of piling more grief on Martha and her children. Like you, Wen, I'd hate to vandalize the fables and institutions that are Hutch's monuments in this town." He shook his head slowly. "I grow softer in my declining years. Besides, I was always too fond of Hutch."

"Are you changing sides?"

"No, I'm laying the predicate for a speech I used to waste on your father when his puritanism was bankrupting him. It's ethics, social history, and Shakespeare—"

"Mr. Singer," Laura said with tender exasperation, "I hope what you have in mind is 'to sleep, perchance to dream.' "

"There is also," said Paulk, "a line that goes, 'I am gone forever [exit, pursued by a bear].' "

"I'm going. But first, let me volunteer to brief the law for this case."

Paulk glanced inquiringly at Laura. Her father looked thinner, drained by fatigue, too old to be reading law against a deadline. Laura's eyes agreed, but on a scrap of paper she wrote, "Yes, let him."

"It's asking a lot," Paulk said, "but I was planning to ask it anyway."

"Good," Singer brightened, "I'll start tomorrow, provided you can say how you expect to defend."

The decision could be put off no longer. Paulk reverted, ruefully, to a design that had forced itself upon his thoughts during the interviews with Priest and, embellishing the scheme as he described it, committed himself. "First," he said, "insanity. I'll need some law on heat of sudden passion, the mind incapable of cool reflection, et cetera. I know, Tigart will be looking for this, but I want to raise about a half of an issue on it anyway."

Singer grunted, disappointed.

"Also, since Shep put this self-defense idea in Ray's mind, I may as well do the best I can with it. It'll be flimsy, only technical if it's possible at all. Nobody will be convinced, but if we can succeed at having it included in the Court's charge, it'll be there to give some soft-hearted juror a way out if he happens to be looking for one.

"Next, there'll be odds and ends—some authority for an inexpert witness to give an opinion on a man's sanity, the law on robbery of a corpse, and I hope you can find me a way to shorten the *res gestae*. They'll contend it runs a couple of months, from the day of the killing on through the arrests. Unless I can cut it down to a day or two, they'll hurt us on what passed between Ray and his wife during the flight. Then, there's this illegal confession, where I'll need a wad of authorities."

"It is clearly inadmissible," Singer said, "but if I know Sharman, you can't keep it out. Even if you should prove duress, which you probably cannot, he'd rule against you."

"That's true, but I'll want to put a good objection into the record. Afterwards, if the confession is all about robbery, as Ray says it is, I'll let them introduce it with no more fuss."

Singer chuckled, foreseeing the strategy and delighted by it. But Laura aroused in indignation. "How could you *not* fuss," she said, "if it really isn't a proper confession?"

Paulk smiled. "Two reasons. One, since it's unlikely I can keep the thing out, I'd be a fool to make a hard *losing* fight which would merely impress the jury with how damaging that statement is. Two, if Anglin actually did leave out part of Ray's story, we may want the statement in evidence so we can have at them about it." He turned back to Old Jack. "The fact is, I consider everything the confession does *not* say as the foundation for Priest's real defense."

Singer broke into a grin. "Then you'll be wanting a passel of case-law on Article 1220."

"Yes."

There was no need to spell out the rest. He would plead insanity and self-defense as feints, puffs of smoke. When he could hold back no longer, he would hit them with the genuine issue, that of homicide justified by adultery. It called for cynicism, ruthlessness with a good name and good legacy. He was accepting a dirty job.

Immediately he felt apprehension. He was stepping across a strange threshold, into that half-lit nether zone of human affairs Singer had tried so often to picture for him. Didn't the shrewd business trans-actions, the deals of practical politics, the realistic practice of criminal law, like all the other essential maneuvers which were neither honor-able nor dishonorable and which the world couldn't afford to outlaw, require a place to occur? The secret arena existed, filling the space be-tween right and wrong. Within it, all was both legal and immoral. In prospect, Paulk saw it as a cold Godless twilight to be ventured on cautiously. With the Gleason defense, he'd been blind. This time he must see and be wary.

"Hard decision?" Singer said.

Paulk grinned. In a way, he thought, his fearfulness was a snobbery. To rout it he could reflect on his belief that even a ne'er-do-well deserved justice, that rich men need not rule the law nor law grind the poor. Perhaps he could destroy delicately, discriminately.

Old Jack limped stiffly around the table and held out his hand. "Good night, Wen. When you see your boy again, congratulate him for me. The poor rube seems to have gotten himself a lawyer." He stooped to kiss Laura, then stalked out through the French doors, the wicker imprint of the chair visible on the back of his head.

Laura crossed her eyes and together they reached for cigarettes. They lit up, gazing at each other like children snitching a few drags behind the barn.

"You're good for him, Wen. He has worried all week, afraid you'd refuse his help. Now, what is my part?"

"Why do you want in, really?"

"It would be something to work at. Besides, they were arguing capital punishment at Guild tonight, and my skin crawled. What bothered me, I think, was how everyone spoke of your client. People hate him without knowing a thing, and they seem willing to hate anyone who raises a hand for him. It made me feel—well, sick, and belligerent." She transferred her gaze to the tip of her cigarette. "Oh, this tastes wonderful. I wish I weren't such a slave."

He said, "You know the Hutchersons well, don't you?"

"Yes—or, I did, until I turned gypsy."

"Tell me what they are like."

"It won't cheer you," she moistened her lips. "Martha is sweet, gracious. It's hard for me to think of her as vengeful. As for the sons, Jess Jr. is the oilman, sort of calm and resourceful like his mother. Charles is the Marine officer, and I'll bet he's great at it. He's the one who made the awful threats back when Mr. Hutcherson was killed. But, you should remember him; he used to come to our parties. Charles was always inviting people outside when he'd had a few drinks."

"And the girl?"

"Yes, Valle. It's worst for her. She isn't pretty, has always seemed overwhelmed by things except around her father. She loved him terribly, if that's the word."

"I don't know what you mean."

"Nor do I, not clearly. I just know she reacted extremely to everything Mr. Hutcherson said or did. If he said 'bread,' she answered 'butter.' Like wearing those ridiculous cowboy boots because he did, and living with his horses although she was scared to death of them. The last time I saw Valle, she was vowing to become a nurse. I remembered then that Mr. Hutcherson had expressed his admiration for nurses in a speech quoted in the newspapers. You see, his death must have wrecked her. But, of course, she's only seventeen. . . ."

As promised, he wasn't cheered. He found himself testing the idea of calling on Mrs. Hutcherson, apprising her candidly of the nature of his defense. Forewarned, the family could stay away from court, could arrange to send Valle away for a while. But, he knew, it wouldn't do. It would amount to revealing himself to Ike Tigart, to losing before he began.

Laura said, "Did you see your photograph in the papers?"

He nodded. Reporters had tracked him down, complained at his noncommittal answers, and departed to produce speculative stories about him. One had supposed him to be a superstitious fellow who carried Jack Singer's briefcase as a luck charm, another had made it a point to associate him with Kelso, Lemons & Hurst despite E. C.'s precautions. The *Tribune* had used an old picture sludged up from the morgue and showing his idiotic grin over the Gleason acquittal.

"The reporters weren't very friendly, were they?"

"I guess I didn't let them like me."

"That particular picture," she said. "Could they have chosen it on purpose, to remind people—?"

"I haven't thought about it," he snapped.

Laura braced. "Wen, I'm not deliberately meddling with your sacred cows. But I admit you're making me feel like kicking their sacred rears."

"I'm sorry, I didn't intend to bark."

"It happens I don't share your reverence for your wife, and you shouldn't expect me to. I won't genuflect everytime something suggests her, and I think—"

"I said, I'm sorry!"

They sat in silence, cooling slowly, startled at themselves. He was tired, frayed, and as his temper subsided, he felt conspicuous and silly. After a minute their eyes met, and she smiled. "Am I fired?"

He shook his head. "I'm wondering if you'd be willing to spend the next two weeks checking my jury list."

"Oh, yes, if you trust me to. Where do I begin?"

"You can get addresses and occupations out of the City Directory. The Credit Bureau will have information, and the crisscross directory will give you the names of a juror's neighbors. If you phone the neighbors, you can learn something of each man's temperament, religion, politics, health, and whether he has any special interest in the case. Usually, they come up with more than you expect."

"Will there be time?"

"Not enough to check the entire list. I've marked off those likely to be excused and all those I already know something about. That leaves about two hundred strangers. Too many?"

"I'll try."

"I could use real detail on the women, and on the Negroes if there happen to be any." A jury of two sexes and two races would be doubly segregated at night; it might, through a long trial, tend to factionalize. The likelihood was small, still, if he wanted twelve minds to disagree, he had to supply them every reason to, even the most remote.

"All right," Laura said, "what else?"

"Would you mind picking out a suit for Priest? He needs something inexpensive and unflashy, but I don't want him to look like he's doing penance. I'll sign a blank check for you. Also, there'll be some letters to Ray's sister, the VA, and his old top-kick in the service."

She walked along with him out to the veranda. He was pleased with her, glad of the sympathy she felt for both Priest and the Hutchersons. She laughed at how he and her father had discussed the connivance issue with restraint, being fuddyduds, she said, as if they thought this to be adult law too risqué for her ears. Bless them, he thought, these Singers. If they kept knocking old wreaths off his shoulders, it was because they cared about him. And if he was grasping that this would be his trial as well as Ray Priest's, it was because the Singers had known it first.

At the steps she stopped to breathe appreciatively of the night. "I almost forgot, Wen. Today I saw a bottle of catsup among your papers. Is it evidence or something?"

"No," he said, "I give it to you."

She smiled, touched his hand, and went padding away on her best undressed feet, back into the house.

PART TWO

XIII

The sidewalks and asphalt streets surrounding Bonita County Courthouse hissed with early heat. It was Monday, the eleventh of May. On
Fifth, people exchanged sleepy good mornings as they streamed in and
out of the post office and, reminded what day it was, paused to look
toward the courthouse. Across the square on Sixth, traffic honked and
clashed and drivers leaned out to see what to blame for the extraordinary snarl.

The Houston Street shopkeepers had rolled down faded canvas
awnings, swept the night litter off their sidewalks and hung their windows with banners reading WELCOME, SHRINERS. Presently they were
assembled at the center of the block in the shade laid by the jail
tower and, leaning on their brooms, they tried to identify the jurors
among the hundreds converging on the square. Occasionally one
of them would mosey off down the block to get a view of the doings at
Fifth and Lamar.

There, under the counterfeit pagodas of Shrine Temple, a parade
was organizing. A paunchy drum and bugle corp, outfitted in kilts
and feathers, was tuning up. Crowds of sequined Camel Herders,
mystic nobles resplendent in their brocade finery, and harassed in-
itiates wearing rouge and sunbonnets and mother hubbards swarmed
over the parade vehicles. There was an aged hand-pumped fire engine,
a Stanley Steamer, and a shortened Model-T that ran on two wheels

83

like a chariot. On the carpeted bed of a truck, three breechclouted slaves primed a cannon and attached its lanyard, and a squad of novices equipped with coal scuttles was being rehearsed on the task of policing up after the Potentate's horse during the march along Main.

The street people commented upon the coincidence. The Shrine's Spring Ceremonial, in which Jess Hutcherson's bombs had been a traditional feature, and the murder trial of Ray Priest, were opening on the same day.

Owen Paulk had spent most of the night at work in the Singers' library. Nonetheless, he felt well enough, still borne up by the momentum of his hectic weeks of preparation. He reached the square at 8:45 A.M. As he walked toward the north door, he saw the news people assembled there, waiting to ambush the principals as they arrived. With Romney Davenport of the *Tribune* and Edward St. Clair, whose voice of doom depressed listeners nightly on television, were several others unknown to Paulk but identified by their cocksure countenances as the visiting big-time press.

To avoid them Paulk turned aside, jaywalked across Fifth, circled around through the Shrine crowd, and entered the courthouse through the seldom-used east door. The lower hall hummed with people. He pushed through unnoticed, slipped across behind the reporters and eased into the sheriff's office. Andy Grosscup's stronghold milled with men in cowboy gear and badges and pistols. Aside from the deputies there were highway patrolmen, plainclothesmen from the police department, Rangers, and the pair of aloof young agents of the FBI. None spoke as he drew a jail pass, checked his briefcase and buzzed for the elevator which, this morning, was operated by a bald-headed trusty.

In the jail office Charlie O'Brien hastily folded his newspaper, hiding the bannerline that proclaimed the State's certainty of a death penalty. "Ray ain't dressed yet, Mr. Paulk," the jailor said. "But if you want to go on back into the tank, I'll take you."

Priest was in a maximum security section, known as the Federal Tank because it conformed to Justice Department standards. The gray cages formed an island inside a broad run-around. In each a steel bunk hung by chains from the wall, a lavatory stood supported only by its pipes, and there was a stark unscreened commode. As O'Brien unlocked the door, Ray straightened from his bunk and nodded. He was naked except for his shorts.

Paulk saw that the barber had visited, as promised. But the result was not what he had hoped for. The vain foretop had been mowed off, the imprudent sideburns were gone. Still, Priest would impress no one as the All-American boy. His cowlick swirled more weirdly than ever. The face was, if anything, coarser than before, and the uninhabited eyes and sagging jaw appeared larger and, yes, almost moronic.

Paulk tapped his watch. "Aren't you running late?"

"Well, my sister came up to see me."

"I thought she was to visit you last night."

"Yes, sir, she was, except they wouldn't let her in. Claimed she couldn't prove she was kin of mine."

"Who, exactly, did that?"

"To tell you the truth—"

"Stop saying that, Ray."

"Yes, sir. Anyways, all I know is it was one of them night deputies, and Angie got pretty mad. You seen Angie yet?"

"I met her bus yesterday." Paulk found it hard to believe Angie Callahan was Priest's sister. Slender, past forty, tastefully dressed; handsome in spite of tight narrow lips and a thin arched nose, she was intelligent and looked it, and her loyalty to "Baby" was both militant and appealing. "I want her to sit with us, if the Judge consents. Come on, get dressed."

Priest extracted the last pin from a new white shirt and slid it on over muscular shoulders still beaded from his shower. He took up a blue necktie from which a tag dangled. The suit was a plain summer gray, the shoes shiny black loafers. Paulk was pleased; Laura had chosen well.

He said, "Was there anything during the weekend that I should know about?"

"Well, that Mr. Anglin was fooling around up here again Sunday. Until pretty late, I heard."

"Talking with Patty Sue?"

"Yes, sir, I reckon. One of the cooks said Mr. Shepherd came up for a while, too."

This was where Paulk missed the courthouse contacts he once had had. No one had tipped him on Anglin's Sunday jail visits; no one had admitted him to the courthouse rumor mill which, no doubt, knew why Patty Sue had seen a doctor.

"All right," he said. "Do you remember all I've told you?"

"Yes, sir, I guess."

"This will take days, and you'll get tired. But don't fidget, don't duck from anything you may hear. You'll be facing the jurors and the witnesses. Don't avoid looking at them. If something funny happens, remember that none of this is laughable to you. Just sit and listen, and don't bother me with anything unless you're positive it's important."

Priest, having gotten slowly into his trousers, sat down to put on his shoes.

"The District Attorney's bunch will be directly across the table from us. Be sure you don't get interested in their papers, or in listening in on their huddles. I want you so inactive you'll look like you belong someplace else, understand?"

"Yes, sir."

"Before I go, have you any questions?"

Priest stood up, stamped the new shoes on the concrete floor. "Well, I'd like to find out if Patty Sue—"

"No," Paulk said impatiently, "despite all that newspaper nonsense, she won't be allowed to attend court." It was odd how not a line of the dull face changed while its distress somehow became apparent. "Anything else?"

"I was wondering if they aim to carry me down there wearing them chains."

"It's unlikely," Paulk said. "But if they try to, let them. It can be reversible error to display a prisoner in manacles before his jury, and we could use a few blunders."

Paulk turned toward the door. "Sir—" Priest said, the flat voice hoarsening.

"What is it?"

"It come to my mind—well, reckon what my chances is?"

So the somber day Priest had never really believed in had come. The boy knew it, was shocked, and the stoicism was dislodged.

"I'm sorry," Paulk said. "I can't promise you a thing, except that I'll do my best."

They looked at each other, for the first time considering between them the same grim likelihoods. Paulk was tempted to offer an assurance he did not feel. Instead he said, "You haven't fed me any hokum, have you? It all happened exactly as you've told me?"

"Yes, sir."

"Very well. I have to go. See you in court."

"Mr. Polk—"

"It's Paulk, dammit."

Priest swallowed without closing his mouth. "Sir, I figure to pay out these clothes, first chance I get."

"Zip up your fly."

The reporters intercepted him in the sheriff's office. They dogged his steps through the hall, bounded about him on the stairs. Was Ray nervous, did he still love his wife, had a psychiatrist examined him, would he be apt to take the stand? They probed for his estimate of how long it might take to get a jury, for the names of his witnesses, for a word on whether he intended to contest the confession. Once he'd have revelled in it; he would have stopped to joke, expound and parry, to make new clippings for Jerry's scrapbook. Now he answered shortly, if at all.

The pale-green fourth floor was a maelstrom. Officers, spectators, witnesses, members of the venire with white summons cards in their hands, collided and jostled and called out inquiries. Along the corridor walls, wedged into the line of church-type pews salvaged from the old courthouse, sat the women of the panel. Most had tucked back their feet, preferring the exposure of their knees to having their toes trampled on. Their presence, Paulk thought, added softness and warmth to the cold hard business of justice, and he smiled at a bewildered little woman because, like Jerry—no, Laura Singer—she had kicked off her shoes.

Someone gripped his arm and he looked up at Andy Grosscup. The high sheriff smelled like a poultice, from the greasy patch on his neck, and he moved as if the pain had made him fragile.

"Wen, they're waiting for you."

XIV

Guarding Judge Sharman's door was Nathan Hart, the gaunt, electric-eyed bailiff. Retired from the Rangers, remarkably agile at seventy-six, Hart unconsciously dignified a lusterless job. Previously, the bailiffs had been worn-out and incompetent deputies assigned from the lower strata of the sheriff's department. Uncle Nathan, as the courthouse girls addressed him, was a complete change of pace. He had been a celebrated officer, and only recently had enhanced his reputation for marksmanship by shooting down a fleeing jailbreaker at seventy-five yards. It was an immortal shot, famous because Hart's one bullet had passed through the felon's buttocks and left *four* neat holes.

Although the sheriff had been chronically cantankerous with his other subordinates since the blunders of the Hutcherson investigation and his carbuncle, his tone with Hart was subdued.

" 'Morning, Wen," Hart said.

"Am I in trouble?"

"I don't think so." Hart opened the door for him. "It's just that everyone else got here early."

Like the courtroom, the Judge's sanctum was exempted from the air-conditioning in deference to the old gentleman's recurrent bronchitis. It was hot and crowded. In one chair sat Herb Cameron, his fingers interlaced and thumbs tumbling over each other. Occupying the other was Hollis Anglin, sniffling from his flu, looking dour and newly out of bed.

Two men stood at the east window. One was Mr. Funderburg, the dumpy little court reporter known to compose most of Judge Sharman's jury charges and dated by how he still wore creases in his coat sleeves. Near him was Billy Shepherd. Shep sparkled from soap and expensive haberdashery but, Paulk thought, he looked tense, his joyousness muted by his role in a litigation of such unfamiliar magnitude. Under Judge Sharman's portrait collection was Ike Tigart.

"Howdy, Wen," Tigart said.

Ike had been hitting his stride just as Jack Singer retired. Effortlessly he had assumed Old Jack's eminence as the dean of defenders, which accounted for why Paulk sometimes took a jaundiced view of him. If he thought Ike needn't have wedded so quickly the dream he once had wooed, he did admit that the groom deserved the bride.

The special prosecutor was nearly as tall as the sheriff and more massive. His stiff clay-red hair, clipped high all around, accented the Prussian roll of flesh that girded his neck and indexed his temperament unmistakably. He was red faced, red handed; his small blue eyes were thoroughly inquisitive, although he could make them friendly and naive to charm a witness into a trap. Ike seldom prosecuted, but Paulk didn't question his ability to focus the community wrath upon Ray Priest, quite as effectively as he often evoked maudlin public compassion for an offender. He knew prosecution from his experience at defeating it, thus he could cross to the other side of the docket without slackening his gait. At the counsel table, Tigart was deceptively relaxed. He would pack a great chew of Beech Nut into his permanently pouched jaw and hold it there hours on end without spitting. It caused an agony of suspense among those who worried and waited and kept puckering their lips for him.

Judge Sharman sat at his desk, coat off, but vest on and buttoned. The superb white hair was awry.

"Mr. Paulk, this case was called for nine o'clock."

"I apologize, sir. I had to stop off."

"Hereafter, I expect every session to begin on time. Unless we press on—"

An explosion trembled the building. It seemed to blast the Judge up from his chair. "Good gracious, Mr. Sheriff!"

"It's them Shriners, Judge. They've got a cannon."

"You needn't tell me what artillery sounds like. Get down there, see if you can quieten them."

"They're just cutting up a mite. It'll be kind of hard to hush 'em down."

Blanched, still shaken, the Judge said he had no desire to affront the Shriners, despite the pool tables they kept in the Temple basement, but he thought they should know he wanted to hold court, and would do so if they didn't mind. As Andy went out, Sharman snatched off his collar and reached for a fresh one. Paulk imagined that the others, like himself, were longing, already, for a judge as good as Sharman looked.

"Now, gentlemen, let's see where we are. We have return of service on more than four hundred veniremen, which threatens us with a lot of milling and confusion. Nevertheless, if we all cooperate, we ought to be able to move right along. Toward that end, I believe we could agree to a definite time limit on the *voir-dire* examinations. What do you think, Mr. Cameron?"

Herb opened his mouth, flushed, and failed to speak. Paulk squirmed for him. It was obvious the special prosecutor would call the turns for the State.

Tigart said, "That suits us fine," and his smile at Paulk was gently sardonic. See, it said, I've gotten in a little spadework while you overslept.

"You, Mr. Paulk?"

"Your Honor, we are entitled to a reasonable time for testing each juror, and I have to claim it. This defendant is in no position to waive any right he has."

"Young man, no one has suggested you waive anything. Nor do I consider myself unreasonable. I think about ten minutes to the side would be adequate. Do either of you object to that?"

"Not at all," said Tigart.

"I do," Paulk said. "From the first, I've felt it unlikely a jury can be had off this list."

"Tut," the Judge said, "it's a large enough panel."

"Yes, sir, it's large. And, in my opinion, abnormal. I think we'd be risking error to conduct the *voir dire* by the clock. But, if that's the Court's decision, I'll have to change my plans. To start with, I'll have to file the defendant's affidavit in challenge to the array."

This, his first trump, surprised them. Sharman glanced at the others, his beautiful face at once saddened and befuddled. It occurred to Paulk that the Judge might never have presided over a challenge hearing. It was a rare proceeding in which Paulk could allege the jury was improperly drawn, picked with view to assuring a conviction, and he could offer proof. Sharman would overrule, no doubt. Still, the Judge saw the prospect of a long hearing, of wasted days instead of the wasted hours of an unlimited *voir dire*.

Paulk moved his gaze to the others. Anglin had turned to him, his sullen mouth pursed in reappraisal, as if he had priorly doubted Paulk was licensed in the law. Shep wore an uneasy, yet rosy, grin; Funderburg winked at him. Tigart met his eye, nodding to concede that the maneuver had worked.

"Very well," the Judge scowled. "However, we can at least agree not to dilly and dally. I see no purpose in examining a juror half an hour before getting to the questions on which he is most apt to disqualify."

Paulk couldn't help wanting to prolong his victory. "Sir, I've no desire to be tedious. I want time because I'm serious in my feeling that this panel doesn't reflect the ordinary output of a jury wheel."

Immediately he knew he had carried the bluff too far, had fallen into the error common to all inexperienced lawyers. The beginner couldn't keep from trying to embellish a point; often he spoiled the hat by trying to add a feather. Sure enough, Tigart called him on it.

"Why, Wen, if you feel that strongly about it, I think you ought to go ahead and challenge the array."

Since he was too far from a window to fall out, Paulk backpedaled lamely. "If it's understood about the *voir dire,* then I'm satisfied."

"It is," the Judge stared at him wearily. "Now, gentlemen, is the Rule invoked?"

"No," Ike Tigart answered, "not by the State."

It took Paulk off-balance. Certainly the prosecution wanted the witnesses barred from the courtroom. But, knowing Sharman's automatic resentment of the side that demanded it, Tigart was saddling the defense with the blame.

'Well, Mr. Paulk?" the Judge prompted.

"Yes, sir," he yielded, "I invoke the Rule."

Sharman glowered and drummed on his docket book at this further evidence of a contrary, upstart defense counsel, one desirous of no rapport with the Court. Tigart smiled sweetly.

"All right," the Judge looked up at the clock, "what else, what else?"

Paulk swallowed. "If you please, I have a question regarding the defendant's sister. She wants to sit with her brother, if the Court will consent."

"You, young man, have just invoked the Rule. Is this woman to be a witness?"

"She isn't under subpoena."

Tigart cut in. "But you do intend to use her?"

"It depends."

"Then," Tigart said, "we'll object to her. His witnesses are bound by the Rule, the same as ours."

Paulk directed himself to the Judge. "I can say I doubt we'll call Mrs. Callahan. However, since she might testify, and since she is the only friend this boy has, I'll ask the State to agree to exempt her from the Rule."

Tigart looked up at the ceiling.

"Your Honor," Anglin stirred as if from a nap, "I don't think we need to seat a weeping woman in the pit, right in the face of the jury. Personally, I believe I'd get pretty tired of sharing the counsel table with a defense waterworks."

"We may all tire of each other," Paulk said evenly. "Frankly, I expect to grow weary of you."

"Here, now! Plain courtesy and decorum isn't too much to ask of all of you. Mercy, if we are quibbling already—"

"Sir, the defendant asked me to make this request. Otherwise I wouldn't have; I care little, either way. But, if Mr. Anglin is worried about what the jury will see, he might do well to think again. The jury will see three or four prosecutors on one side of the table, and the defendant and I alone on the other. Actually, I think this is the picture I'd prefer."

It touched home; the State didn't want Priest to look as ganged up on as, in truth, he was. Tigart adjusted his quid. Anglin snapped a toothpick between his fingers, pouted a moment, then shrugged. "Judge, it makes no difference to me. I don't care if he gets Jesus Christ to sit with him."

Sharman recoiled, his lips blueing with shock. As he fumbled at a reprimand, Tigart stepped forward.

"I feel a great deal of sympathy for the woman," he said. "Have you noticed, Wen, how she calls him 'Baby'?"

The inference was clear. The State regarded Angie Callahan as inconsequential. To Ike she was a zero, useless even as a stage prop.

Still glaring at Anglin, Judge Sharman got up. He reached absently for another fresh collar. "Mr. Paulk, I'll expect you to see that she isn't—isn't demonstrative, do you understand?"

"Yes, sir."

"Very well. Five minutes, gentlemen."

Without a word, Cameron hurried out. Paulk followed, pretending not to notice that The Shepherd was hustling after him. Working his way through the tumult of the hall, he found the stairs and walked down two flights to the telephone booth in the rotunda. He dialed, and Laura answered.

"Is Jack up?"

"No, but I think he is awake."

"Don't disturb him. I just wanted you both to know Mrs. Callahan has her ticket for the show. And tell Jack the challenge gimmick worked, although I nearly muffed it."

"Oh, I'm glad," she said. "And I'm glad you called. I've been tied in knots all morning. Wen—if I came down, could I help at all?"

"You could," he said. "But please don't come. I'd rather not announce that I have the Singers as allies."

"Surely they've already heard about it."

"Probably," he said. "But the jury hasn't. Has Sergeant Blossom shown up?"

"No. I'm wondering if he really means to."

"He'd better," Paulk said. "Or I'll make him take Priest back into the Air Force."

She laughed. "Are you jittery, Wen?"

"Scared is the word, I think."

"Don't be. Remember how right you felt last night? You're just as right this morning."

For a moment, he held the line and waited. In former days, he had placed last-minute calls to Jerry. She would propose some outlandish wager on the case, tease him out of his pit nerves. Back then, every lawsuit had been a plaything.

He said, "You did well with Ray's wardrobe. He looks like a seminary student. How much did it cost me?"

"It didn't. As I told you, I wanted to contribute something. Oh, here comes that slovenly old parlor lawyer, grabbing at the telephone. Good luck, Wen. If you should feel faint, just dampen your wrists and breathe through your mouth. . . ."

XV

The Criminal District Court, 191st Judicial District of Texas, did not piddle with pageantry. There was no "hear ye, hear ye," no standing reception for the Judge. Nor did James A. Sharman wear a jurist robe. In his thinking, robes and ceremony belonged to the nefarious; he had seen both put to evil use by Vigilantes and the Ku Klux Klan. His court came into session the moment he settled into his leather-lined chair and began directing the bailiff through a series of window and shade adjustments, these calculated to reach a tolerable compromise between ventilation, street noise, and sun glare.

Nathan Hart was touching up these adaptions when Paulk arrived. The hall swirled with disgruntled spectators driven out so the venire might be seated. The panel, wilted from having passed from the coolness of the corridor into the courtroom heat, jammed the yellow oak pews, spilled over into the aisle, and lined the walls. Paulk paused at how familiar it all looked.

There, in the row of reserved chairs inside the pit rail, were the deputy sheriffs, newspapermen, and the lawyers trying to make it appear they were superior to curiosity and had happened in just to kill time. On the pit benches beneath the windows sat more lawyers and reporters and the courthouse people who forsook their jobs when something interesting was afoot. At his desk against the jury box, Mr. Funderburg tinkered with a tape recorder, as though he intended to take down the jury examination, which of course he did not, and sitting in the box in her neat sheriff's department uniform was the pretty, blue-haired lady of fifty who served as bailiff for women jurors. She, Mrs. McCormick, was new since Paulk's first criminal career. But what else had changed?

Paulk turned toward the back corner of the pit and there, as expected, sat Mr. Durfee in his special chair. It was Mr. Durfee's distinction to have attended every jury trial in Bonita County during the fourteen years since his retirement from the Santa Fe. His was the amen corner. To Paulk it seemed the old pensioner hadn't moved a muscle since monitoring the Gleason trial. Mr. Durfee affected the same black string tie, the same dowdy black suit and broad gray galluses. There were the wrinkled high-topped black shoes with the rubber soles glued on the bottoms, the trouser legs ridden up to disclose the long underdrawers tucked into the sock tops. And as ever, he wore his Railroad Brotherhood pin and chewed his gum and held ready the advice he hoped would be solicited of him. It was as if court had ground along continuously, through the past five years.

Paulk started to the counsel table where Ike Tigart slouched in the State's front chair. Next was Anglin, then Herb Cameron. The sheriff had drawn his chair up close behind them. At the foot end sat Billy Shepherd, beaming goodwill as though he was beginning to feel more comfortable in his peculiar connection with these affairs. Across the table Ray Priest sat straight and stolid and inexpressive. His sister was leaning forward to whisper in his ear. Seeing Paulk, she smiled.

Mrs. Callahan wore a navy suit, a perky white hat that certainly had been new for Easter, and a look of hope. A jury, Jack Singer would contend, was ever more influenced by what it saw than what it heard. Tigart, Paulk observed, wasn't unaware of the theory. From his open briefcase protruded a scarlet, black-tasseled Shrine fez, duplicates of which crowned the heads of dozens of the waiting jurors.

"Why," Paulk said, "don't we move this case over to the Temple and settle it with black and white balls?"

"Go to hell," Tigart smiled. "Or to the Oddfellows."

"Mr. Bailiff," the Judge said, "where is the clerk?"

Sharman sat fingering his chin, twisting to his left, than to the right, probably debating the arrangement of the flags, while they waited. The American flag hung on a staff at his left, the Lone Star of Texas was at his right. The Judge was never sure this was correct.

Minutes passed before Theodore Holcomb appeared. The district clerk came slowly, gasping accusingly as the courtroom temperature staggered him. The Judge's scathing stare followed his progress to the desk beside the bench, and the clerk returned the fire from beneath fierce white brows. The two old men brimmed with spite for each other. Holcomb despised the Judge for his health and authority and higher salary; Sharman hated the clerk for his seniority in the courthouse, for a political weal that had kept him in office when he was caught paying his medical bills out of filing fees, and he hated him the most, it was said, for thirty years of impunctuality.

Sharman opened the docket book. "Cause Number twelve-ought-sixty-two, *The State of Texas versus Raymond Elliot Priest.*"

Herb Cameron announced, "The State is ready."

Paulk got to his feet. "The defendant is ready. However, Your Honor, I would like to ask what is going on here at the counsel table. Besides the State's four attorneys—"

"Three," Tigart said.

"Besides this army of attorneys, they seem to be bringing the sheriff in against us also. I don't know what he intends doing there, but—"

"May it please the Court," Tigart said, "we'll ask the sheriff to scoot back his chair a little, if his presence is offensive to Mr. Paulk."

"I'm fond of the sheriff," Paulk said. "It's the odds that worry me." He disliked alienating Grosscup so soon. But the jury was somewhere in the crowd; it wasn't too early to establish himself as the underdog.

"Mr. Sheriff," the Judge sighed, "will you move back a bit, please? Now, are the witnesses present?"

Herb responded. "For the State, yes, with the exception of one or two who are available on ten-minute call."

"May it please the Court," Paulk said, "the defendant has no witnesses under subpoena at this time. It's possible we'll have some people to be sworn later."

"Mr. Paulk, do I understand you have announced ready when you've no assurance your witnesses will be here?"

"No, Your Honor. I'm just not sure we'll offer anyone. We are ready to proceed."

"He means," Tigart drawled, "that he doesn't care to identify his people for us. We've no objection."

"Very well." The Judge lifted his gaze to the gallery. "The witnesses will stand."

Along the front rows men and women stood, their faces grave, their eyes tentatively upon Ray Priest as they began to feel the burden of their duty. Ray stared back, calm if uncomprehending, and Paulk was encouraged to think some of his coaching had stuck.

"Raise your hands and be sworn," said the Judge. "You do, each of you, solemnly swear the testimony you are about to give in the case before this court is the truth, the whole truth, and nothing but the truth, so help you God."

The standees bobbed their heads.

"The Rule has been invoked," the Judge continued. "This means that you are under the direction of the Court from this moment forward. The Rule forbids your presence in the courtroom, except for your own appearance on the stand. You are excluded from hearing the testimony of the other witnesses, and you must wait outside, unless specifically instructed otherwise."

The looks of fortitude and dedication fell away, displaced by incredulousness, then anger. This was seduction, a caprice. The witnesses had counted on front-row seats. Instead, by some treachery they were being banished from the grand drama which couldn't have been joined without them.

"While under the Rule, you must not discuss this case with each other, or with anyone except the attorneys. Let me caution you that the bailiff will report any violation of these instructions, and the violator is subject to judgement for contempt."

"May it please the Court," Paulk said, "there are several witnesses here who have refused to talk to me. I'm sure they are in good faith, that the problem is merely a misconception of the defendant's rights. If the Court would explain—?"

"I've got an old textbook," Tigart said. "It tells how to deal with hostile witnesses. I'd lend it gladly."

"Thanks," Paulk said. "But since I'm sure you'll be needing it—"

Sharman snapped his fingers like a schoolmaster, shook his head at them, and focused again on the smoldering witnesses. "You are instructed that it is the defense counsel's right to question you as to what you know about this case, and it is your duty to answer him."

Paulk felt he'd been had. Tigart had shown the witnesses whom to regard as their antagonist, and Paulk himself had set it up by the abortive timing of his request. He studied the special prosecutor's sunny red smile and swore, next time, to weigh and anticipate.

"Now," said the Judge, "since we'll need time to find a jury, I am going to excuse the witnesses until nine o'clock tomorrow morning."

The betrayed witnesses filed out, some glancing back at members of the venire moving into their vacated seats, others turning furious eyes on Ray Priest. Paulk wished witnesses could understand the Rule was essential because there were liars among them.

Sharman addressed the venire. "The clerk will call your names. Please answer up as quickly as possible."

Theodore Holcomb stood up, set his glasses. He read out the names in a tinny, shallow voice that hesitated, faltered, or broke off as he lost his place. The lawyers, following painfully along on their lists, interrupted when the clerk skipped someone or when he gored a name so horribly it seemed the owner's vanity needed repair. The sirens, whistles, and drums of a cavorting Masonry thundered and screamed beneath the windows. Through the first hour, the Judge fidgeted and winced in disgust. Afterwards, in an aspect of sad resignation, he swiveled his chair away, shaded his eyes with his hand, and dozed.

Monotonously the venire shrunk to two hundred eighteen. Eighty-four were unserved, another seventy-three had been excused by agreement of counsel, twenty-six were lost to incorrect spellings and erroneous addresses on Holcomb's jury list, and there were ninety-nine unexcused absentees.

Judge Sharman awakened in a fury. He lectured the attorneys for abuse of the agreed excuse privilege. He undertook to chastise the clerk for his errors. But out of the sanctuary of his long entrenchment, Theodore retorted and the reprimand digressed to a spat between crotchety old men. Suddenly, the Judge called Andy Grosscup to his feet.

"Mr. Sheriff, I am issuing attachments for the absentees. I want them served at once, and I want these people brought here for this afternoon's session."

Grosscup, ashen at the thought of locating ninety-nine missing jurors in less than two hours, went stilting out with Holcomb tripping along behind him. Paulk couldn't help delighting in the pandemonium that would descend, shortly, upon the sheriff's lounging cowboys.

Sneaking a look across the table, he considered the situation. It seemed to work to the advantage of Ray Priest. Certainly, the State's intent had been to force him to expend his fifteen peremptory challenges quickly, freeing them to race along unhampered at filling the box with Hutch's admirers and avengers. Now that the list was shortened by half, Ike would have to think again. Paulk's challenges would go farther, penetrating the panel more deeply.

Sharman ordered the surviving veniremen to stand and be sworn. "You, and each of you, do solemnly swear that you will true answers make to such questions as may be propounded to you by the Court, or under its direction, touching upon your service and qualifications as a juror, so help you God."

Methodically, the Judge began the test of basic qualifications. None of the panel was unable to read and write, none was presently under felony indictment, none admitted to having been convicted of an offense involving moral turpitude. Several who were past sixty claimed their exemptions. Others faded when found to be neither freeholders of the state nor householders in the county. One had served on the grand jury which indicted the Priests. Two more defaulted from having served on other district-court juries during the preceding six months. The dismissal of doctors, druggists, policemen, railroad engineers and firemen, newspapermen and lawyers retired a dozen more.

At each departure, the Judge's anxiety grew.

"Before continuing, I want to make clear that I will accept no business excuses, no requests based on any claim of being an essential employe. Please don't waste the Court's time by offering them." He drew a deep breath and shouted: *"Is there anyone hard of hearing?"*

It brought no response.

"Do any of you have a chronic illness which would make jury service prohibitive, or dangerous, for you? Anyone who requires regular medical treatment, anyone subject to spells or seizures?"

After a moment, a man named Collins stood. His khaki work clothes caused Paulk to search him out in Laura's notes. Collins was a carpenter, resident of the lowly East Side; like Ray Priest, he was a native Oklahoman, and according to a neighbor, he had recently opined that the newspapers were being "too one-sided" against Priest. If there was a defense juror on the panel, this was he.

"All right, Mr. Collins, what's your problem?"

"Well, sir, I've got gall-bladder trouble."

"And you think it would forbid your service?"

"Yes, Judge, I allow it might. Besides, I've been bothered pretty bad with high blood pressure, and my arthritis don't make me any easier."

Sharman frowned. "Is this your physician's diagnosis?"

"Yes, sir, I brung a note from him. I've been laid up with the flu, to where I'm still kind of woozy on my feet—"

"My God," said Ike Tigart, "call the man an ambulance."

Paulk scratched off Collins' name, consoling himself that the State would have cut the man anyway.

"I'll excuse you, Mr. Collins," the Judge said. "Anyone else?"

Besides a chipper-looking diabetic, there were three cardiacs, an ulcer diet, several ragweed sufferers enduring the anguish of the season. A handful of women pleaded young children who couldn't be left unattended. An oilman displayed a subpoena summoning him to Washington for a hearing on petroleum imports. By noon, as the Judge finished, a hundred seventy-three veniremen remained. Paulk grinned. The blue-ribbon jury hadn't disintegrated but, at least, the unpredictable had happened. The panel had diminished to a size he could hope to wade through.

"Disgraceful," the Judge snorted.

"Your Honor," Tigart revolved his chew like a pitcher about to deliver a curve, "since the sheriff is out rounding up the absentees, it seems to me we're in no great peril. However, why shouldn't we head off any possible shortage of jurors now, before we begin, by summoning talesmen?"

Again the prosecutor had caught him napping. Paulk turned to scan the venire. Despite all the dismissals, it appeared none of the Shriners was missing. Neither were those whose impeccable dress marked them as menacing to Ray Priest. It was still a dangerous venire. But, he shuddered, a body of talesmen could be far worse.

If Sharman so ordered, Andy Grosscup would sally forth on the town, gathering up whomever he might choose to encounter. Paulk regretted his early salvo against the sheriff. There was nothing to prevent Andy from lashing back with his pickup jury. Besides, the sheriff had been Hutch's friend. If he wished, he could draft the extra veniremen right out of the Posse clubhouse.

"Perhaps," Sharman was saying, "we should pick up about a hundred more—"

"May it please the Court," Paulk surrendered quietly, "I'm willing to continue with the venire as it is."

"In that case, we'll postpone the matter until we see how many regular members of the panel show up under the attachments." The Judge turned a pained gaze toward the clock. "All right, we'll recess for lunch. You of the venire—I want you back here at one-thirty. Now, where is the clerk? I can't understand why he's never on tap, never, when he's needed. . . ."

XVI

Mrs. Callahan tended to walk too fast, and he took her arm to slow her. As they crossed Houston Street in withering heat that was, nevertheless, refreshing after the stuffiness of the courtroom, she slipped into the surging monologue of stress and ordeal. Rapidly, desultorily, she framed passionate little questions, then answered them herself. If she asked gloomily, he thought, she replied with a determined optimism that touched him.

Wasn't it a shame Baby had to sit through the noon hour in jail without a bite to eat? But, she would bring him back some candy bars; bless his heart, all of his life he had loved Milky Ways. These Texans—they really hated Ray, didn't they; wasn't this what she saw in their eyes? Still, mightn't they change? Surely they would see he was unafraid, see that he was innocent. Oh, she knew Ray had never been one to make a good first impression. But he did look nice, awfully nice, in his handsome new suit.

It sounded like something said beside a casket.

The Little Star was overflowing. He led her on down the block to the corner drugstore and they ordered the chicken-fried steak which was, in reality, a shell of fried flour.

He said, "Mrs. Callahan, can you imagine your brother killing a man, under any circumstances?"

"Oh, no. Except in Korea; he killed men then."

"Which reminds me—did you bring his medals with you?"

"Yes, they're right here in my purse. Why do you ask if I can think of Baby as—in that way?"

"Because he did kill Jess Hutcherson. You've got to prepare yourself for what could happen to him. I want you to understand we can't deny the homicide; we can only try to excuse it."

Tears, or perspiration, had streaked her face powder.

"Mr. Paulk, if Ray did anything bad, it was because of that girl. She's always used him as though he had a handle on him, I know. Sometimes when they were separated and he stayed at my house, he'd cry like a child, all night, so hard that none of us got any sleep. Right now he's more upset about Patty wanting a divorce than he is this trial."

"He has rocks in his head, then."

She put down her fork. "Tell me, honestly—did things go badly this morning?"

"It will be a tough jury."

"I know nothing about trials," she said, "but that woman, being involved—should she be sitting among the jury?"

"What woman?"

"Lily Black, Ray's mother-in-law, from California. I thought you knew her. She's the peroxided woman, the one in the second row giving Ray those dirty looks. She hates him, she has from the first."

Another missed trick. If Patty Sue's mother was in town, he should have known it. As he remembered it from the clippings, Lily Black was a hairdresser who ascribed her daughter's delinquency entirely to the influence of Ray Priest.

"Are you acquainted with her?"

"No. We were in touch for a while after the kids were married, but I never saw her before today. Babe pointed her out to me."

Mrs. Black's name wasn't on the State's subpoena list. It seemed that if Tigart had scheduled her as a surprise witness, he would have kept her away from court, safe from courthouse curiosity. Perhaps she had come to solace her daughter, to be on hand when the reward was paid. Whatever, Paulk was certain he should talk to her. Mrs. Black might know why Patty wanted her husband electrocuted.

"Speaking of the devil," Mrs. Callahan said.

Paulk looked up. Hollis Anglin was plundering through the magazine racks. They watched him select an armload of comic books, pay for them and depart.

"Those are for Patty Sue, I'd bet," said Angie. "She reads the things day and night. Baby says they got into trouble in Georgia, once, because she stole some. Poor Baby, it's been nothing but misery for him since he met her. . . ."

As they ate, she cornered him with more questions. Was he not convinced that the immoral little flip of a wife had driven Ray out of his mind? Would there be much difficulty in proving that Ray had been defending himself against Mr. Hutcherson? Paulk's impulse was to admit these were dummy points, to disclose the truth of his defense. He checked himself. If Priest hadn't confided in her, had doubted his sister's ability to keep still, he dared not risk her either.

He was waving for his check when Billy Shepherd trotted in off the street. Shep hauled up, looked brightly about the store. He found them and came on, whipping his thigh with a folded newspaper, all but sprawling from his fleshy haste.

"Careful," Paulk whispered. "This man has pockets in his underwear."

"Hey, old son!" The Shepherd mopped his face with a silk handkerchief. "Thought you'd be at the Little Star. Hello, ma'am."

Gazing up, irritated, Paulk wished he had sent this jackleg scurrying from the counsel table this morning, along with the sheriff. He had not, and wouldn't, because he hoped the jury might associate Shep's reputation with the prosecution. At least, he didn't have to invite the man to join them.

"Glad to meet you," Shep's ebullient smile was on Mrs. Callahan. "You remember, we had some correspondence early in this merry-go-round."

Angie nodded coldly. Her eyes accused The Shepherd for his abandonment of her brother, for the whiskey on his breath, and probably for what she'd already heard of him during her few hours at the courthouse.

Paulk said, "What's on your mind?"

"Krist, you got away fast; I was aiming to ask you to eat with me." The tone was an admission that Tigart's party had rejected his company. "I was wondering if you've seen the afternoon paper?"

"No."

"Here, boy, look at mine."

Paulk unfolded the *Tribune*. Across the top of the page was the headline, BABY RAY CONFESSES! His breath stopped.

The District Attorney's office today made public the confession of Raymond Elliot (Baby Ray) Priest to the Jan. 14 robbery-murder of Jess Hutcherson.

The document was released just as the selection of a blue-ribbon jury to try the 28-year-old Oklahoma hobo got underway in Judge James A. Sharman's 191st District Court. In it, Priest told how he beat and garroted the famed oilwell shooter to death in a room at the Ranch Inn motel.

Priest, whose pretty teen-age wife also is charged in the murder, offered no mitigation for himself other than to infer that he killed the revered adventurer and philanthropist while suffering a mental blackout.

He said, "I saw Patty Sue [Mrs. Priest] coming out of the bathroom. The next thing I remember, I was standing over Mr. Hutcherson with his gun in my hand. There was a lot of blood on the bed clothes and I had some on my pants . . . I remember there was something around his neck, but I don't remember whether it was a shirt or towel or just what . . . I changed my pants and put on a clean pair and told my wife, 'Let's get out of here.' "

After other excerpts there followed the full text of the confession. Beside it, the story of the forenoon's proceedings was treated as a sidebar.

Paulk swore. "Whose idea was this?"

Shep spread his soft hands. "Me, I don't know. Nobody talked to me about it. Smells like Anglin. Or, Tigart—he ain't above it, either."

Paulk ground his teeth. Before court reconvened, every member of the venire would have read the statement; each would be horrified, inflamed. Tigart had timed it well, catching such jurors as might be sworn during the afternoon and thereafter be isolated from the news. Beyond this, Paulk saw, it would mean little now if he succeeded in keeping the statement out of evidence. The jury had seen it; it could not be ruled or argued out of their minds.

He slid from the booth, strode to the courthouse, sprinted up the stairs. Flushed, he paused at the fourth floor landing to control his breath. Spectators and veniremen filled the hall and courtroom. Some munched the sandwiches they had brought along in order to hold their seats, others assembled around copies of the *Tribune*. Cutting away from a reporter, he crashed against the door of the District Attorney's office. Herb Cameron opened it.

"Fair is fair," Paulk heard himself yelp. "Did you do this?"

"Come on in, Wen; I'm alone." Herb brushed aside the newspaper and turned to lead the way back to his office at the rear. He started to sit down behind his desk, then moved away from it to drop heavily on to a leather couch.

Paulk's anger cooled in sudden concern for his friend. Herb's hair was tousled. His shy naïveté seemed to lie dead on his mouth.

"I'm sorry, Wen. It stinks."

Paulk frowned. "You had nothing to do with this."

"I'm the District Attorney."

"But you didn't approve of it?"

"No," Herb swept back his hair. "I didn't stop it, either." He got up, crossed to the desk. His trousers drew tight and glistened over his rump, his coat stretched bindingly at the armpits, as he bent to bring out a bottle. "Want a drink?"

Paulk shook his head. Puzzled, sidetracked, he watched. Cameron, the teetotaller, poured a suicidal drink, regarded it with a shudder, then tossed it off. Tears bolted to his eyes as he wiped his lips. He sat down and put his face in his hands.

"What's happened, Herb?"

"Things. Things that'd turn your belly inside out. All my own fault, Wen. I accepted the special prosecutor; I hired Anglin, gave him a free hand—"

"Look, I came to scream about reading that confession in the news-paper."

"That's part of it."

It struck him he had chanced upon an unheard-of opportunity. He could ask the District Attorney anything and get a frank answer. As the possibilities exploded on his vision he was exuberant, then sick. It shamed him that he could have thought of pillaging his friend's mind when it lay disarmed and in agony. He said, "I had no business charging in here as I did."

"Sure you did," Herb rasped. "Biggest case of my life, Wen, and now I don't care what happens to it. I hope we bungle it, hope you clobber us."

"Bad as all that?"

"You wouldn't believe it. Listen—"

"Wait," Paulk said. "Let's talk it over after the trial."

Their eyes held. In Herb's, Paulk saw the recklessness fading to abjection, then to consternation over what he had almost revealed. His grin, when it came, was humorless. He said, "Thank you, Wen, I guess I was putting my foot in it."

"Do me a favor?"

"Anything, if I can."

"You could tell me where Lily Black is staying, to save me having to run her down. And you might stall the Judge for me if I'm late to court. Right now I'm going to hide out and bone up on this confession."

As published, the statement was about as Ray had described it, for which Paulk was grateful. As he studied it, however, his thoughts strayed to Herb. What did Herb know that had, in a stroke, wiped the ground from beneath him? It had to be something more stinging than relegation to third position on the State's team, or the news release of Priest's confession.

Too late, he wished he'd found out.

XVII

The novice at law is apt to arrive in court better prepared than the seasoned lawyer. Impervious to long hours, spurred by fear of error, and gifted with superior physical stamina, the beginner leaves few stones unturned. If during trial the young attorney spatters objections about at random in the hope that a few may prove well taken, he at least knows the facts of the case. It's in jury picking, the art of sizing up a stranger in relation to a cause, that inexperience hurts. Here, youth and fervor cannot stand in for days in court.

Jack Singer, in the memoirs he was industriously not finishing, claimed to have practiced law twenty years before he picked his first decent jury. Paulk doubted this, but he was certain it was easier to understand law than to understand people. The problem was to look upon a juror of unknown social, religious, family and economic background and estimate his probable attitude toward a particular defendant and crime.

Taking his place in front of Ray Priest, Paulk sought to compile some rules of thumb. In general, he would want jurors who were first-timers, virgins in the to-do of a capital case, to make sure he swore in no veteran hangmen. Like most defenders, he would excuse Pentecostals and Baptists as too easily convinced of fire by the least glimpse of smoke; as too callous at punishing iniquity. He must cull those who wanted to serve, since the willing juror is almost invariably in sympathy with the State. He would drop the juror he happened to offend on *voir dire,* and all those who exhibited any familiarity with the law. He would avoid cripples, men of small stature, people with ugly faces. These, when exalted to life-and-death power, could become cruel jurors capable of doing to the defendant as had been done unto them. He would remember the technique of *voir-dire* payola, permitting the storekeeper to plug his shop, the father to boast of a son, the status-lover to recite his titles.

Still, the rudimentary guides solved only a few of the questions. Would the man who worked with his hands be merciful to Ray Priest the laborer, or was he more likely to condemn him for shiftlessness? Would a woman be moved by Ray's orphaned and homeless state, or was she more apt to hate him for having widowed the beloved Martha Hutcherson? What of the fathers of young daughters, the baiters of Okies and Yankees, the enemies of whiskey—the list was endless.

Ultimately, he knew, he would pick his jurors by their appearance and his hunch about them. He hated to think Ray Priest teetered between the quick and the dead with the balance to be tipped by an imperfect instinct, but it was so.

Judge Sharman arrived, distributed a look of reproof, and banned the venire to the hall. It left a gallery of housewives, shop girls who probably had called in sick, old men with their tieless collars buttoned and holding the canes that had helped them upstairs from the shade of the trees, and members of the Bonita County Posse, these sitting behind folded arms, impatient to see justice done.

"Call the first juror, Mr. Bailiff."

Paulk drew out his jury list. In the margin opposite each name, he and Laura had set down the geometric marks which represented their preliminary decision on every juror. He used the code because of the tightness of the pit, the proximity of prying eyes, especially Anglin's. Jack Singer's habit had been to notate his jury lists in Greek, but a chicken-scratch system was the best Paulk could do. He hoped he could remember all the symbols.

"Mr. Stanton Jones," Nathan Hart cried into the hall.

The ex-mayor, a gas producer and Democratic committeeman, entered the courtroom briskly. He was fifty, trim in a three-hundred-

dollar suit, and he carried a white rolled-brim Stetson. He stepped up
to the witness chair and smiled expectantly at Ike Tigart.

Paulk watched Tigart lean back, brace a knee against the edge of
the table. Easy does it, he thought. And dammit, it really does, and I
can't.

"State your name, please."

"Stanton M. Jones, 3310 Palo Anne."

Casually, Ike established Jones' thirty-two-year residence in the
county, his business, the fact that he was not acquainted with the
defendant and had never employed any of the attorneys involved in
the case.

"I'll ask you, Mr. Jones, if you knew Mr. Jess Hutcherson during
his lifetime."

"Yes sir, I did."

"How well did you know him?"

"Quite well, I think."

"He was widely known, wasn't he?"

"I'd say he was."

"Isn't it true that from your own knowledge you could tell us that
almost everybody in the Panhandle had some sort of an acquaintance-
ship with Mr. Hutcherson?"

"I think everyone knew Hutch."

"Now," Tigart said, "would you describe the relationship you had
with Mr. Hutcherson as friendly, very friendly—or what?"

"We were good friends."

"Were you ever a guest in Mr. Hutcherson's home, or did he ever
visit in yours?"

Paulk got up. "May it please the Court, I believe the special prosecutor is aware that his double-barrelled question is improper."

"I'm trying," Tigart said, "to conserve time."

"Then," Paulk said, "you might go directly to something that bears
on the juror's qualifications."

"Your Honor," Tigart sighed, "if we're to have these jack-in-the-
box interruptions—"

"Gentlemen," the Judge scowled, "let's not start out with bickering
and table talk."

"I've no desire to bicker," Tigart said, "nor do I require any coaching from Mr. Paulk on how to conduct my *voir dire*. He ought to
know certain rules are suspended during jury examinations. Frankly,

Your Honor, I hoped I might try this cause without running a law school on the side. However, if my young friend here insists, I suppose I should do my best for him."

"Please do," Paulk said, "I'm learning every minute."

"See here!" Judge Sharman, never having been presented with a gavel and block, rapped with his knuckles. He glared at a snickerer in the crowd, then at Paulk as if at an impudent cub.

The implication was disturbing. Paulk knew certain lawyers enjoyed immunity in Sharman's court, that the Judge presided in awe of them. Presently, accepting the reprimand, Paulk felt the old jurist was covetous of peace with Ike Tigart. It promised an active prosecution from the bench, warned him he would have to fight for every point, regardless of how small.

"I believe," Tigart resumed, "that the Court has allowed my question. You may answer, Mr. Jones."

"Answer which one?" Paulk said. "There were two questions, as I recall."

Tigart waved a big freckled hand in a gesture of forbearance. "All right, Mr. Jones, tell us if you have ever visited in Mr. Hutcherson's home?"

"Yes, sir, I have."

"And was he sometimes a guest in your home?"

"Yes."

"There," Paulk said. "See how easy it is?"

Tigart banged the table with his fist. "Your Honor, I won't have this junior pipsqueak—"

"Sit down!" the Judge cried. Then, suddenly moderating, he said, "Both of you ought to behave yourselves. Particularly you, Mr. Paulk. Let's get on, calmly."

Resettling in his chair, Tigart faced the juror. "I assume you have read about this case in the newspapers, is that correct?"

"Yes, sir."

"And, naturally, you have discussed the case with your family and friends?"

"I imagine I have."

Tigart smiled reassuringly. "I'll ask you whether or not, through your friendship with the deceased, or what you may have read or heard about this case, you have formed an opinion as to the guilt or innocence of this defendant."

The ex-mayor turned his hat in his lap. "Well, I think—"

"You needn't say what your opinion is, if you do have one. Just answer as to whether you've formed an opinion."

"Yes, I believe I have."

"This opinion you have—is it so fixed in your mind that it couldn't be changed by what you might hear from the witness stand?"

"Well, I guess it could."

"Your Honor," Paulk interrupted, "the defendant isn't required to offer evidence to change an opinion. I believe the juror is disqualified."

Sharman swiveled toward the witness chair. "Mr. Jones, do you understand that whatever you may have read or heard about this case is strictly hearsay?"

"Yes, sir."

"If you should be chosen as a juror, could you lay aside your hearsay opinion to try this defendant solely on the law and the evidence, uninfluenced by anything else?"

Thus schooled, Jones said, "Yes, sir, I believe I could."

"May it please the Court," Paulk persevered, "since the juror has told us he has a prejudice—"

The Judge shook his head. "He's said nothing about prejudice. I overrule. Continue, Mr. Tigart."

"Regarding your friendship with the murdered man—"

"I object!" Paulk shot up in fury. "That's inflammatory and counsel knows it. If any murder has occurred, we're a long way from knowing it."

"Sustain." The Judge smiled, as Tigart was smiling. It had been a deliberate impropriety, used to draw the objection which, instead of blotting out the word, only drove it deeper home.

"Mr. Jones, in view of this friendship, could you hear this case with a fair and open mind?"

"Yes, I think I could."

Paulk shut his eyes. To qualify as a juror in Texas, it was said, one had to be a nitwit or a liar. Here sat a liar, a good sanctified State's liar. Paulk felt he would trade a dozen like him for one honest, bumbling nitwit.

He sat smoldering as Tigart explained the penalties for murder and carefully qualified the juror as lacking any conscientious scruples against capital punishment. Jones answered thoughtfully, as though reaching a position on the issue for the first time.

"Then," Tigart concluded, "in an extreme case where the law authorizes it and the facts seemed to you to warrant it, you could vote the death penalty?"

"Yes, sir, I could."

"Pass the juror," Ike said.

Paulk feigned scrutiny of his jury list while he gathered himself. Jones, Jess Hutcherson's friend, must not serve. If he couldn't disqualify him, he would have to expend one of the defendant's precious peremptory challenges. It irritated him further that as he shifted his chair forward, he entangled Ray Priest's feet in the rungs.

"Mr. Jones, do you at this moment believe the defendant to be innocent of murder?"

Tigart was ready. "The State objects, Your Honor. This asks the juror to prejudge this case without having heard one iota of evidence."

Paulk said, "I'm simply trying to find out if this gentleman holds the assumption the law requires of him."

"Your Honor, if Junior would be so kind as to let me finish my objection—"

"Oh, by all means."

The Judge stirred from a catnap, blushing at having been caught in arrears on the proceedings. Rather than provoke an adverse ruling by bringing him up to date, Paulk revamped his question.

"Mr. Jones, our law provides that every man charged with a crime is presumed to be innocent, and that he will benefit from this presumption until the contrary has been shown by legal and competent evidence, beyond a reasonable doubt. Do you, at this instant, presume this defendant to be innocent?"

"I've no quarrel with the law."

"Since the law presently regards Ray Priest as innocent, you do too—is that your answer?"

"Yes, sir."

Across the table, Tigart and Anglin conferred in loud whispers. Anglin was smiling, Tigart toying with the tassle on his fez.

"May it please the Court," Paulk said, "I feel we would get along faster if the assistant district attorney and the Great Red One would retire from the courtroom to carry on their visit."

"I'm getting fed up with your smart-aleck remarks, Mr. Paulk—"

"Here, here," Judge Sharman rapped. "I wish you'd address what you have to say to the Court. As for you, Mr. Paulk, you will stop

amusing yourself with these exchanges across the table, and I don't
want to have to speak of it again."

Paulk looked again at the juror.

"I'm sure you know that in a criminal case, the burden of proof is
upon the State. As the Court will tell you in his charge, our law requires
the State to prove each and every material allegation contained in the
indictment. If it fails to do so, beyond a reasonable doubt, the law
demands that you find the defendant not guilty. Do you think this is a
good law?"

"I suppose it is."

"You suppose? Then, you can't say definitely?"

"Yes, sir, I'm definite."

"All right. On your oath, you are saying that if you are chosen on
this jury, and if after hearing the evidence you have a reasonable doubt
as to the guilt of this defendant, you will resolve that doubt in favor of
the defendant by acquitting him, is that correct?"

Jones nodded.

"What is your answer?"

"Yes."

Paulk said, "Our law further provides that the fact this man has been
arrested, indicted, and brought to trial, is no evidence of his guilt and
cannot be construed as such. Do you agree with this?"

"You mean, do I think the officers made a mistake?"

"I meant the question exactly as I stated it."

Tigart groaned. "Your Honor, counsel is arguing with the juror."

"Yes," the Judge said. "Mr. Paulk, I'd appreciate it if you'd favor
us with the more temperate side of your nature."

The titter of the spectators, coinciding with a volley of Shrine fire-
works, heightened Paulk's sense of embattlement.

"Mr. Jones, do you regard the arrest and indictment of this man as
evidence of his guilt?"

"Not as evidence, no."

"But it does bias you to some extent?"

"Not that I'm aware of."

The reply was hypocritical, but Paulk did not blame him for it. No
juror ever really qualified on this point. Everyone knew that if a man
was indicted, his guilt was probable. The contradiction lay between the
law and common sense; there was little to be gained by pursuing it.

"Sir, the defendant in a criminal case is exempt by law from testifying. If Raymond Priest should decline to offer himself as a witness, would you consider that an indication of guilt?"

"No," the juror was growing more cagey, "not if the law says I shouldn't."

It was time for a new tack. In detail he qualified Jones on the suspended-sentence law. Then, principally for Tigart's benefit, he covered the laws of self-defense and insanity, threshing out each minor point, exaggerating the feint while he thrust down the temptation to astonish them all. He could imagine the pole-axed look of the Judge, the lividness of the prosecution, the gasp of the spectators and the news people scampering for telephones if he should ask this, Jess Hutcherson's friend, "Do you know anything about Hutch's fondness for lifting the skirts of other men's wives?" But Priest's chance to live wasn't to be squandered to soothe a chaffed vanity, and he held his questions to the routine. Jones did not falter.

After ten minutes, Paulk resorted to Laura's notes on Stanton Jones. Holding them low between his knees, he said, "When was the last time you served on a jury in this court?"

"I never have."

"During your thirty-two years in this county, this is the first time you have been summoned for jury service?"

"No, I've been called before."

"Oh? On how many occasions?"

"I'd estimate ten or fifteen times."

"Ten or fifteen times," Paulk repeated, "and yet you've never served. In other words, you just can't seem to qualify for a jury?"

"No, that isn't true. I don't believe I've ever been disqualified."

"I'm confused, Mr. Jones. How is it, then, that you've not served on a jury?"

"I was excused."

"For what reasons?"

"Usually in connection with my business."

"You had some sort of pressing business matters, and you asked to be excused, and you were?"

"Yes, that's right."

Paulk scratched his head. "Did someone turn down your request to be excused from this case?"

"No, sir."

Paulk managed to look flabbergasted. "Do you mean that, for this particular case, you didn't ask for an excuse?"

Jones was skewered, and knew it. He reddened, but stared back defiantly. "No."

"Why not?"

"I couldn't give you a reason."

"You still head your own company, do you not?"

"I do."

"Then, your business affairs are less pressing now than they were on those prior occasions?"

"No, I wouldn't say so."

"All right," Paulk said, "why didn't you seek to be excused this time, just as you have in the past?"

"No special reason."

"Isn't it the truth that you have a personal reason for wanting to serve on this jury?"

Tigart was up; Paulk marvelled that he had restrained himself this long.

"Your Honor, the law makes no distinction between jurors who do not care to serve and those who do. I can't see, therefore, that this line of questioning leads anywhere—"

"Sustained."

Paulk stated his exception and went on.

"Sir, I'll ask you if you are a member of an organization known as the Bonita County Posse?"

"I am."

"As such, did you assist in any way in the investigation growing out of Mr. Hutcherson's death?"

"Not that I recall."

"You would recall, wouldn't you, if you had?"

"Yes, sir."

"As a friend of the deceased, did you contribute any money to help finance the investigation?"

Jones glanced at Tigart. "Well, not directly."

"What do you mean by that?"

"As I remember, I was among the subscribers to the reward fund raised by the newspaper."

"Your Honor," Paulk said, "since it appears the juror may have assisted in the apprehension of the defendant, I submit he is disqualified and I challenge him for cause."

Tigart stood, revolving his tobacco in his jaw. "May it please the Court, I don't know what grave inference Mr. Paulk expects us to draw from the fact that Mr. Jones, along with hundreds of others, contributed to a reward that was posted long before the identity of this defendant was known to any of us. To me, nothing is inferred except that this juror stands for law enforcement, which certainly is no disqualification."

Surely, Paulk thought, the Judge realized Jones did not belong on the jury. But Sharman had a stubborn, built-in aversion to seeing any juror escape; he would demand a patent, cut-and-dried reason. Paulk watched him lean, beautifully scowling, toward the witness chair.

"Mr. Jones, would the fact that you donated some money have any influence on you if you should become a member of this jury?"

"No, sir, of course not."

The Judge nodded. "For the time being, and in view of this man's previous answers, I am going to disallow the challenge. Proceed, Mr. Paulk."

It was time to give it up. "Pass the juror."

Tigart hunched forward, with his elbows on the table. His shirttail was bloused out in front; purposefully, Paulk thought. Obviously the big redhead aspired to Jack Singer's reputation for "color" along with the rest.

"Mr. Jones, do you know of any reason why you would not make a fair and impartial juror in this case?"

"No, I do not."

Tigart said, "Pass him back."

Paulk picked up the *Tribune.* "I have here a copy of the *Tribune,* issued at noon today. It displays material purported to be the confession of this defendant. Did you happen to see a copy of this newspaper?"

"Yes, sir."

"Did you read this text published under the heading, 'Baby Ray Confesses'?"

"Yes."

"Yet you still say you could give this defendant an impartial trial?"

"Yes, that is what I said."

Paulk spread his arms, dropped them. "That's all."

Tigart smiled. "The State will accept the juror."

"Let him stand aside," Paulk snapped.

There it was, a defense challenge spent on the very first juror. More disheartening was what it portended. If he couldn't chase a man as openly biased as Jones, whom could he drive away?

With Nathan Hart bawling the name of the next venireman into the hall, Paulk turned to his client. Priest's set gaze, his terrible invariance, revealed nothing. "How are you doing?"

"I ain't hurting none."

Angie Callahan had leaned in; her chin rested upon her brother's shoulder. "Isn't it—sort of slow?"

Paulk nodded. "The first one always is. Now that we've gotten up the script, we'll make better time."

Mrs. Callahan turned her eyes toward the gallery without moving her head. "Have you seen her yet, Mr. Paulk?"

"I forgot to look. Where is she?"

"Front row, watching us now."

Without troubling to be covert about it, Paulk twisted to look at Lily Black. She was a girdled, bosomy woman wearing green linen, pendant earscrews, and tall-heeled sandals with a strap around the ankle. Her loose long hair was bleached waxy white. Patty Sue's mother looked the sort to rear a wayward daughter, he decided, the sort to coax males into telling her she couldn't possibly have a grown child.

"Have you spoken to her?" he asked Angie.

"No. The way she's been staring at us—ugh!"

Paulk nudged his client. "Could she know anything bearing on this case?"

"No, sir, nothing."

"What's your impression of her?"

"Well, she's a mean little bitch."

Paulk left it there. He saw Tigart, trailed by Hollis Anglin, sauntering back from the windows where, while pretending to aid Sheriff Grosscup at mollifying the Judge's testiness over the shades, they had gotten a breath of clean air. Somewhere along Herb Cameron had absented himself, and now The Shepherd, as if assuming his rightful due, sat like a purring fat cat in the District Attorney's chair.

As the next venireman, a bank cashier named Robinson, settled himself nervously in the witness chair, Paulk looked out over the crowd. The struggle over Stanton Jones seemed to have fanned their original curiosity into a sober partisanship. Their eyes made no secret of it; even old Mr. Durfee looked less than friendly. To them, the examination had amounted to an admission of Priest's guilt. From where they sat, it was easy enough to agree that *when the cause goes hard, the guilty man excepts, and thins the jury all he can.*

More often than not, it was true.

XVIII

Through another hour, the *voir dire* dragged along unproductively. The banker and the five who followed him stumbled on the State's primary question. "No indeed," they answered, the accents almost identical, "I believe only *God* has the right to take a life." Anglin's sullen monotone challenged them for cause. The Judge, grimacing over this deplorable lay misconcept of both the law and theology, dismissed each sourly, and Nathan Hart ushered them away.

As he checked the defaulters off his list, Paulk pondered how the Chair had withstood the condemnation heaped upon it by veniremen at every murder trial. Perhaps while opposed to the theory of executions the citizenry stopped short of protesting to the legislature because it could think of no feasible substitute. Many, like Stanton Jones, seemed to have put off decision on the issue until, called up as jurors, they realized they faced "responsibility divided by twelve." It was Jack Singer's idea that the Texan didn't mind bearing a ten-millionth share in any number of electrocutions, "but he'll be damned if he'll assume a one-twelfth share of one."

Some, of course, swore to scruples against the death penalty as the foolproof means of eluding service. Others were sincere. These, Paulk suspected, were horrified by Old Sparky as long as the rapes and murders inflicted tragedy upon others. But, when crime struck down one's own, one no longer spoke of razing the Death House. Which, Paulk thought, supported Old Jack's reasoning that "the Chair disturbs us only because we're afraid we might someday be required to help throw the switch to avenge somebody else." Whatever public sentiment, whatever the ground swells, if any, it was too late for Ray Priest. The hot embrace was there, waiting. . . .

Thomas Ireland, cattleman and Hutch's quail-hunting partner, was the next to qualify on the death penalty. Paulk had budgeted a peremptory challenge for Ireland. But, listening to Ike's examination, he reconsidered. The cattleman answered curtly, seemed nettled over having been seized up at Shrine Temple under one of the Court's absentee attachments. His hostility did not delude Paulk into wanting him on the jury, but it did point to a gamble that might save a challenge.

"So," Tigart concluded a placating examination, "you know of no reason why you wouldn't make a fair and impartial juror?"

"None."

"Pass the juror."

Paulk looked at his notes, then gave Ireland an approving smile that all but appointed him foreman. He said, "The defendant has no questions."

Tigart squinted at him, then leaned to Hollis Anglin. Shep left his chair to join the huddle. While they speculated on what the defense knew about Ireland that they somehow had overlooked, Paulk followed up by trying to appear to be digesting a canary.

After a minute, Ike said, "The State will excuse the juror."

Paulk grinned. Across the table he said, "A challenge saved is a challenge earned."

The Judge shook his head. "We'll have a ten-minute recess. Ten minutes, now—no more."

As the shuffle began, Tigart said, "Okay, Wen. Nice shot."

"Wasn't it?"

"Let's level off, get us a jury."

Paulk shrugged. "If you'd come off this death kick, we might."

"That wasn't what cut the best man we've looked at."

"Jones? He had the wrong kind of hat. I thought I'd hold out for a jury of fezes—or is the plural 'feces'?"

"You've got a fat lip, buddy."

Handing his briefcase to Angie Callahan for safekeeping, he started out. At the pit rail a small mottled woman, elderly yet wearing bobby-socks, blocked his way.

"Young man!" she cried, "I'm crocheting! Can you tell what it is?" She raised a nucleus of crinkly yarn to his face.

"No," he said.

"Something pretty, something very pretty! Know what I'm going to do with it?"

"No, ma'am. Now, if you don't mind—"

She fastened on to his arm. "It's to be a prize for the winner!"

"That's nice. If you'll excuse me—"

She gripped him harder. "What am I to do if the State wins? My, so many lawyers on their side, and I'm making only this one."

"It doesn't matter; let them rip it to bits and each take home a chunk."

The woman recoiled, her sharp chin quivering. He flushed; this wasn't Tigart. A courtroom crank, yes, but harmless, probably somebody's mother. Why didn't all the somebodys keep their idiot mothers at home? He said, "I was joking. I hope I win it."

He bored through a throng of smokers assembling in the hall and on into Mr. Funderburg's office. Judge Sharman had prevailed upon the recorder to share his space with the out-of-town press, but, instead of sharing, the newsmen had preempted the place. Steel tables, typewriters, and direct-line telephones had been installed. The UPI had wired in a teletype machine to move the Priest copy without relay. Mr. Funderburg's rolltop desk had been shunted off into a corner, and he sat beside it and glowered at the reporters as if warning them he meant to hold this much of his own office at any cost. Paulk found the *Tribune*'s Davenport and drew him aside.

"Romney—I'd like to know how Priest's statement got into the paper."

Davenport took off his glasses and rubbed his eyes. "I doubt it would be fair to tell you."

"What is fair about anything?"

The reporter shrugged. "Why don't you make a statement knocking it? You've got no jurors up to now. Whoever they are, they'll see a few more editions before they're locked up. You are welcome to sound off, and I'll try to get you good play."

Although not persuaded he could counter the impact of the noon *Tribune,* he told them what he thought. Release of Ray's confession had been a calculated move to inflame and prejudice. Wantonly, it put before the jury a document almost surely inadmissible in the trial, it predicated critical error, it coerced jurors who might otherwise have been eligible—on and on, blah, blah, blah. As he ranted, he felt like a fathead. Still, he left with a sense of relief.

As he lit a cigarette, Nathan Hart poked an arm through the crowd to hand him a note. Mr. E. C. Kelso had called several times; would he return the call as soon as possible? He put the note in his pocket and, to avoid Billy Shepherd, ducked into the rest room. He stood at a window, smoking, gazing down on the grounds, until the recess was over. Then, at the last minute, he dashed downstairs and dialed Kelso, Lemons & Hurst.

Mrs. Reddock's warm, grass-widow voice caused him a pang of homesickness. Ironically, he seemed to miss his storeroom office, his briefs and coffee breaks, the urbane airs of prestige practice, as previously he had missed criminal law.

"Gosh," she said, "he gave up on you and went out."

"Should I try reaching him somewhere?"

Mrs. Reddock hesitated. "Honestly, I don't know. I'm not supposed to say where he went."

"Okay. Where did he go?"

"To keep an appointment with Mrs. Hutcherson."

"Don't kid me."

"I'm not."

"What's it about?" he said.

"Forgive me," she said, "but that's one thing I really don't know."

For an hour after the recess, the work slogged along. Tigart, equipped with a fresh cud and the recklessness of boredom, strained to make a juror out of everybody. Paulk succeeded in disqualifying a woman on the suspended-sentence law and culled two businessmen whom he maneuvered into admitting to unalterable opinions of guilt. He was forced to spend challenges on Donald Mikesell, the retired chief of police, and an investor who disclaimed prejudice while relating how Jess Hutcherson had financed his first major speculation.

Then the impasse broke.

In thirty minutes they agreed upon four jurors.

XIX

"Tell me about them," Jack Singer said.

They sat at a dinner of cold cuts and tea. Paulk, rid of his jacket and necktie, unaffected by the two tall drinks Jack had mixed for him, was trying to unwind. The Main Street Methodist chimes had been ending their vespers recital when court closed. He had remained in the courtroom a while, to justify his jurors to Priest and Mrs. Callahan. So soon after, it wasn't easy. There was the equal and opposite reaction, the nagging fear that he had erred, that Ike Tigart had bilked and stampeded him. As he bid them good night, he had found The Shepherd waiting for him.

"Got any plans, Wen? We could drive out to Gordon's, get us a steak and maybe a few beers. I'll treat you."

"No, thanks, I've a lot to do."

"Son, you ain't holding that confession business against me, are you?"

"Right now, I hold that against everybody."

Shep laughed. "You're doing all right, boy. Except for Jones, you did great."

Paulk frowned. "What about Jones?"

"Don't get sore. I was just going to say you didn't need to waste a challenge on him. Hell, he was one of the big shots that prowled through that motel cabin, he saw Hutch's body before it was moved. Makes him a witness, see? If you'd asked about that, the Judge would have turned him loose."

He had wrenched himself away, out of the building and down the walk, into the leather seat of Laura's abominable imported roadster. He had ridden across town muttering against the heat drifts along the streets, fancying he saw kids chunking each other with heat balls, mourning his misspent challenge.

Now, rational if still sweltering, he undertook to picture the jurors for the Singers. Mrs. Wilma Chesterson, whose heels had clicked smartly on the tile floor, had been sworn first. The wife of a supermarket executive, she was a do-gooder charming enough not to be insufferable about it. Her son was reputed to have fallen into several spoiled-brat scrapes; she belonged to Federated Women, to the League of Women Voters, to all the Societies for the Prevention Of. She knew Martha Hutcherson, but at the time of Hutch's death, she had been in Bermuda. The public wrath had been a month old before she returned to absorb any of it.

"Which is why you took her?" Singer asked.

"Maybe. Or because her wild boy should soften her toward Mrs. Callahan as well as Ray. Or because she's promoting a home for unwed mothers, or because she qualified without lying."

Or because she had smiled. He didn't mention it, remembering how suddenly *un*smiling Mrs. Chesterson had become with her oath and her retirement to the jury room.

Ancil Andricks was next. Sixty, hulking, and rough-handed, Andricks' coarse gray hair was watered down and wiped straight back; it would rise and wave when it dried. A bricklayer who had bulldozed his way up to contractor, Andricks still got into bib overalls and tin hat to superintend his jobs and, by contrast, was a founding sponsor of the City Symphony. Paulk had seen him as a man certain to have dealt with hundreds like Ray Priest, transient laborers who drew their wages nightly out of perpetual indecision on whether to report for another day. Because Andricks had erected quonsets for Hutch, Tigart had accepted him eagerly.

"And why did you?"

"Well, he was unemotional, I thought. He told me he wanted on the jury, said he felt every man ought to serve at least once, that to him the jury meant learning something and getting a rest."

Again Paulk was withholding parts of his logic. There had been appeal in the square craggy face, the scars and gruffness, in the alliterated name that seemed to write itself in handsome script upon the mind. By coincidence, Andricks had prefixed an answer with "To tell you the truth," but the clincher, Paulk thought now, had been his own yen to see what the man would look like when his hair got dry. If in hindsight his reasoning seemed moronic, it struck him as astute beside that which had precipitated the swearing of J. N. Gay.

Gay was forty-two, swarthy and an accountant. Because he was a scant five feet tall, Paulk had ruled him out on sight. Then he had noticed Gay's unusual attention to the sheriff, his small man's stare as Andy rose to his six-feet-six and crossed the pit enroute to the windows. It set Paulk to thinking. Tigart was six-feet-four; Anglin, like the policemen who would appear for the State, was tall. And Ray Priest was a stubby five-feet-six. Through the *voir dire,* Paulk kept enlarging the comparisons. Hutch had been a giant, and Paulk was, himself, only five-ten.

"All right, Jack, what do you think of him?"

Singer sucked thoughtfully on his teeth. "I'm afraid of runts, Wen. But I didn't see this one. How did he qualify on the death penalty?"

"Too well," Paulk conceded, "didn't hedge a bit. Why is it I felt so good about these jurors when I took them and feel, now, like a fool?"

Singer laughed. "Let's hear about the other one."

William H. Studer—"people call me Willie"—was an auto sales-man. Dark-eyed, nearing his thirtieth birthday, bearded from the day-long wait in the hall, Studer had been the inevitable day's end juror. Briefly examined, he had been accepted summarily because lawyers, like store clerks hustling up a closing-time sale, need a sense of accomplishment while packing up to go home.

"He wasn't acquainted with Hutch," Paulk said, "which makes

him a novelty. But I took him, I think, because he has one of those tiresome, high-pitched voices. It'll drive the other jurors crazy."

Singer nodded. The agreeable, frictionless jury was a hazard to the defendant. Defense preferred, always, the incompatible jury, one with the potential of rifts and factions. Most hung juries occurred because jurymen got fed up with each other. It was the happy jury that lowered the boom.

"I've forgotten," Laura said, "wasn't Mr. Studer among those I didn't check on?"

"He was. That's what bothers me, now, about taking him."

"How did Tigart treat him?" Jack asked.

"Halfheartedly, I think. I overheard him saying to Anglin that they might as well accept him so there'd be enough of them in the jury room tonight to play dominoes."

Singer drew his napkin from his collar.

"Come on, Jack, do you think I'm booting it?"

"I was thinking of the whole business of special venires. The long *voir dire,* the squabbles, the second-guessing. I wonder if a juror isn't overly impressed with the importance of a case before he hears the first word of evidence. For instance, I'd wager these four people are uncomfortable as hell right now. They'll be up there swapping rumors, anticipating consequences, worrying about being thought hard boiled if they vote death and gutless if they don't."

"I hope they are," Paulk said, "and that my Willie Studer is talking a bluestreak." He finished his tea and got up. "Thank you both. I'm sorry I have to run."

"You look tired," Laura said. "Can't I go along, do the driving?"

Already, the night was thirty degrees cooler than the day. A prissy breeze meddled about and there were stars, the first beads of dew, the small gusts of summer sound. It seemed a sacrilege to be at work on a lawsuit. Paulk sank into the cushion, watching Laura wrangle the little car into motion. She had covered her shoulders with a short jacket and left the sleeves to dangle. With her new short haircut, her economy of make-up, she looked pretty, efficient, and serious.

"Do you think your Dad will be all right?"

"No. He'll stay up too late hunting law on connivance. But he wanted me to come with you. He gets ideas, if you haven't noticed."

"Do I know what you mean?"

She laughed. "Sure you do. He'd like us to get married. Oh, don't collapse. I simply thought you were entitled to know. Now, where are we going?"

Awkwardly he got out his note pad. "I want to talk to the guy who found Hutch's gun, at the Arwin—that's a flophouse on Fourth. At the Plaza there's the woman who found the car. Then, Lily Black out at the Flamingo."

"There was an item in the evening paper about Lily."

"What of her?"

"Oh, that she is here, that she's attractive, that she says she never doubted Ray Priest would come to a bad end."

"He may, at that."

"Wen, how is Ray doing?"

"Hanged if I know. He sits, says nothing aside from fuming now and then about not being allowed to see Patty Sue."

"The jury might like him for loving her, after all she's done against him."

"They might," he said. "If they believed it, and they won't, not when they hear all that goes with it."

Laura parked beside a high curb, in a fire lane before the hotel. Mrs. Waddill met them in the lobby. She was a bright plump woman reveling in this respite from her duties as the mistress of an overfilled El Reno household. Although two days earlier she had refused to see Paulk, she talked to them freely now. Hearing out a chronology gilded with the trivia of thought and afterthought, he was puzzled that the State would have subpoenaed the woman at all. She could testify to sighting Hutch's abandoned sedan and to calling police about it; otherwise, she knew nothing.

"I'm sorry, Mr. Paulk, about being short with you the other day. I figured with the other side paying for everything—well, you know."

"It's all right," he glanced at Laura. "The State is taking care of everything, then?"

"My, yes. Mr. Anglin lets me call home every night and talk to my children, pays the baby-sitter. And, I tell you, I'm eating fabulously. I've gained two pounds already. I never knew I was so tired of my own cooking. . . ."

They drove through streets hollow with the ten-o'clock quiet to the run-down, three-story squalor of the Arwin. Leaving Laura in the car, Paulk went upstairs and along an oiled-floor hall posted with fire-exit signs and warnings against loitering and he knocked at a varnish-blackened door. The witness Archie Messer responded grog-gily. Gaunt, dark-skinned, dressed only in blousy drawers, he had been wallowing on an iron bed, diverting himself with a digest-size, girly magazine and a quart of red wine.

Messer told his story as though reciting lines uneasily committed to memory. He had picked up Hutch's fancy pistol from a nest of weeds in a ditch alongside Mrs. Waddill's street in El Reno. He had kept it several days before, on the advice of a friend, he turned it in at the police station. Well, yes, the pistol had fired a couple of times while in his possession but, no siree, he hadn't been trying it out. "Just dropped it and it went off; them automatics are kind of dangerous that way."

The man would swear to this lie, but Paulk saw no advantage in trying to make the perjury apparent to the jury. It was probable Messer had a record, that he regarded any admission of his intent to keep the gun as a candor he could not afford. Since it had no bearing on the issues vital to Ray Priest, Paulk let it pass.

"Mr. Messer, I'm sorry they treated you as a suspect, temporary as it was."

"Well, for a spell there, they had me scairt all right," the witness grinned. "They brung them eyewitnesses over to look at me, and by God, first off they wasn't too sure I wasn't the one."

"Who were these witnesses?"

"I don't recollect their names, except one was called Brownie. Anyways, they been making it up to me since, I'll say that for these Texas laws."

"They should," Paulk said. "I hope they're paying your expenses."

"Sure," Messer said, "I ain't losing nothing. Mr. Anglin is taking care of me. Pretty white of him, since I couldn't stand losing any work. See, when this trial come up, I was drawing eight dollars a day driving a tractor. Mr. Anglin's giving me ten and my keep, so as I won't lose out too much—not that it wasn't a bother to me to have to make this trip, you understand."

"I understand."

He described the interview to Laura as they drove north on Lamar, toward the highway loop that was tourist-court row.

"Wen, can Hollis do that? It's like hiring witnesses."

Paulk shook his head. "The law allows the State to pay per diem and mileage from the state line, and that's all."

"Then Anglin can't keep his promise to these people."

"I don't know, but I expect he will. My guess is there's cash left in that cute little slush fund."

Laura frowned. "It's like cheating."

"I've got a less charitable word for it. Think how eager to please those witnesses will be when it's time for them to get up there and earn their money."

"Dad will be furious."

"Of course."

She smiled. "I mean, very. It's touchier with him than you think. He hasn't told you he contributed to that fund."

"Not Jack."

"Oh, yes, and he's been squirming over it ever since. At the time, he was shocked about Mr. Hutcherson, he felt like everyone else. Now he rants about it, says retirement must be making him senile. You know how he has always hated rewards or anything that resembles them—bounties, he calls them. Actually, I think it's why he offered to defend Ray Priest."

"And the reason he's helping me?"

"No," she said, suddenly reverting to solemn reserve, "I think I explained that pretty frankly a little while ago."

They passed the Ranch Inn, where, he remembered, a Mrs. Johnson appalled at having become her husband's mother-in-law still waited to hear from him—where Jess Hutcherson seemed yet afloat in his own blood—and neither of them turned to look.

"I wonder," Laura mused, "if Lily Black is on a stipend, too."

They drove through a garish floodlit gate into the Flamingo. The motel was a U of balconied brick enclosing a courtyard restaurant, playground, and a glassed-in swimming pool. Lily Black wasn't in her room. At the office, Paulk learned she had left at dinner time in the company of a gentleman. Despite the impression he'd gotten of Mrs. Black in court, Paulk felt a deep cold anger on behalf of the husband, Forrest Black, now fifteen hundred miles away in Glendale. Plainly the Blacks were a freewheeling family. Nevertheless, Paulk smoldered over Lily's date, as he could over every sign of infidelity anywhere.

Laura drove them to a café. After two cups of coffee, they tried the Flamingo again. Mrs. Black still wasn't in. They cruised the highway out to the airport and sat watching the planes arrive and depart. He was nodding when Laura once more steered into the motel.

"Wake up, Wen, she's here."

Paulk stretched, blinked at light from a window, and got out. "Want to go in with me?"

"You'd do better alone."

"All right. I won't be long."

When the door opened, it was but by the length of a night chain. Lily Black's cold-creamed face appeared in the slot. He introduced himself quickly.

"I know who you are," she said. She wore white pajamas under an open wrapper. Out of the hard sunlight of 191st District Courtroom, he thought, she looked younger, not so artificial, and remarkably like Patty Sue.

"May I come in for a moment?"

"I was about to go to bed. What do you want?"

"To talk to you, about Ray's case."

"No sale," she said. Then, flirtatiously: "But I think we could talk of other things, if you'd like to come in for a drink."

"Mrs. Black, if you've come here to testify, I've a right to know what you are going to say."

"Who says I'm a witness, anyway?"

"Since it's so late, couldn't we get together tomorrow at the court-house? During a recess?"

"I offered you a drink, Mr. Paulk."

"I know. Listen, you could help me a lot by telling me about your daughter's marriage."

"Strictly business, aren't you?" Mrs. Black tossed her head, her voice hardened. "All right, I've got one thing to say to you about your friend Ray. If he burns, he's got it coming, and I wish to God I could watch it."

He caught the door on his shoulder as she tried to slam it. She drew back with an oath. "On your way, Junior, before I call a cop."

Rage hoarsened him. "Hear this. If you get on that witness stand you'll answer my questions, and I promise you that you won't like it."

She was shrilling after him as he turned back toward the car. At once he felt sheepish, ashamed. His threat had been stupid, useless. Worse, it meant nothing, except that he'd had a long, up-and-down day.

Laura laughed at him. "You're a babe in the woods, Wen. Don't you know that when a woman throws herself at you, she expects to be caught?"

"I blew it bad, didn't I?"

"You're tired. I'll drive you straight home."

It was past midnight, with only a few police cars slinking about. In the light from the bus station, they saw a newsboy sitting on a stack of morning papers. Laura stopped, bought one, and together they read the black headline reporting the trial's slow beginning. There were subheads on his exchanges with Tigart and the four jurors.

He sighed. "Let's go home."

"Wait, here's something."

She pointed to a series of paragraphs set off in the body of the story. He scanned them, tore his eyes away, then read them again.

"My God, Laura."

> The day's chief surprise came minutes before adjournment when William H. (Willie) Studer was accepted for the jury. Studer, a car salesman who may spend his 30th birthday in the jury dormitory, is a former policeman and, as recently as 1958, was a client of Ike Tigart, the special prosecutor.
>
> Tigart recalled to newsmen that he won a $7,500 settlement for Studer in a damage suit growing out of an automobile collision, but said he felt sure this would have no effect on Studer's jury service. "I know Willie well," Tigart said. "He's intelligent, comes from a fine family, and I know he'll make an excellent juror."
>
> Defense Attorney Owen Paulk, who earlier issued a scathing statement concerning Priest's published confession, could not be reached for comment.

Paulk groaned. By neglect he had admitted a police mentality to the judgement of a jail habitué. Even worse, Studer was among Tigart's satisfied clients. It sickened him to realize that while Ike swore in a ringer, he had occupied himself with conjecture about an irritating voice.

"It's my fault," Laura said. "I didn't get around to checking him."

"All I had to do was examine him."

She ground the gears, driving slowly as he talked. Didn't she see; Tigart and Anglin were running circles around him. Studer was on the jury to stay, unless he dropped dead. How had he let it happen? Cockiness over his stunt with Ireland, numbness from exhaustion, carelessness? Whatever, he had hurt Ray Priest, needlessly, mortally. . . .

"Wen, that's silly. What makes you think you know how this

Studer will vote, or that Mr. Tigart knows? You'd be asking me that, if this were someone else's case. Twelve people penned up together, compromising toward one general mind—"

"Quoting Jack, I take it?"

"Yes," she said sharply, "quoting Jack. And while I'm at it, 'every lawsuit starts out a terrible mess, to be won by whomever works hardest at tidying up.' "

She cut the car off the street into his driveway, braking suddenly as if to jolt him out of the apathy that was descending over him.

"It's spilt milk," she said, "and Mr. Tigart will be laughing at you tomorrow. But, it seems to me that while he's feeling good about this, you might just pick *you* eight more jurors."

With the quick facility of her father, she had laid hold of the one advantage to be salvaged from the fiasco.

"Besides," she smiled, "if anyone in that jury room is going to argue for death, wouldn't you rather it be done in that—what did you call it—that intolerable voice?"

He sat gazing up at his apartment, watching a curtain flapping from a window he'd forgotten to close. "Laura, you should have been the lawyer."

"I've heard you say that to Jerry." Her hands gripped the wheel, her lips set. "So don't—so I wish you'd never say it to me."

It stung. "If you disliked Jerry so much," he said, "why do you insist on discussing her?"

"I never said—oh, go inside, Wen. I get lightheaded when it's this late."

"Gladly." He shoved the door open with his knee. Then, confused, unwilling to start the night uneasy about her when there was Willie Studer to be sleepless about, he turned back. She did not meet him and the kiss was hurried, juvenile, unwanted by either of them. He withdrew clumsily and began groping over the floorboard for his briefcase.

Flatly Laura said, "Better, now?"

"Yes, thank you. I won't cry myself to sleep."

X X

Rest eluded him. The sheets wrinkled, grew hot and abrasive. He switched on the lights and lay staring at the clock and the dismal bachelor disorder of the apartment. Almost nothing in the place, he discovered, was important to him. There were two dusty old pipes, a Bible, and a twenty-dollar gold piece as mementoes of his father, but nothing in sight had belonged to Jerry. In the slow, dead-minded hours it baffled him that this was so, and that he could not have explained it.

He left early, bought breakfast, and stopped off at the Houston Street drugstore for a new ballpoint pen. It was a familiar errand, an effort at reorientation, but with the pen in his pocket he felt no better. Yesterday's errors clung to him as he crossed the lawn to the courthouse. Uncle Nathan Hart hailed him off the elevator.

"Wen, Kelso's secretary is on the phone again, waiting for you."

If E. C. wished to complain (alas) at mention of the firm name by the press, Paulk didn't care to talk to him. Or, if the old Senator had reconsidered, if now he offered aid, he was three weeks too late.

Hart said, "He's on the Judge's line."

"Would you mind telling Mrs. Reddock I'm pressed for time? Ask her to empty out my desk, and say I'll pick up my things as soon as I can."

The 191st Courtroom had been full more than an hour. From the hall, he could see the crochet artist, settled beside the aisle, feeding her needle the thread that unreeled from an ice-cream carton on the floor. The wizened Mr. Durfee sat in his place of privilege, explaining process to a quartet of Possemen clustered about him.

Someone had prevailed upon Judge Sharman to admit an extra table to the pit. Set up in the corner to the right of the bench, it accommodated six eager-eyed shorthand students who were to take down the proceedings as an exercise. Mr. Funderburg, laying out his pads and stylus at his desk, glared at them, his look asking why they couldn't practice as well in some other court where space was not at such a premium. Several unemployed lawyers gossiped inside the rail, waiting to applaud Ike Tigart's stratagems or to be diverted by the bunglings of one Owen Paulk. And he saw Lily Black, conspicuous in a bare sun dress, occupying a seat in the front row.

129

Nathan Hart returned. "I told her, Wen," he said. "But she says be sure to call Kelso anyway."

Paulk nodded. "Did our jurors have a good night?"

"First rate, and tonight ought to be better. I reckon you've heard about the new beds?"

"What beds?"

"Commissioners Court met special last night, ordered a dozen new mattresses for the jury room. They got Verdi's to loan us a hi-fi set for the duration, and the library is sending over some books. Nice, huh?"

"Great," Paulk said. "Now, just what can *I* do to make this jury more comfortable?"

Hart grinned. "Nothing, we've thought of everything. The Judge has just decided I'm to feed them at Gail's instead of the usual slop-chutes. There must be a surplus in the jury fund."

In the courtroom Paulk saw a further sign that the State had been active after hours. A highway patrolman was posted at the foot of the jury box. Handsome, big, strikingly suited to his snug tan uniform and Sam Browne belt and nickeled magnum revolver, the trooper was assigned as doorman, ostensibly to relieve Hart for closer attendance on the jury. Actually, the officer's presence was an added touch for the prosecution. Even more than the Rangers, Texas highway patrolmen looked like law and order.

Angie whispered, "Mr. Paulk, what can we do about that editorial, where they talk about delinquents and thugs and use Ray's name?"

Paulk shook his head. Sometimes he wanted to ask if errors, sin, crime, weren't among life's indispensables; whether morals, religion, philosophy, mercy and forgiveness and the law, could exist except that there occurred the Ray Priests to require them. Where would be the do-gooders like Mrs. Chesterson had there been no Rays to be punished or salvaged? Probably locked up in asylums, he thought—ruined, done in for lack of enough evils to stamp out.

Judge Sharman entered exactly at nine. He paused, scowling at the students as though unable to recall how they came to be here, then climbed to the bench and thumped down the docket book. The *National Geographic* fell out to the floor. As he stooped after it, out of sight behind the bench, he said, "Call the first juror, Mr. Bailiff."

The session dragged along in heat, noise, and tiresome routine. Paulk kept a watch on the table. Billy Shepherd, possibly Lily Black's dinner partner of last night, sat loose and scrubbed up, flashing smiles at whomever happened to glance his way. Herb Cameron had resumed his place, but was silent and puffy and apart. Tigart, relaxed and content with his tobacco, led the examination with patient confidence. Among them, only Hollis Anglin wanted to rub it in. Sniffling from his cold, the assistant patronized Paulk with a graciousness that was infuriating.

As the day wore on, veniremen ascended to the stand, disqualified or were challenged, and departed. Paulk knew he should be choosing jurors as Laura had suggested, but he could not trust his hunches. He saw Willie Studer in every candidate. And, one after another, he drove them away as liars and conspirators.

They came to the oddballs expectable on every jury list: the housewife who undertook to explain the law to the lawyers, the Holiness minister's wife whose personal monopoly on The Cross and The Covenant turned her *voir dire* into a fiery upbraiding of all Bonita County, the inevitable giggler, the embarrassed stutterer, the nervous weeper, the retired printer determined to make his answers a death blow to laws that discriminated against labor.

By afternoon, when Paulk found Anglin's consolations past bearing, bitter duels began. The mugginess, the testiness of boredom, prolonged the clashes. Judge Sharman read, napped, soiled three collars. As the day ended, he flared into beautiful temper. Mercy, how could intelligent men have spent eight hours in examining sixty veniremen without swearing a single juror?

That night, sitting in the Singers' parlor, accepting gin from Jack and coffee from Laura, Paulk recounted the day with bitterness. While it was happening, he had regarded it as a stalemate. In retrospect, he knew better. Tigart had won the day. He had forced Paulk to spend challenges until only two remained. These would have to be hoarded against the next Shriner, the next Posseman or ex-policeman. The defense was disarmed. Tomorrow, then, Ike would complete the jury. . . .

Paulk fought them off until afternoon. At two o'clock, the fifth juror was sworn. She was Iva Billingsley, "oh, just a housewife." Motherly, large, her thin gray hair slain by home permanents and entombed under an old-fashioned net, she kept reaching inside her dress to restore a slipping brassiere strap. Tigart accepted her, Paulk thought, chiefly because it was a rule of Sharman's court that one lady juror pledged the counsel table to receive another; the Judge never permitted a lone woman to be isolated with eleven males, and Mrs.

Chesterson awaited a companion. As for himself, Paulk judged Mrs. Billingsley as old enough to be beyond frivolity, reasonable enough to be living with her first husband, and earnest enough to be badly frightened.

"Let her be sworn," he said.

The sprint was begun. Calmly, they accepted seven others, almost in list sequence. The Judge, startled even though he knew Paulk's challenges were gone, restored to his faith in process, smiled as he sent the twelfth juror upstairs.

"My congratulations, gentlemen, and may I say I trust the cooperative spirit of these past two hours will continue. Now, Mr. Bailiff, if you'll bring in the remainder of the venire?"

He dismissed the tired, unexamined hall dwellers with thanks and the unveiled suggestion that they should converge in a body on Theodore Holcomb to demand their pay. As they drained away, most to compete for standing room in the gallery, Nathan Hart climbed to the bench to whisper to the Judge. Tigart got up and buttoned his coat and strolled out, others left to stretch or smoke. Paulk, seeking to fit his jury notes back into the distended old briefcase, failed to sense the sudden hush until Angie Callahan touched his arm.

He looked up toward the bench. Judge Sharman was standing. Andy Grosscup had risen, as had the body of Possemen. A quartet of attorneys was scrambling up from the extra bench under the windows. Then he saw Ike Tigart in the door, giving his arm to Martha Hutcherson.

He watched incredulously as Tigart brought them in, a whole procession of Hutchersons. Hutch's widow kept her eyes straight ahead. Close behind her came the thin, dark-haired girl, Valle, her small face white, her eyes luminous; then the sons, Jess Junior with a diamond on his hand, and Charles, stiff and ruddy in Marine Corp green. With the air of a funeral director, Tigart conducted them past the counsel table and seated them directly behind Ray Priest. As Martha Hutcherson clasped her hands on her lap and smiled up at those who had surrendered their places, one of the shorthand students began to cry and a murmur coursed through the crowd.

Paulk swung around to Anglin. "You forgot the trumpets."

"Well," Anglin grinned behind a bony hand, "we can't think of everything."

In moments the pit atmosphere had changed. In full view of the jury soon to fill the box were Mrs. Hutcherson's serene composure, the proud respectability of the sons, the pathos of the grieving child. Against such a backdrop, Angie Callahan seemed only dowdy; Priest, neanderthal and evil. Paulk cast about in his mind for a means of countering it. Aside from the effect upon the jury, he feared the thing for himself. He doubted he could defend under Article 1220 with Valle's soft hurt eyes upon him. He trembled at the thought that Tigart perhaps had counted on as much.

XXI

Judge Sharman rapped for quiet. "While the jury is coming down, I want to explain what is expected of the spectators during this trial. You must understand that while in this courtroom, you are under the control of the Court, and it is I who shall establish and enforce the rules of conduct.

"First, let me say I will allow no applause, no demonstrations of any sort. Secondly, I'm sorry to say, we'll have to exclude from future sessions everyone who cannot find a seat. I'm aware of the notoriety of this case, but space is limited. We cannot have people standing around the walls, scarring up the paneling or shutting off ventilation.

"I know that some of the judges of this county permit smoking in their courtrooms, but I do not. It's a filthy habit that I'll not tolerate. Neither do I want you bringing your newspapers here. We can't have newspaper headlines displayed before this jury. Further—you in the back, listen to me, please—it has come to my notice that some of you have been bringing your lunch. We mustn't have any noon-hour picnics in here. If you fear losing your seats, find someone to sit in your place while you're out.

"I will allow no cameras in the courtroom. And, to prevent confusion, I will ask you to avoid fanning in and out the door unnecessarily. Everyone will remain seated when the jury is being retired. I'll not have anyone—you newspaper people included—racing to beat the jury out the door.

"Now," the Judge hastened at the sound of the jury in the hall, "one last word of caution. According to an officer of this court, someone has been selling seats for ten dollars apiece. If this happens again, if anyone hears of it, report it at once to the highway-patrol officer. I'll see to it that a prosecution results."

Sharman paused, reflecting. Then, remembering that these were voters, he brushed back a wisp of white hair and smiled. "I hope my remarks do not infer that you are unwelcome here. Personally, I'm grateful for your interest in this case. I would be very afraid for our freedoms if the citizens cared too little about our judicial processes."

Nathan Hart propped back the door for the jury. Paulk whispered. "They'll look at you, Ray, as soon as they're in the box. Don't duck."

Priest nodded dully. Over his shoulder, Angie said, "What about these people behind us? Can they sit there and stare at Baby, all the way through?"

"We'll see." He turned his attention to the jury.

The four sworn Monday were like old acquaintances. But today's new eight—he knew almost nothing about them. There was Palmer Lloyd, owner of a gas-station chain; Franklin Turner, an electric-plant foreman; M. B. Allen, insurance agent, Methodist deacon and American Legion commander; Hubert Connally, a stooped mail carrier who, thank heaven, had never had the Hutchersons on his route; C. T. Little, the stockyards manager; Sidney Glass, a veterinarian; the nervous Mrs. Billingsley; and E. E. Schuman, a concrete finisher and the last accepted.

Filing into the box, the jurors hesitated at selecting seats. They would keep the same chairs throughout the trial, a curiosity that made this first seating suspenseful for those at the counsel table. Like any electorate, a jury granted leadership to him who would assume it. Usually the juror who claimed the first, front-row chair became the foreman when, at verdict time, a vote was taken. With the prosecutors Paulk watched intently as the women, already paired, chose the corner chairs on the raised second row. Schuman and Allen, Turner and Little joined them.

When Willie Studer and little J. N. Gay led the others along the front row, Paulk shut his eyes. If Tigart's man was about to claim the critical place, he didn't care to see it. Then as the bumping and squeak of leather cushions stilled and he opened his eyes, he felt like shouting. In the key chair sat the stolid, wet-haired builder, Ancil Andricks, with Gay installed beside him, glowering like a disgruntled runner-up.

The Judge choused Andy Grosscup into resetting the window shades and glancing at the clock, addressed the jury. "Ladies and gentlemen, stand and raise your right hands. You do, each of you and all of you, solemnly swear that in the case of the State of Texas against the defendant, you will a true verdict render, according to the law and the evidence, so help you God."

They sat down, turning their heads to look at the audience, the defendant, the lawyers, Martha Hutcherson, before they again faced the Judge.

"Members of the jury, I regret that we've taken three days to come to this point, and to those of you who have been waiting upstairs since Monday, I express my appreciation for your patience. Henceforth, I promise you, we'll let very little of your time go to waste."

The Judge knew the risk of unrestrained comment before an impaneled jury, and he hated even the shadow of error and reversal. Yet it was among his foibles that while he scarcely disciplined his remarks, he believed that he was curbing himself a great deal.

"I have granted a request from the attorneys for a recess until tomorrow afternoon, on the promise that every effort will be made to finish by this weekend. Since few of you have served in a criminal case, I will tell you in general terms what you may expect. The State will call its witnesses first. Afterwards, the defense will offer such witnesses as it may choose, or none at all. When both sides have closed, you will receive the law of the case from me. Thereafter, you will hear the arguments; that is, counsel will address you, with the State presenting the opening and closing speeches.

"The bailiffs, Mr. Hart and Mrs. McCormick, will have you in charge at all times. They are obliged by law to keep you together, to prevent any intercourse with other persons. They are directed to supply your reasonable wants, so long as these would violate no rule of jury conduct. I'm sure you understand that you need ask for no intoxicating beverages, newspapers, radio, or television sets. You cannot have visitors, and if it should become absolutely necessary for you to make a telephone call, a bailiff must attend both sides of the conversation.

"If any of you should require a recess before one is due, you may signify it to me by raising your hand. The entire jury must be retired each time; the law forbids me from excusing you separately. Finally, I strongly urge you to put off any discussion of this case until you have heard all of the evidence. All right, Mr. Bailiff, you may take the jury out."

They filed out slowly, most of them watching their feet. Before turning to the door, Willie Studer glanced toward the counsel table and smiled. Together with Tigart, Paulk quickly smiled back. No hard feelings, Willie, and I should smile and kiss a pig. Priest stared at them through motionless white lashes until the door closed.

"Them people," he said, "they don't look so bad."

Paulk offered no reply. Ray didn't grasp that his trial was half finished, that already he was almost doomed, or almost spared. Maybe it was best that defendants believed the verdict depended solely upon the testimony, the dramatics of argument. It would cheer them little to understand how a jury, once completed, was disposed to one side or the other. The personalities already were reacting to each other, moving toward a jury mind. Whatever the product, its seeds were sown beyond recall.

"Gentlemen," the Judge resumed without waiting for order, "if you've any motions, I think we might dispose of them now. Mr. Tigart?"

"None, Your Honor."

"You, Mr. Paulk?"

"I've nothing at this time. But, may it please the Court, I think a meeting of both parties with the Court, as soon as possible, might benefit all of us."

"Very well." Sharman gathered up a scatter of onionskin notes. "Let's get at it immediately, in my office. This court is recessed until one o'clock tomorrow afternoon."

Anglin stood up, stretched his lank torso. "Whatever you're after, Wen, the answer is no."

"We'll see."

"When I recommended you for this case," the assistant smiled, "I told the Judge, 'Old Wen will be easy to work with.' "

"Thanks, I'll plead this boy guilty tomorrow."

He gave Priest a cigarette, lit another for himself. "I'll try to see you in the morning. We ought to go through the thing once more."

"Yes, sir; I guess I'll still be up there."

"Please, Baby," Angie hugged her brother's arm, "don't joke about running away. Don't even think of it."

"That's good advice," Paulk finished packing the old briefcase. "See you both tomorrow."

The Judge's office, having been shut tight all day, was like an incubator. Sharman had removed his coat, retained his vest, and was fastening on the clean collar he would wear home to Mrs. Sharman.

Tigart and Anglin were waiting in the extra chairs. Herb stood at one window, The Shepherd at the other, and they gazed down through the dusk at the white-tied men and jeweled ladies arriving at the Temple for the closing dinner and dance of the Spring Ceremonial.

As Paulk shut the door, the Judge said, "Mercy," and bent to hunt for a collar button. As he straightened, he looked at Paulk. "Let me say, gentlemen, that I think you've got a good jury, although I see no reason why we should have spent three days at it. Also, I see no reason for all the back-biting and quibbling, and I hope you younger men will—well, make an effort to control yourselves. There are eighty-six other cases waiting on this docket."

Paulk crossed to stand beside Herb; ignored the grin Shep was shining upon him.

"By the bye," the Judge said, "I'll be working on my charge at odd times, and if either of you has any special charges to submit, please get them in early. When the time comes, I don't want to spend a half a day rewriting the thing."

There were sly smiles; the Judge went to great lengths to assert that he, not Mr. Funderburg, actually compiled the critical document.

"Now, Mr. Paulk, what's your problem?"

"The Hutcherson family. I want to know whether Mr. Tigart intends to replay his pageant daily, and if he intends to seat them under the jury's nose every day."

Ike brushed his red crewcut with a palm that was mysteriously callused. "Son, are you going to tell us they've no right to attend court?"

"I've said nothing of rights, but I will now. This was a cheap vaudeville stunt, meant to put pressure on the jury. I won't have it continued on through the testimony."

"Indeed?" Tigart's brows lifted. "How is it any different from having your Mrs. Callahan in the pit?"

"You'll recall, and so will the Court, that I proposed that *before* we started. You had advance knowledge, and gave your consent."

Tigart shrugged. "It's sauce for the goose. If there's room for the kith and kin of the defendant, for shorthand students and half the Bar Association, then there's space for Hutch's folks."

The Judge was looking at neither of them. His cheeks were faintly flushed. It was likely he had known of the grand-entry plan and consented to it.

"Then," Paulk said, "you expect to give us encores?"

Sweetly Tigart said, "With the Court's permission, yes."

Sharman was fussing with a thread clinging to his vest. He said nothing.

Paulk refused to address any of them directly. At large he said, "All right, I'll get them out of there. We've got the witnesses under the Rule. So, before I leave here tonight, I'll get out subpoenas for all four of them."

Eyes lifted, mouths fell open. Paulk glared at them. The whip handle felt good in his hand. "I mean it," he said. "If we can't seat them where they belong, we'll exclude them entirely."

The silence told him he had not been anticipated; that he would have his way. After a moment Anglin said, "That would work two ways, if we happened to subpoena Angie."

"Do it. I'll trade her out for your four."

"Now, just a minute," the Judge cleared his throat. "It seems to me we can satisfy everyone without locking out either of these families. After all, we're talking about some sort of imagined advantage that may not exist—why couldn't we agree to seat one member of each family, say, with equal prominence?"

Tigart switched on the light at the Judge's washbowl, studied his beard in the mirror, before he responded. "I'm not going to be unreasonable."

"What do you say, young man?"

Paulk shook his head. "I realize that Ike ought to have a Hutcherson there to see him earn his money. I won't object, providing that one takes a normal place in the gallery."

This pushed them hard. Anglin was ready to explode. "Then the sister goes into the crowd, too."

"No." It paid them a little for Willie Studer, the published confession, the Masonic jury. "It's Mrs. Callahan's brother we're trying. If there's a Hutcherson on trial here, we're yet to hear about it."

For an instant, he feared he had said too much. His stomach fluttered as he watched the special prosecutor. Tigart had opened his pants and was stuffing in his shirttail, treating them all to a glimpse of peppermint drawers.

"Your Honor," Ike said, "I cannot tell Hutch's folks to come to court, or to stay away. But I will explain Junior's tantrum about it and suggest that they pamper him. I won't guarantee what they'll do, and I'm not going to persuade them one way or the other."

Even the heavyweight like Tigart needed to save face, and Paulk let him. He had what he wanted. However Ike put it, he knew there'd be no Hutchersons under the jury gaze tomorrow, no gusts of wronged breath on the back of Ray Priest's neck. He caught up his briefcase and left, wondering if Mrs. Hutcherson's friend, Laura Singer, would share his satisfaction over this first small conquest.

XXII

On Thursday, just at noon, a tall thunderhead came trundling in from the southwest. Having flushed out the farmers to stand like gray-faced scarecrows in the fields of heading wheat, having sent their families to the storm cellars, the cloud paused squarely over the city. Flexing its twisting black arms, dangling a few ugly yellow tassels, it weighted the town under the suffocating still of a green darkness. It was spring; there would be many such days. But for the start of the trial, Paulk would have liked sunshine, and a breeze.

The courtroom's fluorescent lamps were lit. People sniffed the dense air and whispered to each other that if hail and a twister were coming, the courthouse was as strong a shelter as any. Judge Sharman climbed to the bench, gazed out the open windows a moment, as if deciding to fine the weather for contempt, then nodded down on the pit.

"The defendant will rise. Mr. District Attorney, you may proceed."

Cameron approached the jury rail with a copy of the indictment held between his hands. He began reading it, his voice firm, precise in its fidelity to the language. But, Paulk thought, the vigor, the zest of office, seemed to have died out of him.

"In the name and by the authority of the State of Texas, the Grand Jurors for the County of Bonita, state aforesaid, duly organized, im-paneled and sworn as such at the January term, A.D. 1959, of the District Court of the 191st Judicial District in and for said county, upon their oaths in said court do present that Raymond Elliot Priest, hereinafter called the defendant, on or about the fourteenth day of January, A.D. 1959, and anterior to the presentment of this indictment in the County of Bonita and State of Texas, did then and there unlaw-fully, voluntarily and with malice aforethought, kill Jessup C. Hutch-

erson by then and there beating and striking the said Jessup C. Hutcherson with a pistol, against the peace and dignity of the State.

"Count Two. And the Grand Jurors aforesaid, upon their oaths as
aforesaid, and in and to said court, at said term thereof, do further
present that Raymond Elliot Priest, hereinafter called the defendant,
on or about the fourteenth day of January, A.D. 1959, and anterior to
the presentment of this indictment, in the County of Bonita and State
of Texas, did then and there unlawfully, voluntarily, and with malice
aforethought, kill Jessup C. Hutcherson by then and there beating and
striking the said Jessup C. Hutcherson on the head with a pistol and
by then and there *strangling and choking* the said Jessup C. Hutcherson
with a shirt, against the peace and dignity of the State.

"Count Three. And the Grand Jurors aforesaid, upon their oaths
as aforesaid, in and to said Court, at said term thereof, do further
present that Raymond Elliot Priest, hereinafter called the defendant,
on or about the fourteenth day of January, A.D. 1959, and anterior to
the presentment of this indictment, in the County of Bonita and State
of Texas, did then and there unlawfully, voluntarily and with malice
aforethought, kill Jessup C. Hutcherson by then and there beating
and striking the said Jessup C. Hutcherson *on the head* with a pistol,
against the peace and dignity of the State.

"Signed, Beaumont W. Wilson, Foreman of the Grand Jury. Filed
on the twenty-seventh day of March, A.D. 1959, and endorsed a True
Bill by Theodore Holcomb, Clerk, 191st Judicial District of Texas."

Paulk doubted the jury grasped the dearth of alternatives. It was
murder by beating, murder by beating and strangling, or murder by
beating on the head. Which was unequivocal murder with malice, anyway you cut it. He got up to stand beside Priest, regretting the harsh
angular look of him in the dreary light.

"To which the defendant pleads not guilty," he announced. "All
right, Ray, let's sit down."

"Mr. Tigart," the Judge glanced at the clock, "you may call your
first witness."

Ike said, "Mr. Hollis Anglin, please."

The assistant blew his nose as he settled in the witness chair. The
sullen, sleepy air was about him, giving him an appearance of vast
reluctance.

"Have you been sworn?" asked the Judge.

"No, sir."

"You do solemnly swear the testimony you are about to give in the case before this court is the truth, the whole truth, and nothing but the truth, so help you God."

"I do."

Tigart propped his knee against the table and squinted at the ceiling. "State your name to the jury, please."

"Hollis Anglin."

"And you are the assistant district attorney for the 191st Judicial District?"

"I am."

"Were you serving this county in that capacity on March 28th, 1959?"

"Yes, sir, I was."

"Mr. Anglin, I'll ask you whether, on that date, you had a conversation with the defendant, Raymond Priest."

"I did."

"Where did this meeting take place?"

"In Bonita County jail."

"Will you tell the jury how you happened to see the defendant that day?"

"I called on Mr. Priest to find out if he wished to make a statement in connection with this case."

"And did he make a statement that day?"

"Yes, sir, he did."

"What, if anything, did you tell the defendant prior to—?"

Paulk said, "That's leading, Your Honor."

Tigart hunched his shoulders, letting the jury see at once which side meant to impede by tediousness about small matters. "All right," he said. "Mr. Anglin, will you tell us the circumstances under which the defendant made his statement?"

"I told him he wasn't required to make any statement whatsoever, and that if he decided to do so, the statement would be used against him in his trial. I also told him he was being offered no promises, no inducement of any sort."

"Then, you exerted no persuasion of any kind?"

"That's correct."

"And, having heard the statutory warning, the defendant proceeded to make his statement?"

"Yes."

"To your knowledge, Mr. Anglin, did anyone else promise the defendant anything or make any threats in connection with this statement?"

"No, sir."

Tigart got up, handing a sheaf of dog-eared pages to Mr. Funderburg for marking. As the special prosecutor lumbered along the jury rail, bearing the document on to Anglin, Paulk watched J. N. Gay. He hoped that to the little man, Ike looked ten feet tall.

"Mr. Anglin, I hand you State's Exhibit One. Have you ever seen it before?"

"I have."

"Can you tell us what it is?"

"This is the original copy of the statement given to me by Raymond Priest on March 28th, 1959."

"How have you identified it?"

"By its contents, by my signature, and by the signatures of the other witnesses."

"What signatures do you see on this document?"

"It is signed by Raymond Elliot Priest and attested to by the witnesses, Mr. Isaac Tigart and Sheriff Andrew Grosscup."

"Did you see the defendant sign it?"

"Yes."

"Do you know whether or not he did so voluntarily?"

"Yes, sir, he did."

"Tell us, if you know, whether Mr. Priest was fully apprised of the contents of this statement before he signed it."

"He was. It was read aloud to him."

"Were the witnesses you have named present during this reading?"

"They were."

Ike returned to the counsel table, picked up a carbon of the statement, and slid it toward Paulk. "May it please the Court, we will offer State's Exhibit One in evidence at this time."

Paulk pushed the copy aside without a glance at it. From the *Tribune* he knew the statement by heart. The need now was to reduce its importance in the jury's eyes. Without waiting a signal from the Judge, he said, "Mr. Anglin, how long have you known this defendant?"

"Not long."

"Were you acquainted with him prior to this jail meeting on March twenty-eighth?"

"No."

"Was that the first time you ever saw Ray Priest?"

"It was."

"Then, just how did this creative-writing session happen to come about that day?"

"I don't believe I have testified to any 'creative writing,' Mr. Paulk." Anglin was laconic, bored.

"I'm trying to find out," Paulk said, "whether you went up to jail that day because Priest sent for you, say, the way a man in trouble is apt to send for an old friend."

At least, Anglin flushed. "I did not."

"Then, you weren't invited?"

"No."

"This meeting in which you did *not* do any creative writing, then, was initiated by yourself; is that correct?"

"Yes."

"Tell us how long this meeting lasted."

"I don't remember. About two hours, I imagine."

"Were you, the sheriff, and the special prosecutor alone with the defendant during that time?"

"We were."

"Was there an attorney up there to represent this man?"

"Not that I know of."

"You'd know of it, if there had been, wouldn't you?"

"I think so."

"All right. Please tell the jury just how this document was developed."

"If you'd be more direct—" Anglin gazed back blandly.

"I'll do my best," Paulk said. "Tell me, did Ray just sit himself down to the typewriter and whip out this long tale and hand it to you?"

"No, certainly not."

"Well," Paulk picked up the statement, "here it is, on paper—and recently *in* the paper—and I think we ought to know just how it got there. Tell us who did do the typing."

"I did."

"Then, you sort of collaborated in the creation of this thing?"

"No. I was the typist."

"Tell us, Mr. Anglin, just how you laid hold of the information you wrote into this statement?"

"I wrote in nothing. I typed out what the defendant told me."

"I see. Ray just sailed off into a long monologue, and you sat there pecking away, getting it all down; is that it?"

"I questioned him, and took down his answers."

"Oh. In other words, you asked Ray the questions that happened to come to your mind, and you put down his replies in an order that seemed best to you, and you came up with this piece of purple prose?"

"You may think of it that way if you like," Anglin smiled.

"What I like doesn't count. I want to know whether you asked all the questions, every logical question that might have been put to this defendant concerning the events of January fourteenth?"

"Insofar as I know, I did."

"Do you suppose that while you were writing this, anything material to this case could have escaped you?"

"No."

"I'll ask you to tell the jury, Mr. Anglin, whether you included in this statement every answer you received from the defendant."

"I did."

Here it was, the typical certified State's lie, doubly insidious because it well could pass unsuspected. As Jack Singer said, a defendant's lies, being anticipated, seldom deceived. But the State's perjuries were ever successful. A policeman lied to cover a mistake, other witnesses perjured themselves from vindictiveness or merely out of common know-it-all vanity, or an assistant district attorney lied to protect the admissibility of a confession, and juries seemed never to guess it. Always, jury gullibility favored the prosecution because, as Singer expressed it, "a witness called by the State takes the stand with the Great Seal of Texas stamped on his ass and it's hell to peel it off." Nobody could be taught to be leery of anything offered in the name of Texas.

Although Anglin's flat denial was no surprise to him, Paulk hesitated, contemplating his course. He wanted the record to include, as the basis for an appeal, a well-grounded objection to Ray's confession. At the same time, he wanted the statement admitted. It was a tight-rope. He must build toward a solid objection, then make certain he was overruled. It called for a touch, a timing he wasn't sure he had.

He said, "As an assistant district attorney, Mr. Anglin, have you taken other statements in connection with this case?"

"I have."

"Have you obtained a statement, or statements, from Patty Sue Priest?"

"Object," Tigart got up quickly. "This is going far afield, it's irrelevant, and bears on no issue in this case."

"That's so," the Judge sighed.

"Your Honor, I believe Mr. Paulk is trying to decide whether he wants to object to this exhibit. If he is going to object, let him say so and let's have the jury retired."

Sharman nodded. "If you are objecting, Mr. Paulk—"

"May it please the Court, until now I've been trying only to discover the authenticity of this document. But if the special prosecutor wants to send the jury out, wants us to thresh out this business in the dark—"

"Hold on," Tigart screeched his chair back. "I object to the insinuation that we want to handle anything in the dark. Mr. Paulk knows the law requires the jury's retirement, and his remark inferring that I'm trying to get rid of them was calculated as prejudicial. I move it be stricken, and that the Court instruct the jury not to consider it."

"Sustain," Sharman was scowling. "The jury will disregard the defense counsel's remark about hiding things in the dark, or whatever it was he said. All right, Mr. Hart, you may take the jury upstairs."

So far, so good. As the jury shuffled out, he scanned the crowd. Lily Black was scorning him through thick mascara. On back, sitting in front of the Posse delegation, was Martha Hutcherson. She was listening, her fine dark head inclined, to the whisperings of Mayor Jones.

The Judge said, "Proceed, Mr. Paulk."

"Mr. Anglin," he began cautiously, "this so-called confession does not include everything the defendant told you during that interview, does it?"

"It includes what was material." Anglin was spraddled, scattered out drowsily, now that the jury did not watch him.

"And you, along with the special prosecutor and the sheriff, decided just what was material?"

"We didn't see any reason to include the defendant's comments on jail food, or the weather."

"Is that all you omitted?"

"Of course not. A good deal that was extraneous was said during those two hours."

"Did you at any time tell Mr. Priest that some of what he said was being left out, quote, 'because this is running too long'?"

"I don't recall any such remark."

"But you may have made it?"

"I doubt that I did."

"It's unfortunate that your memory is less vivid in this respect than on the other details. Let me ask you if you recall whether you gave Mr. Priest the opportunity to add to his statement, or to make deletions, after you had written it down."

"I imagine we did, that's routine."

"You imagine, but you can't say positively?"

"Yes, I am positive."

The State was committed to a position; it was useless to think Anglin might modify it now, or ever. Paulk said, "Tell us, Mr. Anglin, whether this was the first statement the defendant made following his arrest as a suspect in this case."

"As far as my personal knowledge goes, it was."

"Then you just don't know anything about a statement the defendant might have made up there in Peoria, Illinois?"

"Not of my own knowledge."

"You never heard of such a statement?"

"I heard of one, yes. As a matter of fact, I saw it."

Paulk was surprised. "Then, the statement you took in jail was the second one made by this defendant?"

"It was the first legal one, I believe."

"Will you explain what you mean by that?"

"Certainly. The officers in Illinois failed to include in the first statement the name of the person who gave the defendant the statutory warning. We therefore accepted a second statement."

"Was this technical error the only reason you took a second statement?"

"It was."

"Then, it's your testimony that the facts as set forth by the defendant were identical in the two statements?"

"No. The first one was very brief. The second includes more detail."

"Mr. Anglin, who took that statement up in Peoria?"

"I don't know."

"You mean you haven't seen the signatures on it?"

"I suppose I did, but I paid little attention."

"I see. You just didn't notice Ranger Captain A. B. C. Smith's name there, if it was there?"

"That's right."

Paulk glanced at his client. Often it was during the clinical struggle over a point of law that a defendant began to panic. A man saw legal science laboring along too impersonally. With sinking heart he discovered that neither the court in which he sat nor the law it argued had taken into account the uniqueness of himself and his crime. Justice had neither anticipated, nor failed to anticipate, his birth and life and deeds. He was another white rat, a specimen. But Priest remained undisturbed, peculiarly strong in his nothingness.

"As an attorney, Mr. Anglin, you are aware that when one statement is given involuntarily, all subsequent statements from the same defendant must be regarded as involuntary?"

"Naturally."

"If this defendant was questioned through an entire day and night, if he was told he would be forbidden food and sleep until he confessed, could his statement be regarded as voluntary?"

"No."

"And if a two-hundred-pound Texas Ranger stood on his feet, causing him pain, and if this officer threatened to stomp his guts out unless he gave a statement in writing, would there be a question of undue persuasion?"

"Of course."

"And if an officer told the defendant that having made an oral statement, he might as well make a written one, and if a written statement did result, would there be a question of duress?"

"Certainly."

"During your association with this prosecution, Mr. Anglin, have you learned that any of these things happened to this defendant while he was under arrest in Peoria?"

"I have not."

He wasn't making much of a record. To call Captain Smith would be to extract more untruths in support of the confession. If he put Priest on, he risked a premature disclosure of the defense.

"Well, Mr. Paulk?" The Judge was impatient.

"Your Honor, the defendant will object to State's Exhibit One as inadmissible because it is not the original statement given by him; it was made subsequent to a statement coerced from the defendant under the pressure of fatigue, hunger, and both threatened and actual violence, and it was drafted to exclude certain relevant, highly material facts which were properly admissible as mitigation."

Sharman pursed over the nerve of it. "You are objecting with no offering of evidence?"

"May it please the Court, I realize we are in an odd situation here. But, not having been permitted to examine this statement in advance, I've had no chance to prepare. It's risky to admit this exhibit now when, later on, there'll be direct testimony as to the duress exerted—"

Tigart threw up his hands. "Counsel is asking a ruling based on evidence he *says* may come, and we're supposed to accept his word that it exists and will be sufficient to bar this confession. I don't see that he has even raised an issue."

The Judge nodded. "Anything further, Mr. Paulk?"

"No."

"Very well. Bring down the jury, Mr. Hart. I'm overruling your objection. You may have your exception."

Paulk said, "Is it the Court's ruling that this statement will not be open to explanation by the defendant?"

"Young man, if there is an issue as to whether the statement is voluntary and complete, you may put it before the jury at any moment you please."

The lights dimmed, and heads turned to study the gloom outside as the jury, led by Ancil Andricks, tramped back into the box.

"Continue, Mr. Tigart."

"Your Honor," Paulk said, "I hadn't concluded my cross-examination."

"Get on with it; we're wasting time."

Paulk said, "Mr. Anglin, your only interest in this case is that imposed on you as a prosecutor, is that correct?"

"It is."

"Then, I'm mistaken in my belief that you've been retained by the codefendant in this case for her divorce action against Ray Priest?"

Tigart came up shouting. "I won't stand for any more of this, Your Honor! He intends to dirty up this record by worming in a lot of junk that has no bearing on this case, and I move the Court instruct him on his conduct."

Sharman jerked his chair around and gazed in shock at the assistant district attorney. "Are you acting as attorney for Mrs. Priest?"

"No," Anglin answered coolly. "She asked me to handle her divorce, but I've no intention of doing so."

Paulk caught the stir in the jury box and said, "No more questions."

Tigart lost no time. "Mr. Anglin, when you went up to see the defendant in jail, did you know what his story was going to be?"

"I did not."

"The statements set forth in State's Exhibit One are those of the defendant, just as he made them?"

"They are."

"That's all."

Anglin was smooth, his voice without inflection, as he began reading Ray's statement to the jury. The audience strained forward to miss none of it. Despite himself, Paulk had to admire Hollis Anglin. The statement contained the sort of grammatical errors Priest might have made; here and there lay an authenticating piece of Oklahoma vernacular. As the recital went on, he began to feel grateful to the *Tribune*. Had the statement been undisclosed, it might now have been sensational. As it was, part of its impact was lost to familiarity.

It was during the recess, with Anglin glaring curses at him, that Nathan Hart showed him the note.

"You say one of the jurors dropped it?"

"On the stairs," Uncle Nathan grinned. "I don't know which one it was. But, read it."

The writing was in pencil, on the back of a blank check. "Free country," it said. "Tell a lie, and you go to jail. Tell the truth, and they stick you on the jury."

Perhaps this jury wasn't as extraordinary as he thought.

XXIII

Tigart lay deep in his chair. "State your name to the jury."

"Ellis Browning, of Crossroads, New Mexico."

"What do you do, Mr. Browning?"

"I'm a cattle trader, got me a little feed-lot business, and I run the lounge and bar there in Crossroads."

Brownie was one of the exceptional big-case witnesses who probably deserved the sympathy he claimed for himself. Spare, weathered, he recently had acquired a look of harassment. During the manhunt, he had been snatched from his tavern at odd hours and flown across the country to inspect new suspects; he had been required to pore through police mugbooks in a dozen cities; he had been pursued by the grand jury, the Hats, and the State's hypnotist, all insisting he had to remember more than he did. From his own interview with the man, Paulk felt that Brownie was no longer able to separate his actual recollection from those matters that had been suggested to him.

"Speak a little louder, if you please," Ike said.

In good order, the special prosecutor established that Brownie's place was a quarter-mile west of the Texas–New Mexico line, on the north side of Highway 66; that he had known Hutch twenty-five years, that he was tending bar when, at about 3:30 P.M. on January fourteenth, Hutch's sedan drew up in his driveway.

While Tigart laid his predicate, Paulk undertook a visual poll of the jury. In the back corner Mrs. Chesterson, the welfarist whom he had hoped might see Ray Priest as someone ripe for reconstruction, scowled with a concentration that left no trace of her warm, *voir-dire* charm. Beside her Mrs. Billingsley, faded colorless in the glum thunderstorm light, was leaning forward, frozen by the earnest juror's apprehension of missing what counted, absorbing what did not. Gay, the angry little gamecock, sat on a double cushion, his eyes a warning that he would be hard to convince. Andricks, his watered hair drying despite the saturation of the air and, sure enough, rising up on end, looked bulky and comical in the foremost chair. There was Franklin Turner, swinging his chair from side to side; Studer darting his gaze over the crowd as if counting the house; then the others, the men with serious faces, attentive now in a way that seemed to make them more dangerous.

To which of these ought he to play his case? Andricks? Maybe Gay, possibly the two women. It was too early to decide. Whatever, he must guard against disclosure of the cold hate he felt for Willie Studer. *In the sworn twelve, a thief or two, guiltier than him they try. . . .*

"Tell us," Tigart said, "how you happen to know the time Mr. Hutcherson and the two young people arrived at the bar?"

"Well, my place being right on the time zone, I keep two big clocks going. The one on the east wall shows Texas time, and the one on the west keeps New Mexico time. That hour's difference warts people, so I'm always looking at them clocks and explaining to somebody."

Brownie said he had been explaining his clocks when Hutch and the Priests came in. Hutch, he said, had raised a hand and yelled at him. "Of course, I hollered back."

"Do you remember what each of you said?"

"Offhand, I don't. But we usually cussed each other on sight—that's how him and me always was."

"All right. What, if anything, did Mr. Hutcherson do next?"

"Him and this young couple sat down in the front booth and ordered some drinks."

Ike would have liked to vault across the business of the drinks. But since he couldn't, he had chosen to minimize it on direct, taking the edge off Paulk's cross-examination.

"Do you know who served them, Mr. Browning?"

"Yes, sir, I did."

"What did they order?"

"They asked for a whiskey sour and two beers."

"Which of the three placed the order?"

"Hutch did, he was buying. He taken the whiskey sour—that's what he always liked at my place—and the boy and girl, they taken the beers."

"Did you hear any discussion between them while you were waiting for their order?"

"Well, some."

"Tell the jury what you heard."

"I don't recollect the exact words, but at first this girl wanted a whiskey too, and this young feller told her 'no,' that she could have a Coke. Then she told me she'd have a beer."

"This young man you speak of—do you see him in the courtroom?"

"Yes, sir."

"Will you point him out for the jury?"

"He's the feller sitting there at the table, the one in the light gray suit."

"You are pointing to the defendant, Raymond Elliot Priest?"

"Yes, sir, that's him."

"Very well. Did Priest object when the girl asked for beer?"

"Not that I heard, he didn't."

"What else, if anything, was said while you were at the booth?"

"Well, Hutch hoorawed me some, about a horse trade him and me had up in the air, and he talked about his trip, and how the wheat looked—stuff like that."

Tigart referred to a note pad. "Now, Mr. Browning, out of your long familiarity with Hutch, can you tell us whether you noticed anything unusual about him that day?"

Paulk said, "We'll object; that calls for a conclusion of the witness."

The Judge pushed up his glasses. "I believe the witness is qualified to answer, since he says he knew Mr. Hutcherson intimately for many years. I'll overrule."

"Note my exception." Paulk glanced at Mr. Funderburg and smiled. As a rule, the old reporter was poker-faced, content, as his stylus set down their extended chronicles of trouble. Today he was sour, wincing over every unessential word. He hated the news machines clattering away in his office, the table of students who were remembering only occasionally that they had come to sharpen up their shorthand, the heat that caused him to smudge his pads.

"Well," Browning said, "Hutch looked all tuckered out, and told me he was. Said he'd been up two nights running on account of a wild well, said he guessed he couldn't take it like he used to."

"Is that all he said to you about his physical condition?"

"That's about it, just that he wasn't feeling up to snuff."

Tigart left it there, guiding Browning along in the other details of Hutch's stop at the bar. He had served the drinks, and after a time, Patty Sue Priest left the booth to play the jukebox. With a can of beer in one hand, a cellophane envelope of peanuts in the other, she had danced alone to the music. Yes, Brownie said, it was something a teen-ager might do; well, to the best of his recollection, she had played three or four rock-and-roll records, maybe five, and in between, she had returned to the booth and Hutch had given her more nickels.

Paulk listened carefully, pleased that Tigart waded through this phase a trifle too rapidly.

"Did you observe, Mr. Browning, just how it happened that the girl stopped playing the jukebox, stopped enjoying the music?"

"Yes, sir, I heard what was said."

"I'll ask you to tell the jury what that was."

"Well, this man, Priest, told her to come sit down."

"Is that all he said to her?"

"No. He said, 'You better sit down, quit attracting attention to yourself.' He said, 'You've got everybody looking at you, and you ought to have better sense.' "

Paulk marked an X on his note pad. Here it started, the State's

portrait of a man conceiving a crime, growing wary of those who might
become witnesses.

Ike said, "Are you positive he used the phrase, 'quit attracting
attention'?"

"Yes, sir, I am."

"And that he told her she 'ought to have better sense'?"

"Yes, sir."

Tigart paused to turn knowing eyes upon the jury before, with a
sad wag of his head, he resumed. Browning told of serving a second
round of drinks, of a conversation in the booth in tones "so low I
didn't get the drift," of their preparations to leave and an order for
a fifth of whiskey, more peanuts, and six cans of beer they would take
with them.

"Then, all three of them came to the cash register?"

"Yes, sir."

"Who paid for the drinks?"

"Hutch did."

"In cash?"

Browning smiled. Everyone knew Hutch paid all obligations in
cash fished from any pocket, or, sometimes, dumped out of his hat.
"Yes, sir," he said. "He dropped a fistful of bills on the bar and sez
to me, 'Take out what's yours, Brownie, and leave me a little dab to
get myself home on.' "

"What, if anything, did you say to this?"

"Not much. I asked him what his hurry was, told him I'd like to
talk a horse swap."

"Did Mr. Hutcherson make any response to this?"

"He said he had to get on home, was going to be late to dinner like
it was, and that he was having some car trouble. Hutch had a pretty
little appaloosa mare I figured I could use—"

"Did he tell you the nature of his car trouble?"

"He mentioned it, said if he killed the engine, he'd have to get a
push."

"Where was the defendant during all this?"

"Standing there, waiting."

"Near Mr. Hutcherson?"

"Yes, sir, just two or three feet away."

"Then, Ray Priest was two or three feet away when Hutch put this
fistful of money on the bar?"

"That's right."

"Mr. Browning, I'll ask you to describe that money for us."

The witness shrugged. "It was just a big wad, like Hutch always carried."

"How big, if you please?"

"Enough to choke a mule, I'd say."

"Did you notice the denominations of any of those bills?"

"Some, I did. I took mine out of a twenty. I seen there was more twenties, a hundred or two, and some fifties."

"You know, then, that Mr. Hutcherson was pretty well heeled that day?"

"It was a right smart of money."

"Would you say he had as much as a thousand dollars?"

"We'll object," Paulk said. "He says he saw only some of the bills. It calls for a conclusion."

"Sustain the objection," Sharman almost yawned. His lids were heavy; he had to fight them on warm, dull afternoons.

"Mr. Browning," Ike said, "I'll ask you if anyone else could have seen this money while it was heaped up there on the bar."

"Sure, everybody in the place was looking at it."

"*Everybody?* You include this defendant, Ray Priest?"

"Yes, sir; I reckon he was as pop-eyed as the rest of us."

Tigart made the point swiftly while Paulk hunted lucklessly for grounds on which to protest. It bordered on opinion, unless Priest's eyes literally had popped, as well they might have. Anyway, he was too late. He grinned at the jury and let it ride.

Hutch and the Priests had passed about forty-five minutes in the bar, Browning said. When they left, Patty Sue was carrying the fifth of Seagram's, Ray had the beer. Priest got in the car to drive, Hutch sat on the right side, and Patty Sue was between them. The car, apparently left idling throughout, moved off to the east, toward Texas.

"Now," Ike drawled, "during the time you observed Ray Priest, did you notice anything extraordinary in his manner?"

"Well, he did hit me as kind of queer—"

"I object," Paulk shot to his feet. "The special prosecutor is burdening this jury with insinuations he knows are improper and which would be improper even if they were relevant, which they are not."

Sharman jerked up straight in his chair. By some miracle, the sudden dispute had registered on his coma. He swiveled toward the witness, clearing his throat as he came.

"I doubt the question was improper, but the answer certainly was. Mr. Browning, you may tell all you saw and heard, but you cannot interpret or offer any opinions here. Under the rules, you are permitted to say what may have happened to cause you to think this man queer, but you cannot state that he was queer, regardless of how confident you may be of this deduction. The jury will disregard the statement that the defendant was queer."

The Judge had tripled the damage. Paulk groaned. "Your Honor, the defendant objects—"

"I've already sustained your objection, Mr. Paulk."

"May it please the Court, I'm objecting now to the comments of the Court as prejudicial to the rights of this defendant, as inflammatory, as lending weight to the improper remark of the witness, and I move the Court instruct the jury to—"

"Overrule." Sharman's hands seized his lapels, quivered at this impudence. Behind Paulk, Anglin snickered. Tigart's sweetest red smile was upon him.

"The defendant excepts to the ruling."

Sharman ignored him. "Proceed, Mr. Tigart."

"Your Honor," Paulk shouted, "I want to preserve my bill."

"You may have it. Now, sit down."

He had charged a windmill. Until now, Judge Sharman had prosecuted only a little. Henceforth, he would prosecute a great deal.

Tigart spoke softly, presenting a deft contrast. "Mr. Browning, tell the jury just what it was you noticed about Ray Priest."

"Well, the funny thing was, he was always sort of turned away, so as you couldn't get a real good look at him."

"We'll object," Paulk didn't bother to rise. "The answer assumes a motive and state of mind in the defendant, one the witness could have had no access to."

Grudgingly, under an apprehension of error greater than the sufferings of his dignity, the Judge sustained.

Tigart said, "You got a good look at Hutch that day?"

"Yes, sir."

"Did you get a good look at the girl?"

"Yes, sir, I did."

"But for some reason, you never got a good look at this defendant?"

"Just a fair look, that's all."

Quickly, Ike wrapped it up with Browning's account of how he had picked Priest out of a sheriff's department line-up.

"Your witness, Mr. Paulk."

Paulk sat a moment, evaluating the witness and the testimony. He disliked antagonizing an honest man. But men had never been able to fight politely.

"Mr. Browning, you've come here bearing no grudge, no malice toward anyone despite your long friendship with the deceased, isn't that true?"

"Yes, sir." Brownie's eyes, narrowed by their lifetime encounter with the High Plains winds, opened with relief.

"As a good citizen accepting your moral and legal responsibilities, you've come forward for no reason except to help us find the truth, isn't that correct?"

"Yes, sir, that's so."

He could feel the tense readiness across the table, the prosecutors poised to spring up in full cry. He supposed they recognized the old Jack Singer technique, the buttering of the bun before biting into it.

"To help us understand this case, will you tell the jury whether in January of this year you went to El Reno, Oklahoma, and there identified a man as the one you saw with Jess Hutcherson?"

Browning recoiled as if slapped during a handshake. "No, I didn't exactly identify anybody over at El Reno."

"What do you mean by 'didn't exactly'?"

"Well, I mean they showed me a man over there, and first off I thought he was the one. But after I taken a second look, and thought it over some, I knew they had the wrong feller."

"Then, at the time, only a few days after Mr. Hutcherson visited your bar, you didn't have as clear a picture of the accused as you do now?"

"I had a clear picture, all right."

He could bore in, he knew, maybe impeach the identification. But there was little purpose in it since, later, he would be conceding freely that Ray Priest had passed that day with Hutch.

"During the investigation, did you make any other trips to view persons who were under arrest?"

Cautiously, Browning described junkets to Kansas, Colorado, Minnesota, and two to California, adding firmly that on these occasions, he hadn't come close to identifying anyone. Next, in a tedium of feet and inches, Paulk led him to draw an oral floor plan of the tavern, to describe the arrangement, the lights and shadows, the position of the critical booth in relationship to all else.

"Then, if I understand you correctly, all the time the defendant sat in the booth, his back was turned toward you?"

"Yes, it would have been."

"So that to have exposed his face to your view, the defendant would have had to have sat there with his head twisted around backwards?"

"I reckon that's about it."

"But from your position behind the bar, you had an almost constant, full and unobstructed view of Hutch and the girl?"

"Yes."

He paused, aware of Mrs. Hutcherson, wishing he might postpone this first innuendo, the little spatter of dung that would begin his defense. But he didn't dare wait. His case must emerge from the State's own witnesses, and he could not recall them.

He said, "Does this mean that instead of sitting with her husband, Patty Priest was sharing a seat with Jess Hutcherson?"

Brownie's poorly knotted necktie bobbed. "Well, she wasn't in that booth, most of the time."

"But when she was?"

"Yes, she sat beside Hutch."

"Did that strike you as peculiar, Mr. Browning?"

"The State will object," Anglin said. "That calls for a conclusion."

"I'm asking for no conclusion," Paulk cut in. "I just want to know if he thought this peculiar."

"Your Honor," Tigart rose to join in, "I think Junior wants—"

"It seems to me," Paulk said, "that the opinions of this witness as to the defendant's manner were admissible a few minutes ago, and that his opinion as to the conduct of the deceased is equally admissible now."

"If you'll stop butting in, ole buddy—"

"That's enough," the Judge was snapping his fingers like a schoolmarm. "Behave yourself, young man. I'll sustain the objection."

Paulk settled back to his chair, satisfied. It was probable his question tantalized the jury all the more because its answer was disallowed.

"Mr. Browning, was there any sort of disturbance in your place that day?"

"No, none at all."

"Was this defendant noisy, rowdy, offensive in any way?"

"No, he was pretty quiet."

Slowly Paulk qualified Browning as an expert. Yes, after fifteen years at tavern keeping, Brownie had grown familiar with drunks; yes, he was competent to recognize intoxication, to discern changes in conduct that could be credited to liquor.

"In view of your experience," Paulk said, "would you say this defendant had drunk too much that day?"

"No, he wasn't drunk."

"As a matter of fact, no one in the party consumed any hard liquor except Mr. Hutcherson himself, isn't that right?"

"Well, the young couple, they just had beer."

"I believe you testified that Mr. Hutcherson drank two whiskey sours, these taken twenty or twenty-five minutes apart?"

"That's my recollection of it."

"Do you know who mixed Mr. Hutcherson's drinks?"

"I did."

"Tell us, Mr. Browning, what ingredients you use in a whiskey sour."

"I put lemon juice, sugar and bourbon, fixed up on cracked ice."

"How much bourbon?"

"Usually, an ounce to maybe an ounce and a half, depending on who the customer is."

"Usually, you say? Were Mr. Hutcherson's drinks that day the 'usual' ones?"

"Well, Hutch always craved his a little stronger."

"How much stronger?"

"For him, I'd put two ounces of whiskey."

"Which is what you did on January fourteenth?"

"Yes, sir."

"Then, in his two drinks taken less than thirty minutes apart, Mr. Hutcherson consumed four ounces of bourbon whiskey?"

"Sure, but for Hutch, that wasn't—"

"Just answer the question, please." The Judge, chagrined that so distinguished a man should have known demon whiskey, seemed to be dividing his distaste between Paulk and the witness.

"What change, if any, did you observe in Mr. Hutcherson after these drinks?" Paulk said.

"Wasn't much; Hutch could handle it."

"Is it your testimony that after missing two nights' sleep, the deceased was able to drink four ounces of whiskey in a brief space of time and remain unaffected?"

"The State objects," Tigart rumbled up from his chair. "The tastes and capacities of the deceased are not in issue here. None of this has any bearing on the guilt or innocence of this defendant; the whole line of examination is immaterial."

"May it please the Court," Paulk spoke meekly, "the State opened the inquiry into what transpired in the bar, including the matter of the drinks. Since they've gone into part of what this witness saw and heard, we are entitled to show the rest of it."

Sharman agreed because he had to. Paulk nodded at the witness. "You may answer."

Falteringly, Browning admitted that Hutch had seemed to cheer up, had grown livelier and more talkative, after his whiskey sours. "But he wasn't staggering, nothing like that."

"All right. Calling your attention to that bottle of whiskey Mr. Hutcherson paid for before he left—can you tell us which of the three ordered that?"

"Hutch did."

"What did he say when he asked for it?"

"I can't remember, exactly. 'Brownie, gimme a bottle of Seagram's,' or something like that."

His prosecution of Hutch had started; how, or when, he couldn't have said. Shortly, the State would be defending a dead man, as angrily as it attacked the living one. The realization lay in the faces of the jury, the agonized eyes of the Judge. The transition seemed to revive Paulk while it darkened the air. He felt pulse and meter, vague syncopations, eerieness; as if while hearing a dirge, he marched. He wiped his forehead.

"Did he say anything else?"

"Well, not much. He told me that since he had this young feller to drive for him, he guessed he might have a few drinks on down the road."

It was better than he had expected. "Now, I believe you testified that Mr. Hutcherson told you he was feeling ill that day?"

"No, I never said that. I said he told me he was plumb wore out."

"Then, insofar as you know, he wasn't sick?"

"He never said he was."

Paulk steered him through a description of the small stock of patent medicines he kept in the bar, there for tourists who stopped off with headaches and upset stomachs. No, Hutch had purchased nothing from the drug rack; yes, of course Hutch knew the seltzers and aspirin were displayed for sale.

"Now, Mr. Browning, in reference to this twenty-minute floorshow Mrs. Priest performed in your establishment—can you tell us just what sort of a dance it was?"

"I ain't much of a hand when it comes to dancing."

"I understand that," Paulk smiled. "I'm just trying to find out whether she did a waltz, bebop, a hoedown—maybe a ballet?"

"I don't know," Browning squirmed, "she sort of danced around, that's all."

"Try to recall for this jury what movements she used."

"Well, I guess you'd say she kind of whirled and shook and kept time with her feet."

"I believe you've testified that she was holding a bag of peanuts in one hand and a glass of beer in the other?"

"No, sir; it was a can of beer—she drunk hers out of the can."

"All right. And she was singing along with the jukebox?"

"Humming, that's what I said. Just part of the time."

"What other sounds did she make?"

"None that I heard."

"It's my impression, Mr. Browning, that the newspapers quoted you as saying that 'she groaned, down deep in her throat, sort of like an alley cat,' and that she made a sound with her lips that kept time to the music."

"Well, that's right, she did do that."

"Will you describe that lip sound to the jury?"

"I don't reckon I can, not very good. It was a kind of a—a sucking noise, I'd say."

"Didn't you tell the newspapermen that it sounded, quote, 'like a bunch of little kisses'?"

"I don't remember saying that."

"But, is that how it sounded?"

"I guess that's as good a way to put it as any."

Paulk gave the jury a moment for its imaginings. A pretty teen-age girl, watched by men who were drinking, dancing and waving her beer and peanuts, expending volleys of kisses on the smoky barroom air.

"You said, I believe, that Patty wore her hair very long?"

"Yes, sir, down to here—down to her shoulders."

"And those were bare shoulders, were they not?"

"She had her clothes on, if that's what you mean."

"When I talked to you a few days ago, didn't you tell me that her blouse was cut very low, and that during the dance, it slid down off her shoulders?"

"Yes, sir, I seen that much."

"Then, through this whirling, shaking, groaning, kissing dance, this girl's hair was flouncing about over naked shoulders?"

"Your Honor," Tigart rose wearily, "I'm fascinated by Mr. Paulk's interpretation of this dance he didn't see, but since it is immaterial to any issue in this case, I'll have to object in the interest of saving time."

Sharman sat stiff and wide-awake, his old Southern heart shriveling over the reality of such wantonness in women. But he wanted to hear the rest; he listened as avidly as any old rake. The knowing familiarized him with the enemy, confirmed him in the clucks of tongue by which he sorrowed for this ungallant world of his latter years. Hoarsely he said, "I'll overrule."

"Well, sure," Browning said, "her hair bounced around."

"What style skirt was she wearing that day?"

"It was a big one, had red trimming on it."

"By big, you mean it was a full skirt?"

"I reckon that's what you'd call it."

"Your Honor," Tigart said, "we're shooting off into the blue, killing good time. Mrs. Priest's wardrobe has no bearing whatsoever on the guilt or innocence of this defendant."

The Judge spoke before Paulk could stand. "The defendant has the right to go into everything this witness saw while these people were in his saloon. Proceed, Mr. Paulk."

Sensing that Brownie needed some help, Paulk said, "This performance wasn't typical of your place, was it?"

"No, sir." The witness exuded gratitude; perhaps his wife was in court. "I don't allow no messing around; fact is, the whole thing was pretty embarrassing."

"Were you embarrassed because Patty Priest displayed more of her person than you thought appropriate?"

"Yes, sir, she did."

"Tell the jury just what she did expose?"

Browning swallowed hard. "Well, swirling around the way she was, her skirt swung out pretty far."

"Then, her legs were exposed to the view of anyone who happened to be watching?"

"Yes, sir."

"How much of her legs?"

"I'd say, above the knees."

"She showed her thighs, you mean?"

"Yes, sir."

"And at times, her skirt flew higher than that, didn't it?"

"Yes."

"Speak a little louder, please."

"Yes, sir, it did."

"Isn't it a fact that you and others present saw her panties each time she whirled?"

Browning bit his lip, then nodded.

"What is your answer?"

"I seen what she had on underneath."

"Very well. Now, as the proprietor of the Crossroads Bar, what, if anything, did you do to end this unusual performance?"

"Wasn't much I could do. What I mean is, I was aiming to speak to her, but her coming in with Hutch and all, I couldn't figure out what to say. Anyhow, her husband straightened her out."

"Did anyone else speak to her?"

"Not that I know of."

"Then, with yourself, Mr. Hutcherson, and four or five other patrons present, only this defendant took action when Patty's dance got out of hand?"

"As far as I know."

"Tell the jury what Ray said to his wife."

"He told her to sit down and keep still."

"Wasn't this the occasion on which he told her she was 'attracting attention' to herself?"

"Yes, he told her that."

Surely Ray had said more than this, and Paulk was tempted to probe for it. But at the last instant, he curbed himself; he need not risk his strength by fishing for some minor improvement. He saw that the jury mouths were looser; the eyes less positive. It was almost time to quit.

"Remembering that scene as you saw it, Mr. Browning—the dance, the bare shoulders and legs, the music, the cat groans and the little kisses—can you tell us whether it would have been exciting to a healthy man drinking a whiskey sour?"

"Object!" Tigart screamed up in red rage.

Paulk closed his eyes. There it was, earlier than planned. He might as well have read Article 1220 into the record. The room was deathly still, breathless. Then reporters scurried for the door, the crowd aroused, and someone sobbed. *It's true,* Paulk told himself. *Whatever happens, this is truth.*

Judge Sharman coughed as he called for order. "You object to what, Mr. Tigart?"

"Conclusion," Ike boomed. "He's after a conclusion, an opinion, invading the province of the jury."

"Sustained."

"My apologies to the Court," Paulk said. "Mr. Browning, your obligation as a witness in this case has caused you a great deal of personal inconvenience, isn't that correct?"

The barkeeper was cagey now, having been initiated to Greek gifts. He said, "Some."

Paulk elicited the facts of costly trips, a neglected business, an extra employe hired to fill in while Brownie was away.

"Then, it has cost you hard money to come in from New Mexico and help us out?"

"Well, it would have, if I hadn't got—"

"We'll object to this as material to no issue," Anglin chopped off the reply.

Paulk grinned at him. "I believe I'll withdraw the question, Your Honor." The subscription fund, the curious reimbursal of witnesses, could wait. "Are you aware that a reward has been offered in this case?"

"I've heard of it, yes, sir."

"I'll ask you whether you have filed your application to share in that reward?"

"Well, since they're paying it out, and if anything is coming to me—"

"Pass the witness."

Tigart launched a harsh redirect, combing again through the incident of the money, fighting to erase the lingering picture thoughts of a dancing, abandoned girl. His voice shot curtly through the unwholesome light; it was as if he blamed Browning for Patty's bouncing hair and flashing legs.

Paulk glanced up at the jury, wondering. Couldn't they accept, now, that Hutch, the idol, was a man? Did they sense that Ray Priest, the killer, wasn't totally inhuman?

Tigart brought a brown-wrapped parcel from under the table. Holding it before him, he drew from Browning a description of the clothing Priest had worn that day: brown jacket, a billed cap, tweed trousers that were "sort of muckledy brown." With broad flourishes, Ike shook the trousers from their wrapper and had them marked State's Exhibit Two.

"Have you ever seen this pair of trousers before?"

"Yes, sir, I seen them in the District Attorney's office."

"Did you see them at any time prior to that?"

"I might have; they look like them the young feller was wearing in the bar that day."

Tigart considered. Obviously, the tentative identification had surprised him. Paulk got up.

"May it please the Court, if the State is preparing to offer these trousers in evidence, I'll object on the grounds that—"

"Oh, sit down!" Tigart snapped. "I know you're clairvoyant, but I won't have you anticipating me on what I intend to do and when I mean to do it."

"Gentlemen, gentlemen," the Judge scowled. "You, young man, cannot object to an exhibit not yet offered. And you, Mr. Prosecutor, I wish you'd address yourself to the Court instead of to counsel. All right, are you offering these trousers in evidence?"

"I am."

"State your objection, Mr. Paulk."

"Your Honor, these pants can't be admitted if they show any bloodstains, as I understand they do, under the general holding that such displays are prejudicial and inflammatory when they elucidate no disputed issue. Further, the witness has shown he is unable to state he has ever seen these trousers elsewhere than in the District Attorney's office."

Sharman turned to the witness. "Did you say you saw these trousers worn by the defendant last January fourteenth?"

"No, sir, I said I saw this pair or a pair just like them."

The Judge lifted his brow at Tigart. Doggedly, holding the trousers by one leg so that they hung in a mammoth split, Tigart said, "We offer the exhibit, Your Honor." Having failed at obtaining identification, the special prosecutor was forcing a ruling against himself, once more priming the jury with the idea that the defense would bury as much evidence as it could under the technicalities of procedure.

"Ruling?" Paulk said.

The Judge shook his head. "I'll not admit the exhibit on such tentative identification. As to the objection to the bloodstains, if there are any, we'll consider that if and when the exhibit is reoffered properly."

Ike smiled, transferred his tobacco to the other cheek, and dragged the trousers across the floor as he returned to his seat.

"I've one other question," he said. "Mr. Browning, since certain aspersions have been cast here, I want you to tell this jury what, if anything, you learned of Mr. Jess Hutcherson's moral caliber during your twenty-five-year acquaintance with him."

"Sir, Hutch was the best man I ever knew."

"That's all."

Both question and answer were objectionable, but Paulk felt it ill-becoming to his cause, at this point, to say so. Instead he slouched back, mimicking Ike's country-lawyer posture, and said, "Mr. Browning, on the night of January fourteenth, you were at home over in New Mexico, isn't that right?"

"Yes, sir, I was."

"Then you have absolutely no knowledge of what took place over here in our county, in the Ranch motel, that evening?"

"No, sir, I couldn't say what happened."

"Thank you. We'll excuse the witness."

Tigart said, "Let him stand aside."

Paulk turned to Ray Priest. The strange eyes seemed harder, the slack jaw had almost closed. "Damn you, lawyer; ain't no call to stick in that crap about my wife."

Paulk looked at Angie.

"Baby!" she scolded, her hand on Ray's arm. "Shame on you, talking that way to Mr. Polk. . . ."

XXIV

Through a queer paradox of linkage and leverage, the boy reclined in the witness chair as if it were a couch and glanced about, confident of appreciation. He was John Soloman, age fifteen, dressed continentally, oozing self-love. A streak of his brown hair had been bleached platinum. The remainder was upswept into a pampered coiffure that included an Elvis curl above the brow. John's father operated a gas station on Highway 66 but was, essentially, a wheat farmer, one of those burnt dry men comfortable only in boots and khaki. His son could scarcely have known him. This was the new generation farm boy, the rural cat produced, or by-produced, by the age of subsidies and soil bank. John owned no work clothes, he had never saddled up a plow horse for a Sunday ride or spent a July heading maize. Instead, he appeared to have been bred for staying out all night and racking off the glasspacks of his customized Ford and country-slicking the city girls into desperate situations.

Judge Sharman took one look. "Sit up straight," he snapped. "Get rid of that gum, or whatever it is you're chewing." As the boy colored, the old jurist struck a second blow. "Don't stick it on the chair. You can just hold it in your hand until you get out of here."

Johnny spat the gum into his hand and looked stunned. His lark in court was spoiled before it began. At once Tigart opened the examination.

Along with a friend, Jake Swann, Johnny had been tending his father's station when, near dusk, the horned Cadillac sedan pulled in. Hutch, whom he recognized as his father's old friend, rode on the right side, Ray Priest was driving, and Patty Sue sat between them. It took about ten minutes to put twelve gallons of gasoline in the car, check the tires, clean the windshield. When Johnny started to raise the hood, Hutch had waved him away, explaining why the engine could not be turned off. Afterwards Hutch had passed his credit card and a dollar tip out the window. Then Priest had switched on the headlamps and "dug out," pelting the station with gravel as he sped on to the highway.

"Did Mr. Hutcherson say anything else to you?"

"He asked me what Dad was doing, and he wanted to know if the wheat looked good."

"Pass the witness."

Paulk was puzzled. Although the testimony continued the identification sequence, it gained the State nothing more. Could Ike have been too cursory in his interrogations before the trial; was he unprepared for what this cross-examination might cost him?

Paulk doubted it, but decided to plunge ahead.

"Johnny, were you able to see the occupants of the car quite clearly?"

"Yes, sir, especially when I was wiping the windshield."

"I'll ask you to describe how the girl was dressed."

"She had on this light-colored blouse, and I think it was a dark skirt."

"You aren't sure about the skirt?"

"I'm sure, but my buddy argued it was short shorts."

"Let's see, this was on January fourteenth—what sort of weather were you having out there that day?"

"It was windy, getting pretty chilly."

"Tell the jury how you happened to disagree with your friend as to whether this girl was traveling, in midwinter, in shorts."

"We'll object," Tigart said, "to any discussions between this witness and some extraneous party as hearsay. And I'll ask the Court to place Mr. Paulk under oath if he intends to keep asking questions in a way that amounts to testimony."

"I'll sustain," the Judge scowled. "Mr. Paulk, you are permitted to lead. But leading doesn't mean soaring off into the blue."

Paulk said, "In reference to this skirt, Johnny, exactly what did you see?"

The urbane sneer, the adolescent pretense to a supervirility, reappeared. "I saw that she wasn't minding it very well."

"What do you mean by that?"

"Well, her dress was up, way high."

"Then, her legs were uncovered?"

"Yes, sir."

Because Tigart remained silent, Paulk vaguely scented a trap. If Ike was ready to admit the adultery issue, it meant he held the proof of connivance with which to defeat it. Maybe that proof began here. Paulk wished he'd excused Johnny Soloman without questions. As it was, he could only finish what was begun.

"Where was Mr. Hutcherson when you noticed this unminded skirt?"

"He was sitting beside her."

"Can you tell us the position in which he sat?"

"He had his right arm, his elbow, out the window, the way people do when they drive."

"All right. What about the other arm?"

"He had it—kind of along the seat back."

"Behind the girl?"

"Yes, sir, over her shoulders."

"I'll ask you whether or not anything occurred to cause you to pay special attention to Mr. Hutcherson's left hand."

"Yes, sir, it did."

"What was it?"

"While I was doing the windshield, I saw his hand move, sort of come down some."

"How far down, Johnny?"

"Down over her front."

"His hand was touching her?"

"Yes, sir."

"Where?"

The boy said, "Here," indicating his chest.

"It's your testimony that you saw Mr. Hutcherson put his hand on the girl's breast?"

"Yes, that's what I saw."

"That's all."

Tigart said, "Son, you're just a pretty hawk-eyed fella, aren't you, able to see so much at dusk and in the darkness of an automobile—?"

"Your Honor," Paulk said, "Counsel is impeaching his own witness."

"I'm doing no such thing. And I'm getting fed up with this butting in every time I try to ask a question. . . ."

Through the hassle and the Court's lengthy but feeble reprimand, Paulk watched the jury. The women had lowered their eyes, Mrs. Billingsley using the moment to adjust her straps. Andricks had forced a thick finger into his nostril. Gay seemed excited. Studer, together with the rapt spectators, stared at Paulk. Some seemed confused as they fought off belief. Others pinpointed him with their hatred. Criminal lawyer, faker, liar, their looks said; Hutch was never that kind.

Tigart set out afresh. "Did you see a bottle of liquor in the car that day?"

"Yes, sir."

"Where was it when you first saw it?"

"The girl was holding it on her lap."

"Did it remain there, all the time these people were in your driveway?"

"No, the next time I noticed, the driver had it."

"Is this the man, the one you see seated behind Mr. Paulk, who was driving Mr. Hutcherson's car that day?"

"Yes, sir, that's him."

"All right. Johnny, you've told us this girl's dress was disarranged—that is, unless she was wearing shorts—and you've testified that you saw Mr. Hutcherson touch her with his hand. I'll ask you whether, to your knowledge, anything took place in the car as a result of that touch?"

"Nothing I know of."

"Was there a rumpus?"

"No, sir."

"Any loud talk, any blows struck?"

"No, nothing like that."

"Did this defendant, the driver, appear to make any protest whatsoever?"

"Not that I saw, he didn't."

The courtroom murmured. Here was Ike's hidden hook; you had to discredit the testimony of this repugnant boy, else assume Priest had assented to Hutch's sampling of Patty Sue. Paulk remembered Singer's warning: "If the Soloman boy seems useful, he also is dangerous."

"No more questions," Tigart said.

To shore up the major point, Paulk decided to gamble on a smaller one. "Did you see the defendant drink from that bottle?"

"No, sir."

Good; on this Ray hadn't lied to him. "Were you in a position to see how the defendant got possession of the liquor?"

"He just reached over and took it."

"What you saw, then, was Ray Priest taking whiskey away from a young girl?"

"That's right; they were all laughing over it."

He had pressed too far. Quickly he said, "Did you see any of the three take a drink?"

"No, sir."

"But you did have some reason to believe someone in that automobile had been drinking?"

"I smelled it on somebody, but I couldn't say which one."

Priest had been firm in saying Hutch took at least two drinks during the stop. Still, to impeach the Soloman boy on this detail would mean stripping the credibility off the rest, especially the precious testimony as to Hutch's yen for Ray's wife, and he let it pass. "We'll excuse the witness," he said, and he watched John Soloman withdraw regretfully, burdened with such undischarged facts as might, from his view, have been related tellingly, might have gotten his picture in the papers.

Nathan Hart cried the name of the next witness into the hall. He was Robert Nunnally, whose quick unnatural stride inferred both court fright and a grim resolution to do his straightforward best. About fifty, short, Nunnally had trousers which crimped in about his waist to reveal that, recently, he had been much heavier. His face was sunburnt over lines suggesting habitual good nature. Paulk judged him to be among those intelligent persons mistrustful of lawyers, shy of courts, and presently impatient to be done and away. For ten years he had been host and manager at the Ranch Inn Motel. Since the Hutcherson upheaval, he had been having a try at farming in western Oklahoma.

Tigart established that Nunnally had been on duty alone in the motel office when, at about 8:20 P.M. January fourteenth, Hutch and the Priests arrived. The witness studied the registration card, marked as State's Exhibit Three, and identified it by his initials as set down in a box headed 'Clerk.' The other blanks, he said, had been filled in by Patty Sue Priest, who came into the office while Ray and Hutch waited in the car. Tigart gave Paulk a moment to examine the card, then announced, "We offer State's Exhibit Three in evidence."

Paulk said, "May it please the Court, on the basis of this predicate, I don't know whether I have an objection or not. If I may ask a *voir-dire* question of this witness—?"

"Sure," Ike waved his tolerance, "go ahead."

"Mr. Nunnally, aside from yourself, was anyone else present when Mrs. Priest filled out this card?"

"No, sir."

"Thank you. Your Honor, the defendant objects to the exhibit as a hearsay instrument, executed outside the presence of the accused."

Sharman said, "Is that all of your objection?"

"Well, yes, it is, but I'm always open to suggestions."

"This is no place for flippancy, young man. I overrule. The exhibit may be admitted."

"Note my exception."

In a concise, painstaking direct, Tigart reconstructed the arrival of the Cadillac and its occupants. Priest was driving, Patty rode beside him, and Hutch sat alone in the rear seat. The girl entered alone to sign for the room, paying in advance with a twenty-dollar bill, depositing the change in her bosom. She had registered them under the name R. E. Priest, Chicago, Illinois. The time, date, room number, the rate of ten dollars, had been set down by Nunnally, who also wrote in the car tag number as *ZK5563.* The latter, he said, was in error; the *six* was correctly an *eight,* in the light of his later knowledge. After the registration, he said, he called a porter named Preston who directed the party back to Cabin 4.

Tigart brought up a floor-plan sketch of the cabin and drew Nunnally through a lengthy corroboration of its accuracy. The suite included a rectangular front bedroom, a small arched hall leading to the rear bathroom and to a second bedroom. When the dimensions and furniture placements had been proven up, Tigart offered the sketch as State's Exhibit Four. Paulk saw no reason to object.

"Now," Tigart returned to his chair, "did you see any of these three people again that night?"

"No, I did not."

"Did you ever see any of them again?"

"I saw the young couple later on, in jail."

"What difficulty, if any, did you have recognizing them?"

"None at all; I knew them at once."

"Tell the jury whether you see the younger man in this courtroom."

"Yes, sir; he's the one seated there, in the light suit."

"All right. When did you next see the older man, if you did?"

"Mr. Hutcherson? I saw him the next morning."

Nunnally had been finishing his shave in his apartment behind the motel office when the colored maid, Rose Houston, called him to come to Cabin 4. She was almost incoherent with shock, so that it was necessary for him to explore the rooms for himself. Hutch's body lay on the bed in the rear bedroom, covered by the spread except for one darkening foot. The manager, uncertain as to which was proper, had telephoned both the sheriff and police from the front bedroom. Then he had remained there, looking out the front window, until the officers arrived.

"During those ten minutes, Mr. Nunnally, did you return to the back room?"

"No, I didn't; it looked pretty horrible in there—"

"We'll object to the comment by the witness," Paulk said.

"Sustained."

Tigart said, "Was anyone else present during your wait?"

"The maid, Rose, was there for a little while. She left shortly after I phoned the law."

No, he had touched nothing except the telephone; well, yes, upon finding the body, he had drawn back the spread enough to see what was underneath. He remembered that the furniture was all in place, the lights turned off, that the bed in the front room was only slightly mussed, as if someone had sat upon it, and he had seen two or three beer cans on the nightstand. No, the covers of the bed had not been turned back, the pillows were uncrushed. He had noted a fresh cigarette burn on the carpet.

"Can you tell us which officers arrived there first?"

"Yes, Sheriff Grosscup and some city detectives came at about the same time. I think the sheriff was first into the cabin."

"Pass the witness."

The examination disturbed Paulk for what it did not produce. He could assume that Ike preferred to put the gore of the death scene before the jury through a witness who had known Hutch, one like Andy Grosscup, whose description might gain impact through the revival of that day's emotions. But what of the rest? Surely Nunnally knew how he had come to assign them to a two-bedroom suite. It appeared Tigart liked the reason, meant to save it for redirect.

Paulk said, "I believe you've told us this party signed in under the name, 'R. E. Priest, Chicago, Illinois'?"

"Yes, sir."

"As a hotel man, would you say that 'R. E. Priest' was a reasonable and proper representation of the full name, 'Raymond Elliot Priest'?"

"Why, yes, I would."

"During your experience as a host, Mr. Nunnally, have you encountered instances wherein a person contemplating some illicit or unbecoming conduct has registered under a false name?"

"Certainly, that happens."

"Yet, in light of your present knowledge, you now know, do you not, that the defendant's true and correct name was given on the registration card you've just identified for us?"

"Yes."

"Calling again for the benefit of your experience, I'll ask you whether or not it is a fairly common practice for people from the smaller cities to speak of the nearest large city as their hometown when they are travelling?"

"Some do that."

"Then, a person from Arlington might give his hometown as Washington; one from Highland Park probably would register as being from Dallas?"

"I've seen people do that, yes."

"Then, if a Mr. Priest from Peoria checked in as Mr. Priest from Chicago, this would be a common occurrence; as correct, substantially, as motel registrations usually are?"

"Well, sir—"

"The State will object," Ike said. "This is spiraling off into yonder, calling for a conclusion."

"Sustain the objection."

So far, so good. Now he might as well delve for the worst, dull the teeth of Ike's redirect. "Mr. Nunnally, how did you happen to give this party a two-bedroom cabin?"

"Mrs. Priest asked for two bedrooms."

Paulk rather relished the answer. It implied connivance toward adultery, sure enough. But whose connivance? Patty Sue, not Ray, had made the request, and had done so outside her husband's hearing.

"This defendant wasn't present when she made this room reservation, was he?"

"No, he was sitting outside, in the car."

"Did you have any other conversation with Mrs. Priest?"

Nunnally nodded. He had offered to show the suite, and Patty had told him she was sure it was acceptable. He had asked her why Chicago people had a Texas tag on their car, and she had explained that the car belonged to a friend who had driven them to the motel from the downtown bus station. Again, Paulk was pleased. The jury saw that Patty Sue, the State's Girl Friday, was an inventive liar.

"From your familiarity with Cabin 4, I'll ask you to tell the jury whether a person lying on the bed in the front room, with his head at the foot of the bed and his feet toward the headboard, would be able to see into the hallway?"

Nunnally cocked his head in consideration. "Yes, I think he could."

"Would he, from the same position, have a view of the door leading from the bathroom?"

"I'd say he would."

"Thank you," Paulk said, "that's all."

Tigart shuttled three eight-by-ten glossy prints across the table to Paulk. One pictured the office and entrance driveway of the Ranch Inn, another looked out from the motel courtyard toward the exit and the highway, and the third framed a frontal view of the flat-roofed building and carport that was Cabin 4. Paulk shrugged, passed the photographs back, and sat sketching bulldogs with spiked collars while Ike put them in evidence as Exhibits Five, Six, and Seven. As the photos passed through the jury box, disappointing each juror in turn as he looked at them, the special prosecutor turned a thoughtful red smile upon the witness.

"One other question, Mr. Nunnally—what was Patty Sue Priest wearing when she came into your office to register?"

"She had on a blouse, no coat, and a pair of shorts."

Paulk jolted up from his note pad.

"Pass the witness," Tigart grinned.

A full skirt, according to Browning. A careless skirt, said Johnny Soloman. Yes, a skirt, Priest had insisted. But, glaring at Nunnally, Paulk couldn't believe the man was lying. Could Patty have changed clothes in the car, in Hutch's presence, and Ray have forgotten it? Or, was it possible the witness was honestly mistaken, that long interrogations before the grand jury had brainwashed him into a positive memory of something which never existed?

He turned to his client. Gazing into the static eyes, he endured icy recollections of the Gleason affair, of the night he lost Jerry. In the heat and ill light, under the gaze of Martha Hutcherson, he felt purpose draining from him. Ray could die, everyone did; why was it so vital that a pimp survive? The thing answered itself. This was as much a conspiracy as a prosecution. What was it Singer had said? "Drink the slime, my friend, if there's no other way to be rid of it. . . ."

"Mr. Nunnally," he said, "was it customary for women tourists to appear at your motel wearing shorts in the dead of winter?"

"No, maybe that's why I noticed it."

Doubt hardened into rage. "Tell us, weren't you fired from your job at the Ranch Inn shortly after this killing?"

Nunnally met his eyes squarely. "Yes, I was."

"Have you filed your application to share in the reward posted in this case?"

"Why, no sir, I have not."

Temper's error had worsened his position in an instant; he saw Ancil Andricks shut his teeth on a pencil, Willie Studer was gazing at the ceiling. He felt the blaze of his face as he grasped for recovery through the State's extra-legal witness fund. "Since leaving the Ranch Inn, you've farmed in Oklahoma?"

"Yes, sir."

"Isn't this plowing time?"

"It sure is."

"Then, you really can't afford being over here, away from your fields—"

"The State objects," Tigart said dryly. "This line of questioning is irrelevant, immaterial, and bears on no issue in this case."

"I'll sustain."

"That's all," Paulk said. In hindsight, he could see the shorts-versus-skirt issue for what it was, a dispute of detail, one of those normal discrepancies inherent in every case. Every other lawyer in town, he thought, would have known to leave it alone.

"Recess ten minutes," the Judge said. "Let's everyone keep his place until the jury has been retired."

XXV

Once the testimony starts, the attorney's appraisal of his jury position becomes the least reliable of any. Viewpoint sweeps away his objectivity, and he knows it. He can't resist accosting whomever has attended court, soliciting estimates and opinions: "He made a good witness, didn't he; do you think my point was clear enough; where do you think we're hurt?"

Although resolved not to, Paulk made the rounds. Old Mr. Durfee fingered his string tie, clucked and walked away which was, in itself, a bad sign. Mr. Funderburg leaned against the wall, frowning. "I can't say, Wen, that's the truth. Usually there's an atmosphere, a feel that predicts what will happen. But this one strikes me funny. Say, the Judge and Theodore Holcomb are going at it hammer and tongs over paying the venire, did you know it? I could iron it out, but I'm not about to, not unless that old goat shows some sense and kicks all those newspaper screwballs out of my office. . . ."

He caught Nathan Hart returning from the jury room upstairs. Uncle Nathan smiled, "Sure, you're in fair shape, although it'll take people a while to get used to hearing this rough stuff about Hutch. One thing, you've got you a congenial jury. While ago, a couple of the men put a chunk of ice down Mrs. Chesterson's back."

When The Shepherd bore down on him, beaming, he did not retreat. "Naw, son, nobody has hurt you yet; you're doing great, just like I told the Judge you would."

"Then it was you who put me up for this appointment?"

Shep pulled away, saying something about keeping a date with his client. Paulk went down to the rotunda, passing a woman who stared at him and said, "Dirty, dirty," and he telephoned the Singers.

"The radio is having bulletins every few minutes," Laura said. "It sounds rugged. Oh, I hope Valle isn't there. Dad? No, I can't say, but of course he might have suggested you to the Judge. You know how he's always felt. . . ."

The work resumed with David McCarney, chief of the police identification bureau. Thirty years old, handsome, explicit with his night-school diction, McCarney typified the new breed of policemen. With FBI school and the Texas A&M police shortcourses behind him, his qualifications were impressive enough that Paulk stipulated them.

McCarney sat with a fat file folder on his knee as Hollis Anglin advanced the questions. The officer told of arriving at Cabin 4 about 9:20 A.M. He had shot about one hundred pictures, made the measurements and rough sketches later developed into the scale drawing presently in evidence, and, when his assistants arrived, he had supervised the fingerprint work. Pretending reluctance, as if policemen did not hate the sheriff's department, he conceded that "other agencies" had permitted certain confusions at the scene, thus penalizing his staff and its effectiveness.

He had identified twelve sets of prints lifted from the cabin. Five of these, he said, matched the prints of the deceased. Hutch had imprinted the bedstand, the rear bedroom doorknob, a water tumbler, the commode handle, the whiskey bottle and a panel of the bedroom door.

"As to the other seven sets," Anglin said, "what comparisons, if any, did you make?"

"The primary comparisons were with prints taken from Raymond Elliot Priest and Patty Sue Priest following their arrests."

"What was the result?"

"I found no match."

"Then, insofar as you could discover, if this defendant was in those rooms that night, he left no fingerprints whatsoever?"

"That is correct."

The implication was of a professional criminal, one shrewd enough to wipe away all trace of himself. Which, Paulk conceded, was the State's best tack when it lacked prints yet wished to create the illusion of a perfect, unbroken line of proof.

Anglin grinned with satisfaction. "Your witness."

Paulk said, "How was it, Officer McCarney, that you found a hundred sets of prints in those two small rooms, if you know?"

Well, it was obvious a great many people had walked through the rooms. Were Mr. Hutcherson's the only ones identified? No, there were several others. Whose, for instance? McCarney evaded, then granted that some of the prints belonged to Sheriff Grosscup, to Ranger Turnbow, to "various other personages," by which he meant Hutch's important, intruding friends, the men of the Bonita County Posse. Paulk drew out an explanation of how new fingerprints erased or smudged older ones, then got into the record the fact that the ID men had picked up some eighty-eight prints too damaged to be readable.

"With so many people parading through those rooms, touching things, depositing all those prints, wouldn't it be likely that they rubbed out the fingerprints left by the defendant?"

"Yes, sir; that is probably what happened."

Paulk saw Ike Tigart's smile before understanding what he had done. He had put Ray Priest in Cabin 4 for them, more definitely than they could have done it for themselves. Although it mattered little, since he would make no issue over Ray's presence there, he disliked knowing that Ike still outmaneuvered him.

"Pass the witness."

Tigart slouched hugely across to Mr. Funderburg, holding three photographs face down for marking. As he handed them up to the witness, Paulk scooted forward in his chair. These would be the grisly views of Hutch's bloody body and exposed brain. While Ike knew he stood small chance of getting them in, he could compel Paulk to fend them off. Once more, Tigart would show the jury a defense attorney determined to deny them the evidence.

"I hand you State's Exhibits Eight, Nine, and Ten, and I'll ask you if you know what they are."

"Yes, sir—"

"Your Honor," Paulk said, "I'm learning a great deal, just as the special prosecutor promised I would, while the State's army comes at me in relays and waves. However, I'll have to object to this intervention by my teacher. Under the Rules of Procedure, Rule Forty-three, I believe, it remains the privilege of the assistant district attorney to conclude the examination he originated."

It was the simplest error, the more embarrassing to Ike because it was the last he expected to make. The spectator attorneys swapped smiles, and Tigart glared at them. He appreciated only such humor as was initiated by himself. Quickly, Anglin picked up the questioning. When he had established the authenticity of the pictures, he offered them in evidence and turned to await Paulk's challenge.

"As the Court well knows, the objection I'm going to make must be heard in the absence of the jury."

Sharman called for the pictures, glanced at the top one, recoiled. "All right, Mr. Bailiff, we'll have the jury retired."

The jury left unwillingly. They had guessed the nature of the pictures, they had tingled from anticipated horror. Only the women appeared grateful for this respite, and even they seemed ingenuine about it. Their disappointment, for which he would be blamed, couldn't be helped. He crossed to the bench, took the hideous photos, and was ready to speak when the trooper closed the door. He noticed Priest, the craftsman behind the depicted gore, pushing two sticks of gum into his mouth.

"May it please the Court, the defendant objects to the admission of these photographs as a specie of demonstrative evidence, tending neither to prove nor disprove any issue in this case and, therefore, prejudicial and inflammatory. By the general rule, I believe, photographs of the body of the deceased may be admissible when they serve to prove, or to solve, a disputed issue. But here, we have no issue on which they may be construed as relevant. We have not disputed that this man was killed and is dead. Nor have we raised any issue as to the condition of his body, its position, or the extent and character of the wounds. This portion of my objection is drawn from Underhill on Criminal Evidence; also, Section 53, Page 1002 of 44 Texas Jurisprudence, which states that a photograph is inadmissible when it is neither necessary nor instructive and when it would tend to create confusion.

"*Newcomb vs. the State,* 95 Southwestern 1048; *Willis vs. the State,* 90 Southwestern 1100, and Section 280, Page 405 of 18 Texas Jurisprudence, hold that a photograph which doesn't serve to illustrate, which does not enable the jury to apply the evidence, is not admissible. These authorities are particularly emphatic in outlawing photographs that present a view calculated to inflame or prejudice the minds of the jury.

"I repeat, there is no controversy in this record as to the fact of death, or as to the manner of it. I submit that in the absence of any dispute, there is nothing that these photographs can illustrate, instruct upon, or solve."

He sat down. Thanks to Jack Singer he was sound, preponderant with law. He watched Tigart get up. Ike was smiling tolerantly, preparing to try bluffing it through.

"Your Honor," he spoke around a quid that somewhat muffled his voice, "I think the parties can agree that these photographs are admissible if properly obtained and if they illustrate or shed light on any circumstance material to this case. I believe it's time we faced up to what we're dealing with here. So far as we know, there are only two eyewitnesses to this killing. One, the defendant, is not required to testify. The other, as his wife, cannot appear for the State, and as a codefendant, she is disqualified to appear for the defense. Although we have a confession in evidence, Mr. Paulk has told us he intends to raise an issue as to its legality. Thus we seem to be trying a circumstantial evidence case. Up to this point, at least, we can regard it as such, and there is no law or logic that should forbid the rules of circumstantial evidence from applying.

"The law is quite plain in authorizing the admission of any and all evidence serving to illuminate the offense, to excuse or mitigate it, or to support the allegations set forth in the indictment. A good many years ago, before my bookish antagonist cracked his first legal text, Justice Davidson declared that in situations of circumstantial proof, one must turn on all the light. Along with others, he laid down the precedents by which this may be done. The 'all the light' principle is fundamental. It is not optional, its mandates cannot be abridged at the discretion of the trial court."

Tigart gathered up the pictures. A fascination with them had gripped the courtroom. People edged ahead, stretched their necks, stared morbidly.

"In deference to the record—and, to assist the Court—let me state what these photographs show. State's Exhibit Eight is a view of the dead body of Jess Hutcherson, illustrating the wounds, the condition of the bed and nearby walls, reflecting the location of the deceased, revealing that the body was in a sleeping posture, and showing what Count Two of the indictment alleges was the weapon, the garment knotted about the victim's throat.

"Exhibit Nine, a broader perspective of the body, provides an exact and enlightening representation of the position of the furniture and the deceased's clothing in relation to the corpse. State's Exhibit Ten casts light on several material issues. As a bust view, it places the wounds, reflects their size, number and severity, and it does so with absolute accuracy.

"Your Honor, each of these photographs sheds light, and I can see nothing objectionable to doing that. Whatever inference the reasonable mind might draw from these pictures could amount only to a proper and legally correct deduction. Defense counsel has not, and cannot, attack these pictures as faked, as distorted by photographic tricks, or as exaggerations. In view of this, it seems sufficient to me that these exhibits bear entirely on relevant physical facts. We see in them exactly what was seen in Cabin 4 that morning, which is no more than the jury is entitled to."

The objection was safe. While Ike argued common sense, Paulk

had argued law. Even Judge Sharman had discovered how often the
two were incompatible.

"If the Court please," he said, "the defendant has one further
ground for objection. Aside from being demonstrative, highly inflammatory and prejudicial, aside from the fact that they relate to
no disputed issue, these pictures must be regarded as secondary
evidence and therefore, inadmissible. The State has subpoenaed eyewitnesses to all such conditions as these pictures are purported to
illustrate. This constitutes the best evidence. Secondary evidence on
the same facts can become admissible only if the aforementioned
best evidence becomes unobtainable."

They'd all been through it before. Sharman didn't hesitate. "Bring
the jury in, Mr. Hart. Gentlemen, the defendant's points are valid,
except for that secondary evidence business, and I'm going to rule out
those—"

"Your Honor," Tigart cut in, "we'll ask the Court to defer his
ruling, since we wish to withdraw these exhibits until a later time."
It was sharp, professional. If Ike could not win, then he could postpone losing, perhaps not to lose at all.

"The defendant insists upon a ruling before we proceed."

"Just a minute, young man," the Judge reacted, "I'm not here to
take ultimatums from counsel. There's nothing to rule about, if these
exhibits are withdrawn. We'll hear your objection again if and when
these pictures are offered in evidence."

Paulk flushed. The difficulty with Sharman was how, at the least
likely moments, he might behave like a Judge. You never knew when
to expect it.

As the jury reoccupied the box, Anglin sneezed and said, "No more
questions."

Paulk scanned the chamber. Lily Black, momentarily lapsed from
her radiating hostility, applied an emery board to her fingernails.
Nearby, the elderly woman sped along with her crocheting. On back
he saw the Possemen clustered more tightly about Martha Hutcherson. Her widow's veil was raised, her face looked aged, less handsome, in the meagre light. Why didn't she leave, go home to her teas
as Woman of the Year or to nap away this slanderous, sodden afternoon? He dreaded the next chore.

"Mr. McCarney, what were your police duties prior to your quali-
fication as an identification expert?"

"I was a traffic officer."

"As a patrolman, did you develop any familiarity with the streets, highways, and block numbers of this city?"

"Yes, sir, I did."

Paulk led him to map orally the course of Highway 66 through the city; how it entered from the west, crossed downtown, turned north along Lamar, past the courthouse and post office, then coursed eastward again past the Ranch Inn.

"I'll ask you now if you know the location of the Jess Hutcherson residence."

"Yes; it's out in the west part, on Bellaire—that's the nine-hundred block of Bellaire."

"Is that a north-south street?"

"Yes, sir."

"And does it intersect with Highway 66?"

"It does, just inside the west city limit."

"In respect to this intersection, how near is the Hutcherson house?"

"It's pretty close. About a half a block, I'd say; something like two hundred feet."

"Then, a party driving into town from the west along Highway 66, would pass within two hundred feet of the Hutcherson home?"

"That's correct."

"And if this party arrived at the intersection of the highway with Bellaire, and chose at that point to continue on to the Ranch Inn Motel, how far would he have to drive?"

"I've never measured that."

"Approximately how far?"

"Well, it would be all the way across town—at least six miles, I'd say."

"It's your testimony, then, that a motorist entering the city from the west would almost immediately come to the Bellaire intersection with the highway; that at this juncture, if his destination was the Hutcherson home, he had only about two hundred feet to go; and, if his destination was the Ranch Inn Motel, he had at least six miles to travel?"

"Yes."

He glanced at the jury, wondering if he'd left any confusion. Hutch had been tired, late for an engagement. Yet he'd not dropped off his passengers at the intersection. Why had he driven past the intersection, almost past his home, to check into a motel with Ray and Patty Priest?

"We'll excuse the witness."

Anglin wished no truck with it. At once he said, "The State excuses Mr. McCarney and, may it please the Court, we'll call Hansford Preston."

The Negro was well-made, solemn. His wine eyes were alert and intelligent. If the prevalent fear of the witness stand was upon him, he disguised it with a wonderfully carefree smile. Handy, as he was called, was the porter who had shown Hutch and the Priests to their rooms. Under Tigart's examination, he told of directing the parking of the Cadillac, unlocking the cabin door, switching on the lights. Hutch was the first to enter, he said, and had gone straight back to the bathroom. Patty followed, tossed cigarettes and a comic book on the bed, and commented upon what a comfortable suite it was. Priest had inquired about a place to eat, and Handy had recommended Dusty's Cafeteria, directly across the street. Dusty, Handy volunteered, "liked to give me a little something for sending him customers."

Tigart congratulated him on the arrangement and said, "After all of you were inside, what happened next, if anything?"

"Well, the ageable gentleman came out of the bathroom and gave me a tip."

"How much did he give you?"

"A dollar."

"Was this defendant, the man you've identified here as being a member of that party, present at that time?"

"Yes, sir; he helped me pick up what was spilt."

"Just what was spilled, Handy?"

"Well, while the ageable gentleman was tipping me, he dropped a bunch of money on the floor. This other fellow, the man sitting yonder, helped me gather it up for him."

"Did you notice the denominations of this money?"

"There was a heap of it; came out loose from his pocket when he pulled out his hand. I saw a hundred-dollar bill, and a fifty, and I picked up some twenties."

"And this defendant gathered up the rest?"

"Yes, sir."

"What, if anything, was said about this mishap?"

"I didn't say nothing."

"Did the defendant?"

"Well, he told the ageable gentleman, 'Boss, you're gonna lose this if you ain't careful.' "

Jurors nodded; Ike's showing of an incentive to rob was going well.

The porter had been summoned back to Cabin 4 about five minutes later on Priest's complaint that the television set, placed on a stand at the west end of the front room, was out of order. Handy had found it unplugged. He had waited long enough to watch Ray tune in the Wednesday night fights, to hear his grousing because the bouts were almost over, then had hied back to the motel office to watch the fights himself.

"Did you see any of these people again that night?"

"Yes, sir, the young feller sent for me again around nine o'clock, after the fights were over." Priest had asked to borrow a screwdriver, had inquired if the porter knew anything about automobile starters. Preston had stood by as Priest raised the hood. Then, he said, "the ageable man" yelled out the window that they should leave the car alone, that he would have it repaired in the morning. "The young feller gave me back the screwdriver, said he reckoned we better do like the boss said."

"The defendant did use that word, 'boss'?"

"Yes, sir, two or three times."

"Was this the last time you saw the defendant that night?"

It wasn't. At about ten o'clock, with the newscast starting on the office TV set, Handy had seen the black Cadillac creep into the driveway. Priest and the girl were pushing it, with Ray walking along on the left side, reaching an arm inside to steer. He had hailed the porter out to help push the car on out on to the highway. The porter said he had started to a service station to hire a truck to push the car off when a passing automobile stopped and offered a shove.

"What happened then?"

"The Caddy started, and they drove on off, headed east."

"Now, who was in the car when it left?"

"Just them two, the young feller and the lady."

"During the time you were helping push the car, did you have any conversation with the defendant?"

"Yes, sir; some."

"I'll ask you to tell the jury what was said."

"Well, he was cussing the car, said he was in a hurry, said him and his wife aimed to go pick up a friend of theirs and they was already late."

"Is that all he told you?"

"No, sir. Another thing was, he said, 'Don't be messing around our cabin in the morning, on account of we want to sleep late.' "

"And did he make any mention of the 'ageable gentleman'?"

Preston nodded. "No, sir, not much. All he said was, 'the boss, he's already asleep.' "

Tigart repeated it gravely. "Already asleep." He leaned forward heavily, chin in his hands, letting the words enlarge themselves with the jury. "Did you get a good look at this couple before they departed?"

"Yes, sir, we had plenty of light in the driveway."

"Did you observe any change in their appearance?"

"Well, I saw that they'd cleaned up, put on different clothes. The man had put on some black pants, and the lady had on a dress and a sweater."

"And she hadn't been wearing this dress when she checked in?"

"No, sir. First time I saw her, she had on shorts."

This time, Paulk's misgivings as to the veracity of his client were less acute. He made no acknowledgement as, with a gesture of triumph, Tigart surrendered the witness.

"Mr. Preston," Paulk began softly, "you haven't been employed at the Ranch Inn since the events you've described, have you?"

"No, sir, that was my last day. They fired Mr. Nunnally and all the rest of us the next afternoon."

At Tigart's objection to the question and the answer the Judge sustained. Paulk set out anew—prompting Handy to say it was Priest who had sent for him, that during none of their three conversations had the defendant tried to conceal himself, sought to protect himself against later recognition.

"All right. Now, what was the defendant's manner as you observed it that night?"

"Well, I guess he had pretty good manners."

There was a mirthless titter, like the response to a sick joke, and Paulk hurried on. "My question referred to his conduct, Mr. Preston. Did he appear nervous?"

"Not that I noticed."

"Did he appear excited?"

"No, sir, not that I could tell."

"Was there anything in his behavior to suggest to you that he might have been drinking?"

"No, he didn't act like it."

"I'll ask you whether there was anything strange or suspicious about his behavior as you observed it?"

"No, sir."

He had worked near the core of his defense once more, and he hesitated. His tongue was dry. The gloomy false twilight of the afternoon belonged with what must come next, he thought. Was there really a purity in truth? A little raspily he said, "What about this older man—the 'ageable gentleman,' the 'boss'—did you see anything out of the ordinary in his conduct?"

"We'll object," Tigart groaned. "That has no bearing on the guilt or innocence of the defendant. The deceased isn't on trial here, and I think it's time the Court enlightened Mr. Paulk on that fact."

Judge Sharman's scowl was a broadcast of how dearly he would have loved to sustain. Yet, in view of previous inquiry, the objection was groundless, and he had to say so. "But while I'm overruling, Mr. Paulk, I want to warn you that we'll have nothing introduced here just for the sake of dramatics or sensation. We've ladies on the jury, others among the spectators, and—"

Paulk came up shouting. "The defendant takes exception to the Court's remarks. Sensation, dramatics—that's an unfair commentary by the Court on the weight to be given this evidence, and I want—"

"Sit down and proceed."

"Sit down? I'm entitled to—"

"Mr. Paulk, this Court will not be accused of unfairness," the old eyes glinted fiercely. "I fine you twenty-five dollars. And you will sit down, or I shall have the bailiff accommodate you to your chair."

Paulk sank down, surrounded by a crackling silence. Stung, trembling, he realized he had run afoul of the chivalry, the old Southern prudery that Sharman enforced upon his court once his own curiosity had been satisfied. As he calmed himself, he seemed to glimpse a peculiar balance in his predicament. Whenever his compassion for the Hutchersons began to temper him, someone cuffed Ray Priest another sneak blow and in his rage he could continue heartlessly.

"Well," the Judge growled, "is your cross-examination finished?"

"May it please the Court, I'd first like a ruling on my objection to the Court's comments."

"You are overruled."

"Then I want to reserve my bill."

"You're welcome to it. Now, get on with whatever it is you've got to get on with."

He managed a smile as he addressed the witness. "Mr. Preston, you may answer my question now."

"Yes, sir. Well, the older gentleman didn't speak very clearly."

"Did you notice anything else about him?"

"Yes, sir; he was staggering a little."

"And he dropped his money while trying to tip you?"

"Yes, sir."

"Did you see him drink anything there in the motel room?"

"Yes, he took a drink."

"You testified, I believe, that Mr. Hutcherson entered and went directly to the bathroom, isn't that correct?"

"Yes, sir; he did."

"Where was the defendant and his wife while Mr. Hutcherson was in the bathroom?"

"They were standing in the front room, beside me."

"From the position the three of you had, were you able to see into the bathroom?"

"Yes, sir."

"How was this?"

"Well, he didn't close the door."

"Then, you could see, and did see, what Mr. Hutcherson was doing in there?"

The wine eyes studied him, studying also a way to frame the answer. After a moment, Handy said, "We saw him. He opened up his pants and took a leak."

Paulk ignored the gasp of the crowd. "By this you mean the 'age-able gentleman' urinated in plain sight of Patty Sue Priest?"

"Yes, sir."

Paulk heard a cry, then a thump, in the gallery. Someone said, "watch it" as he whirled to look. The Posse had come to its feet, was crowding around. Instantly the Judge left his chair, pounding, admonishing at large for order. Then the Possemen, aided by the highway patrolman, were bearing Martha Hutcherson from the room, upright between them, their arms about her waist. Paulk watched coldly, still unfeeling from the numbness of his reprimand, until it ended. When he glanced at the jury, he saw the women had flushed with excitement. But, like the men, they were gazing at the witness. They were shocked, but not shrinking from the surprise image of the great Jess Hutcherson exposing himself to a teen-age girl. Maybe, he thought, it was a better jury than he knew.

He said, "I've no more questions."

The Judge announced the time and asked the State to put on one more brief witness, if feasibly it could, to close the day. Crimson and sober, Tigart called the maid, Rose Houston. As he examined her, motion continued. Spectators fidgeted like captives, minds were listless. People tried to prorate their credence and anger; they needed to withdraw and, alone, to assess.

The maid, relating her discovery of Hutch's body, used extreme descriptions obviously adopted from the newspapers, so that her testimony sounded wholly unnatural. She had entered Cabin 4 "little knowing" what awaited her, she had only "chanced on the remains," she had been "petrified with horror" at seeing the bloody wall and headboard, the stained spread, the uncovered dead foot.

Paulk sat through it reminded of his neglected client, Mrs. Johnson, who had been Rose Houston's replacement at the Ranch Inn. Was that poor woman still uncapitulated to the idea of her ex-husband as a son-in-law?

"Pass the witness," Tigart said.

"Mr. Paulk?" the Judge cued him impatiently.

"No questions."

The Judge began assembling his notes and magazines. "Nine o'clock tomorrow, gentlemen—here, you newspapermen, you people in the gallery. How often must I tell you I want you to remain seated until the jury has cleared the room? Mercy, we can't have these sprints for the door. If it's necessary to cite some of you. . . ."

Across the table, Tigart said, "You want a glandular case? All right, when it's over tell me how you liked it."

Paulk sat still while the crowd pushed into the aisles, while the pit sitters gathered in sets to talk. Beside him Ray Priest stretched, stood up, lighted a cigarette off a kitchen match and stared at the deputy who was untangling a pair of handcuffs.

Angie touched his arm. "Don't worry, Mr. Paulk. My husband is sending part of his check, and I can pay the Judge that twenty-five dollars."

He smiled at her. Bless you, he thought. Bless them all, the women.

XXVI

The rain broke, cut off, then pelted down again. Cool, marvelously freshened air surged through the courtroom, driving its staleness into the hall. He made his way out through the stragglers, the trial fans who always loitered in hope of overhearing the real truth as whispered between lawyers. Others scrambled for the elevators and stairs, rummaging plastic raincoats from their purses and pockets. At the stairs, Paulk remembered his briefcase and returned for it. The Shepherd had picked it up, was coming after him.

"Hey, son, doing anything tonight?"

"I've got a date."

"Fine, fine; so have I. Thought if you cared to, we might get together, find something to eat, chew the rag—?"

Paulk made no effort to conceal his disgust. "Courting Lily Black, Billy?"

Shep chuckled, blooming with good fellowship. "Between us, I'd rather it was her daughter. Tell you what, Wen, since you wanted to talk to Lily, why don't you meet us at Gail's? I'll have her tamed down a little—suit you?"

He moved away, leaving Shep the reply of nothingness. At the first landing E. C. Kelso stood brushing the rain from his shoulders, waiting.

"Almost missed you again," Kelso was unsmiling. "Why didn't you return my calls?"

"I'm sorry, sir. I've been busy."

Passers on the stairs turned curious looks upon them, and they drew back to the landing window. For a moment, while E. C. dried his face on a checkered handkerchief, Paulk watched the rain. Although it was after six, there was more light now than there'd been all afternoon; the cloud was drifting slowly to the northeast, its thunder like the rumble of giant casters. The shower would be brief; they could expect a clear night.

"Wen, what's this Mrs. Reddock tells me, about your moving out?"

"That's it, sir. Seems best, doesn't it?"

"You'll practice criminal law?" Kelso frowned as he licked a cigar. "Frankly, I didn't think you'd let this get under your skin."

Paulk felt no subservience, no beholding inferiority, which left him little patience. "What was it you called about?"

"Well," the old Senator grunted, "the day you did phone in, I had gone out to Martha Hutcherson's; I suppose Mrs. Reddock told you that?"

"Yes."

"She sent for me, Wen. Partly because of you, partly because we're old friends. She had heard some rumors about your defense, and she was concerned, wanted to know something about you."

"What did you tell her?"

"The facts: that you hadn't wanted the case, that you had a genuine sympathy for everyone involved. I told her I knew you, Wen; told her you'd handle the thing honorably and well. When I left, she felt much better. Martha had been pretty upset, especially as to her daughter. Valle is a strange, high-strung child—"

"Please," Paulk said, "I've a lot to do, a plane to meet."

"Of course," Kelso wheezed at lighting the cigar. "The upshot of my visit was that Martha wants to meet you, talk to you."

"Why?"

"She's a great woman, Wen, not the kind to think of persuading you one way or the other. You'd be surprised at her outlook, I think. She honestly, generously, wants to help you understand a few things."

"That was before today. They had to help her from the courtroom this afternoon."

"I know that, I saw her twenty minutes ago. She'd still like to see you."

"How does Tigart figure in this?"

Kelso shook his head. "If Ike had anything to do with her invitation, I don't know about it. Look, I wouldn't be a party to anything phony."

"I know that," Paulk said, "I'm sorry. When?"

"Soon, anytime you can. She's at home, keeping no engagements—hasn't, I understand, since the whole mess began. I'd like to tell her you'll come."

"All right, sir, I'll try." He turned toward the stairs, immediately ruing the promise.

"One more thing, Wen," Kelso's voice was deep, only half hearty, "something I want to say for myself. These last three weeks, we've missed you around the office. I've not felt good about things, or that my judgement was what it was when you got stuck with this case."

"It doesn't matter."

"Yes, it does. Terry and I have talked it over. To be brief, we've decided upon an arrangement. Hell, I may as well speak out; we're setting up your partnership."

Paulk opened his mouth, then closed it. Something seemed out of order. A partnership had been eventual; he had known that. But not imminent. The firm was deliberate, progression at Kelso's was geared to the pace of inheritance. A month ago, he would have approximated his partnership as fifteen years away.

Kelso laughed. "Effective at once, Wen. As I say, we've missed you. I know this is a bad time to spring it, to start talking about terms. On the other hand, it may be the best moment for all of us. You're at a crossroads, Wen, one of those career points where a man needs a pair of positives to choose between. I want to see you safely over it, see your talent in the field where it belongs. If you want, just say I'm bidding against Jack Singer."

Naturally, E. C.'s sources would have told him about all the evenings in the Singer parlor; it was probable he knew the case as thoroughly as Paulk himself.

"Don't misunderstand," Kelso went on thoughtfully, "I admire Jack as much as you do. I remember a Bar sectional meeting down in Fort Worth a few years ago, where several of us talked to a bunch of new, GI Bill lawyers. Jack made one of the most incisive speeches on criminal law I've ever heard. One thing he said that day sticks in my mind; I'll never forget it. He was talking about the necessary, knowing defense of the guilty. It can be destructive of the defender, he said, unless he's a man of two philosophies, two souls. The single-minded man, he said, can fall into a nether world, a place Jack spoke of as 'the twilight of honor,' and once there, he's unlikely to emerge."

Paulk spoke tightly. "In your opinion, then, I've—"

"No, Wen, no. I'm saying only that I hope you will call on Martha Hutcherson, and after that, I want you to call on me. Good night."

Kelso, Lemons, Hurst & Paulk. On a frosted glass door, tomorrow if he wanted it. He imagined Terry Hurst claiming a place at the counsel table, reshaping Ray Priest's defense, taking the lead—the firm graciously, mildly disposing of its first and last criminal case. Still, the offer was importunate; the old patriarch's timing had been breathtaking. He knew because he wanted, simply, to accept.

Laura's tinker-toy car, looking sloven under a bedraggled top that leaked the rain, stood beside his. With relief he got in beside her. Their dinner, had in the library because old Jack would not leave the special charge on insanity he was composing in longhand, was ending before Paulk felt like opening up. Laura heard him out in serious, common-sense silence. But Jack was riled. "By God," he said, "I wonder if I ever did say anything as assy as that? I'll bet that prim old hack is misquoting me! But, is he or isn't he, what's the difference? Wen, you don't think you could do much for truth and due process, do you, by stepping out and leaving the courts to the Billy Shepherds and the Hollis Anglins?"

The rain had ended, a few stars were becoming visible, when Laura drove him out to the airport. He sat deep back, limp from a drowsiness that increased as time wedged itself further between him and his day in court, watching Laura with her cigarette, until the flight arrived. The rocking, three-legged jet discharged forty passengers on a flood-lit apron. Master Sergeant Bernard Blossom was the only one in uniform.

He wasn't what Paulk had expected. Trim, tall, handsomely tanned, the sergeant doffed his cap for Laura. He had a thick topknot of curly black hair and a rather heroic scar proceeding out of it, almost down to his brow. He retained Laura's hand as he said, "You needn't have gone to such trouble, Paulk, but since I see her, I'm glad you did."

Although no older than Paulk, Blossom had a ladder of hashmarks climbing up his sleeve. He was among those wartime draftables who had found the military to their liking and were confirmed for thirty years. Paulk didn't like him. Blossom chatted brightly with Laura until they were parked at the Cattleman's and he appeared not to notice the hotel until Paulk forced his way into the talk; began to probe for what the sergeant knew of Raymond Priest.

After a half-hour of it, Paulk was wondering if he had ever needed Article 1220 at all. The man could prove insanity, he would make an impressive witness. The story of Ray's near suicide seemed, in itself, almost sufficient.

"One other thing," Paulk said, shutting off the sergeant's proposal that Laura initiate him to Texas, "did you get Priest's medals?"

"Couldn't do it. I wrote in, nothing happened."

"Wen," Laura said, "I thought Mrs. Callahan brought them."

"She thought so too. All she has is a stick of ribbons, the stuff you can pick up in any hockshop. Ray never sent in for the actual medals, and I can't use anything else."

"I'll lend you mine," Blossom said. "I've got a Purple Heart, some Air Medals, and I brought them along. It would be all the same."

"Not quite," Paulk said.

Laura was laughing softly at his weariness, or perhaps his surliness, as they left Blossom haggling with a redcap. "Where to, now?"

"Jail. I've got a lot to say to Priest before he gets on the stand."

"You mean, that's coming soon?"

"It might. Tigart is ginning along; he might finish tomorrow."

Except for the sheriff's office, only the topmost levels of the courthouse were lighted: the jail and the jury dormitory. She ground the little car onto the sheriff's parking area and shut it off. She had stowed the sodden top, unaided, at the airport. They sat looking up at the glowing windows.

"Wonder what they're doing up there?"

"Which?" he said, "jail or jury?"

"The jury."

"Having hi-fi and dominoes, I suppose. Or, since there's the women, it may be bridge. I hope Willie Studer loses his shirt." He slid out, bumping dead-leggedly against his own car, spotting a soaked parking ticket on its windshield.

"I'll wait for you," she said.

"No, I might be very late."

He stepped back as she cranked the car. "Look, Laura—I dozed through some of that bright talk a while ago. Do you or don't you have a date with my witness?"

She smiled. "I don't."

"He made quite a pitch."

"Oh, yes. He's direct, handsome, has a uniform—and something tells me he is very, very married."

The loneliness he'd sensed in her that first night was in her voice. He bent down. She smelled of damp upholstery and undried hair as he kissed her. She was soft, then retreating, and he wondered why her cheeks should be wet from the rain. Afterwards they gazed at each other, unseeing in the dark.

"For me, Wen?" she said. "Or Jerry?"

She thrust the car ahead, bucked it across a row of traffic-dividing concrete turtles, and was gone. Paulk stood, tingling, scarcely half awake. Abruptly he knew he had had it for today; the talk with Priest would have to wait. He stilted along the puddled sidewalk, away from the courthouse, toward the corner drugstore and the coffee he'd need to get him home. He was sitting in a hard booth, sifting through a rubble of exhaustion for some hint of what he felt about Laura, when he saw the mirage.

A girl sauntered to the magazine rack. She took up a muscle magazine, thumbed it through, then reached for a love thriller. She was chesty, small, restless in a skirt widened by cones upon cones of rainbow petticoats. Her loose long hair glistened yellow. Patty Sue's hair had been dark brown. But, no mistake, this was she.

He heaved himself up, pondering the citizen arrest of an escapee; then sank back as he saw Hollis Anglin. The assistant district attorney hung bonelessly on a fountain stool, bearing a sleepy frown upon a boy who mixed a pair of malteds. Paulk shook himself, goading himself for an answer. Was Anglin this much fool; had Andy Grosscup gone mad, had they granted Patty Priest a furlough? This was an accused felon, under a murder indictment and, as the subject of a proof evident, someone unbailable. What back-office law justified her liberty, allowed her a midnight soda on Houston Street?

He watched, frozen lest he be seen, while the girl selected several comic books. She joined Anglin at the counter and drank her malted rapidly. She stood by as Anglin paid, then followed him, silent as a squaw, out to the street. Through the smeared glass front Paulk saw them cross to the courthouse lawn and disappear under the black elms. At once he suspected a delusion, some fantasy arising out of the tiredness that was almost a stupor. He was stumbling, but furiously awake, when he hurried back to his car.

XXVII

He breakfasted at the Little Star just at sunrise. Winking on the scratchiness of his eyes, he read through the morning paper. There was a photo of Priest leaving the elevator, another of Tigart and Anglin huddled over the unadmitted death pictures. There was Lily Black, "worried mother," smoking in the hall; a shot of Uncle Nathan squiring the jury down Lamar in its after-dinner stroll; and there was even a view of himself, the "embattled defender," distorted from having been taken through the glass of the courtroom door. The accompanying stories puzzled him.

The lead piece was pitched on Hutch's carelessness with his money; the State's strong proof that Ray had seen it and the powerful implication of a plot for robbery. The adultery issue was there, but so briefly, so cryptically treated that it could be missed. With the third cup of coffee, he was able to regard this as not quite dumbfounding. Of course, yesterday's events would have sent the *Tribune*'s policy-makers into conference. There was a Jess Hutcherson Wing to the Bonita County Hospital, the Jess Hutcherson Expressway would soon be completed. A Hutcherson Center had been dedicated on the west side only last year, and a Jess Hutcherson Memorial Scholarship Fund was to become operational this fall. Like Amon Carter in Fort Worth, Cullen in Houston, Hutcherson was advertised. He was a brand name and editors had to think twice before they mishandled him.

Ray Priest was finishing a tin plate of Andy Grosscup's powdered eggs when Paulk arrived. He got up at once, accosted the jailor for his razor, and went to the lavatory in his cell. Shortly his face was lathered and he still hadn't spoken.

"All right," Paulk sighed, "get it off your chest."

"Ain't no sense to it, making Patty look so bad."

Paulk sat down on the mildewed bunk. "I've assumed all along that you'd like to go on living. This testimony isn't being diluted to protect Martha Hutcherson, and it damned sure can't be doctored up to please your wife. Listen to me—if you can't smell your hair burning already, then you better take a couple of deep breaths."

Priest dragged the razor upward from his throat. His shoulders looked drawn, thinner each time Paulk saw them.

"The State may get through today, Ray. So we've got to talk about your testimony. First, I want you to remember to give me a direct answer to my questions, and to add nothing else. In other words, let me be the authority on what's good for you and what isn't. We'll let the State dig out what hurts, if they can."

He thought ahead as he spoke. Here was another of the borderlines. You advised. To a degree, you suggested and coached. This was legal, ethical. Yet a scant step away was the criminal act, subordination of perjury. "Have you got that?"

"Yes, sir, I reckon."

"I want you to tell the truth exactly as you've told it to me." And lie, he meant, if and wherever you've lied to me. "Answer, then shut up and wait for the next question. Don't try for any acting awards. Don't try to give us anything you don't really feel, and don't try to emphasize anything. Let me decide what's worth repeating. If you don't understand a question, say so.

"I want you to pay no attention to the crowd, or to how it reacts to what you say. Speak up, and tell it to the jury, not the lawyers. And don't fancy up your language—use the words that you use every day."

He started a cigarette, feeling that he spoke into a well.

"Another thing—if you're asked who you have talked to about your defense, name everybody, including me. Defendants are always afraid to admit their whole story isn't extemporaneous, so they lie and get caught at it. You've talked to Billy Shepherd, to a raft of officers, the prosecutors and me. Say so, and it'll save a peck of trouble. You understand?"

Priest grunted, rinsing his razor.

"Tigart will treat you rough, and you've got to be careful. Think, don't lose your temper. The moment you get up on that stand, your character and reputation become a legal issue. You can be attacked to test your credibility as a witness, and you will be. Your record will be introduced, even though it's of misdemeanors, because they involve moral turpitude. You're going to be racked up as a pimp and wife-beater, and there's nothing I can do to prevent it.

"At times you'll think I ought to be up objecting when I'm not. I can't protect you with a bunch of hot-air objections, and I'm not going to fight when it will hurt more than it can help. When there's nothing at stake but your feelings, I'll let them chew on you. We'll save our hell-raising for when they're hurting our case."

Priest wiped on a ragged towel, came across to nudge Paulk aside and draw his trousers from beneath the mattress, where they'd lain pressing all night.

"That all, Mr. Polk?"

"I think it is."

"I was wondering," Priest said, "wondering if you'd seen Patty Sue?"

"Yes, I have. Look, Ray—do you intend to give me the whole story from the stand? If not, I can't put you on."

"Well, I been thinking back, sort of, remembering some things. There's some stuff I thought of—"

"Hold it right there," Paulk's throat tightened. "You've been telling me what happened for three weeks. I believe it, and we're out on a limb with it—*as is*. Dammit, Ray, your wife is divorcing you, she's bounty hunting."

"I ain't sore. Maybe it's you got her wrong."

"Maybe so," Paulk got up, anxious to be gone. "Anything I can send you?"

"Well, I wish't I had some money. I'd as leave send my wife some candy, seeing as everybody else is doing it."

"All right, I'll attend to it. Is that all?"

"I guess I could eat some peanuts myself."

"Can't Angie get them for you?"

"To tell you the truth, she's peeved at me. She don't like Patty much."

"Seems to me Patty is supposed to be the peanut eater."

Priest glanced up, the listless eyes staring Paulk down as, unfailingly, they could. "You'd know about stuff like that, Mr. Polk, if you'd ever been out on the bum. A few peanuts can take a man a long ways."

Paulk stopped at the door; touched, exasperated. "Ray, I've got to know whether you intend to stand hitched. Maybe I ought to tell you I saw your wife last night. Out of jail with," he swallowed back Anglin's name "—out with a friend."

Priest's jaw closed. "I don't see how—"

"Nor do I, but I'll try to find out. In the meantime, you'd better decide to scramble for yourself."

Priest's oath seemed to come whispering out of the steel, to drift about them in the whirlpool of human odors never cleansed from the cellblock. Hoarsely: "How did she look?"

"Not pregnant, if that's your worry. She's bleached her hair."

The prisoner sat down, brushing his hands over his naked chest.

"Well?" Paulk said.

"She always wanted to do that; always said she would. Me, I told her a hundred times, hell no. I said, a woman's hair needs to be plain and natural. . . ."

XXVIII

While a pair of pigeons fought and flirted on a sun-heated window ledge, the 191st District Court assembled for the wintry business of Friday, May 15. Judge Sharman, his linty vest buttoned crookedly, commented with elation upon the breeze that rattled the slats of the shades and gently ruffled the gold-fringed flags at either side of the bench. Then, repenting the pleasantry as if it unbecame him, he turned to lash Andy Grosscup about the glare. Paulk assumed his place on time despite the delay of an interview by Romney Davenport. The *Tribune*'s celebrated by-line had approached him mildly, almost deferentially, he thought.

"How many witnesses will you have, Mr. Paulk?" "Not many; two or three, I imagine." "Will Priest be one of them?" "I can't say; that depends on how matters stand when the time comes." "Do you think it's probable you'll offer him?" "Yes." "Would his testimony follow the—the line indicated by your cross-examinations?" "Of course, if I know what you mean. If this boy is called, he'll tell the story, all of it, the good and the bad. Our side isn't holding out anything."

He watched ten smiling women file in to occupy a reserved pew near the front. These were the jury wives, come to gaze with possessive pride upon the sudden judicial glory of their husbands, ushered in by Nathan Hart, who declared he didn't know the origin of the order which had saved space for them. At the counsel table, Hollis Anglin hunched forward, sniffling, massaging sunken eyes. Herb Cameron wandered in off course, looking pallid and glum and disassociated. The Shepherd trotted in from the Judge's office, waving and glowing as he plopped into his chair. Tigart appeared last. He seemed to preen himself as he disgorged his briefcase. If Ike shared the general fatigue, he hid it well. Behind Paulk, Angie Callahan, looking a little frumpy and pathetic under her wilted Easter hat, stared at this massing of her brother's enemies and shook her head.

"All right," the Judge signaled to Tigart, "let's proceed."

Ike drew a tagged pistol from an envelope, started the procession of testimony needed to establish it as the death weapon. First witness was Tolbert Shanahan, a squinting and warmly uninhibited gunsmith. As a partner in Tol's and Joe's Gun Shop he identified State's Exhibit Eleven as the .45-caliber, government-model Colt automatic he had

198

traded to Jess Hutcherson back in August of 1948. Later, in 1955, he had customized the pistol with a pair of grips he had hand-carved from the elkhorn Hutch brought home from an Alaskan hunting trip. Tol's initials were etched into his work.

"See here!" the Judge flinched as the muzzle of the gun came to bear upon him, "is that thing loaded?"

"No, Your Honor, it is not."

"Well, maybe you know, but let's not wave it around that way. A lot of people get killed with empty guns, and it's a sad needless waste. Safe beats sorry. . . ."

Paulk cross-examined briefly. Repairs? Yes, Tol recalled filing off the seer to give Hutch the hair-trigger he liked. On five occasions, he had installed new barrels. Yes, this did suggest that Hutch, or someone, had fired the pistol a great deal. Why the gun trade in the first place? Tol couldn't say, aside from the fact that Hutch's previous gun had been plain blue while this one was nickle-plated, and "Hutch always did get a kick out of flashy things."

"Mr. Shanahan," Ike drawled into his redirect, "tell the jury, if you know, how much this pistol weighs."

"Thirty-nine ounces."

"Isn't that rather heavy—say, heavier than a blackjack or a billy club?"

"Yes, sir, it's the heaviest handgun I know about, except for some of the relics, or maybe a few of the older magnums."

Archie Messer came next. Fresh shaven, dressed in a cheap new suit with the tag prints apparent on the cuff, smelling faintly of cheap wine, Messer described with grinning agreeability how he happened to find the gun, how he turned it in at El Reno police headquarters. He lied earnestly about the two empty shells in it, sticking to his tale of how dropping the pistol had caused two accidental firings. On cross, Paulk let the fabrication stand. He also passed over Messer's record of drunkenness arrests and spared the witness from an explanation of his temporary status as a suspect. With the overtures made, Paulk delved for the only vital assist Messer could give.

"Then, the four days you've spent here in Texas, away from your tractor, have cost you $32 in wages?"

"I guess it comes to that, but a man has got to do his part."

"I'll ask you to state whether you're being compensated, in any way and by anyone, for these lost earnings?"

Tigart stood up. "Your Honor, I believe the law allows a witness one dollar and fifty cents a day and six cents a mile for travel within the state. I'm sure Mr. Messer will receive this, as he should. But, it seems to me, inquiring into it is just squandering good time."

"You are objecting, Mr. Tigart?"

"No," Ike shrugged. "If Mr. Paulk insists, I don't mind."

Nicely enough, it told Paulk the witness would deny Anglin's generosity; it warned this was a dry run.

"You may answer," the Judge said.

"I ain't dead sure I got the question."

"The question," Paulk said, "is whether anyone promised you any money for coming here to testify."

Messer glanced at the assistant prosecutor. "Why no, they didn't."

"I'll ask you whether or not, at the Arwin Hotel last Wednesday evening, you discussed your testimony with me?"

"Yes, sir, I done that."

"At that time, didn't you tell me you were being paid ten dollars a day for appearing here?"

"I don't recollect nothing like that. The fact is, I was doing a speck of drinking that night—you know, being off in a strange town and all."

As much in temper as technique, Paulk recanted his kindnesses. He compelled Archie to an admission of his police record, challenged his motives in testing and almost keeping the pistol. The State's slush fund was eluding him again; it was another miscalculation. The fault was that he anticipated truth while the good ones, like Jack Singer, always expected evasion.

The pistol history dragged on. Tigart proved up its return from Oklahoma, its delivery to the city chemist, Dr. Ivan Neilson. The timid, barely audible Neilson came on to recite in formulistic exactitude each test performed on the weapon. Ultimately, he had proven scrapings off the gun butt contained human blood, but the sample was too old and small for any determination of its type. Afterwards, he had returned the pistol to Chief Hardeman.

The chief, brusque, powerful, physically as overwhelming as the volume of city ordinances behind him, followed to complete the identification for the record.

"Then," said Ike, "the pistol handed to you by Dr. Neilson has been in your constant custody since that time?"

"Yes, sir."

"And it is the same pistol you have just inspected, the one marked State's Exhibit Eleven?"

"It is."

"Thank you. We'll pass the witness."

"Chief Hardeman," Paulk said, "you were in charge of the investigation of this case for a period of several weeks, isn't that correct?"

"Yes."

As an experienced witness, Hardeman answered slowly, amplifying nothing. By bits, Paulk led out the facts of the special bureau, special staff, the special coordinating steps which had distinguished the search for Hutch's killer.

"Chief, wasn't all this rather unusual?"

"Yes."

"During your years of police work, have you ever participated in an investigation so uniquely organized?"

"No, sir."

"Now, I suppose this extraordinary operation involved some extraordinary expense, did it not?"

"Some."

"I'll ask you if you know whether this expense was paid out of a special bank account."

"Yes, it was."

"Please tell the jury how this account came to exist."

"My understanding was that the money was put up by friends of Mr. Hutcherson."

"Chief, did your bureau keep any record of how this donated money was spent?"

"Absolutely. We accounted for every cent of it."

"How was the money used?"

"Different ways. Mostly, I'd say, to pay travel expense for investigators checking leads, running down tips, in various parts of the country. There were some office salaries, rent, correspondence and communications costs. We also leased vehicles from time to time, and paid fees for expert advice."

"I see. Now, how large was this slush fund, or whatever it was?"

"It varied from time to time."

"At its peak, how much was there?"

"Offhand I couldn't say."

"Actually, at the time you set up this Get Ray Priest Bureau, didn't the fund total more than ten thousand dollars?"

"I believe it did."

"Then in addition to the usual resources of the police, sheriff, FBI and Ranger departments, you had ten thousand dollars to spend on gathering evidence against this defendant?"

"If you want to put it that way, yes."

"Did you spend it?"

"Part of it was spent."

"But some of that money was left over, after the job was done?"

"That's right."

"What became of this surplus?"

"When we broke up the bureau, the decision was to return the balance to the contributors, on a pro rata basis."

"And was this done?"

"I assume so."

"You assume? Don't you know definitely?"

"I think so; to my own satisfaction, I do."

"Chief Hardeman, who wrote the checks on that account during the investigation?"

"The assistant district attorney, Mr. Anglin. I countersigned most of them, but this wasn't necessary. Mr. Anglin was authorized to make the dispersals and keep the accounts."

"When the bureau was dissolved, did Mr. Anglin still have authority to draw on the account, for purposes of the investigation?"

"Yes."

"Then, you assumed he drew the checks that were to divide the balance between the contributors?"

"I'm sure he did."

"But you didn't see him do it?"

"No."

"Is it possible that money was not returned to the donors, that some of it was used, or is being used, to meet certain expenses of this prosecution?"

"I'm in no position to say."

"Can you tell us, then, on your oath, that this fund is presently inoperative?"

"No. I feel certain, however—"

"No more questions."

Judge Sharman patted down a yawn. "Ten minutes, gentlemen."

Through the recess, Paulk stood in the rotunda's phone booth, smoking and listening to Jack Singer. The wry voice seemed to bring Jack's wopshot grin through the instrument. Singer was enjoying every clash, in absentia, just as he staggered on the liquor he served someone else.

"Wen, your idea that Hutch might have been committing a felony when he died raises some interesting questions."

By law, carnal knowledge of a girl younger than eighteen was statutory rape under every condition except marriage, with consent no issue. "Since Patty was seventeen," said Singer, "it was statutory rape even if she tripped Hutch and fell under him; that is, on the face of it. But on the other hand, as a married woman she had reached her majority in certain respects, and I'm inclined to think her marriage might have removed her disability for consent. The whole thing might mire down in a mess of law, more law than Jimmie Sharman could say 'Mercy' over, I'm afraid. It's up to you. I'll dig it out if you want."

If Hutch had been in the act of a felony when Priest killed him, then what? As Paulk thought it over, Singer trailed off into one of his reveries where law and a generous memory blended in almost scholarly confusion.

Juries knew, Jack was saying, that most women who claimed rape had brought it on themselves. "I recall getting a boy off because his girlfriend had crooned sex songs to him all evening. Wen, you should have heard me singing those tunes to my jury. Another time, I had this farm boy who laid out in his field between two rows of sorghum with his shotgun, watching until his wife and his brother went sneaking down to the cellar—but, excuse me, that story isn't really in point. I'm trying to say I think you're taking Ray's protective attitude toward Patty too much to heart. If Hutch raped her, he barely did. You've got to grant she was willing, and as guilty as Hutch. Of course, if you want to go into it—?"

"Let's skip it," Paulk said. "I can't see myself arguing that to the jury, even if it wasn't so threadbare."

"Good. Now, what can I do next?"

"Nothing," Paulk looked at his watch. He'd thought to tell Jack about Patty's mystifying excursion from jail, but there wasn't time. He said, "I guess you know by now that I muffed things with Archie Messer?"

"Don't sound so whipped," Singer laughed. "Hindsight is what kills a lawyer. Come to think of it, that's the very thing everyone dies of, isn't it? Good luck, son; give 'em hell."

XXIX

Mary Waddill, her compact figure reflecting the happy bulges of "somebody else's cooking," testified to the kitchen-window curiosity which had led her to summon police to Hutch's abandoned sedan. Anglin's questions permitted her to tell of standing by while officers searched the car. She had witnessed discovery of Hutch's wallet, the blasting caps, the silver saddle and the rest of the Posse parade regalia. Paulk excused her without cross-examining. He wasn't sure whether he feared she, like honest Archie Messer, would lie about the baby-sitting fees being paid for her by the State, or whether he was beginning to lose heart for any further proof of the destitution of trial ethics.

Tigart called Mitchell Wiley, lieutenant of detectives, to follow her. Wiley's name had not been included on the State's list, and Paulk sensed another blocking maneuver. Since it was necessary to put on an officer from the death scene, Ike had selected an innocuous one. It was as if he knew Paulk had hoped for Ranger Captain A. B. C. Smith. No doubt, Smith had been the "Texas stranger" of the confession duress at Peoria; Paulk had an outline for the Ranger's cross-examination waiting in Jack Singer's briefcase. It was likely to expire there.

Referring always to the scale drawing of Cabin 4, the lieutenant described the arrangement and condition of the rooms, yet skirted any statement as to the situation or appearance of Hutch's body. He got in the facts of the tweed trousers marked K. F. Stanfield, the beads of diluted blood in the lavatory, the beer cans in the front bedroom.

"Lieutenant," Tigart turned his tobacco to the other jaw, "I'll ask whether, aside from those trousers, you found any other items of clothing in those rooms?"

"Yes, we found the clothing of the deceased."

"Please tell the jury what items you found, and where you found them."

"Mr. Hutcherson's trousers were folded and hanging over the back of the bedroom chair. His underwear was in the seat of the chair, and his boots were under the edge of the bed, one standing upright, the other lying on its side. There was a sock inside each of the boots. His coat was on a hanger in the closet."

"Is that all of it?"

"No, sir. Mr. Hutcherson's hat was on the dresser, beside his watch. Then there was his shirt, tied around his neck."

"Was the room searched while you were present?"

"Yes, sir; we went over it thoroughly, several times."

"Did you locate Mr. Hutcherson's wallet?"

"No, sir."

"How about his credit cards, driver's license, identification?"

"None of those things were there."

"What about his money?"

"It was missing."

"You found no money whatsoever?"

"That's correct, not a cent."

"What about Mr. Hutcherson's automobile?"

"It was gone too."

"I see. Your witness, Mr. Paulk."

The thefts, like the unlucky fact of flight, had to be admitted. Ike's smug consciousness of this irritated Paulk. Each time, the Great Red One gave the jury a lingering meaningful look, one assuring them that this telltale point was in itself a complete annihilation of the defense. Paulk retaliated bitterly.

"Lieutenant, while describing all these wondrous sights, didn't you overlook something?"

"Not that I can think of."

"Let's see if you can think of a whiskey bottle."

"Well, yes, there was a bottle."

"Where?"

"In the bedroom."

"In the *back* bedroom, wasn't it, on the floor?"

"Yes."

"And one of the missing items you failed to mention was the liquor that bottle had contained, isn't that correct?"

"Yes, it was empty."

"That's all."

Judge Sharman, already in his third collar of the day, scowled at the clock as the policeman passed under it and on out the door, and he ordered the noon recess. Paulk hurried out as quickly as the jury was clear. An awareness of something urgent and unfinished was upon him as he crossed Houston and claimed a counter stool in the Little Star. He drank coffee, smoked a cigarette. Then, pressed, ambivalent, he made a telephone call. Shortly he was in his car, driving out to Bellaire and abominating it.

The Hutcherson house was among the few old dwellings in a spawning young country. New shingles had replaced the original roof tile, stone cornices had been sliced off the tall brick faces. There were steel windows and aluminum screens and a stockade fence to enclose the gardens. The effect was of a house as new as antique; odd, yet commodious and not incompatible with the city and land as Paulk knew them. The maid who answered his ring spoke his name, led him into a foyer, and asked him to wait. As she bustled away, up a carpeted stair, he looked about at plaster walls hung with massively framed paintings, carved mouldings, scrim draperies and a few pieces of dark heirloom furniture.

He felt eyes upon him before he saw the Marine leaning in a doorway. The man was flushed, his eyes glittered. He wore tight khaki with a tarnished gold leaf on the open collar and he rotated a glass in his hand. "Well," he said, "my father's bloodsucker. You'll pardon me if I don't offer my hand."

Charles, Laura had said, was prone to ask people outside. If it happened now, he thought, he'd not much care. He said nothing.

Major Hutcherson drank, belched in deliberate insult. "Matey," he said, "this was my mother's idea, not mine. My personal approach would be to take you by the stacking swivel—"

The maid reappeared, coming partway down the stairs. "Mr. Paulk, if you'll come up, please?"

He glanced at Charles, then nodded to the relieved servant and followed her up to a second-floor sitting room. Martha Hutcherson waited on a satin love seat, her back to the door. She faced a glass wall and the roof terrace beyond. Before her a table held a candle-warmed demijohn and a tray of sandwiches.

"Please come in," she said, "I'm grateful you are here."

There was, indeed, something queenly about her, something immediately majestic in her quiet dominance of her own setting. Her head was erect, shoulders square under the same dark dress she had worn to court. As he chose a chair opposite her, he discovered her hair showed no gray despite the years apparent on her hands; that beneath the dark tranquility of her eyes lay a disciplined agony almost surely predating the hard abradings of the trial.

He said, "I've explained to your maid why I picked such an awkward hour. I hope she told you."

"Oh, it's the best time, if it isn't costing you your lunch. Here's coffee and a snack—please serve yourself; I never take anything at noon."

As he filled a crystal-thin cup, he knew she made her measurement of him, sized him for whatever persuasion she had planned. He frowned, wondering why he had come.

"Did you know, Mr. Paulk, that we have a mutual friend? One who champions you beautifully?"

"Laura Singer," he said idiotically, and she nodded.

He tasted the coffee. Martha Hutcherson took up a cigarette, lit it before he could offer to, and held it between her thumb and two fingers in a mannish, unaffected way that lent credence to the tales of her nerve with Hutch's explosives during the oil boom days. On her left hand he saw a large solitary diamond, probably the renowned stone sent her from Iran. Although her hand seemed still, the gem winked and flashed. He took it to mean her qualms equaled his.

For a minute, they waited, each upon the other.

"Why did you send for me, Mrs. Hutcherson?"

His bluntness caused a small smile. "That's not so easy to explain as it might have been a few days ago."

"Mr. Kelso spoke to me only yesterday."

"Yes, I know, he told me of your conversation, and I feel I owe you an apology for it. I didn't know he was linking his partnership plan to my invitation. Please understand the two aren't related. Poor E. C., he's an old friend. He has been as distraught as I, or he'd not have let it appear as it did. When Mr. Tigart told me he had suggested that you be appointed to defend this man—"

"Ike nominated me to the Judge?"

"Why, didn't you know?"

Singer, Herb, Anglin, The Shepherd. And now, Tigart. The case seemed to have come to him by acclamation. Everyone had wanted him. Everyone, that is, except the man most concerned, Ray Priest.

"If I've said something to shock you—?"

"No," he smiled. "I'm surprised at Ike, that's all. What were you saying?"

"I don't really know. I was trying to get into an explanation of what I have in mind. May we be direct, quite frank, with each other?"

"Certainly."

"Then I'll say first that we—my children and I—were prepared for an ordeal when this trial began. But we did not expect the developments of these past two days. Wait—I'm not setting out to lecture you. Rather, I intend to beg a bargain, something we all could live with. I can't pretend I'm not humiliated, sick, angry with what has been insinuated against my husband. But believe me, I'll ask you nothing for myself, or for my sons. The boys are men, strong men, thank God; they will not be pulled down. It's Valle who counts. Surely you know she was a late child, pampered and kept a baby by her father. She's seventeen, but she so idolized Jessup that—well, her world excluded everything except what he wanted for her, so that she has developed no armor of her own."

He kept silent. This picture of consequence wasn't welcome. Still, he had driven himself here to receive it; to accept chastisement, he supposed, as a relief from the long vague forebodings.

"I confess, sir, that when you barred my family from the trial, I was furious. Now I thank you for it. It's kept Valle out of the courtroom. From the day Jessup was found, she's been unable to get hold of herself. She's had such wild notions that we had to take her out of school."

"I'm sorry, Mrs. Hutcherson, but—"

"Please let me finish. While I'm admitting you to the family secrets, I may as well say this whole terrible affair happens to have been my daughter's introduction to the facts of life. Yes, I know that in this enlightened age, this sounds ridiculous, but it's true. Jessup wouldn't have her told anything, he wanted her innocence preserved as long as possible. I was never so Victorian, but my husband—anyway, Mr. Paulk, consider what can happen to a young girl when her first contact with the sex facts occurs as sewer gossip involving her dead father with a girl of just her same age."

He looked out upon the young plants of the terrace, the spring shoots as fragile as Valle's father must have caused her to be. He said, "The facts of the case exist. I didn't invent them."

"Oh, I'm accusing no one. I've tried to keep my thinking straight. But through Mr. Tigart, I have learned something of Raymond Priest, of the appalling creature he is. Am I wrong to prefer my daughter's future, or even my husband's good name, to the welfare of a solicitor for prostitutes?"

"We're trying him for murder," he answered flatly, "nothing else. It's his life, Mrs. Hutcherson."

"And what of Valle's?"

"I'm afraid we aren't getting anywhere. If you'll excuse me?"

"Just a moment more, please. Jessup had his faults; he could be blustery, impulsive, reckless, especially in the last two years of his life. I know this, so I can say I'm not sure that your idea of what happened that day isn't partly true. He was concerned about himself, drinking a little too much—I promised to be candid, didn't I? He had talked to his doctor several times—"

Paulk said, "You shouldn't tell me this."

"Perhaps, but I will; I don't want you to think my anxiety over Valle is only a ruse. Jessup was aware of his age, beginning to fret over his— his capacities as a man. Knowing this, I excused certain things, outside his normal pattern of conduct. This is why I'm willing to concede something, if I must. Mr. Tigart tells me he believes you'd be satisfied if this Priest is allowed to live."

Paulk turned to look at her. She was pale, stiffer now; a horse trader.

"I can help you save him," she said.

"I beg your pardon?"

"I said, I'll help you." The poise was yielding to desperation. "If, for Valle's sake, you'd drop everything except the insanity matter, I would visit this Priest in jail. I would testify for you. I'd say I believe he is insane, and that I think it would be wrong to execute him."

He stared, his mind leaping ahead to a test of it. No, she wasn't qualified to give an opinion on Ray's sanity. But would Ike, whom she had hired, object? Nor could she legally comment upon the disposition of the case, a direct invasion of the jury province. But if she wished to, who would prevent her? Not Ike, not Judge Sharman. He shuddered. It could be done.

Her voice grew cold. "You are determined to save this man's life.

I shall do what I can to preserve my daughter's sanity. This way, we might both succeed."

He said, "Does Tigart know about this?"

"No."

"Or, that you asked me to come here?"

"I've mentioned none of this to him."

He shook his head in disbelief. "Kids heal quickly, Mrs. Hutcherson. Could you be exaggerating your problem with Valle?"

"No. Understand me, Mr. Paulk. I loved my husband for many years, perhaps I still did the day he was murdered. But, be shocked if you will, I do not love him now—partly because he is beyond the reach of anything I may feel, partly because I am a woman and I shall live out my life fearing his last act was a corruption of our marriage. Soon I may even hate him. Whatever, if his name comes down off a few cornerstones and letterheads and grants-in-aid, let it. It's Valle I have left, and hope to save."

She had put a label on the regimented anguish he'd sensed beneath the serenity.

"Mr. Paulk, I've said this to you only."

"I wish you hadn't."

"My proposal—what's your answer?"

"There is none."

He left quickly, his mind grappling, sinking under a helplessness that smothered every dogma he knew. How did he reject life for Ray Priest; forfeit him, unilaterally, to a concept he couldn't even state? But was he to enlist with the Anglins, knowingly to affix puppet strings to a court of law? Deeper, inseparable from the thought, he felt pity for Martha Hutcherson and, as if appended to it, a curious sorrow for himself. It was as though he and she suddenly shared losses, confusions, a common consciousness of infinite unanswerables. If while loving her husband, she hated him also, Paulk wasn't truly astounded. Had he not yearned wrathfully for Jerry? How many nights had he immersed himself in Texas jurisprudence to hide from the voices that screamed, *Hate her, hate her for dying!*

XXX

Announcement of the first witness of the afternoon confirmed Paulk in his estimate that the State was almost through. Now would come a showing of the horror of Cabin 4, the ghastliness Tigart had so carefully reserved for his close. Paulk could do little. Before a jury it was always the violent deed, not its causation, that reduced the accused from man to monster.

The witness was B. J. Kittinger, mortician, who did not look his profession. He answered crisply, forcefully, as Tigart ran through a lengthy predicate to qualify him as an expert in instances of mutilation death. While doubting the legality of Kittinger's right to opinion, Paulk kept silent. The jury was intent, excited; he could not wisely put them off. He looked at Ancil Andricks, his hair newly wet down; at Gay, open mouthed and waiting. The women leaned forward, as eager as afraid. Juror Turner rocked himself on his swivel; Glass had a note pad on his knee. Studer was housecleaning his mouth, using one of the mint-flavored toothpicks given away at Gail's.

The best of the prospect, he thought, was that none of the Hutchersons were here.

"All right," Tigart said, "what, if anything, did you do when you arrived at the Ranch Inn on the morning of January fifteenth?"

"I parked the ambulance and went directly to the back bedroom of Cabin 4."

"And what did you see there?"

Kittinger shook his head. "It was a terrible, gruesome sight—"

"I'll object," Paulk jumped up. "That's a conclusion, highly inflammatory, prejudicial to the rights of this defendant."

"I'll sustain," Judge Sharman said. "The jury will not consider the witness' statement that 'it was a terrible, gruesome sight,' not for any purpose."

Tigart drew his head back, closed his eyes as if upon a carnage visible to them all, and he said, "Just tell us what you saw, Mr. Kittinger."

"I saw Mr. Hutcherson's body lying on the bed."

"Will you describe for the jury the condition of that bed?"

"It was bloody. There was blood spattered up the headboard and

211

wall, on the bedclothing. The pillow was completely soaked, and there was a large pool of uncongealed blood filling up the depression made by the weight of the body. I also saw that the mattress was soaked through, and some of the blood was dripping through, making a puddle underneath on the floor. The body appeared to have drained entirely—"

"Will you," Tigart headed off Paulk's objection, "tell us what you observed about the bed as to the portion of it not taken up by the body?"

"Well, it looked like any bed."

"What was its state of disarray, if any?"

"It wasn't disarranged. The bedclothing looked undisturbed, except about the body."

"What about the pillow on this undisturbed side of the bed?"

"Some blood had spattered over onto it, but it wasn't crushed."

"As far as you could determine at that moment, then, only one-half of the bed had been used?"

"Yes, sir."

"Now, it was your mission that day, was it not, to take charge of Mr. Hutcherson's body?"

"Yes, sir."

"And I'll ask you whether you were instructed by the officers there to observe the body carefully before moving it?"

"Yes, sir; the Ranger suggested I do that, and I did."

"What did you see as to the position of the body?"

"It was lying on the near side of the bed, the side closest to the door. The head was on the pillow, face up; the body fully extended on the back, and at a slight angle, so that the right foot hung over the edge of the bed."

"Did you notice the position of the arms?"

"Yes, sir; they were along the sides, in a sort of natural position."

"By this, do you mean the arms were in a normal pose, as might be expected of a person asleep?"

"That's leading," Paulk snapped. "I'll object to it, and to any answer that might be made if the question should be rephrased. This witness hasn't been shown competent as to the normal sleeping position of the deceased."

The Judge's gaze had levelled on Ray Priest. He said, "I believe the question is leading, but it seems to me the witness should be allowed to tell what the pose of the body was, and to tell it in the terms that make it clearest to all of us. Let's get on."

"May it please the Court, the defendant would like a ruling."

"Sit down, young man; you've been overruled."

"Note my exception."

Tigart said, "Were the hands at the sides?"

"Yes, sir."

"They gave no appearance of having been raised to a position of defense?"

"No, sir."

"Now, Mr. Kittinger, will you tell us just what you saw as to the condition of the body itself?"

"Well, the first thing I noticed was the blood. There was a lot of it, on the head and face, down over the chest. The mouth was open somewhat, and I could see that a dental plate was missing. There was a garment—a shirt, it turned out to be—tied around the throat, and so wet with blood you couldn't make out what it was without looking a second time. Then, I could also see the wounds."

"All right. What, if anything, did you do, there in that room?"

"My assistant, Mr. Ballew, and I put the body on a carriage."

"To your knowledge, and in your presence, was anything found as result of this removal?"

"Yes, sir; we found the missing dental plate. It was under the body. Fact is, it had caused a U-shaped indentation on the back."

Tigart grimaced. "What did you do next, Mr. Kittinger?"

"We took the body to the funeral home."

"Did you, personally, have any occasion to further examine Mr. Hutcherson's body after reaching the mortuary?"

"Yes, I did. The officers were there, wanting to know the nature and location of the wounds. They also wanted the shirt. I accommodated them."

"Tell the jury what you did about the shirt?"

"I untied it and gave it to the policemen."

"Did you have any difficulty with this?"

"Yes, a great deal. The shirt was tied very tight."

"In what sort of a knot?"

"A double knot, the kind we always used to speak of as a 'granny' knot. It was saturated with blood, very hard to untie. Finally, I had to get up and stand astride the body to work it loose."

At Mrs. Chesterson's quick, strangled gasp, Tigart paused. Turning toward the paling, white-lipped jurors, he joined them in contemplation of the horror. Then, gruffly: "I'll ask you to describe what, if anything, you discovered about the wounds."

Kittinger's voice had hardened. He had been a lodge brother of Jess Hutcherson. "Two of the head wounds were very severe. They—"

"May it please the Court," Paulk rose, "the witness hasn't qualified in medicine, or in pathology. I submit that he cannot testify as to these matters, certainly not to the severity of any wounds."

Sharman scorned him. "He's got a right to tell everything he saw and did. Overrule."

"I'll except, Your Honor. And, to save time, I'd like the record to show that we are objecting to every question and every answer in this line of inquiry, and that in each instance I am reserving my bill."

"Very well, you're welcome to your objections and exceptions. But I'm not saying what my ruling will be on every question, since I don't know what is going to be asked. Proceed, Mr. Tigart."

Ike said, "You may continue, Mr. Kittinger."

"One of the severe wounds was on the right front quarter of the head, beginning about four inches above the right eye. The other was at the top of the head, slightly forward from the center. Both were very deep into the brain. There were other cuts and abrasions—a cut through the right ear, cuts on the nose and around the mouth, besides the marks on the throat."

"Did you restrict yourself to a mere visual examination of these injuries?"

"No, sir. I used an instrument, a probe, to investigate the skull fractures."

"What, if anything, did you learn from this?"

"That the skull was badly crushed around each of the head wounds. Each wound had a number of bone fragments in it. My probe entered the wound above the eye to a depth of two inches. It penetrated, freely, the larger wound to a depth of about five inches."

"You mean two and five inches into the brain?"

"That's right. His skull was crushed like an egg shell."

"Now, just a minute!" Paulk left his chair. "I'll not have this—"

"Pass the witness," Tigart said. For a moment, Paulk glared at him. Facing away from the jury, the special prosecutor could indulge in a sweet scarlet smile. "He's all yours, Junior."

"I heard you the first time."

"It's good," Ike drawled, "that your ears are open, if your eyes are not."

"Maybe you'd like your eyes closed for you—"

Judge Sharman came shouting into it, belatedly, almost hysterically. When at last it ended, Paulk's fury still blazed.

He turned from Anglin's grin to address the witness. "Mr. Kittinger, did you keep a journal, or take notes, on your activities of January fifteenth?"

"No."

"But you can tell us all these details, under oath, right down to feet and inches?"

"That's correct."

"Do you possess a photographic memory, Mr. Kittinger?"

"I have an excellent memory."

"Is it so excellent that you couldn't be mistaken about any of these things—the body, the bed, those motel rooms?"

"I'm not mistaken."

"If I were to ask you for such details on some other death case, one you handled four months ago; say, on the day after this one, could you swear to them with equal certainty?"

"Possibly not. When something like this comes up, I'm careful to remember because I know I may be called to court."

"I see," Paulk scratched his head. "I assume, then, that you also memorized for us all the details of that bedroom?"

"Yes, sir; I did."

"Will you tell us what the furnishings were?"

"There was the double bed, a bedstand beside it, a green upholstered chair in the back corner, a luggage bench under the window, and a dresser against the west wall."

"Was there a rug?"

"I believe so."

"What color were the window drapes in that room?"

Kittinger checked himself. "Well, maybe I didn't notice that."

"To err is human," Paulk said. "What color were the walls?"

"Under such circumstances, you don't notice those things."

"I thought you noticed everything. Can you tell us where the light switch for that room was located?"

"Usually the switch is right inside the door."

"Usually, perhaps. But what about this one?"

Kittinger had flushed slightly. He was correct, but did not know he was. He said, "I don't recall seeing the switch."

"Actually," Paulk said, "you are telling us you have a perfect memory but that it just doesn't remember very much, isn't that right?"

"Your Honor," Tigart said, "the State objects. The witness has not testified that his memory is perfect."

"Sustained."

"Just tell us," Paulk pressed, "how your memory happens to be so good when it comes to blood and so poor as to everything else?"

"I'm sure," the mortician answered hotly, "that I wouldn't know."

"Nor would I. Now, strain your memory a little, if you will, and tell us how you came to examine that half of the bed not occupied by the body of the deceased."

"I just saw it, that's all."

"No one directed your attention to it?"

"Someone might have. I can't say they did or didn't."

"Is it possible, Mr. Kittinger, that while you were present, some discussions were being had as to whether Mr. Hutcherson had been alone in that bed?"

"Anything is possible, but I don't remember any discussion."

"Your memory sort of blows hot and cold, doesn't it?"

"It does not."

"I believe you've testified that you knew Mr. Hutcherson well, had been his friend for many years?"

"That's right, and I'm proud of it."

"Does this friendship have any effect upon your memory, do you think?"

"Certainly not."

"Were you influenced by this relationship when you told us the other half of that bed looked unused?"

"No."

"In your capacity there as an extracurricular detective, or whatever it was, did you search that bed for hairpins?"

"Of course not."

"Did you put your nose to those pillows and sniff to discover if they smelled of cologne?"

"No. The one was soaked with—"

"Yes, with blood," Paulk's ire spilled out in sarcasm. "Allow me,

Mr. Kittinger, to help you get that word in as often as you like, which seems to be pretty often. Now, did you make any tests, like a good private eye, to determine if those bedsheets held a trace of body powder?"

"No."

"Did you make an effort to learn whether that bed contained any long, dark feminine hairs?"

"No, that wasn't my—"

"Then, your assumption that the deceased went to bed alone is based merely on your observation of an uncrushed pillow?"

"Mostly, yes."

"Mr. Kittinger, as a man of experience, have you ever heard that at certain times two people may occupy the *same* half of a bed?"

"I suppose, if you want to deal in dirt—"

"No autopsy was held in this case, was there?"

"No."

"No pathologist was called in, no post mortem carried out to ascertain exactly the condition of all the vital organs?"

"That's correct."

Paulk had intended forcing an admission that this failure to post the body had precluded forever any knowledge of whether Hutch's death had been preceded by a sexual orgasm. It was reverse English, a backspin to say the State could not prove the adultery had not occurred. But, as his lips framed the words, he gave it up. The talk with Martha Hutcherson had tamed him this much, and he wasn't sorry.

"Can you tell us why, when the law provides for an autopsy in circumstances of this sort, that none was conducted?"

"I understand the family opposed it."

"As a matter of fact, you know they opposed it because you talked to them about it, didn't you?"

"Yes. I've known them a long time."

"You interceded with the coroner, did you not?"

"Well, a lot of people feel pretty strongly against any post on their loved ones."

"All right. Then, to your own knowledge, no official report as to specific cause of Mr. Hutcherson's death is now, or ever has been, available to any of us?"

"That is true," Kittinger said, "but anybody with one eye and half sense could tell—"

"Just a minute, please; I'm not asking for your opinions, as numerous and all-encompassing as they seem to be. Just tell the jury, if you will, whether the body was covered when you first saw it in that motel room."

"It was, partially. The bedspread was drawn up to the waist."

"In performing your duty there, did you remove that bedspread?"

"Naturally."

"At that time, what did you see as to the state of dress of the deceased?"

"He wasn't dressed."

Paulk lowered his voice. "He wore no trousers?"

"No." Kittinger replied in a near whisper. The Court, the jury, were craning toward him.

"No pajamas?"

"No."

"No underwear?"

"No."

"No socks?"

"I told you, he wasn't wearing anything."

"Naked; not a stitch on him?"

"That's right," the witness bit out.

"Thank you," Paulk said. "You may stand aside."

"Wait a minute," Ike's wave halted the mortician half risen from the chair. "By your leave, Mr. Paulk, I happen to have a little re-direct—?"

"By all means, Mr. Special Prosecutor."

Tigart ignored him. "Mr. Kittinger, do you know many people who sleep with their clothes on?"

"None," the witness drilled his vengeance into Paulk. "I think almost everybody disrobes before going to bed."

"I think so, too," Ike said. "That's all." He ducked into a nodding, murmuring conference with Hollis Anglin. Then, as the assistant district attorney got up to saunter out the door, he announced, "The State will call Dr. Henderson Silversmith."

Short, middle-aged, his manner typically remote out of the physician's contempt for legal affairs, Silversmith took the oath and sat down to peer crabbedly at his watch. Most doctors make poor witnesses. To them the rules of evidence are absurd; a trial is tomfoolery, a waste of time. Accustomed to interrogating, they dislike being interrogated; used to the succor of technical language, they resent the

court insistence on understandable answers. They are apt to grow
querulous, to talk down to lawyers and jurors. This one, Paulk thought,
would be no exception.

He declined to stipulate Silversmith's qualifications, forcing Tigart
to lead him through a slow enumeration of his colleges, internships,
and staff jobs. When the predicate was lain, Ike established that Dr.
Silversmith had examined the body at Kittinger's and was the signer
of the death certificate.

"In plain bread-and-butter words, Doctor," Tigart said, "I want
you to describe to the jury the location and extent of those principal
head wounds."

Forbearing, the witness tapped his fingertips together. "As I said,
the fractures were extreme. Number One, located in the frontal area,
slightly in advance of the coronal suture, depressed an area of approximately ten centimeters' diameter. I found several bone slivers separated and projecting through the longitudinal fissure of the brain into
the *corpus callosum*. Number Two, a fracture of the right upper region
of the frontal bone, seemed to suggest a definite triangular shape. It,
likewise, was of deep penetration, with slivers of bone piercing the
right frontal lobe of the brain. Collaterally, there were numerous ir-
regular fractures extending radially from each of the wounds, these
joining and continuing on to the sides and back of the skull, into the
temporal and parietal regions."

"In your judgement, Doctor, how might such wounds as these have
occurred?"

"By blows—blows of great force, such as might be delivered with
a hammer or similar instrument."

Tigart passed the pistol to him from Mr. Funderburg's desk. The
doctor took it gingerly in a soft white hand.

"I'll ask you to grip this pistol, State's Exhibit Eleven, by the
barrel and tell us whether, in your opinion, a man holding it in this way
and striking with it as if it were a hammer might inflict the skull fractures you have described?"

"Yes, I believe he could, if he struck very hard."

"Bearing in mind that this pistol has been shown to have a weight
of thirty-nine ounces, that it is made of steel, you would still say it
could cause the skull damage you found only if wielded with extreme
force?"

"That is my opinion, yes."

Tigart had him examine the butt of the pistol, then say that he believed the floor plate of the ammunition clip could account for the triangular form of the smaller wound.

Then: "Doctor, having finished your examination of Mr. Hutcherson's body, did you reach any conclusion as to the cause of his death?"

"I did."

"State this to the jury, please."

"The skull fractures were the primary cause, contributed to, of course, by the accompanying hemorrhage."

"Which of the fractures—Number One or Number Two?"

"Either of them, whichever occurred first."

"You could not determine which fracture was first?"

"No, sir."

"So that we may understand you, Doctor—are you saying that, since either of these blows would have been fatal, the recipient of them was either dying or already dead when the second one hit him?"

"That is correct."

"Doctor, you were present, were you not, when the shirt was removed from the neck of the deceased?"

"I was."

"Yet you did not attribute death to strangulation?"

"That is easily explained," Silversmith marshalled his patience. "The garment was drawn down securely enough to have served as a tourniquet. If it had been present prior to the cranial wounds, the bleeding could not have been so profuse."

Tigart nodded gravely. "Doctor, suppose there had been no head wounds, suppose the shirt alone was there, knotted just as it was— what would have been the result?"

"Mr. Hutcherson would have died from strangulation."

It was a nice, damaging point. Paulk stole a look at the jury. Was this murder with malice; had Raymond Elliot Priest been "fatally bent on mischief" that night? If they had reserved doubts, they weren't doubting now. Before them sat a still, fish-eyed man who had killed Jess Hutcherson thrice, who had garroted a corpse. Tigart had cut a course for their deductions. If the initial blow had killed, then the second one and the attack with the shirt had but one implication. Priest had wanted to make sure of his job.

Judge Sharman drew up from his reading upon the primitive existence of the Icelandics and glowered, his umbrage flowing over Priest and into the jury box.

"Pass the witness," said Tigart.

Paulk, although not surprised, was impressed. In wavering faith, bordering on despondency, he opened his cross-examination with no plan in mind.

"Doctor, you are not a pa' ogist, are you?"

"No."

"You've never specialized in post mortem examinations?"

"No, sir."

"You performed no autopsy that day, did you?"

"I did not."

"Actually, your investigation was quite superficial in comparison to a regular formal autopsy, was it not?"

"You may say that, if you wish."

"I don't wish to say anything, Doctor. I want you to say it, if it's true."

Silversmith braced. "I've already said I didn't conduct an autopsy. And, I might add, I wasn't authorized to do so."

"Then, you've arrived at your conclusions solely on the basis of what you learned from a perfunctory, external examination?"

"I'd not consider it perfunctory. In view of the obvious skull damage, it was pointless to search any further."

It seemed the time to deflate him. Paulk said, "Sir, are you the county doctor?"

Bonita County's doctor, the healer of jail inmates and those other prisoners of the welfare rolls, was by custom some washed-out MD accepting the meagre public salary because he had failed to acquire a practice. The witness reddened as he said, "I am not."

"Are you connected with the City Health Department?"

"I am not."

"Or with the office of Justice of the Peace?"

"Of course not."

"Will you tell the jury how, lacking any official capacity, you happened to be called to examine Mr. Hutcherson's body?"

"He was my patient, and had been for many years."

"You were, then, preferred by his family?"

"I would gather that I was."

"As Mr. Hutcherson's physician, were you familiar with his physical condition?"

"I was."

"Was that good or bad?"

"Mr. Hutcherson was in very good health."

"When was the last time you had occasion to investigate this matter of Jess Hutcherson's health?"

"When I gave him his last regular checkup."

"And when was this?"

"I can't say; I don't have my office records with me."

"Approximately how long was this before his death, Doctor?"

"Two or three weeks, probably."

"That would make it in December of 1958?"

"I think so."

"At that time, you found him sound, suffering from no disorders of any sort?"

"Yes."

"Doctor, do you know what Mr. Hutcherson's physical dimensions were?"

"He was about six feet tall, usually weighed around two hundred ten."

"Is it fair to assume that he was an exceptional physical specimen, particularly for a man of his years?"

"Yes, he was quite extraordinary."

Now it had to get rougher. Paulk said, "Doctor, what advice, if any, did you give Mr. Hutcherson the last time you saw him professionally?"

"I don't have my records here, as I said. Besides, I'm not at liberty to disclose confidences—"

"Your Honor," Paulk got up, "to save time, I submit that the Court might instruct the witness on what the law requires of him."

The Judge, having started to doze, aroused with a jerk and somehow managed to lay hold of the situation. Disconnectedly, apologetically, he told Silversmith the privilege he claimed was nonexistent in law, that doctor-patient communication could not be withheld. The doctor flushed as he listened. He was, Paulk thought, preparing to enforce his privilege by other means if it was denied him by statute.

"Did you caution Mr. Hutcherson on anything regarding his health?"

"If I did, I don't remember it."

"Did you give him a prescription?"

"As I told you, I can't remember. I see a lot of patients in a day."

"May it please the Court," Ike Tigart said, "I'll object to this side trail as irrelevant, immaterial to any issue in this case, and touching upon matters not introduced in the direct examination."

"Yes," Sharman said, "I've been waiting."

Paulk spoke plaintively. "Your Honor, the State has inquired into the cause of death and, at the same time, the record shows that there was no autopsy, no absolute finding. I believe the defendant is entitled to go into the matter of the health of the deceased, insofar as is possible through this witness, in order for the jury to determine what weight it will give to the testimony given on direct. May I point out, also, that since we have accepted every detail of the deceased's physical condition several hours after his death, the defendant is entitled to show what that condition was prior to it. There is no question of materiality or of remoteness."

"Nor," said Tigart, "is there any issue as to what Mr. Hutcherson's health was back there two or three weeks before he was killed."

Tigart was right, Paulk conceded to himself, but he felt sure he would be allowed to continue. The Judge, fully awake now, thinking back, would wonder what sort of pills Hutch had been taking, what sort of problem he had had. The curiosity was harmless from the standpoint of the bench, since to err in favor of the defense was, in effect, not to err at all. Sharman pulled at his lip and said, "I'll allow the answer, so long as it bears strictly upon the deceased's condition at times in reasonable proximity to his death."

The ruling was so absurd that Mr. Funderburg whistled softly and wagged his head. It was a gift, the sort Sharman might shortly withdraw, and Paulk hurried on.

"Doctor, we can issue a subpoena for your records, if you feel it's impossible for you to remember otherwise."

Silversmith's eyes were seething. "Thinking about it," he said, "I believe I prescribed a tranquilizer."

"Thank you. Now, what was there about Mr. Hutcherson that prompted this prescription?"

"Nothing serious. He was overworked, tired, hadn't been sleeping well."

"He told you, himself, of these problems?"

"Naturally."

"Did he tell you, also, that he had been drinking excessively?"

"He most assuredly did not."

"He made no mention of drinking?"

"This was five or six months ago—"

"I realize that, Doctor. But try to recall, if you will, whether Mr. Hutcherson made any other complaints to you."

"I've told you, it's not possible for me to recall everything."

"Didn't you tell him his restlessness, his sudden appetite for liquor, were symptoms of an emotional upheaval connected with his advancing age?"

"I doubt, sir, that I would say that to any patient."

"Isn't it a fact, Dr. Silversmith, that you advised Jess Hutcherson to stop worrying about his virility?"

"I did not!"

Tigart leaped to his feet, shouting. From the Posse section a man rushed at the pit and was intercepted by the patrolman as Nathan Hart jumped from his chair to protect the isolation of the jury. The Judge, scrambling for something to pound with, bawled for order.

Paulk sat down, waiting it out, looking at the floor. He felt hollow. A moment ago, the questions had seemed to occur to him out of sheer intuition. Now he knew better. He had used Martha Hutcherson's confidences, broken a trust he should never have accepted. The admission chilled him. What had he gained? The likelihood, he knew, was that he'd hurt Ray Priest, as gravely as he had injured himself.

XXXI

The session reconvened at half-past four. The Judge began it by rescinding his ruling and purging the record of most of Paulk's cross-examination. With Tigart nodding his approval, the Court withdrew questions and answers from the jury consideration, framing his instructions in a way that made them an indirect reprimand of defense counsel. He closed his remarks with a sigh.

"Very well, you may proceed, Mr. Prosecutor."

Tigart nudged Herb Cameron. Without rising, the District Attorney said, "May it please the Court, the State rests."

A wave of disappointment rippled the crowd. Was this the State's case; was there to be no surprise, no clinching bit of evidence beyond that so often hashed over in the newspapers? Few, if any, understood that with a confession in evidence, the State needed only to show that the alleged offense had, in fact, occurred. It would take them a while to grasp that Tigart had more than met the requirements of proof. Corroboration of Ray's written admission lay everywhere, by a preponderance, since every witness had escaped impeachment.

"Mr. Paulk," the Judge said, "since it's late, I'm wondering if you can't call a witness who could be examined in just a few minutes—"

"Your Honor," Tigart interrupted, "before we continue, the State will offer a motion, a copy of which was delivered to you yesterday, I believe. If we might have the jury retired, I think we can handle this in the time that remains."

"Yes," the Judge remembered, "yes. Mr. Hart, take the jury upstairs. We'll not need you again, ladies and gentlemen, until nine o'clock tomorrow."

As the jury vanished, Billy Shepherd and Tigart stood to converse over the head of Herb Cameron, their bellies against his ears. Andy Grosscup went out, ducking to get through the door, and Paulk glimpsed Hollis Anglin in the hallway. A fat deputy sheriff, great hat in hand, appeared to gaze in as if waiting a signal. Ray Priest whispered, "What are they fixin' to do?"

Paulk got up. "May it please the Court, if the State's motion is in writing, then I'd like my copy of it immediately."

Tigart smiled. "You may have my copy in just a moment," he said sweetly. "But you won't need it now, since the motion is no part of this case."

Paulk shrugged and as he sat down, Tigart said, "Now, if the sheriff is ready—?"

"Jesus!" Ray hissed.

Paulk twisted around to him, saw that the dull eyes were peculiarly alight and directed at the door. He turned back, just as Patty Sue Priest entered the courtroom. Her lips were parted, her eyes wide and excited as they beheld the crowd. She had drawn the long bleached hair back into a pony tail; her blouse was buttoned up to her throat. Beside her, a hand cupping her elbow, was Andy Grosscup, walking guardedly to avoid tangling his legs in her flared skirt. Anglin followed. As Paulk darted his gaze about for an explanation, Billy Shepherd greeted his client. Glowing, absurdly courteous, he guided Ray's wife past the counsel table and posted her under the bench.

"Your Honor—"

"Please keep your peace, Mr. Paulk."

He looked again at Priest's hungering face, then at the girl. She stood with her head slightly lowered, with The Shepherd beside her, his stomach thrust at the bench as if for judgement. It was Cameron who got up to read the motion.

"Number twelve-zero-sixty-three, the *State of Texas versus Patty Sue Priest;* in the District Court of the 191st Judicial District of Texas, Bonita County, Texas.

"To the Honorable Judge of said Court:

"Now comes Herbert Cameron, District Attorney, representing the State of Texas, and moves the Court to dismiss the above styled and numbered cause for the following good and sufficient reasons, to wit: Further investigation discloses that the evidence against this defendant is insufficient to support the prosecution of this case to a successful conclusion."

Paulk, cursing them, also cursed himself. How could he have been too busy to discover the significance of Patty's evening leave from jail?

"Wherefore," Cameron read on, "the petitioner prays that said cause be dismissed. Signed, Herbert Cameron, District Attorney, 191st Judicial District."

Now Tigart passed across a copy of the motion, unfolded to the ready-prepared Order of Dismissal.

Judge Sharman scribbled on his docket book. "I'll grant the motion," he said, "and the Order will be entered in the minutes."

Paulk was helpless.

". . . and the Court, having heard and considered said motion, is of the opinion that the reasons therein assigned are good and sufficient to justify a dismissal of said cause. It is therefore ordered by the Court that said motion be, and the same is, hereby sustained and the defendant go hence without delay and said cause be, and hereby is, dismissed. . . ."

Shep shook her hand. They came about, smiling. Patty waved at Lily Black, whose mouth was forming words meant to be lip-read. Never once looking at her husband, she departed unhurriedly, free except for the federal charge on which she could expect probation. Tigart had paid Patty off under a bargain The Shepherd must have negotiated long before Paulk became involved.

"All right," said the Judge. "Nine o'clock tomorrow."

Priest caught Paulk's arm. "They've turned Patty loose, ain't they?"

"Except for the federal charge." Suddenly the blank, gaping ignorance infuriated him. "Dammit, Ray, if that pleases you, you're too dumb to—"

"Please," Angie Callahan slid between them, just catching her weary hat as it skidded awry. "Poor Baby, he can't help it. This is the first time he's seen her since last January, and she wouldn't even look at him; don't you see?"

"I see," he watched Priest's face, "and I hope he'll think about that tonight. Mrs. Callahan, he's got to understand what this dismissal means, why it happened. They couldn't use her as a witness against her husband. But by killing this charge, they've made her eligible to testify for the defense. She's an eyewitness, and they're going to challenge us to call her, force us to admit in front of this jury that we don't dare put her on. Make him see that, Angie. When his turn comes, he's got to tell *everything*."

Anglin loitered about the table, grinning. "Do you want to state your appreciation orally, Wen? Or will you be putting it in writing?"

"Go blow your nose, you bastard."

At the door he found himself wedged between a fat steamy woman and Herb Cameron. Cameron said, "Have you got a minute?"

The affection he'd always felt for the District Attorney meant nothing at the moment. He said, "Don't tell me a thing, Herb. This time I'd listen."

He plowed clear of the mob pressing toward the elevators and, as he reached the stairs, pondered Hollis Anglin. Somehow, the assistant's advance knowledge of the dismissal wasn't substantial enough as an explanation for Patty's night freedom along Houston Street. There had to be more.

He pushed open a glass door, bumping it against the several old men gathered in the sun to begin their rehash of the court day, and there Billy Shepherd waylaid him.

"Hey, son, what's the rush? Since my client is clear, I've got an idea for you. I figure, what the hell—"

"Leave me alone, Shep."

"Aw, come on, Wen."

"I mean it. Go shove Lily Black into a closet, or something. Just stay away from me."

XXXII

"It's bad," he said, "for Jack to get as furious as all that. Which is why, I suppose, you dragged me away?"

"Partly," Laura smiled. "But he'd have heard it all anyway. Actually, I was more afraid for you."

"How so?"

"Couldn't you tell? Dad was planning to get you drunk."

"Let's turn around, then, and go straight back."

She shook her head. The wind, humming past them as the roadster surged along the newest freeway, hadn't displaced the least strand of her hair. He wondered how she happened to be carrying a spare cigarette over her ear.

"It's the loveliest night yet," she said. "No one should miss it. Shall we pick up Sergeant Blossom?"

He groaned.

A few blocks later, she was serious—her voice marked with caution. "You liked Martha Hutcherson, didn't you?"

"Her, yes. But not what she had to say, or what I did with it this afternoon."

"I'm pleased you feel that way."

"Maybe I'd be," he said, "if I knew why."

"Sometime I'll tell you why, I'm afraid. You know, she telephoned me not long after you left."

"About me?"

"She spoke of you. Oh, really, she just wanted to talk to someone about Valle. Surprised me. Anyway, I'm to come to tea."

"Laura, I wish to God it could be different."

She squealed the car off the paving, on to a gravel drive. "Look," she said, "this will be a gasser. Three features!"

He raised to peer up at the floodlit, muraled backside of a screen tower. "You're joking."

"No, sir. We're going to the movies. Hand me a dollar, will you?"

Minutes passed before she bothered to fetch the small, raspy speaker into the car. He gazed ahead, transfixed by exhaustion, as four golden chariots drawn by white horses four abreast and manned by yelling naked Greek teamsters went charging through a hail of spears. After the first volley from the crossbows, he rested his head on her arm and slept.

XXXIII

Theodore Holcomb and the Judge were working out on each other as the court settled for the Saturday proceedings. The engagement broke off rancorously when, exactly at nine, Nathan Hart and Mrs. McCormick brought the jury to the box. All the regulars were present. In addition, Paulk saw a line of latecomers forming up, in defiance of Sharman's fetish about standees, around the walls. Scanning the room he encountered Lily Black's look of triumph, then old Mr. Durfee's vigorous and meaningless nods. Briefly his gaze met Martha Hutcherson's. He hoped it told her he was sorry she had come.

"Proceed, Mr. Paulk."

He looked at his client. Until you put a man on, you never knew how the witness chair would affect him. Sometimes the theoretical "good witness" succumbed to self-consciousness and fright; a few people, curiously, were incapable of speaking the truth convincingly. Now and then the weak witness you had dreaded became strong and positive under examination. Always there was risk, and when the questionable witness was the defendant, the call amounted to an act of daredeviltry.

"May it please the Court," he said, "let the defendant be sworn."

Priest looked gaunt and small (observe, Juror Gay) as he listened to the oath. Across the table, Tigart had removed his Masonic ring, strung it on a watch chain, and was swinging it thoughtfully, as a pendulum. In the other hand he held a pencil which he tried to poke through the ring. Beside him, Anglin was leaning, whispering.

"I do," Priest said, and sat down.

"State your name to the jury."

"Raymond Elliot Priest."

"Where is your home?"

"Peoria, Illinois."

"How old are you, Ray?"

"Twenty-eight."

Paulk took an envelope from his pocket. It contained his unpaid gas bill. On the back was his ten-word outline for Priest's testimony. He hoped he could follow it. Leisurely, he put his client through the tale of his childhood—his birth at Sand Springs, Oklahoma, to a waitress mother already abandoned by her husband, his pillar-to-post boyhood, his school troubles and earliest hobo jaunts across the country.

Gradually Paulk grew more at ease. Ray was answering directly, and if the vacancy of him discomforted the jury they did not show it. He spoke feelinglessly, so that the pathos of his existence became a thing concluded rather than heard. Even to Paulk, Priest had never sounded as credible. Although his ignorance, his wasted opportunities, were quickly apparent, Ray exhibited an amazing memory. He could state the names of companies and foremen on scores of jobs, he knew the number of days he had passed as sawmill hand, janitor, bar swamper, messenger boy, harvest hand, gandy dancer, pieceworker. He could pinpoint the dates of his journeys, describe the turns in a hundred highways, he recalled every lawn and junk car where he had slept.

"These things took place before you were seventeen?"

"Yes, sir."

"Ray, were you arrested during any of these travels?"

"Yes sir, several times."

"On what charge?"

"I got vagged."

"In every instance, the charge was vagrancy?"

"Yes, sir."

"Did you understand the reason for these arrests?"

"Well," Ray said matter-of-factly, "it's agin the law to be in a town without no money or a job, unless you live there."

Paulk could have cheered. His man looked and sounded as he was, a nobody born without expectations, accepting the dregs of everything as life's normal due. The sluggish mind, the apathy, were turning into assets.

At the insistence of his sister, Ray said, he enlisted in the Air Force in November of 1949. "She figured it was a chance for me to learn a trade." "Did you learn one?" "Yes, sir, they sent me to gunnery school." A gunner by trade? I guess you could say that.

Carefully Paulk developed Priest's war record. He had gone to Korea in obsolete B-25s. He flew ten months of sorties, shared in the kill of a MIG-15, suffered leg wounds from ground fire, and once had bailed out, fracturing both ankles. Most juries accorded a certain stature to the combat veteran, but Paulk's goal reached beyond this. He doubted that Bonita County, in its passion against Ray, had ever paused to regard the prisoner as a man. He wanted them to grasp that Ray Priest bled when hurt, ate when hungry, slept when tired.

He introduced as Defense Exhibits the medals borrowed from Sergeant Blossom, and did so nervelessly. It seemed only a petty duplicity, now, not worth a second thought. Again, Priest reacted well. He acknowledged the Air Medal and Purple Heart with the same uninflection that had conceded his arrests. Paulk hoped the jury saw how Ray, unlike countless others, had never banked upon his decorations as the free passes to a Utopian evermore; how he was unaware of them, presently, as any mockery of the broken hopes that had brought him to this peril.

Ray told candidly of the three years after Korea when he had held no job longer than a month. He had stayed with Angie until the unemployment benefits expired. Afterwards he had hitchhiked around the country, lengthening his vag record, sharing cothouses with drunks and homosexuals, drifting toward his second Air Force enlistment.

"During those years," Paulk said, "just what was the trouble?"

"I dunno, I couldn't get settled down. I was kind of nervous after the war, and I kept having them headaches."

"Were these severe headaches?"

"Well, they were the kind that lasts two or three days."

"Did you see a doctor?"

"No sir, I never had money for doctors."

"Didn't you do anything at all about them?"

"Well, once in a while I taken a drink."

"I see. Now, did these headaches have anything to do with the number of jobs you gave up?"

"I reckon so. Quick as I got to a place, it seemed like I didn't want to stay there, and my head would hurt, and I'd quit and go away."

"Then your nervousness was involved in this also?"

"Well, it messed me up to work around machines, or where there was noise. I couldn't work in no factories."

Through most of 1955, Priest had stayed with the Callahans in Peoria. Then, by answering advertisements, Angie had found him a job in California. Late in September, he had set out for Los Angeles. When, weeks afterwards, he arrived, the job had been filled. Priest had "sort of hung around," picking up odd jobs of short duration. It was that fall, in a bar on Figueroa, that he first saw Patty Sue Black.

"How did you come to meet her, Ray?"

"I seen her come in by herself, and we just got to talking."

"Was that the extent of your contact with her that night?"

"No, sir. I bought her a beer, and we danced a few times."

"Did you see her again after that?"

"Yes, sir, about all the time. I taken her with me, to this room I had. She said her old man had kicked her out, and she didn't have no place else to go."

Since it was going well, Paulk elected to weaken himself a little now, rather than bypass facts which Tigart could produce more damagingly in a later inning. He said, "Did you think it proper to take a young girl to live with you?"

"Well, she didn't want to sleep on the street. Besides that, she told me she was twenty, and another thing was, I asked her to marry me."

"What was her answer to this?"

"She said she'd think about it, sort of see how we got along."

"And did you marry her?"

"Yes, sir, the next February—that was in fifty-six."

"Were you in love with her?"

"Yes, sir."

"Where did the wedding take place?"

"At Louisville, Kentucky."

Paulk considered his client a moment. It was as good a time as any to find out whether Patty's bleached hair, the dismissal and courtroom snub, had made a whole witness of him. "Ray, I'll ask you to tell the jury what events, if any, led up to this marriage."

If Priest's expression changed, it was too slight to gauge. "Wasn't much of anything. I bought a license, and when I showed it to her, she got mad. She said it was because I didn't like some of the guys she'd been going around with. A couple days later, she ran off with a boy-friend she had. I went to his place, and we had a little trouble over it, and they took Patty and me to the police station. When they let us out, we got married."

For an instant, Paulk zoomed over the heights; he would get the candor he wanted. Then it struck him this was a great deal more than he had wanted, and he hurried on. In the ensuing months, Priest said, he and Patty had lived in Peoria with the Callahans, in Glendale with the Blacks, and on the roads that pursued whatever job he heard about. At last, "to make a living," Ray had signed into the Air Force at March Field with Sergeant Blossom as his top-kick. Carefully, Paulk proved up again the headaches, the "spells," the compulsion to escape.

"On these occasions when you went AWOL, was it always to go to Los Angeles to visit your wife?"

"Well, she wasn't in L. A. all the time."

"Where was she?"

"Different times, she was gone different places. I'd hear about her taking off, and I'd head out looking for her."

Stolidly he identified Lily Black as his tipster: "She'd let me know Patty was gone, so if I got leave, I wouldn't be coming to her house."

In April of 1958, the Air Force had transferred Priest to Fitzsimmons General Hospital at Denver. There had been two months of tests: X-rays, brain wave, sessions with sodium pentothal, long visits with doctors who "didn't do much of anything outside of asking questions." At the end of it, the Air Force had expelled him.

"Was it a 'blue' discharge, Ray?"

"Sort of like that."

"I'll ask you to tell the jury the exact terms of this second discharge, if you know them."

"They wrote it down, 'lack of adaptability to the needs of the service.' "

Paulk nodded as to a good pupil. It had taken hours to hammer the precise quotation into Ray's head. "All right, what did you do after being discharged?"

"I hung around Denver for a while."

"Did you have any reason to do this?"

"Yes, sir, I wanted to see if I could find Patty Sue."

"I'll ask you to tell us why, when your wife was missing, you searched for her in Denver?"

Priest evaded. "I just figured she might be there."

"Had she ever indicated that's where she might go?"

"Yes, sir, she did, lots of times."

Paulk pressed him; he could not now let him turn back. "Just what did Patty say to you about Denver?"

"Well," Priest yielded, "whenever she was sore at me, there was two things she would say. One was, she'd say she aimed to dye her hair. The other was that she might run off to Denver and be a hustling woman."

"What, if you know, did she mean by 'hustling woman'?"

"You know. It's a girl that hustles dates."

"A prostitute?"

"Yes, sir."

The jury responded as he'd hoped. They squirmed, looked at each other, tried not to realize the misery of this man while in fact they realized it wholly.

Quietly Paulk said, "Do you know why she'd chosen Denver?"

"She said a hustling woman could make real good money there."

Priest had failed to find Patty Sue. He had been back in Peoria, working, under the admonition of his sister to forget his wife, before he heard from her again. Patty's father had written him to say—

"We'll object," Tigart said, "to anything Patty's daddy might have said in a letter. It's hearsay."

"Sustain."

Paulk had all but forgotten the special prosecutor. Ike still dawdled with his ring and chain, played the game with his pencil.

"Very well," Paulk said. "After receiving that letter, what, if anything, did you do?"

"I headed back to California to see my wife."

"This was in September?"

"Yes, sir, but it was after Christmas before I got there."

"What was the delay?"

"Well, they vagged me at Salt Lake City, and I was in jail sixty days."

"When you reached Los Angeles, did you find Patty Sue?"

"Yes, sir."

"Where was she?"

"They had her in the Detention Home, like Mr. Black said."

"What did you do about that?"

"I commenced trying to get her out."

"And did you obtain her release?"

"Yes, sir, they let me take her out when they got through checking up to see if I was her husband."

"During the course of this effort, did you learn why your wife was in the Detention Home?"

"Yes, sir. Some cops caught her in a rooming house."

"What, if you know, was the specific charge?"

"Well, they called it cohabiting with a man."

Paulk glanced at his notes. "Then, in December of 1958, you were again in California. Did you have a job out there?"

"No, sir."

"Did you have a place to live?"

"No, sir. Patty's mother wouldn't let us in, said she didn't want no more to do with us."

"What did you do for food and shelter?"

"We stayed at a mission for a while. Then we left."

"Where did you go?"

"To Albuquerque. A fellow told me about a job in Florida, and we decided to go there. He gave me a ride as far as Albuquerque for helping him load his truck."

"When did you leave Los Angeles?"

"The eleventh of January."

"And your wife was with you?"

"Yes, sir."

"And this was the trip on which you met Jess Hutcherson?"

"Yes, sir."

Paulk frowned, studying his watch as he said, "Ray, did you kill Mr. Hutcherson?"

"Yes, sir, I did."

As the jury jaws dropped, Paulk said, "Your Honor, since it's nearly eleven, I'd suggest we have a recess."

XXXIV

After the break Paulk veered off toward proof of the circumstances of Ray's confession. With the jury balanced on a crest, big-eared for the defense version of the slaying, he could work in the less engrossing points necessary to his legal position and know they would be heard. At a later juncture, such essentials might go for naught, buried under the reflections on a climax that was already past. If the waiting annoyed them, let it. Jurors, being people, would absorb the sensational facts whenever they could be had.

He drew out the story of the "three laws" entering Angie's house, prodding Ray awake, refusing him permission to call out to the clothesline to his sister; of the long day of interrogation and missed meals, the persuasions and threats of the night, the trick of the oral statement brought off by the FBI agent, the arrival of the "Texas stranger" to stand on Ray's toes and threaten to stomp his guts out, and, finally, the signing after thirty sleepless, foodless hours. He elicited from Priest a description of Ranger A. B. C. Smith before moving on to the second confession, State's Exhibit One, the prosecution's fast shuffle of an ignorant man.

"Ray, in making this second statement, did you tell Mr. Anglin about your headaches?"

"Yes, sir." He had, he said, told them also of his nervousness, his war experience and decorations, his stay at Fitzsimmons Hospital, his problems with Patty Sue. In detail, he said, he had informed the State's attorneys of his conversations with Jess Hutcherson and of certain events of that day. But none of these things had been included in the document.

"When you discovered so much was left out, why didn't you protest to Mr. Tigart and Mr. Anglin?"

"Well," Priest echoed the answer he had given weeks ago in jail, "them being lawyers, I guessed they knew what they were doing."

Paulk nodded, leaving the issue there. Referring to his outline, he proved up the defendant's height and weight. Aside from the contrast of Ray's one hundred forty-five pounds to Hutch's two-ten as a prop to the self-defense plea, he wanted it evident that Ray had lost fifteen pounds in jail. The jurors who required a sign of remorse could interpret this as such; the others, Paulk hoped, might regard it as another index to the spirit of a merciless prosecution.

The preliminaries were done.

"Ray, I believe you've testified that with your wife, you left Los Angeles on January eleventh of this year, riding a truck to Albuquerque, New Mexico. Tell the jury what happened on that trip."

Slowly, staring at Ancil Andricks, Priest told of reaching Albuquerque on the thirteenth, making supper on oranges taken from the truck's cargo, spending the night in a one-dollar hotel room before setting out again. They had hitched rides through Tucumcari and were stranded "someplace a long ways out" when they first saw the Cadillac with the steer horns mounted on the front.

"And the driver of this car was Mr. Jess Hutcherson?"

"Yes, sir."

"What, if anything, did he say to you when he stopped?"

"Well, he asked me if I'd ever driven a car like his, and I said

I never had, and he told me to get in anyway and drive for him because he was tired."

"Was there any further conversation between you?"

"He told me about the starter trouble, and not to kill the engine. He also told me to 'rear back and let 'er eat,' that he was in a big hurry to get home."

"Did he specify the speed at which he wanted to travel?"

"No, sir, not exactly. He just said, 'let your conscience be your guide, boy,' and he said not to worry about the highway patrol because if we got any tickets, he could fix them."

"What, if anything, did Mr. Hutcherson tell you about fixing tickets?"

"Well, he said he was a big man over here in Texas, said he drawed a lot of water. Besides that, he told us he was an officer himself."

"Did he say what kind of an officer he was?"

"Yes, sir. He taken a deputy sheriff's badge out of his pocket and showed it to me, and he showed me the pistol he had there in the car."

Anglin looked up from his note pad, Tigart from his preoccupation with the pencil and ring. It hadn't occurred to Paulk that Patty Sue might have failed to tell them about this. The badge had been that of the honorary deputy, issued to Hutch as to all members of his riding club.

"Ray, what did you think about catching a ride with a man who flashed a gun and badge and told you he was an officer?"

"To tell you the truth, it kind of worried me. Sometimes you get vagged, just for hitchhiking."

"All right. As you drove on, was anything else said?"

"Well, Mr. Hutcherson talked a right smart. He wanted to know who we were, where we was headed, if we had any money to get there on."

"What did you tell him?"

"I told him we had two dollars, and that we was going to Florida to get a job."

"Did he make any comment upon that?"

"He said there was better jobs in the Panhandle than Florida ever heard of. He said when we got to Texas, he'd fix me and my wife up with a place to sleep, and he'd help me get a good job. He said he might even hire me himself."

"Did you agree to accept this offer?"

"Yes, sir, I did, but I didn't figure he meant it."

"Why not?"

"Well, he acted like he'd been drinking quite a bit, and I figured it was the whiskey talking."

"Now, Ray, will you tell the jury what, if anything, Mr. Hutcherson was doing while you drove?"

"Mostly, he was shooting."

Again the State's side of the table grew active. Priest was catching his cues well.

"Tell us about the shooting."

"Well, he had his pistol out the window, and he was trying to hit the fence posts."

"Was there any conversation about this?"

"Yes, sir. He told us he was good with a gun, but said he hadn't had time to practice and needed to catch up."

"Then, you were driving along Highway 66, at high speed, in company with a stranger who was shooting from the car—weren't you disturbed by the situation?"

"It scairt me some. But he said he was a law, so I figured he could do it if he wanted to."

The target shooting had continued through three clips of ammunition, and until they neared the Crossroads Bar. Paulk led Ray to say it was Hutch who proposed the stop. From there on, he selected his questions so that Priest's recapitulation of the bar visit matched the version put into the record by Ellis Browning. Actually, the discrepancies, if plentiful, were minor. By skirting the small disagreements, Paulk could appropriate Brownie's evidence to corroborate the defendant. It was a basic nicety of his plan. Unless he could support Ray's story by the prosecution witnesses, he couldn't support it at all.

He emphasized the drinking, the fact that Patty Sue and Hutch had shared one side of the booth, and Hutch's smiling concentration on the girl as the reason Priest had put an end to her dance.

"And you say your wife was angry when you told her to stop making such a display of herself?"

"Well, she said I didn't want her to have any fun."

"Was this all that was said?"

"Yes, except for Mr. Hutcherson. He said a pretty girl needed to have a good time, and she oughtn't to hide her light under a bushel."

Priest's look grew colder as Paulk guided him through their return to the car and toward the dispute over where each of them should ride.

"Then, because Mr. Hutcherson asked you to, you got under the wheel again?"

"That's right."

"Tell the jury what the argument was about, then."

A stare preceded the answer. "Mr. Hutcherson said he thought he'd ride in the back seat where he could stretch his legs, and he wanted Patty Sue to ride back there with him."

"Did she get into the back?"

"No. I told her to stay up front with me."

"What happened then?"

"Nothing. Mr. Hutcherson said it wasn't anything to get hot over, that we'd just all ride in the front seat again, and that's what we did."

As they drove, Priest said, Hutch took an occasional drink of whiskey. If Patty Sue drank, Ray didn't see it. He had himself consumed part of a beer.

"Aside from the drinking, was Mr. Hutcherson occupied in any other regard during this segment of the trip?"

Priest moistened his lips with a blunt tongue. "Well, I seen he was messing around with my wife."

"What do you mean by 'messing around'?"

"Well, he kept putting his arm around Patty Sue, kind of hugging her up."

"Was that all you saw?"

"No, sir, he goobled around different ways. Sometimes he felt of her leg with his hand, and I heard him asking her how come she wore her brassiere so tight."

"What, if anything, did you do about this?"

"I told him to knock it off. He said he was sorry, that he was a little drunk and there wasn't no harm done since we was all good friends."

Tigart banged his fist on the table. "Your Honor, I'm sick of this hodgepodge of lies and slander and self-serving declarations and I want it stopped. We're turning this man loose to—"

"Overrule," Sharman said. It startled Paulk as much as Ike. The old jurist was pale and scowling but, perhaps, beginning to reconsider his alignment. Paulk hurried on, conducting Priest through the gasoline stop, again avoiding the points that didn't tally with the testimony of the State's witness. He produced the facts Johnny Soloman's account had verified, then steered Priest on to the remainder of the trip.

Hutch had climbed over to the rear seat and begun spinning anecdotes of his career with explosives. Because it was getting dark and the traffic compelled him to watch his driving, Ray said, he was uncertain whether Hutch had any further contact with his wife. "But I did see Patty hanging her hand over the back of the seat."

They drove into town, Priest said, at about seven-thirty.

"I'll ask you whether, at all times, you operated that automobile under Mr. Hutcherson's direction?"

"Yes, sir, I did."

"And after you reached town, did he continue to direct you?"

"Yes, sir. He said to go on through town on the highway, that he knew some motels out on the other side."

"Why, if you know, did he want to find a motel?"

"He said it was to get Patty and me a place for the night."

"At any time during the drive, did you learn whether Mr. Hutcherson had a family?"

"Well, he mentioned that his wife was looking for him for supper. And when we was talking about my Air Force time, he told me he had a son in the Marines."

"From any of these conversations, did you learn where Mr. Hutcherson resided?"

"Yes, sir, right after we got into town he pointed down a street and showed me a house and said it was where he lived. That was when I stopped the car, because I thought he wanted to turn off and Patty and me was supposed to get out."

"Did he put you out of the car there?"

"No, he said go on through to the motel."

"Did you drive on?"

"Yes, sir."

"Where were you the next time you stopped the car?"

"Right yonder," Priest pointed toward the windows, "at the post office. He said to pull in, he wanted to get his mail."

"And did he pick up his mail?"

"No, sir."

"Tell us why he didn't, if you know."

"Well, he told me to take his box key off the car key ring without shutting off the engine, and when I done that, he wanted me to go inside and get his mail for him."

"Why didn't you do as he asked?"

"I didn't care for the looks of it, myself. He wanted Patty Sue to stay with him in the car, and me to go into the post office alone. I wasn't going to do that."

"Why did you refuse, Ray?"

"Because of how he'd been acting up towards Patty. I thought maybe he aimed to ditch me and take her off with him. I didn't see why Patty couldn't go in and get the mail."

"Did he offer to go for the mail himself?"

"No, sir."

"All right, what did you do?"

"We just sat there and talked about it a while. Finally he said, 'to hell with it, let's get going,' and we drove on out the highway to a place he knew about, that Ranch Inn Motel."

Again Paulk hewed to the State's line as established by the motel manager, Robert Nunnally, and the porter, Handy Preston. Skimming over the conflicts, especially the issue of whether Patty Sue wore a skirt or shorts, he put the party in Cabin 4 and waded safely through the clutter of witnessed events that followed.

"Then, when you arrived at the Ranch Inn, it was your belief that Mr. Hutcherson intended to leave you there and return to his home?"

"Yes, sir."

"I'll ask you to tell this jury when you first learned that your wife had rented a two-bedroom cabin."

"I didn't know it until I walked in there."

"Didn't you wonder about the situation when Mr. Hutcherson told you to shut off the car, since you knew it wouldn't start again?"

"Well, I knew he was coming inside, but I figured it was just to use the bathroom."

"Actually, you saw him use the bathroom, didn't you?"

"Yes, sir."

"And the porter saw it?"

"Yes, sir, he was standing right there."

"And your wife saw him too?"

"Yes, sir."

"Did you speak to Mr. Hutcherson about this behavior?"

"Well, I told him I wished he wouldn't do stuff like that in front of my wife."

"Did he answer you?"

"Yes, sir; he said he forgot to shut the door, said he didn't mean nothing by it."

After Handy Preston put the TV set in order, Priest said he sat sipping beer and watching the prize fight. Hutch, he remembered, had retired to the back bedroom, taking the whiskey along with him. Patty Sue had wandered about the suite, complaining of boredom. "She kept going back to Mr. Hutcherson's room, then coming back to mine. After a while, I told her to sit down and stay with me . . . yes, sir, she done it. She taken a chair and read some comic books we had."

"And you did not, at any time, drink any of the whiskey?"

Judge Sharman's concern swelled at each mention of the whiskey. The old cavalier turned his beautiful scowl upon the crowd, his saddened eyes begging them to profit from this tragic example. See, his manner said, this is liquor's ugly drama; without the drinks, a catastrophe might have been averted. It freed Paulk to underscore Hutch's drinking by repetitions Tigart could protest only futilely.

When the topic wore thin, he directed Priest through a showing that he had made no effort to pass unnoticed at the motel. Then, because Ike would contend that Ray had tried to repair the car because it was vital to his scheme for flight, Paulk produced an account of the incident.

"Now, Mr. Priest, tell this jury why you made such a long and earnest effort to correct the car trouble."

"Well, I figured I owed him something, since he had given us a ride and paid for us a room. I wanted to fix it for him if I could."

"When he told you to leave the car alone, what did you do?"

"I went back inside and laid down on the bed."

"In the front room?"

"Yes, sir."

"What, if you recall, was your position on the bed?"

"I laid down with my head toward the foot, so I could see the television."

"Was anyone else present in that room?"

"Patty Sue. She was reading some more."

"And Mr. Hutcherson was in the back bedroom?"

"I reckon so; Patty said he was."

"All right, what happened then, if anything?"

"I went to sleep. I was pretty tired."

"Had you taken off your clothes?"

"No, sir, just my shoes."

"Can you tell us how long you slept?"

"I reckon it was about an hour, maybe some less."

"What caused you to wake up?"

"I dunno, it seemed like it was being hungry. We hadn't et nothing that night."

"When you awakened, was anyone in the room with you?"

"No."

"Were the lights still on?"

"Yes, sir."

"How about the television set?"

"It was still going."

"What, if anything, did you do next?"

"Well, I turned the TV off, and I laid back down to sort of figure out where I was, and then I looked around for my wife."

Juror Glass was taking notes. Behind him, Turner swiveled from side to side. The others, even Willie Studer, were still, intent, and, Paulk hoped, believing.

"Did you see your wife?"

"Not first off, I didn't. After a couple of minutes, I seen her come out of the bathroom."

Paulk tried to keep the excitement out of his voice. "I'll ask you to tell us now what you observed about your wife at that moment."

Priest's white lashes blinked over cold, suddenly dilated eyes.

Gently Paulk said, "You'll have to answer this, Ray."

"Well, I seen she had her clothes off."

"She had removed her outer clothing?"

"No, all of it. She was—nekkid as the day she was born."

"I'll ask you if—"

"Just a minute, Mr. Paulk." The Judge sounded heartsick. "In view of the direction this testimony is taking, I believe it's my duty to say a few words to you who are here as spectators. Particularly you ladies—you should have the opportunity to absent yourselves if you wish, and you may do so now."

There was an embarrassed stir. Cheeks colored, eyes were lowered, but no one left the pews. Sharman reddened.

"Very well," he said. "It's my right to enforce my own conscience upon you as I see fit. Therefore, I will insist that all you unmarried ladies, and those of you who are under twenty-one, retire from the courtroom at this time."

The idle lawyers encircling the pit winked at each other as shop girls, typists and pairs of teen-agers got up and, with scarlet faces and high heads, marched to the door. Other women squeezed in from the corridor to claim their places. Curiously, no one ogled. It was as if everyone took pains not to look at anyone else. During the shuffle, Paulk thought of Martha Hutcherson and Valle. If the widow remained in her seat, he had no desire to know it.

"Proceed," said the Judge.

Paulk said, "Ray, did Patty's nudity alarm you?"

"Not right then. I figured she was coming in to bed."

"Did she come to your room?"

"No, sir."

"What did you do about this?"

"Nothing. I laid back down. I thought maybe she had turned around and gone back into the bathroom."

"How long did you wait for her?"

"Maybe five or ten minutes."

"When she didn't appear, did you do anything about it?"

"Well, I finally got up and went and looked in the bathroom."

"Was she there?"

"No."

"All right, then what did you do, if anything?"

Priest's fists had closed on his knees; the heavy chin might have trembled. "Wasn't but one place else she could be. I pushed open the door to Mr. Hutcherson's room."

Paulk heard the whir of the electric clock. "Was the room dark?"

"No, sir, the light was burning."

"I'll ask you to tell this jury exactly what you saw."

Priest appeared to waver between rage and a bleak resignation. After thirty seconds he said, "I seen them in bed together."

"You saw the deceased, Jess Hutcherson, in bed with your wife?"

"Yes, sir. He had her—"

"Was your wife still undressed?"

"Yes, sir."

"And how was Mr. Hutcherson dressed?"

"He was bare-nekkid, too."

Sharman rapped to curtail a stir that didn't begin. Except for the sound of his knuckles, the room remained deathly still.

Paulk said, "Tell the jury what their position was."

"She—my wife was lying on the bed, and he was on top of her."

"Did they appear to be embracing?"

"It was more than that."

"How near to them were you, Ray?"

"Maybe four or five feet."

"With the lights on, standing just four or five feet away, could you see with certainty exactly what they were doing?"

"Yes, sir; he was doing it to her, right then."

"By 'it' do you mean the act of sexual intercourse?"

"Yes, sir."

Paulk sat back, allowing it to sink in, realizing he had never been as convinced of the adultery as now. When Priest seemed ready, he said, "Can you tell us what happened next?"

Ray rubbed his forehead; it was the gesture Paulk had hoped for during the headache testimony. "I know I seen red, and I went after him. The rest ain't very clear to me."

"When you 'went after him,' were you armed?"

"No, I didn't have nothing."

Paulk couldn't help a skepticism of what came next. Some men would recall every word and move of such a moment; others might truly black out. Ray claimed a touch of both, partly remembering, partly forgetting. Nevertheless, it had to be risked if the self-defense plea was to be served.

"How did Mr. Hutcherson react, if he did?"

"It ain't too plain. I know he rolled off of her and he was cussing. He hollered he was going to kill me, and I saw him pull his gun out from under the pillow."

"All right, what did you do?"

"Well, I know I got the gun away from him, and I guess I hit him with it."

"Do you remember hitting him?"

"No, but afterwards I could see he'd been hit."

"Did you see anything tied around his neck?"

"Yes, sir."

"A shirt?"

"I never did know what it was. I kind of thought it was a towel."

"Can you tell us how this shirt, or towel, got there?"

"No, sir."

"What was your wife doing during this clash between Mr. Hutcherson and yourself?"

"I don't know; I was pretty excited." His first clear recollection, he said, was of standing beside the bed, holding the gun. "I saw the blood, and I seen there was some on my pants."

"How did you feel at that time, Ray?"

"I dunno. Scairt, I guess, and sort of wobbly. I remember I wanted to get moving, be a long ways gone."

"Did you get moving?"

"Well, not right off. My wife came in there and said I ought to change my clothes, and she handed me some to put on. I went to the bathroom and cleaned up, and when I came out, Patty Sue was ready, and we took off."

He hadn't looked into the bedroom again. No, he'd not drawn the bedspread up to cover the body; he'd not toured the rooms to wipe away fingerprints, nor had he seen any money.

"On your oath, then, you are telling this jury that you did not take Mr. Hutcherson's money?"

"I didn't take it. I never stole anything in my life."

During the flight, Priest said, he sometimes pushed Hutch's car up to 110 miles per hour. "I kept thinking what cops do to anybody who hurts an officer."

"Then, you still thought of Mr. Hutcherson as a deputy?"

"Yes, sir; he never told me any different."

Priest, despite his road-map mind, could not name the place they'd stopped for gasoline.

"How much gasoline did you get?"

"I asked for five gallons, because two dollars was all I had. But my wife said to the fellow, 'fill 'er up.' She said she could pay for it."

"And did she pay?"

"Yes, sir."

"Did you see the money?"

"Yes, sir, she had plenty of it."

"Did your wife offer any explanation as to how she came to have this money?"

"She told me Mr. Hutcherson had given it to her."

"Did you then, or later, have the opportunity to discover just how much money Patty Sue did have?"

"Not exactly, but it was several hundred. I know that when we split up the next morning, she gave me a handful to travel on, and when I got around to counting it, it was a hundred and eighty."

"After giving you the hundred and eighty dollars, did your wife still have some money left?"

"Yes, sir, she kept a heap more than that."

Ray described their second stop; a Coke for Patty, hamburgers for himself, with Patty paying for them. Then they had driven an hour on the wrong road, turned back, continued east to arrive at El Reno shortly before daybreak. It was there they agreed to separate and meet at a rooming house in Atlanta. Patty had caught the bus. Ray had loitered around the El Reno freight yards until a railroad detective cited him to a ride on a truck. Priest hadn't reached Atlanta until Sunday morning, three days after the flight began. Patty wasn't at the rooming house. Searching, he had at last found her in a bar where he'd once worked as a swamper.

"What, if anything, passed between you and your wife that day?"

"Well, she showed me a newspaper she had. It said Mr. Hutcherson was dead, and they were hunting for us."

"Was that the first time you knew he was dead?"

"Yes, sir."

"Did this knowledge have any effect upon your plans?"

"Sure, I didn't much know what to do. I talked to my wife about giving up; telling 'em what happened. She thought we ought to get as far away as we could."

"And what did you decide?"

"Well, we finally agreed to go on down to Florida, just like we aimed to in the first place."

At Tampa they had moved in with friends. He'd failed to get the job he'd heard of in Los Angeles. Then, after a week, Patty Sue had vanished.

"What did you do about this?"

"I went looking for her."

"Where did you look?"

"I went to Denver."

"Was this because she had threatened to go to Denver to become a 'hustling woman'?"

"Yes, sir. I had to look somewheres."

"Did you find your wife there?"

"No, I didn't see her no more."

Paulk paused, reviewed, trying to make sure he'd missed nothing he needed. Judge Sharman cleared his throat. "Mr. Paulk, since it's twelve-thirty, I think we might recess for lunch. Unless, of course, you've about finished."

"May it please the Court, I've just a few more questions."

"Very well, proceed."

"Thank you. Mr. Priest, I want to call your attention once more to last March twenty-eighth, the day you made your statement to Mr. Anglin and Mr. Tigart up there in jail. During that interrogation by these gentlemen, did you tell them all the facts you've given us here today?"

"Yes, sir, I did."

"But these matters aren't included in the statement read here as State's Exhibit One, is that correct?"

"Yes, sir, they left out a lot of things."

"Did you tell them about Mr. Hutcherson's 'goobling around'?"

"Yes, sir."

"About seeing your wife in bed with him?"

"Yes, sir."

"About Mr. Hutcherson threatening to kill you and reaching for his gun?"

"Yes, sir."

"Now, did either of these gentlemen, Mr. Tigart or Mr. Anglin, say anything to you that day as to why these facts were not set down by them in the statement you signed?"

"Mr. Anglin did. He said they couldn't put down everything, or it would run too long."

"Weren't you under arrest, in custody, when this occurred?"

"Yes, sir."

"Ray, I'll ask you if you've ever been convicted of a felony."

"No, sir, I never was."

"Have you ever owned a gun?"

"No, sir."

"Ray, I want you to tell the Court and the jury whether at any time on January fourteenth you planned to rob Jess Hutcherson?"

"I did not."

"Did you at any time intend to kill him?"

"No. All I done was let him give me a lift—"

"What, to the best of your knowledge and recollection, was your intention when you saw Jess Hutcherson in the sex act with your wife?"

"I aimed to get him off her. She—she was my wife, not his." It was better, surer, than Paulk had expected.

"What, if you know, was your purpose when he pointed his pistol at you?"

"I guess I didn't mean to stand there and get shot."

"What was your state of mind at that time?"

"I ain't sure what you mean, Mr. Polk."

"The question is, were you thinking coolly, deliberately, calculating your actions?"

"A man sees his wife like that," Priest spoke almost below hearing, "I guess he don't have any mind."

"Were you financially able to employ an attorney to represent you in this case?"

"No."

"Now, I'll ask you if you know a reward was offered for your arrest and conviction?"

"Yes, sir; I've heard of that."

"Do you know who turned you in to the police?"

"My wife, they said."

"Do you know, also, that your wife has applied for the reward?"

"Yes, sir."

"Knowing these things, Mr. Priest, do you bear any ill will toward Patty Sue?"

"No, sir, she's my wife."

Paulk nodded to the bench. "That's all."

XXXV

Ike Tigart returned from lunch fresh-shaven. The short red hair had a new trim, looked flatter on top. He had put on a fierce orange tie and flushed his mouth of its tobacco. The special prosecutor, Paulk thought, was determined to give the Hutcherson family their money's worth. Although wild, shouting cross-examinations were supposed to be passé, gone with the days of illiterate jurors, Ike wore all the signs.

Paulk stared a last warning to his client. Priest, waiting on the stand, refused to look at him. A knot hardened in Paulk's stomach.

"All right," the Judge nodded.

Tigart was cumbersome, formidable, as he picked up the pistol and approached the witness. "You!" he cracked the word like a whip. "You are the man that killed Jess Hutcherson, aren't you?"

Priest nodded.

"Smashed him with this gun, bashed his skull into his brain, garroted him with his own shirt, bled his veins white—*you* did these things, didn't you?"

Priest stared back, blank and silent.

"Well, didn't you?"

"I hit him, if that's what you want me to say."

Gripping the automatic by the barrel, Tigart chopped downward as if striking with a hammer. "Is this how you hit him?"

Paulk said, "May it please the Court, none of us is deaf. I want the prosecutor to take his seat—"

"Oh, dry up!" Tigart wheeled. "I'll cross-examine just as I please, without any static from you."

"Your Honor—"

Ike cut off the appeal, whirling back to the witness. "How many times did you hit him? Three, four, twenty times?"

Now Paulk was shouting. "Your Honor, I move we adjourn until this maniac can compose himself."

"Damn you, Junior, if you don't shut your trap—"

Sharman was up, signaling frantically for the sheriff, crying "See here!" Nathan Hart slid in front of Tigart. Suddenly, all was quiet. The Judge glared down, shaking his head as if unsure of what he'd seen and heard. One of his frail knuckles seemed to be bleeding.

"Now take your seats, both of you. Mr. Tigart, you will cross-examine from your chair, except when you've got something for the witness to identify. We aren't going to turn this into a sideshow."

A tense, hushed minute passed before Tigart again held the gun up to Priest. "*Mister* Priest, will you tell us whether this is the weapon you used to kill Jess Hutcherson?"

"I reckon it is."

Ike tossed the pistol to Mr. Funderburg and tramped back to his chair. "Now, *sir*," he said sweetly, "since we've heard so much about your sensitivity to noise, I'll ask you to describe just what it sounds like to beat a man's head to a pulp."

"I don't know if they was any sound."

"Oh? I believe you've told us that factory noises—actually, the sound of work—give you a strange impulse to get away. I'm wondering if the sound of those death blows affected you the same way, caused you to run from Cabin 4 at 110 miles an hour?"

Priest swallowed. "I don't remember no sounds."

"Maybe we can stimulate your memory a little. When the butt of that pistol crashed through Mr. Hutcherson's skull, did you hear a thud?"

"I don't know."

"Or," Ike had Patty's statement spread before him now, "do you recall that it sounded like—let's see, here—'like when you stomp on mud'?"

"May it please the Court," Paulk sighed, "the witness has already said he knows of no sounds. I suggest that—"

"Sustain."

"When you'd finished your killing, what did you do with the gun?"

"I guess I kept it."

"As a matter of fact, you cleaned it up and put it in your belt and took it with you, didn't you?"

"I reckon I did."

"Tell the jury why you took the gun with you."

"I wasn't thinking very good. I don't know why."

"Is it possible you intended to use it again if somebody tried to stop you?"

"I wasn't out to hurt nobody."

"Is it possible that, having just reached the status of a celebrated killer, you felt obligated to pack a gun?"

"I never thought nothing like that."

Tigart pawed out the confession and forced Priest to acknowledge it. He compelled Priest to concede that nothing on which he now defended himself had been included in it. "Did you hold back these things just to confuse Mr. Anglin? Are you telling us the assistant district attorney of the 191st Judicial District is a crook who was out to get you any way he could? No? Isn't it the plain truth, Ray, that these claims are missing from this document because, back there on March twenty-eighth, you hadn't thought them up?"

"That ain't true."

"If I understand your testimony, Ray, there were only three people in that bedroom that night, is that correct?"

"Yes, sir."

"One is dead, one is on trial—would you like to have the third party, your wife, get up here and tell us what happened, now that she is eligible to testify?"

"Objection!" Paulk came up, stammering with fury, "that's a rotten stunt, putting before this jury something they cannot legally know. I want—"

"Sustain," the Judge ruled hastily. "The jury is instructed not to consider the question for any purpose."

"I haven't finished my objection," Paulk steamed toward the bench. "If this axman can tell the jury Mrs. Priest is available as a witness, then I can tell them he dismissed the murder indictment against her yesterday just to pave the way for this breech of the rules! If the State is challenging me to put on a hostile, reward-happy witness who has already given a half-dozen versions of what she saw—"

"Your Honor," Tigart said, "he's making a speech!"

"May it please the Court, the defendant moves a mistrial."

Sharman grimaced. "Now, Mr. Paulk, you"ve objected, and I have sustained you. Mr. Tigart, if you have anything to say about which witnesses may not appear in this case, you'll withhold those comments until you offer your argument. Let's get on, not bicker away the rest of the day."

Paulk said, "I've asked a mistrial."

"The motion is denied."

"We except to the ruling. I want my bill to note that the Court has acknowledged the improper conduct, the error by the State—"

"I've sustained an objection," Sharman said, "but I've said nothing at all about error. Get on, Mr. Tigart."

Paulk surrendered bitterly. The damage was done. The jury understood that Patty Sue could be called by the defense, but wouldn't be because the defendant didn't dare. The insinuation of guilt was strong and without remedy. Only Priest appeared not to realize it.

Displaying a nice blend of anger and disgust, Tigart clipped along into the robbery issue. He wrung from Priest the details of the money incidents at the bar and in the motel, building well before he asked, "Did you comment to your wife about Hutch's pocket roll?"

"Not that I remember."

"Perhaps I can refresh you as we go along. At the bar, didn't you tell your wife, 'A man who flashes that kind of dough is just begging to get shut of it'?"

"No."

"Your clean, All-American mind just doesn't run in those channels, is that it? The money didn't impress you?"

"I never said anything about his money."

"What about when you were outside the cabin, tinkering with the car? Do you recall saying to your wife, 'Honey, we could live high on the hog on a wad like the boss is toting'?"

"I didn't say it."

"All right, Ray. Just when *did* you decide to rob Jess?"

"I done told you, I never did."

Weren't the hijacking plans, the decision to kill if necessary, complete in his mind when, to insure a dependable means of escape, he worked on the automobile? Wasn't it Hutch's money he had spent during his flight?

"All I spent was what my wife gave me."

"Oh, I see. You never dreamed that was Hutch's money?"

"I knew what she told me, that's all."

"Until this stop for gasoline, then, you just had no idea whatsoever that all that cash was in the car with you?"

"That's right."

"You want us to believe that you killed Jess Hutcherson, stole his pistol, stole an eight-thousand-dollar automobile, and drove away thinking you were leaving his money behind?"

"I ain't asking anybody to believe anything except what happened."

"I suppose you can't remember handing your wife three or four hundred dollars and saying 'There's plenty more where this came from'?"

"I didn't do that."

"Very well. Since Mr. Hutcherson was dead, why *didn't* you take that money?"

"On account of I ain't a thief."

"By your peculiar standards, then, running off with a Cadillac isn't a theft?"

Paulk said, "I'll object to this badgering by the special prosecutor, and to his questions on collateral matters not in issue. The defendant is not on trial for car theft or pistol theft or any other theft." It was an amateurish protest, and he knew it.

Tigart smiled. "Your Honor, the State is seeking to show flight, guilty knowledge, possession of the fruits of a crime, all of which are clearly admissible by proximity to the homicide and as part of the *res gestae,* not to mention the fact that defense counsel went into these things on direct examination. Of course, if we've time to waste, I'm willing to coach my young friend in the ways of the law—"

Paulk said, "I don't choose to study under a fatheaded windbag."

"That'll do!" The Judge snapped out of a light doze. "Let's get some work done, if you please."

Tigart lifted his shoulders to his ears and mugged the jury as he resumed. "Ray, while you were speeding along the highway in this car you didn't steal, carrying this gun you hadn't stolen, enjoying this money you didn't take, getting away from this killing that wasn't murder, did you have any conversation with your wife?"

"I reckon we talked some."

"Tell us, what did you say to her about killing Hutch?"

"Nothing that I can think of."

"I wonder if you remember saying to her, 'You better believe me, I sure took care of that sonofabitch.' "

Priest blew an accidental spit bubble as he retorted, "I didn't ever say nothing like that."

Tigart bored on in, artfully weaving Patty Priest's statement into the record. Under cross-examination's special privilege of leading the witness, Ike framed his questions so that they overwhelmed the answers. Ray's wife seemed to have armed the prosecutor with a mass of incriminating *res-gestae* remarks, and there was nothing Paulk could do to block them. The jury, he feared, was lapping it up.

Abruptly Tigart switched to the manner of the killing. Had Ray clubbed Hutch to death instead of shooting him because clubbing was quieter? Why, after Hutch's head was bashed in, had Priest tied the shirt around his neck?

"I don't recollect any shirt."

"Were you trying to make sure you'd done a good job of it?"

"I told you, I don't know why anything was like it was."

"Tell us, just what were you doing when you drew that bedspread over his body? Did you think that would hide him?"

"Wasn't me done that. I never touched the bed—"

"Why, if you killed in self-defense as you now claim you did, why didn't you step to the telephone and call the police?"

"Well, after that scene I saw—"

"Why, Ray, if your mind was so unsound you couldn't tell right from wrong, did you pack up and run?"

"Well, a man sees another feller on his wife—"

Again Tigart cut off the answer. Paulk might have objected, but he decided he liked it better this way. Priest, if he began volunteering explanations, could be dangerous to himself. Besides, Juror Gay was frowning at the special prosecutor and, to Paulk, it appeared Ancil Andricks was becoming annoyed. The stolid denials, then, were enough.

Why had Ray permitted Patty's sensual dance to continue twenty minutes before he interfered? Why hadn't he stopped Hutch's so-called "goobling around" the instant it began? Why had he been laughing, enjoying himself at Soloman's service station, if he was distressed by this fondling of his wife? Why, in heaven's name, hadn't he fought for her?

"Him having a badge and a gun, I didn't see there was much I could do."

"The better part of valor," Ike said in sarcasm as he peered at his notes. "Now, I believe it's your testimony that you drank two beers at the bar, another in the car, and maybe some more after you got to the motel, is that correct?"

"Something like that."

"Since you left the Crossroads carrying a six-pack, and since you've told us Mr. Hutcherson drank only whiskey, and since the officers tell us all the beer cans found in the motel room were empty, can we assume that you drank eight beers that day?"

"I wouldn't say I had that much."

"Did you take some beer with you after the killing, just to nip at along the road?"

"No, sir, I did not."

"Did Patty Sue help drink up that six-pack, then?"

"She sure didn't. My wife don't drink much, ever."

"But you still doubt that you drank it all?"

"If I did, I know I wasn't drunk."

"Eight beers don't make you drunk, Ray?"

"Not scattered out over eight or ten hours they don't."

"How many does it take to make you drunk?"

"I don't know how many."

"During all your years in bars and flophouses and honkytonks you haven't found out just what your capacity is?"

"I guess I've got an idea."

Ike was playing the flipside of Paulk's own tune, picking up points with the Judge.

"If anybody was drunk in Cabin 4 that night, it was you, wasn't it?"

"No, I wasn't drunk."

"Ray, are you telling us you are capable of crushing a man's skull, then strangling his corpse, while you're cold sober?"

"That wasn't what I said."

Tigart swung aside, into a new bombardment. "You were a pretty sorry soldier, weren't you? How many times AWOL? How many stretches in the guardhouse? Were these military crimes brought on by your headaches, or are they supposed to have resulted from your wife's good judgement in trying to get away from you? You weren't wounded in the head, were you? You were a bum, loafer, a perennial sponger off your sister long before you ever went to Korea, isn't that correct?"

"You ought to have some of my headaches your own self."

"I think," Ike said, "that I'm suffering one this very minute."

"And I," Paulk felt bearish, "am suffering a pain in the neck. Would the Court please instruct the Great Red One to reserve his personal comments for his autobiography?"

"This is research, Mr. Paulk. I'd like my memoirs to disclose just why, out of seventeen million veterans in this country, this butcher is supposed to be singled out for pity!"

"I object to—"

"Gentlemen! This disrespect, this snarling and table talk has got to stop. Mercy, if you have no charity for each other. . . ."

Tigart returned to work moodily. "Ray, your discharge from the hospital up at Denver wasn't a medical discharge, was it?"

"No."

"Up there, they examined you for two months, studied you from stem to stern, without finding you were insane?"

"They said 'unadaptable,' or something like that."

"You don't like it when I ask you about robbery, do you?"

"I sure don't, because I ain't a thief."

"Is that because you think it's wrong to steal?"

"Yes, sir."

Paulk closed his eyes. The snare was well constructed. He'd not warned Ray of it, and the poor fool had grabbed the bait.

Ike said, "I take it, then, that you know right from wrong?"

"I reckon I do."

"Are you aware that under the law of this state, a man who knows right from wrong is fully responsible for his acts?"

"When I get one of them spells—"

"Don't you think it's wrong to shatter a sleeping man's skull?"

"That wasn't what—"

"Isn't it wrong to sit there lying under oath to this jury?"

"I told you, I—"

"It's wrong, isn't it, to—"

"Your Honor," Paulk shouted, "this bellowing moose is cutting off the defendant's answers and making assumptions in his questions that are no part of the testimony or the record. I want the witness heard, even if we've got to ice down this swollen head."

Again the wrangle, the wan mediation, the resolution that was without force. With a real judge, Paulk thought, he might have protected Priest. Here it wasn't possible. When it was over, Ike was again ruffling through Patty's typewritten statement.

"Ray, when did you get the idea to accuse Jess Hutcherson of adultery as a way to save your hide?"

"It wasn't no idea."

"Didn't Hutch tell you that day that he was sick?"

"He said he was tired."

"Didn't he go into that motel after telling you he was too sick at the moment to drive himself home?"

"I never heard anything like that."

"You still want us to believe that a man like Jess Hutcherson would take a teen-age girl into a motel room, and would take her to bed with her husband in the next room and the door unlocked?"

"That's what he done."

Tigart took up his ring, swung it, darted a pencil at it, and missed. "All right, supposing this thing did happen, your wife was willing, wasn't she?"

"She was not!"

"Are you saying your wife was being raped?"

Priest clenched the arms of the chair. "I seen what happened."

"Did you hear her scream for help?"

"Well, at first, I was asleep. I don't know if she hollered."

"The next time you saw her, was she bruised, scarred up?"

"Not that I saw, she wasn't."

"When you walked in on them, as you claim you did, was your wife fighting Mr. Hutcherson?"

"I don't know, everything happened so quick."

"As long as this ring is moving," Tigart said, "I cannot jab this pencil through it. Now, I'll ask you—"

"I object!" Paulk jumped from his chair. "The special prosecutor is injecting his cute remarks again, trespassing on the prerogatives of the jury. I move it be stricken, and that the Court instruct Mr. Tigart to retire to the pool hall if he wants to continue his obscene demonstrations. I—"

"Hold on," the Judge waved a hand as if fending off assault, "let's don't get another one of those things started. I'll sustain the objection, and the jury is instructed not to consider that ring and pencil business for any purpose."

Tigart's voice took on a sympathetic, confidential tone. "Ray, tell the jury exactly what you said when you offered to sell your wife to Jess Hutcherson for the night."

"I never did that!"

"I take it you'd just never stoop so low as to swap your wife for a night's lodging?"

Tigart burrowed into the papers for the long, blue-mimeographed FBI rap sheet Paulk had been dreading. Priest recognized it also, and his jaw muscles hardened.

"How many times have you been arrested, Ray?"

"I don't know."

"How about the figure 'seventeen'—does that ring a bell?"

"I don't hear any bells."

"You've been locked up in jails in how many states?"

"Not very many."

"What about *nine* states—does that figure sound about right?"

"It might be; I never counted."

"I'll ask you whether you've ever been arrested in the state of California for pimping?"

"No, sir; vagrancy, that's all they said."

"Were you arrested in October, 1958, at Salt Lake City, Utah, on a charge of procuring men for a prostitute named Mickey Halton?"

"They was a mistake about that."

"Were the police mistaken on those arrests in Los Angeles, Cleveland, Tulsa, Kansas City?"

"Vag was what it was."

Tigart snorted. "Do you know what pandering is?"

"I guess so."

"And procuring?"

"Yes."

Behind Paulk, Angie Callahan was crying.

"Do you suppose there are any police files around the country that mention these things in connection with you?"

"I ain't seen any files."

"Have you ever heard of a place in Atlanta, Georgia, called the Bachelor Inn?"

"I've heard of it."

"What sort of a place is it?"

"It's a rooming house."

"Isn't this the place where you agreed to meet your wife after you had abandoned Mr. Hutcherson's car in El Reno?"

"Yes, sir."

"You'd been there before, hadn't you, in July of 1957?"

"I don't remember if I was there then or not."

"I was afraid your memory might dim a little, so I am prepared to help you. Didn't you live with your wife in Room 37 of the Bachelor Inn through July of that year?"

"We might have."

"Were you working in Atlanta?"

"Well, I went there looking for a job."

"Of course, looking," Tigart said. "How did you pay the rent?"

Paulk was tense, irate with his client. Whatever Ike had, Priest had failed to tell him about it.

"The way I remember," Priest said, "we had a little money."

"Did Patty Sue have a job?"

"No, I don't like my wife to work."

"During that July, didn't you buy a suit of clothes and make a down payment on a used automobile?"

"I might have."

"Isn't it fact, Ray, that you spent a lot of time that summer sitting in a chair in the hall, just outside the door of Room 37?"

"Not that I recollect."

"Didn't you spend some time out around the state capitol, talking to men who were in and out of there on business?"

"Well, I tried to get me a job out there, I remember that."

"Your wife was about sixteen years old then, wasn't she?"

"I imagine that's about right."

"A lot of fellows visited your room that month, didn't they?"

"Not many I know of."

"I'll ask you whether, during July of 1957, you brought as many as twenty men a day to that room and whether you sat out there in the hall to collect from them as they left your wife?"

"That ain't—"

"I object," Paulk didn't trust himself to look at Priest, lest the jury read on his face the loathing he felt. "The witness has answered repeatedly that none of these things happened. Further, the prosecutor is inquiring into *alleged* events too remote to have any bearing on this case."

Tigart smiled. "May it please the Court, the suspended-sentence application puts in issue here this man's reputation as a peaceful, law-abiding citizen. Moreover, having become a witness, he is subject to examination on all such matters as touch upon his credibility."

Paulk gazed out the window to cover his defeat. The State had chosen to meet the adultery issue, head on, with proof of connivance. He wished they'd clung, instead, to a pooh-pooh of it all.

"Ray, how old was Patty Sue when you latched on to her and took her to live with you?"

"Fourteen. But I didn't know it."

"In your meandering around the country, on that fleabag and beer-hall circuit of yours, you always took her with you?"

"I never ran off and left her."

"I believe you've told us she had turned fifteen, and you were at Louisville, Kentucky, when you finally got around to marrying her, is that correct?"

"Yes, sir."

"And the ceremony, I think you said, took place shortly after the two of you were dismissed from jail?"

"That's right."

"I'll ask you what happened between Patty Sue and yourself to precipitate that wedding?"

"Nothing I know of happened."

"Didn't you take her around behind the city hall and beat her up with your fists?"

"I did not. I always treated my wife good."

Ike put a thick red finger on something in Patty's statement. "If the bride went to the altar with a black eye and a broken tooth and two fractured ribs, you just don't know anything about it?"

"It wasn't like that."

"You've always treated her with kindness?"

"That's the truth, I always did."

"Never had any fights with her?"

"I guess married people fuss sometimes."

"Then you did 'fuss' with your wife occasionally?"

"Once't in a while, but it never amounted to nothing."

"Never amounted to nothing," Tigart echoed him. "It was of no consequence, then, when you took a notion to beat her up?"

"I never said I beat her up."

"Did you ever strike her?"

"A few times, maybe. But not like you make it sound."

"When you were living with your mother-in-law at Glendale, didn't you receive a dividend check on your GI insurance?"

"Yes."

"What did you do with the money?"

"We used it for different expenses we had."

"I'll ask you whether you spent that money on a binge, then knocked your wife senseless for asking what you'd done with it?"

"That's a lie."

Ike stretched, shaking his head at the jury. "Ray, your marriage hasn't produced any children, has it?"

"No."

"But it might have, mightn't it?"

"I guess so."

"Isn't it a fact that during your second Air Force enlistment, Patty wrote you she was pregnant?"

"Yes, but it turned out she wasn't."

"Tell the jury whether you went AWOL, joined your wife at her mother's home, and pounded her in the belly with your fists until she had a miscarriage!"

"That ain't so!" The answer was lost, stifled under repugnance like a stench. Jurors winced. Women gasped, then craned to watch Angie Callahan cry.

"Now, Ray, it's all a vast mystery to you that your wife would turn you in for this killing, isn't it?"

"They don't let me see her, so I can't find out anything."

"Do you think she might be afraid of you?"

"Wouldn't be no reason for that."

"When you were down there in Tampa, hiding from police, did you ever say to her, 'You better keep quiet if you don't want the same dose I gave that Texan'?"

"I never said that."

"Calling your attention, just once more, to the Ranch Inn and January fourteenth, isn't it a fact that you took Mr. Hutcherson's gun from his car while you were out there tinkering with the engine?"

"I already told you, the gun was under his pillow."

"Didn't you wait until you knew Mr. Hutcherson was asleep, and didn't you creep into his room and without saying one word, begin beating his brains out?"

"That was *my* wife! I seen—"

"Your Honor," Tigart turned his back, "I'm sick of this witness. No more questions."

XXXVI

The outlook was only dismal. He wished he had kept Priest off the stand. Until the cross-examination, he had imagined that a few hard minds were being pried open. Now, in the aftermath of Ike's cruel surprises, Ray again was a fiend, a monster. The conclusion filled the room like a part of the fetid air, like the smells of brilliantine and hatred and too many bodies. The axiom was that if, while presenting your own evidence you did not appear to be winning, then certainly you were losing. It seemed now that he had fared better with the State's witnesses than with Ray, which promised defeat as surely as defeat guaranteed death.

He tried to beat off the depression when, at four o'clock, he called Sergeant Bernard Blossom. Handsome in crisp Air Force blue, embossed with ribbons, the sergeant responded with earnest concentration. He affirmed Priest's fine Korean record and bravery in action and edged in his personal belief that the defendant had entered upon his second enlistment as a combat-fatigue case.

It was this, Blossom said, that led him to bend the regulations to grant Priest a chain of second chances. Informed of Ray's problems with Patty Sue, he said, he had known where to search when Priest went over the hill. He had sent out telegrams, made phone calls, until he located him. Then, instead of sending Air Police, he would cajole Ray into returning to the station. On most occasions, he said, he had wired Ray the money for train fare. Never, he declared with apparent pride, had Priest been hauled back under guard.

Paulk used him to show the jury why the hospital records on Priest could not be had. He introduced correspondence between the Sergeant and himself, following up with an account of Blossom's last effort to wheedle the records from Fitzsimmons via a personal visit. By walking a tight wire across hearsay, Paulk managed to show that such records could be had only by subpoena, and that his Texas subpoena was without effect in Colorado.

Next he conducted the Sergeant through a description of Priest's day-to-day conduct during his second enlistment. Priest had been incompetent even for the most menial assignments. "He didn't seem to know where he was, or what he was doing. He was moody, morbid,

263

always begging for leave so he could go see his wife. Several times, I saw him cry when I told him it was impossible."

"You say that for most of a year you were aware of this boy's problems and tried to help him?"

"Yes, sir. I kept trying, until it seemed to me he was getting worse instead of better. Finally, I turned him in to the wing medical officer. They later transferred him to Fitzsimmons."

"What, if anything, caused you to think Priest ought to be in the hospital?"

"A number of things. He complained of fierce headaches. He was nervous, resentful of the other men. Sometimes he seemed incoherent, just half conscious. One thing I remember is that suddenly, he forgot how to make up his bunk. One morning he just couldn't do it, and he never did it right after that."

"I'll ask you whether the defendant made any effort to explain to you why he could not make a good airman?"

"Yes, sir, many times. He connected everything with his belief that his wife was running away with other men."

"Where did you send these messages to him when he was AWOL?"

"Usually, I tried his mother-in-law's home at Glendale. If I missed him there, I knew he'd turn up sooner or later at his sister's in Illinois."

"I see. Now, Sergeant, was there anything in particular that finally led you to send this boy to the hospital?"

"Yes, sir; there was."

"Please tell the jury what that was."

Blossom took a small note pad from his pocket. "On September sixteenth, I denied his request for a seventy-two. An hour later, at about 3:00 P.M., I was called to the squadroom where several of the men were restraining Airman Priest. They told me—"

"The State will object to anything the Sergeant may have been told, as hearsay."

"I'll sustain."

Paulk said, "Just tell us what you saw and heard when you arrived."

"There was a noose around Ray's neck. Another piece of it, a parachute reiser, was hanging from a rafter. He was fighting, cursing them for cutting him down."

"What, if anything, did he say to you at that time?"

"He asked me to let him finish what he had started."

"Did he say why he wanted to hang himself?"

"He said he had to do it because his wife had gone to Denver."

Paulk glanced at the jury and its quandary. Could Raymond Priest have procured for his wife in Atlanta, yet attempted suicide at March Field out of heartbreak over her efforts to become a whore? It was a muddle out of which he was asking the jury to deduce that Ray had not assented to his wife's interlude with Jess Hutcherson. If there was a chance, Paulk thought, it lay in the fact that the Atlanta wretchedness had been denied, while Blossom's testimony would stand.

He said, "Pass the witness."

Anglin began the cross-examination with the standard debunkings. You aren't a psychiatrist, are you, Sergeant? Never been to medical school, have you? Don't know what this man did with himself after his discharge, do you? Know anything about what the defendant was doing last January fourteenth? Then the assistant tried a few long shots.

"During your nursemaiding of this man, did you ever hear him threaten to kill anyone?"

"He threatened himself."

"Did he ever, in your hearing, threaten to kill his wife?"

"No, sir."

"Or his mother-in-law, Mrs. Black?"

"No."

"All right, Sergeant, you've told us how you 'bent' Air Force regulations to cover this man's desertions. In view of your familiarity with those regulations, do you know what might have become of Ray Priest if you hadn't made an exception of him?"

"I think so."

"What would have happened to him?"

"He'd have done a lot of time in the guardhouse."

"Actually, under his record of repeated desertion, he was more likely to have been put away in a military prison, isn't that correct?"

"Yes, sir, that might have happened."

"If he had gone to prison, he wouldn't have been free to kill a man, would he?"

Blossom retained his composure, but it was obvious this had never occurred to him. He said, "Possibly not."

"If you had it all to do over again, knowing what you know now, do you think you'd be thwarting military law to shelter this defendant under your tender, motherly wing?"

"I imagine I'd handle the problem differently."

"I should hope so," Anglin said. "That's all."

Paulk turned to his client, whispered across him to Angie Callahan. "It's now," he said, "if you still want to get up there. I don't think what you can say is vital, we can do without it. You make the choice."

The eyes widened in the tired, loyal face. She said, "They ought to understand about Baby. I can make them see how it was, I'm sure of it."

"All right." Paulk faced back toward the bench. "The defendant calls Mrs. Angie Callahan." Watching her receive the oath, noting the determined set of her shoulders under the bedraggled dress, Paulk felt a tightening of his throat, a recurrence of his strange envy of Ray Priest. As before, she made him think of the all-redeeming qualities. Courage in a man, faithfulness in a woman. . . .

As he put the questions establishing her relationship and association with Priest, he was aware that she was going to lie. Exaggerate Ray's good, at least such good as she supposed him to possess, minimize his evils as just small frailties for which he wasn't responsible. The Godly perjury of people who love, Singer called it; the lie justified by every star in heaven and profane only to the law.

Angie looked much thinner than a week ago. On her face lay the shadows of the nightmares wherein Baby marched along a stone corridor to the death chamber. As Paulk bore her along he was encouraged. The defense would close on an effect like a mother pleading for her child.

"Then, after all these years of caring for Ray in your home, you knew him as you did your own children?"

"Oh, yes. He was always more like my son than my brother."

"I'll ask you whether you know this defendant's reputation for truth and veracity in the community in which he resides?"

"Of course I do."

"Is that reputation good or bad?"

"It's good."

"Do you know his reputation as a peaceful, law-abiding citizen in his home community?"

"Yes, sir."

"Is that reputation good or bad?"

"It's good."

Having met the requirements of the suspended-sentence law, Paulk was all but done. "Mrs. Callahan, tell the jury when you first noticed the change in Ray that you've mentioned."

"When he came home from Korea. Then, it seemed to get worse after his marriage."

"Just what was this difference?"

"Well, he never seemed to feel well. He had headaches, he couldn't sleep at night, he didn't want to talk to any of us. He stopped going to church with us, although he used to go all the time."

"Were these the only differences that disturbed you?"

"There were others. To tell you the truth, I never knew of Baby taking a drink until after he came home from the war."

Ray gave up old friends and old pastimes; he surrendered jobs because responsibility seemed to panic him. He grew angry when urged to check in at a VA hospital. Once, she said, she and her husband had tried to trick him into seeing a doctor. This was after a wild night through which Ray wept over the frustrations of a coast-to-coast junket in search of Patty.

"One other question, Mrs. Callahan. If your brother should regain his freedom sometime in the near or distant future, would you welcome him into your home again?"

"Oh, yes! We love him."

"Pass the witness."

Tigart had a fresh quid in his jaw. He churned it into place as he leaned to listen to Hollis Anglin, then smiled at the witness. The cordiality of his voice put Paulk on the alert.

"Mrs. Callahan, you'd do anything you could to help your brother, isn't that correct?"

"Yes, I would."

Tigart nodded. "I think we all understand that this has been a terrible ordeal for you, so I'll be as brief as possible. There are just a few things I want to clear up. Tell us, has this defendant ever mistreated you in any way?"

"No, sir, he has not."

"Was he considerate of you and your family?"

"Yes, he is one of us."

"I believe you have three daughters, isn't that correct?"

"Yes."

"And what are their ages?"

"My eldest is just past twenty. The next one is fourteen, and the youngest, Judy, is going on seven."

"Do these three girls live at home with you?"

"Yes."

"How large is your house, Mrs. Callahan?"

"It's small—we have five rooms."

"With Ray spending so much time with you, weren't you pretty crowded?"

"We made out all right."

"When Ray was there, where did he sleep?"

"Well, usually I'd move the three girls into one room, and Ray would take the front bedroom."

"Didn't this make his presence something of a burden on all of you?"

"Oh, no, we never thought of it that way."

Tigart left his chair by performing a slow push-up off the table and ambled toward the stand. He held out several pale blue pages. Paulk strained forward, his knees suddenly quivering with premonition.

Tigart said, "I hand you a letter dated April tenth, 1958, and I'll ask you to state whether it is in your handwriting."

Angie accepted the letter, glanced at it. She reddened, then grew ashen.

"Is that your handwriting, Mrs. Callahan?"

"It—looks like it."

"And is that your signature, 'Angie,' on the bottom of the third page?"

"Yes. But that was a long time back—"

"If you will, Mr. Funderburg," Ike turned to the reporter, "we'd like this letter marked for identification. State's Exhibit Twelve, if I'm not mistaken."

"May it please the Court," Paulk said, "I've not been allowed to examine this letter or whatever it is, and I believe I'm entitled to see it before we continue."

Tigart smiled. "Defense counsel ought to know we can't properly offer this in evidence through his witness, and we aren't doing so."

Sharman nodded his agreement and yawned. "Proceed."

Whatever was in the offing, Angie was in terror of it. As the special prosecutor lumbered back to his place, her eyes appealed to Paulk.

He stared back, communicating his inability to help, warning her to control herself.

"Mrs. Callahan," Tigart said, "are you acquainted with Mrs. Lily Black?"

"No, not actually."

"But you do know who she is?"

"I know she is Baby's mother-in-law, but I've never met her."

"Have you ever corresponded with her?"

Oh God, Paulk thought. How could he have passed over Lily Black, been unwilling because of one rebuff to try her again?

"Well, we wrote to each other some, after the kids were married."

"What did you write about?"

"Different things, about the kids and how they were getting along, that's all."

Tigart bent over the letter. "Did you ever say to Mrs. Black in a letter, 'This is nothing new for Ray, he has never cared about working as long as he could get money from somebody else'?"

"About this letter," Angie said, "there are a few things I can explain—"

"Then you do recognize this letter as one you wrote to Mrs. Black?"

"Yes, but I'd like to—"

"Your Honor," Paulk gave it another try, "I'm going to object to this on the grounds of remoteness and irrelevancy, also because anything this witness might have said in a letter is hearsay and outside the knowledge or hearing of this defendant. This so-called letter has not been introduced, I've not seen it and I've no way of knowing whether anything in it is material to any issue in this case."

The Judge was attentive, now, intrigued by the letter. "I'll overrule. You may object, Mr. Paulk, to any question you feel is improper, but I don't see how you can object in advance."

"Note my exception."

Tigart said, "You may answer, Mrs. Callahan, as to whether you stated in a letter that your brother wouldn't work as long as he could get money without working."

"I don't know how I can be expected to remember what I wrote a long time ago."

"Did you not write, 'Baby has never made any real effort to settle down, and I doubt he ever will'?"

"If I did, I didn't mean it the way you make it sound."

"Try to recall whether you told Mrs. Black in a letter, 'I've always had to send him money to come here on, money to leave on, money for his cigarettes, and I know he has taken money out of the tea can in my cabinet whenever he felt like having a few beers.'"

As if they thought it indecent to look upon Angie's agony, the jury faces turned toward Paulk and Ray Priest. Paulk longed to duck under the table, to pound the floor with his fists.

"I'll ask you, Mrs. Callahan, whether you wrote, quote: 'My husband has always said Baby was heading for serious trouble, and however I hate to admit it, I'm afraid he is right.'"

"Yes, I might have, but if you'd let me explain—"

"And did you not write, further, 'I've been uneasy at having him in the house, especially for my daughters, since their bedroom is right next to his'?"

Paulk saw the witness he had so carelessly offered cover her face with her hands. As she began to sob, he thought of his fight to win Angie a place in the pit, his cageyness as to whether she would appear as a witness. The special prosecutor had played him as a sucker. Tigart had wanted her testimony, had known how to get it.

"Did you not write these words: 'Dear Lily, whatever Ray amounts to, he is still my brother. Everyone has a cross to bear, and I suppose he is ours. I guess there's nothing more we can do except hope and pray'?"

Angie looked at Priest and emitted a strangled little cry. The courtroom, its pulses racing with this first real and devastating impeachment, watched Mrs. McCormick hurry across the pit to the stand. Nathan Hart brought a glass of water. Angie drank while Mrs. McCormick whispered to her, an arm around her shoulders. After a minute, Ray's sister blew her nose, dabbed her eyes, and faced Tigart again.

The Judge, scowling an open rebuff at Paulk for such incredible mispreparation, asked, "Can you continue?"

"Yes, sir."

Ike shook his head sadly. Let the jury see he was merciful, disinclined to twist the knife. "That will be all."

Paulk spoke up immediately, grasping at straws.

"Mrs. Callahan, since the special prosecutor cut off your answers, I'd like you to complete them now. When you wrote of your brother's inability to keep a job, to what period of his life were you referring?"

She answered eagerly. "To the time after Korea, when noise and headaches bothered him."

"When you mentioned his taking money from a tea can, were you accusing him of theft?"

"Oh, no, that's what I wanted to explain. That was family money; odds-and-ends money, we call it. We kept it in the cabinet for everyone to use. Ray would put money in there sometimes, just as the rest of us did."

Paulk nodded. "Now, I believe there was an insinuation that you feared the defendant might be headed for serious trouble, something Mr. Tigart didn't allow you to explain?"

"Yes, I wanted to say that Mrs. Black and I had been writing back and forth about the marriage problems they had. What I said was referring to that. I was afraid they were going to have a terrible divorce —that's serious trouble, to my mind. I wanted them to make a go of it; I knew Ray really cared for her."

If he was inducing lies, subordinating perjury, he felt no compunction about it. What was honor if it bound a man to die by conspiracy and blood-lust instead of law? Think fast, he cautioned her with his eyes, and he said, "And what were you trying to say about the defendant's bedroom being near that of your daughters?"

Her tears began again. "I—Baby couldn't sleep nights. He'd pace and moan and cry. It kept my girls awake, since their room was right next to his. At their ages, it kept them in a pretty bad state, hurt their schoolwork—that's what I was telling in the letter."

"Were you ever, at any time, afraid Ray might harm your children?"

"Oh, never! He loved them, like his own sisters."

"These concerns of yours developed—all of them—after your brother's return from the war and his marriage to Patty Sue?"

"Yes, sir."

"Thank you, Mrs. Callahan. You may stand down."

It was a poor and negative moment, a fuzzy and dangerous place to end. But he had nothing more. He sat listening through the vesper peal of the Main Street Church chimes, trying to appreciate this coincidence of timing. Then, without rising, he said, "We'll rest."

XXXVII

He pleaded exhaustion and the need for solitude in declining his Saturday-night invitation to the Singers'. He had bargained a copy of Judge Sharman's charge out of Mr. Funderburg, its real author, and he wanted to study it alone. In a way, he worried, he was wronging his friends. Jack deserved to see that his magnificently drawn special charges were included and would go to the jury; Laura was entitled to have him eat the dinner she had prepared for him. But it seemed he'd already leaned too heavily on Jack's experience and Laura's special empathy for him, if that was what it was.

He went to bed early with the lengthy charge open on his lap. He jotted notes in the margin as reminders for his summation and cocked an ear to the night. The first mosquitoes, bred in the puddles left by Thursday's storm, whined in through the window screen. The air was cool, mysterious with the smell of barbecue smoke and the spring purr of the streets. If Jerry was in and out of his thoughts, it wasn't Jerry his wife who should smile and kiss a pig, but Jerry, a name from history and somehow entwined with the trial. The sterility of it, he decided, defined the extent of his fatigue and the martyrdom he shared with Ray Priest.

He awakened in a zombie state and shaved, nicking severely the trench of his chin, then read the Sunday papers. At last the news writers had acknowledged his defense under Article 1220. Priest's testimony had received full play, the Hutcherson sensibilities notwithstanding. He hoped it was a sign. Since the *Tribune* customarily seconded popular opinion instead of founding it, there was the implication that a segment of the public was accepting the fact of adultery or was, at least, conceding an issue existed and had to be fought out.

He passed the morning at the kitchenette table setting down notes for his speech. Although most lawyers agreed that closing arguments had scant, if any, effect on the outcome of a case, he applied himself unsparingly. Effective or not, his voice would be the last raised for a man over whom almost no one had wept.

At noon he turned on his radio for the news. Crowds were prowling through the courthouse, on the lookout for a Sunday session although they knew Judge Sharman had never once consented to one. The jury, said the announcer, had breakfasted early, refreshed itself with a long

272

stroll, then had marched to the Main Street Methodist worship hour and occupied front pews saved for them. Paulk was irked that the jury should visit the place of Hutch's funeral, there to be eyed and pointed out and to grow saturate with the knowledge of what Hutch's aggrieved congregation expected of them. As he paced, groping for a means to allege misconduct, the telephone rang.

"Wen?" Billy Shepherd chortled, "you doing anything?"

"Yes. What do you want?"

"Something important has come up. I'm at the Little Star, and I think you better get down here."

"Shep, I thought you were out of this thing."

"Honest to God, son, you'd better shag. Right now."

Paulk got into his car tabulating his grudges against The Shepherd. The original appointment, the dismissal on Patty Sue, Lily Black, and the letter Shep surely had known was coming. He had worked up a thorough truculence by the time he parked on Houston and left his car to the mischief of the starlings.

Shep waited in the foremost booth of the café, gazing out benignly on Paulk's arrival. Two great bloody steaks were on the table. If this was Shep's way of getting someone to lunch with him, Paulk swore, he'd bat him into next week.

"I see you're on a diet."

"Sure," Shep grinned, "I'm drinking nonfat water. Hope you don't mind; I thought we'd have time to eat." His lip jutted out as he peered out at the street.

"Expecting somebody else?"

"In a way. Hey, you look pooped, and peeved. Hell, boy, in my boots you'd of done the same. Anyhow, that dismissal ain't hurt you as bad as you think."

"You didn't get me down here to convey your sympathy."

Shep chuckled. "Try your sirloin. At four bucks, it oughta be good. I called because—well, there's a couple of things. My axes are ground now, see, so I can do as I please, lend a hand to my friends. You've had a raw deal from the start—"

"Get to the point."

The Shepherd was dumping sauces over everything. "If I can bank on you to forget where these tips came from—but, of course I can. First, did you happen to hear they've had a doctor up to look at Patty?"

"I heard about it. Why?"

"They didn't let me in on that," Shep said, "which bothered me. Another thing, I noticed Anglin has been hanging around the courthouse every weekend." He forked up an enormous first bite, chomped it assessingly, and, with a piece of paper napkin sticking to his chin, sighed. "Man, this is fine. Bachelor like me—I forgot, you're one too —we get tired of eating alone, hey?"

"So, Anglin works on Sundays."

Shep nodded. "Next thing, it looked odd to me that Patty never asked me to bring her things, not even cigarettes. My clients always chisel me for that stuff. I bet you've been supporting Ray, huh?"

Until now, Paulk had discounted the tales about The Shepherd's performances at the table. Watching, he was fascinated. Shep dined hideously. There were gulps, smacks, grunts and slurps and sensuous little groans. The pink fingers plunged into the mouth for cleansing, came out with a fleshy pop. Through the grinding, sucking vulgarity emerged his words, pushed out through loads of food which, rather than swallowed, were flushed down periodically by great draughts of milk.

"Reason was," Shep choked, "that she was getting smokes, lipstick, reading material, all compliments of the State. Another thing that worried me, Patty kept trying to hold out on her case. You know, Wen, that people have accused me of testing virtue now and then, and maybe I have. But I never had any ideas about this girl, wasn't any reason for her to lie to me. Then, last Monday, Herb Cameron fell apart—you saw that, the same as me. I knew it had something to do with Anglin, and I got nosy. Hell, I didn't aim to have him cutting in on me to get Patty's divorce."

To conceal his interest, Paulk bent to his steak despite a nausea that made eating impossible. Shep twisted to squint out the window.

"Anyway, on Wednesday, when I found out my dismissal deal was going through, I went upstairs and told that girl she could level with me or I'd bail out; told her I'd tell Tigart to take his swap and jam it."

The same consciousness of broken boundaries he'd known while in Martha Hutcherson's sitting room troubled him. He said, "I'm not sure I want to hear this."

The Shepherd dropped his napkin and waggled his clean, lotion-scented jowls. "Judge it when you've heard it, son. The short of it is, Patty explained. Take it or leave it, since her third day in jail she's been shacking up with Hollis Anglin."

"You're guessing!"

"Nope, check it out if you want. I did. Anglin got worried about his sniffles, was afraid he'd caught a dose, so he sent a doctor up there to make sure she was clean. They started out going to the jury dorm on Sundays. Anglin would check her out of jail, and Andy thought he was taking her to the DA's office for more questions. After we got some jurors in the dorm, he was stupid enough to take her out at night. What'll knock you over, Wen—a couple of times they went to the Ranch Inn. And once, by God, just for kicks, they used Cabin 4."

The drugstore incident fitted. Paulk shuddered, trying to cope with it.

"You'll find they signed in out there as 'Mr. and Mrs. Carlson.' There's a maid out there, a Mrs. Johnson. Tells me she's a client of yours. Well, she saw 'em."

He thought of Herb, his friend. Betrayed and finished. Herb was incapable of burying this, or of living with it.

"Herb knows this?"

"I figure he does," Shep said. "What else would be eating on him?"

"Who else?"

"You, me. Not Ike. You know him, he'd probably horsewhip the little squirt right in front of the jury." Shep was polishing his plate with a folded slice of bread. "It's your move, Wen. But it strikes me you could get Anglin recalled, since he's already been a witness."

"Then what?"

"Then, I think, the case would blow up. The jury might slap 'em down by turning the boy loose."

"If there's no conviction," Paulk studied him, "Patty loses the reward, and you lose your fee."

"Hell, that's so, ain't it?" The Shepherd grinned. He gazed out the window. "All right, son, you've missed out on your steak. Lookee yonder."

Paulk leaned to see a car stopping on the sheriff's lot. Three men got out. Shep said, "That would be Ike, Anglin, and the good head-shrinker."

"What?"

"That's right, the psychiatrist, Eiderhoff. Two tips, I told you. They've hired the Doc to paw over your man, then testify in rebuttal tomorrow."

Paulk scrambled up, seizing his hat.

"Wen, the way to stop this—"

"I know how to stop it."

He dashed across the street, sprinted on to the courthouse lawn. He was gagging for breath, yet swearing, when he burst in upon them.

XXXVIII

"Is your rebuttal ready, Mr. Tigart?" said the Judge.

Ike signaled to Andy Grosscup. The Bonita County sheriff was a cringing tower of law and order as carefully he fitted his gangling body into the witness chair. His carbuncle had so immobilized him that when his eyes cut toward the jury, he still faced the counsel table. Andy avoided nods as he identified himself, as he described the composition of his department and confirmed a force of fourteen active deputies.

From this, Ike entered upon a history of the honorary deputy program. Traditionally, Andy said, the prominent citizens of the county received these commissions. They carried no real enforcement authority, although he had called upon such badge holders, particularly those in the Bonita County Posse, to ride in search of lost children or to help fight prairie fires. They assisted, he said, in a volunteer status, wholly *ex officio*.

"Mr. Jess Hutcherson held one of these honorary badges, did he not?"

"Yes, sir; he had one a long time before I taken office."

"Then, if at any time Mr. Hutcherson chanced to mention to anyone that he was an honorary deputy sheriff of this county, he was making a true and accurate statement?"

"He sure was."

Tigart turned next to the confession, which Andy had witnessed. The sheriff said Priest had not been coerced into signing it, that the statutory warning had been given, and that the prisoner knew the statement's contents before he put his name to it. From there the testimony told Andy's role in the case.

"If I understand correctly," Tigart said, "this defendant has been

in your custody and care constantly since the twenty-seventh of March,
is that right?"

"Yes, sir."

"I'll ask you whether during that time he ever complained to you
of headaches."

"No, sir, he never did."

"Ever ask you to get him a doctor?"

"Not a time, no, sir."

"In your daily contact with him, have you ever seen him when he
was irrational in his speech?"

"No, sir."

"Or behaving strangely?"

"No, he's acted all right."

"Sheriff, on the basis of your prolonged acquaintance with this
defendant, have you formed any opinion as to whether he can tell right
from wrong?"

"We'll object," Paulk said. "This calls for a conclusion. The witness
hasn't been shown qualified to diagnose mental disorders."

Tigart smiled. "May it please the Court, I believe the previous ruling
was that an Air Force sergeant was qualified to express an opinion on
this issue. I submit that the sheriff is no less qualified."

Sharman was quick with Monday freshness; the weekend seemed
to have strengthened him. "I'll allow the answer. You may have your
exception, Mr. Paulk."

"You may answer, Sheriff."

"Well, I'd say he knows right from wrong. Leastaways, I never seen
him do anything to make me think he was crazy."

"All right. I'll ask you, Sheriff, if you were in your office yesterday
afternoon?"

"I was."

"And did you see this defendant, Raymond Priest, in your office?"

"Just a minute," Paulk said. "I'll object to the admission of any
hearsay as to what might have transpired in the sheriff's office yesterday. Whatever transaction was had there is immaterial and irrelevant."

"We'll show the relevancy, Your Honor, in a few seconds."

Sharman scratched. "Gentlemen, I've no way of knowing what is
coming, or what is being objected to."

If the jury was to hear it, Paulk thought, it best be from him. "May
it please the Court, the special prosecutor wants to show that he tried

to sneak a psychiatrist up to jail yesterday to putter around with my client, and that I arrived there just in time to prevent this violation of the defendant's rights."

The Judge lifted his brows. "Appears to me, young man, that you're being pretty specific about a matter you say you want kept out. Mr. Tigart, is this your intention?"

"Roughly. But it deserves a more accurate exposition."

"Very well," the Judge was confused. "If you'll restate your objection, Mr. Paulk, I'll rule."

"I'm withdrawing it, Your Honor. Occurs to me I'd like this jury to know all about the State's latest shenanigan."

"We don't need any smart-aleck analysis from Junior as to what took place," Tigart said. "I move his remark—"

"Here, here, you attorneys. We needn't get off into one of those. I suggest you continue with the witness."

Ike prodded the sheriff through an account of the Sunday afternoon scene, down to Paulk's explosive arrival just as Ray Priest was being introduced to Dr. Eiderhoff. Andy credited Paulk with threatening to seize Assistant District Attorney Anglin by the throat and use him as a bludgeon upon Special Prosecutor Tigart. Which, Paulk reflected, was probably as accurate a piece of testimony as had been heard to date.

"Your witness, Mr. Paulk."

"Sheriff Grosscup, you gave me no notice whatsoever that a medical examination was being arranged for this defendant, did you?"

"Well, Wen, once I get a man in jail, the rest ain't my lookout."

"Did you notify me?"

"No."

"To your knowledge, did anyone else advise me of this in advance?"

"No."

"Did this defendant ask to be given an examination by a doctor?"

"No."

Paulk chipped the ice from his voice and for ten minutes worked to extract the sheriff's account of the trip home from Peoria with Ray. During that flight, didn't you speak on the radio? Didn't you seek to put this defendant on the air? Wasn't he under arrest, and without counsel, at that time? Did you not, upon arrival, detain the defendant on the wing of your airplane, so that he might be photographed while wearing chains? Is it customary, Sheriff, to display your prisoners in this manner? Did you ask the defendant's consent for these things?

"Very well. Sheriff, when you issue these honorary deputy badges you've told us about, do you also issue sidearms?"

"Why, no, of course not."

"Is it your wish that these honoraries carry pistols?"

"No, like I said, they ain't really officers. It's just a form of recognition, that's all."

"These honorary deputies are not authorized to make arrests, are they?"

"No."

"Would one of these honorary commissions give a man the right to cruise along a public highway firing at fence posts?"

"Well, no, it wouldn't."

"That's all."

"We'll excuse the witness," Tigart said. He bent to a short whispered consultation with Anglin, then twisted to look at the crowd. "The State calls Mrs. Lily Black."

Paulk saw the bleached and leggy hairdresser, this utterly improbable mother-in-law, rise from her seat in back of the jury wives and approach the stand. Lily was aware of the audience. She minced her steps, tossed her head, smiled upon the pit as she arrived to take the oath. Since the letter surprise, Paulk had been wondering what he might do with her. Angie had received letters in return, but she had not saved them. He had nothing but Angie's memory of them, which would count for little. He took such satisfaction as he could from Judge Sharman's rebuking scowl upon the excessive make-up, the tight bare-backed dress, the sleek legs crossed and calling attention to themselves via a foot that bobbed up and down. Clearly, Lily regarded herself as the dazzling, magnetic female on whom all the movie trials turned, the creature of climax and sensation.

Quickly, Tigart produced her identification of Angie's letter, put it in evidence and, with Lily attempting tears in the background, he read the full text to the jury. Then, having destroyed Angie, Ike began an inquiry into Lily's infrequent but violent battles with Priest over his mistreatment of Patty Sue.

"Now, Mrs. Black, would you say your daughter's letter to Ray about her pregnancy had an immediate result?"

"It sure did. Ray came to my house the very next night, without any leave papers. He rang the doorbell, and Patty was—"

"Just a moment," Ike said. "You were present when he rang the bell?"

"I certainly was, Patty and I were in the living room. My husband was away."

"All right, what took place there that night?"

"Well, Patty answered the bell. When she opened the door, Ray stepped inside, and without saying a word, he slapped her. Then he grabbed her arm and yelled at me to stay out of it and he pulled Patty back into the bedroom and slammed the door. He commenced to—"

"Object," Paulk said, "to anything that might have occurred in one room while the witness was in another."

"I'll sustain."

"All right," Tigart said, "did you hear anything after that door closed?"

"Yes, sir. I heard some licks, and I heard Patty crying and begging him not to hit her anymore."

"What, if anything, did you do?"

"There wasn't anything I could do."

"How long were they in that bedroom?"

"It seemed like a long time. Maybe half an hour."

"Were you there when they came out?"

"Yes, sir. Only, Ray didn't come out; he went to bed. Patty came out."

"I'll ask what, if anything, you noticed as to your daughter's condition when she emerged from that room?"

"She looked—well, she had a black eye, and her lips were swollen. She was holding her stomach. She said he had—"

Paulk said, "We'll object to this as hearsay, conversation outside the hearing of this defendant."

Tigart did not wait for the ruling. "Mrs. Black, did you observe any other marks on your daughter that night?"

"I'll say I did. I helped her undress, put her to bed in my room. There were big red spots on her stomach, and she was all doubled up, couldn't straighten out."

Lily claimed to have been awakened at 4:00 A.M., to have found Patty in convulsions. The next day, the miscarriage had been confirmed at a hospital. Watching the woman's extreme awareness of

the crowd, catching the now-it's-my-turn glances she stabbed at Ray
Priest, Paulk decided she was lying. The best guess was that there had
been a miscarriage, that Ray had indeed slapped his wife a day, or
week, or month before; that the rest was vehement imagination. But
if the jury suspected her, it gave no hint.

Tigart progressed from this tale to a similar one. Priest had gotten
a large VA check, had blown it on a binge, had choked Patty in a
quarrel about it, leaving the imprint of his fingers on her throat.
Twice, Priest leaned forward to whisper, "It's a lie, Mr. Polk; I
treated my wife good."

Ike lounged back, couching his cropped red head in the palms of
his hands. "Now, Mrs. Black, just what did you do about these things,
if anything?"

"Well, for years, I tried to help them get straightened out. My house
was always open to them. He never had any money, or any job, and
I'd let them stay with me."

"Is that all?"

"No, sir, my husband and I were always trying to find Ray a job
after he got out of the Air Force."

"I'll ask you whether the defendant cooperated with you in this?"

"No, sir, he never did. We had a lot of arguments about it."

"Arguments? What did the defendant say about going to work?"

"Mostly, he'd say he didn't care about a job."

"Tell this jury when was the last time you had an argument on this
question."

"It was in December of 1958, just before they left on this trip
and got into this trouble."

"What, if you recall, did Ray say to you on that occasion?"

"He said plenty, said he didn't care whether he got the Florida job
or not. I told him he ought to be ashamed, that he had a wife to
support."

"And what did the defendant say to that?"

"He said there wasn't any reason for him to work, not as long as
he had Patty."

"Did he explain what he meant by that?"

"He sure did." Lily turned to the jury. "He said, 'Why should I
worry, as long as Patty can make me a good living with her body.'"

Heads snapped up. A jury chair creaked. Angie gasped. Paulk felt
the prickle of his neck and he realized he almost believed her. If on

Saturday he'd thought his position must improve because it could not worsen, he'd been an idiot.

"As a mother," Tigart said, "what was your reaction to such a suggestion regarding your daughter?"

"I was shocked, although I couldn't believe he meant it. I told him that if he loved Patty Sue as much as he was always saying he did, he just couldn't have ideas like that."

"Did he reply to this, Mrs. Black?"

"Yes, sir. He said, 'Why not?' Then he said, 'Even Jesus Christ loved a prostitute.' "

On a strangled outcry, Angie fled to the door. The courtroom froze. Along with the others, Paulk feared even a breath of the soundless blasphemed air. Perspiring, he began wresting his mind from it, wishing he'd never heard of Ray Priest.

Tigart said, "Pass the witness."

"A lie," Priest was hissing behind him, "she made it up, I swear to God!"

Paulk gave him no notice. For due process, he told himself. Just for that, now, and for himself. He glared at Lily Black, willing her to dissolve.

"Are you a natural blonde?"

"The State objects, Your Honor."

"Sustain," the Judge grated. "You know better than that, Mr. Paulk, and I want you to behave yourself."

He welcomed the reprimand; he needed it in reinforcement of his uncertain ire. He said, "Tell this jury whether, at any time, I attempted to talk to you about this case?"

"I know you said that was what you were after."

"When I called at your motel, did you refuse to talk to me about your testimony?"

"I'm not used to having people call on me at midnight."

"My question was, did you refuse to talk with me?"

"At that hour, certainly."

"I'll ask you whether your only response to me was the remark that you hoped this boy burned and you hoped you'd get to see it?"

"I'm not sure what I said to you. Not when you were telling me you intended to tear me up if I took the stand."

Every last ill-begotten chicken, it seemed, came fluttering back to roost. "It's your testimony that I threatened you?"

"That's what it sounded like."

"Very well. Now, since you've already been such a source of enlightenment, I'm wondering if we've tapped you for absolutely everything you know that might be of value to the jury. Let's see—isn't your daughter, Patty, the product of a broken home?"

"She is not."

"Then, you are presently living with your husband?"

"I am."

"But you have been separated from your husband on several occasions, isn't that correct?"

"I don't think that's any of your business."

"Have you ever visited an attorney to discuss a divorce action against your husband, Mrs. Black?" It was an impulsive jab, but one her look and demeanor seemed to call for.

Lily was startled. She hesitated, and he could see that she speculated on how much he knew and upon the likely consequence of a lie. After a moment she said, "That was a long time ago, and it didn't amount to anything."

"Just routine for you, is that it?"

"I didn't say that."

"Is your husband here in Texas with you?"

"No."

"You're all alone here?"

"That's right."

He drew a giant breath so he might shove forth his next question in an unstoppable rush. "Then, the person who brought you back to the motel the other night was not your husband?"

Tigart's ferocious objection reverberated off the glossy oak panels. When the red fury subsided, Paulk felt surer of his instincts, less untrusting of the hunches that had to serve when there was no plan.

He said, "Mrs. Black, I call your attention to this letter you just happened to bring along from California, and I ask you if this is the only letter you ever received from Mrs. Callahan?"

"No, we wrote back and forth."

"During this correspondence, how many letters did you receive from the defendant's sister?"

"Six or eight, I suppose."

"Six or eight. Did you save them all?"

"No."

"But you saved this one?"

"That's right."

"Why did you hang on to this particular one?"

"No special reason."

Paulk repeated her answer. Then, "This wasn't a one-sided correspondence, was it?"

"I don't know what you mean."

"I mean, did you write to Mrs. Callahan?"

"Of course I did."

"Do you remember what you wrote to her in regard to your daughter and this defendant?"

"Not word for word."

"But, in substance, you do remember what you wrote?"

"Naturally."

"All right. Did you, in a letter to Mrs. Callahan last summer, tell her it was your belief that Raymond Priest was insane and ought never to have been discharged from the Air Force in his condition?"

"No, that isn't what I said."

"Tell us, please, just what you did say."

"I said the Air Force didn't have any business turning Ray loose."

Lacking the letter, working without the smallest wedge of information, he had to be satisfied with this. He said, "Do you think you've been a good mother to Patty Sue?"

"Yes, and I tried to be nice to Ray, too."

"How often did you visit your daughter when she was serving her term in the Detention Home out there?"

"Well, I was working long hours at the time."

"Did you visit her at all?"

"I never got off work until after seven—"

"Did you visit her?"

"No, but she wasn't out there very long."

"Because Ray got her out?"

"That's right."

"In other words, you wouldn't drive across town to see your daughter then, but you've come halfway across the country to be with her now?"

"You can see I am here."

"Yes, I do see. Now, Mrs. Black, you've heard a great deal about the reward in this case, haven't you?"

"Depends on what you call 'a great deal.' "

"Have you learned, from any source, that your daughter may receive a large sum of money if Ray Priest is convicted?"

"Everybody knows that."

"Now, these stories about the terrible beatings you claim this defendant inflicted on your daughter, the ones where you stood by and did nothing—did you relate them to anyone before you found out Patty was in line for a jackpot?"

"Your Honor," said Tigart, "we must object to the question, and to this line of inquiry, as irrelevant to any issue—"

"Yes," the Judge nodded, "I doubt this is material, especially in view of the answers she's made up to now."

Paulk spread his hands, shook his head. Despite his earliest resolutions as an attorney, he was becoming, he supposed, as much a ham and mugger and showman as Tigart. Still, how else might a lawyer fight on when the facts surprised and confounded him, when his position in law suddenly shifted beneath him like river sand, when his crusader's wrath was flickering and burning low? He stared his scorn at Lily Black, hoping to induce a reflection of it in the jury box, before he said, "Let her stand aside."

Sharman tracked Lily's retreating figure with a glowering disapproval which Paulk welcomed as an appropriate commentary upon her credibility. As Nathan Hart put her out into the hall, the Judge said, "Mr. Tigart, where do we stand?"

"May it please the Court, I believe we'll offer only one additional witness. This one will require very little time, if you'd like to postpone the recess."

"Good," Judge Sharman glanced at the clock, "proceed."

Tigart turned, as if to guard both the jury and the door, and he said, "Mrs. Martha Hutcherson, please."

Now what?

Amid the murmurs, the sudden adjustment as people sought clear lanes of view for the entrance of this, the offended, the sufferer-in-chief, Paulk was inert. Why Mrs. Hutcherson; wherein was she competent to rebut anything? Then, tingling, he remembered lunch with Shep. He seized on the notion that henceforth, he need not be surprised by anyone.

He caught up a yellow note pad and the newest of his ballpoints. Rapidly he sketched a heart and within it he wrote, HOLLIS LOVES

PATTY. Underneath he scrawled, MOVE FOR A RECESS, *NOW*. He scooted the pad across the table, butting it against Tigart's chest.

XXXIX

He left the courtroom at the rear of the flow. At the far end of the corridor, the prosecutors were filing into Herb's office, Anglin first, as if he would choose the ground on which to defend himself. The Shepherd looked at them, then at Paulk, before bustling away toward the stairs and the safety of distance. Paulk considered a moment. He would give them five minutes. He turned into the rest room. Standing at the window, the place of the finest view, he gazed out upon his town. Somewhere along, spring had touched itself up. The elm buds had unfolded as miniature leaves, the grass had lost its last winter yellow and awaited the season's first mowing. It didn't surprise him as it might have. The world, he was discovering, could be changed in an instant. Not change, but only the awareness of it, came slowly.

He finished his cigarette, crushed it out on the terrazzo, and went to the office. He rapped lightly, then let himself in. The reception room was vacant. At the rear, Tigart's hoarse voice halted on an expletive and went silent. Paulk walked on back to Herb's inner room. The District Attorney sat behind his desk, hands folded over his stomach, still the forlorn bystander. Tigart was pacing, the big freckled fists clenched against his thighs, veins raised in his temples. Hollis Anglin sat on the divan, elbows on knees, his face covered by quivering hands.

Paulk stopped in the door. He could see his heart sketch on the desk. "I'm sorry, Ike."

The big man halted, turned to look at Anglin. Paulk wondered suddenly if Tigart had hit him.

"All right," Ike said, "what do you want?"

It acknowledged Paulk's power over them. He thought of all the abuses, the finagling. Still, the upper hand did not feel good. He wanted to finish and get away.

He said, "What do you intend to do with Martha Hutcherson?" There was no need for sparring, for appraisal of position.

Tigart swore. "We expected her to testify that Hutch had no use for pajamas, that if he went to bed naked in the motel, it was quite normal for him. We also meant to show that she disapproved of Hutch's drinking, that when he had had a few, he often checked into a motel room instead of going home. Another thing, she can tell us that Hutch habitually slept on his back, in about the posture his body was in when it was found. That's it."

Paulk leaned against the door facing, evaluating. This was sound, correct rebuttal. Yet legally, something was wrong with it.

Ike said, "Well, Wen—let's get through with this. What's your proposition?"

"Seems to me," he was thinking as he spoke, "that this sort of testimony assumes Hutch's character to be in issue. Except for what happened while he was with the defendant, it isn't. If you go into his habits and foibles here, through his wife or anyone else, you're opening the flood gates. I can go back then and prove up every tavern he ever walked into, every woman he ever winked at. Isn't that right?"

Tigart shrugged. "I don't think so. Not with Sharman up there, you can't. But this is beside the point now. What do you want. Before I— before I kill this little bastard."

"Keep Mrs. Hutcherson off altogether."

"My God, I can't do that. We've already called her."

Paulk felt cold, his legs were unsteady. He was among them now, in that zone of law that was neither dark nor light. There was only numbness, the daze of having rammed headfirst through an old, strong barrier. He met Ike's eyes. The special prosecutor, he was certain, knew nothing of his visit with Martha Hutcherson. If this was true, perhaps there was yet a chance for Ray by letting her appear.

"I'll do this," he said dubiously. "You can use her as you planned except for one thing. I don't want her saying Hutch always slept naked."

Tigart brushed the short hair; its coarseness whispered. "What if I tell you to go to hell?"

Paulk said, "You should. But if you do, I'm going to recall lover boy here, and I'm going to put Patty on. I can stand all you can get from her in order to show them just what sort of prosecution this has been. You name it."

He felt colder, almost sick.

Tigart strode across the room. With the big hands gripping together behind him, he stared down at Hollis Anglin. Paulk looked at Herb. The District Attorney had not moved. Herb had known since last Monday; this was what had broken him.

"All right," Ike said. "That is, if Herb agrees."

The District Attorney barely nodded.

Paulk said, "One thing more ought to be understood. Even if you go along, I'm going to cross-examine her as I please. Late as it is, I'm going to get this boy a break if I can. Does that change your mind?"

Ike's chin was on his chest. He shook his head without lifting it. Then Cameron opened a desk drawer, gazed bleakly into it, shut it slowly, and said softly, "Hollis, you're fired."

Tigart was cursing, walking again, as Paulk left. He shut the door behind him. He felt curiously lonely, deprived even of his own company, as he dragged along back to court.

Martha Hutcherson wasn't herself on the stand. Not serene, not the woman of poise and quality, of iron and lace. She breathed too rapidly, watching the clock, as Tigart put his questions. Paulk suspected that until now she hadn't thought what might happen to her, hadn't realized that her proffered compromise could make her a witness for the defense. Through the brief direct, he sorted his questions, set them in order. Did you not volunteer to trade me your testimony for a suppression of this adultery issue? Did you not tell me your husband drank excessively during his last two years? Was he not, according to your own statements, agitated over the decline of his virility? Just how long, Mrs. Hutcherson, had your husband's conduct been abnormal?

Ike said, "To the best of your recollection, how many times had your husband slept in a motel instead of coming home?"

"I can't give a specific number. But it was dozens of times."

"Thank you." Tigart got up beside Anglin's empty chair, looked at Herb, and sat down again. "That's all."

Paulk advanced his chair a yard in order not to crane at her around a corner of the bench. Mrs. Hutcherson's gaze travelled over the jury, up to the clock, before it met his. In her eyes he detected a desperation apart from the traps with which she had armed him. It seemed she cared only to be done. As mentally he phrased the first of the blows he could strike for Ray Priest, he felt the recurrence of the peculiar affinity for her that he had known as he departed her house that day. It was as if they were joined under a single burden of pain which neither of them, alone, could bear.

The fire died on his tongue. A voice said, "No questions," and strange as it sounded, it was his own.

He was standing as Tigart helped her from the stand, escorted her to the door, and whispered in her ear before she hurried away through the standees in the hall. Ike's frown was fixed on Paulk as he returned to the table. He stood over it a moment, the fighter baffled that his opponent had pulled a punch.

"Your Honor," he said, "the State will close."

The Judge started with delight. "You, Mr. Paulk?"

"May it please the Court, the defense closes."

Mr. Funderburg dropped a stylus, rocked back in his chair and, stretching his arms high, exhaled his benediction: "Ah, all over except the shouting!"

Sharman's hands fluttered over his papers as he gathered up loose ends. Would either party have objections to the Court's charge? If not, he would proceed to read it to the jury and, gentlemen, wouldn't that clear the way to wind up with arguments during the afternoon? Well, on second thought, a short recess before hearing the charge, say, five minutes. Mr. Bailiff, may we have some fresh water in the decanter? And, Mr. Sheriff, if you can do something about that glare—?

Staring after Martha Hutcherson, ignoring the Judge, Paulk began feeling the backlash. The glow of *beau geste* dimmed and disappeared, leaving the reality behind, unobscured. He had let Martha Hutcherson go, the questions unasked, his man unrescued. In sudden harsh clarity he saw himself as among the appointive fakers, the Bar's uncaring accessories to legal murder, the sundown back-patters who waived away lives.

How, why? Earlier, without a backward glance, he had bartered off the Anglin fiasco to Ray's advantage, committing blackmail with only a sense of righteousness. Yet with the witness who might have meant Priest's life, he had yielded and fizzled out. Could he blame it on Old Jack, for confusing him with platitudes on honor in the law? Or Laura, whose compassion had infected him? Or Jerry, no longer near to prompt and toughen him; or the girl Valle, not innocent when the very sound of her name had become a bribe in his ears? He could not. It was he, Owen Paulk alone, compensating, being weak and maudlin and sorrowful over a miserable set of facts. He had kept his personal stand-off with his profession and, like Mrs. Hutcherson's answers, Raymond Priest was lost.

The torment turned him to his client. Shouldn't he say it; tell Ray that behind the barrier of decency was a cheapened and fatal lawyer, stinking to his own nostrils from the blood already spoiling on his hands?

Angie touched his arm. "Are you ill, Mr. Polk?"

"It's Paulk," he said, and he got up and fled.

PART THREE

XL

The door stood open. Fresh air-conditioned currents poured in, chilling the Judge while brightening everyone else. With the Rule expired, the witnesses pressed for standing room from which to observe what their swearings had wrought. There were more lawyers shoehorned into the pit, more housewives and pensioners, more of every sort except the Hutchersons, whom Paulk missed if, indeed, they had come.

As the Judge cleaned his glasses, a narrow aisle began to break, grudgingly, and along it, out of the mass of the corridor, came a wheelchair. Jack Singer trundled in, grinning crookedly everywhere. He shook hands with a dozen attorneys who surged to greet him. Then, while the Judge watched in an air of awe and misgivings, Jack rolled across the pit and parked himself on Paulk's quarter, immediately beside Raymond Priest.

"Why," Paulk spoke behind his hand, "aren't you up and walking?"

Singer winked and turned his grin on the jury.

Jack's appearance was as little expected by Paulk as anyone. He wanted to hug him. Here was the dean, the retired champion of the difficult but just and rational cause, seated beside Ray Priest. If shamed by his presence, Paulk felt better. Singer was at work. The wheelchair apprised the jury of why he hadn't defended all along, and to clinch it, Jack clapped Priest on the shoulder. Next he fastened a depreciating pixie look on the Judge, his eyes chiding: Now, Jimmie, just what have you been doing to the unfortunate little folks while I've been gone?

Sharman gruffened. "Your attention, please. We've admitted you standees reluctantly, on the assurance that you'll cause no disturbance." He scowled down at Mr. Durfee, who had plodded forward boldly and was leaning to speak to Jack Singer in a whisper punctuated with whistles and hisses. "All of you, and each of you, must cooperate. . . ."

Singer tapped Paulk's arm. "Which is Tigart's policeman?"

"Front row, right end. Is Laura with you?"

"I thought you saw her. She's back there, sitting in the window."

Laura was smiling as he turned, and she raised her hand to him.

"Wen, what's this mess about Anglin?"

Because the Judge was swiveling to face the jury, smoothing the pages of the charge, Paulk didn't have to answer.

"Ladies and gentlemen of the jury, the instruction you will receive from me at this time explains the law of this case and the rules which shall govern you in your deliberation. You will take a copy of the charge with you to the jury room, and I strongly suggest you reread it as soon as you have elected a foreman and before you begin your work. I implore you, as well, to listen carefully now."

Normally, Paulk was relieved, reassured, by the recital of a correct jury charge. In the statute books the law could seem colorless and dense. But, raised to life by its application to a particular event and person, read aloud by one enamored with it, the law shined, its beauty like the poetry of scripture. Under the stringing sentences and nettlesome archaic appositives was a proof that men did, after all, have a knowledge of themselves. But today, there was no wonder of revelation; he felt no peace or pride at his place in the pit.

"In this case," the Judge read, "the defendant, Raymond Elliot Priest, is charged by indictment containing three counts, with the offense of murder with malice aforethought, to which he has pleaded not guilty. The District Attorney has elected by his motion to prosecute this case upon the third count of the indictment. The law of the case, by which you should be governed in your deliberations upon a verdict, is hereinafter given, to wit:

"Our statute provides that if any person shall, in this state, unlawfully and voluntarily kill any other person, he shall be deemed guilty of murder. Murder is distinguishable from every other species of homicide by the absence of circumstances which reduce the offense to negligent homicide or which excuse it, or which justify it."

Sharman's voice deepened, his fine head inclined as he opened the definitions. He seemed to savor every phrase, to dote on his marvelous law as on a grandchild.

" 'Voluntarily,' as used in this charge," he intoned, "means an act done with purpose, design and intent . . . 'malice aforethought,' as used in our statutes and in this charge, is the voluntary and intentional performance of an unlawful act by one of sound memory and discretion and possessing the purpose, means and ability to accomplish the reasonable and probable consequences of said act. Malice aforethought includes all those states of mind under which the killing of a person takes place without any cause which will, in law, justify, excuse or extenuate the homicide. It is a condition of mind which shows a heart that is regardless of social duty and fatally bent on mischief. . . ."

He defined express malice, implied malice, imputed malice, then came previous design and the matters of the sedate and self-possessed mind, reasonable sufficiency and reasonable doubt. Because the gallery was growing restless, Paulk shifted to look at the jury. They listened avidly, but the shadow of bafflement was edging across their faces. It frightened him. If only attorneys could hear the law, what was a jury?

In a long paragraph, the Judge related the terms to the Priest indictment and proceeded into the suspended-sentence law which, Paulk saw, was rejected by the jurors the instant they heard it. There followed a special charge on confessions, the one Singer had labored over through many evenings. It read about as Jack had written it: "Astute," he grinned, "and garnished with just the right amount of fog." In substance, the jury was told it must resolve the issue as to the legality of the statement before deciding whether to use or discard it as a consideration.

"Paragraph Six," the Judge read. "In this case, the defendant has offered a showing of justification under the right of self-defense. Our law holds that a reasonable expectation or fear of death, or of serious bodily injury, excuses and justifies any person in using such force as is necessary to protect his life or person from any danger thereto. It is not essential that there should be real or actual danger if the person acts upon a reasonable apprehension or appearance of danger as it appears to him from his standpoint at the time. . . ."

Paulk took no heart from the section. His few distractionary pebbles of self-defense proof seemed to vanish under the avalanche of law they had brought down on the jury. Nor did the next section, amplifying the law of insanity, lessen his gloom. Sharman was submitting Old Jack's two special-issue questions, telling the jury it could answer "yes" or "no" as to whether it believed Priest had been insane when he killed and was, or was not, insane now. The plan had been to offer any reluctant juror a face-saving escape, to provide a way for him to vote acquittal and yet be certain that Ray, instead of being released, would go to confinement in a mental hospital. Since Lily Black, since the suspicions raised by the affair of the Sunday psychiatrist, the special charge sounded like spent hope and wasted scholarship.

Singer's perfect composition, he thought sadly, made it a masterpiece. Perhaps, if he'd not waxed soft with Martha Hutcherson—

The Judge drank a glass of water, frowned, and began his Paragraph Eight by quoting in full Article 1220. Paulk took up his copy to follow the instruction carefully. If anything still mitigated for Ray, this was it.

"... 'adultery,' as that term is in the law and herein used, means any single act of sexual intercourse between the two parties under consideration. If at the time and place alleged in the indictment, at night, on the fourteenth day of January A.D. 1959, in the back bedroom of Cabin 4 of the Ranch Inn Motel in the County of Bonita, State of Texas, the defendant Raymond Elliot Priest killed Jessup C. Hutcherson by beating and striking him on the head with a pistol, and if at the time of such homicide the said Jessup C. Hutcherson and the defendant's wife, one Patty Sue Priest, were nude and together in the bed of the deceased in the said room, and if it then and there reasonably appeared to the defendant that his wife and the deceased were then and there committing, or had committed, or were about to commit, the act of adultery with each other, and if the defendant had not connived in, or assented to, such connection between his wife and the deceased, then such homicide was justifiable under the provisions of the law, and if you so find and believe from the evidence that the homicide was committed under such circumstances, or if you have a reasonable doubt thereof, you should acquit the defendant and say by your verdict, 'not guilty.' "

By his somber tone, the Judge disclosed that while he, no less than anyone, reproached those who had raised the issue, he acknowledged all else as chaff by comparison. Paulk stole a look across the table. Herb Cameron seemed to be tracking the first fly of the season as it spiraled over the heads of the jurors. Tigart slouched forward, his cuffs shot far out of his coat sleeves, and he bemused himself with his swinging ring and thrusting pencil.

"The words 'before the parties have separated' do not mean still united in copulation, but rather only that the parties are still in company with each other. To avail himself of the Article, the defendant need not show adultery as defined by any other statute or section of the Code. It is sufficient if he show a single defilement of his marriage bed, and you are so instructed."

Only twenty minutes had passed. The Judge moved on to Ike's requested charges, the terse bits of law aimed at erasing a skein of minor quandaries. The prosecutor wanted the jury to understand that intoxication was no excuse for crime; that Hutch, by statute, had the right to carry firearms in his automobile while travelling, that the facts of Ray's war record and orphaned state had been admitted for the purpose of determining his credibility as a witness and could not be considered, legally, as bearing upon his guilt or innocence. Lastly, at Tigart's request, the Judge defined the limits concerning the letter used in the impeachment of Angie Callahan.

"You should not, and must not, consider or discuss the same as any original evidence or any fact or circumstance against the defendant, nor for any other purpose, if you consider it at all, except to aid you, if it does, in determining the weight to be given the testimony of Mrs. Angie Callahan as given on direct examination of her by the defendant's attorney."

Paulk raised an eyebrow at Singer. Why, after sensational success with the letter, was Tigart now uncertain of it? It seemed Ike feared a jury anger over his cross-examination of Angie; that he wanted the Court's charge to justify him.

Sharman droned on—no, the old jurist never droned—through the forms of the possible verdicts (due to Jack's insanity special issues, there were six of them), and arrived, still in reverence over every word, to the closing general instructions.

The jury must not consider the indictment as any evidence of guilt nor discuss it as such; it could consider Ray's police record as bearing on his credibility as a witness but could not regard it for any other purpose. He explained the procedure for communicating with the Court, for obtaining repeats of the testimony. "You shall not, however, contact this Court or anyone else for legal counsel, advice or explanation, or for the interpretation of any matter whatsoever, whether contained or not contained in this charge.

"After the argument of counsel, you will retire to select one of your number as foreman and to consider your verdict. As you find, so say, and write your verdict on a separate piece of paper. When you are unanimously agreed, your foreman shall so certify by signing the verdict, and you shall inform the bailiff that a verdict has been reached.

"If you should find the defendant guilty, beyond a reasonable doubt, and if you should agree by your deliberations that the punishment shall be less than death, you are instructed that you should not and must not attempt to arrive at the punishment to be assessed by a ballot as to the number of years each juror is in favor of assessing and then dividing the total of said preferences by twelve. Nor should you, or can you legally, arrive at agreement by lot, or by chance, or by devising any other means or formula for determining punishment, aside from conscientious deliberation of the law and the facts as given and introduced and not withdrawn from your consideration by the Court.

"You are limited in your deliberations upon a verdict to the consideration and discussion of such facts and circumstances only as were admitted in evidence, or as are reasonably deducible from the evidence, and you cannot legally, and should not, consider or discuss any fact or circumstance not thus in evidence or reasonably deducible therefrom. Neither juror may lawfully relate to any of the other jurors any fact or circumstance of which he may have, or may claim to have, knowledge or information that was not introduced in evidence, nor may any or all of you discuss anything except the evidence introduced by the parties, admitted by the Court and not withdrawn by the Court from the consideration of the jury.

"In this case, as in all criminal cases, the burden of proof is upon the State. The defendant is presumed to be innocent unless and until his guilt is established by legal and competent evidence, beyond a reasonable doubt, and if you have a reasonable doubt of his guilt, this doubt must be resolved in favor of the defendant and you will acquit him and say by your verdict, 'not guilty.'

"You are the exclusive judges of the credibility of the witnesses, of the weight to be given to the evidence, and of the facts proved. But you are bound by your oath and by the law to receive the law of the case from the Court, as it is herein before given in this charge, and insofar as the evidence is concerned, you will be governed thereby."

Sharman read his signature and sank back, slowly, in his chair as if loath to leave these jewels of jurisprudence in the keeping of persons less loving of them than he. He looked down at the attorneys, then out at the crowd, seeking some sign that his splendrous law had thwarted, once again, the black tides of iniquity that forever sucked at the foundations of his bench.

Through a lopsided smile, Jack Singer silently formed the words, "That's good, Jimmie."

The Judge cleared his throat, swept his gaze up to the clock. The charge had taken thirty-two minutes. "Lunch," he said sharply. "We'll resume at one-thirty. Mr. Bailiff—where are you, Mr. Hart? You may have the jury."

XLI

Singer giggled at them as he flounced up from the wheelchair and all but skipped down the stairs. Paulk, with Laura and Angie, followed him to the Little Star. None of them could eat. Mrs. Callahan, humiliated and grieving over her misfire as a witness, humbled by the company, looked at her plate. Laura was detached, gazing at walls, gravely avoiding conversation. Jack rambled on, not quite enthusiastically, about the old days and cases. To Paulk it seemed they all skirted about the thing uppermost in their thoughts. No one mentioned Ray Priest. He was glad when time pressed them back to the courthouse.

He excused himself at sight of Herb Cameron in the rotunda. He accepted Herb's invitation for coffee and they stood together at the concession stand, switching the hot paper cups from hand to hand, reflecting, behaving like men at a wake.

"Funny," the District Attorney scratched the thin honest-blue seat of his pants, "how a guy can kid himself. I didn't fire Anglin when I found out what was going on; told myself I'd wait until it was over, so it wouldn't blow up the case. But this morning, when you passed us that note—it hit me I had decided to let the whole thing ride."

"I'm not proud of that note, believe me."

"We had it coming."

"Wonder," Paulk said, "what happens next?"

"Next I'll make our first argument, in place of Anglin, and I think I'll let that close me out. I've decided to resign, first thing tomorrow."

"I wish you wouldn't. Especially since I've got to go job hunting."

"You're not going back to Kelso's?"

Paulk shook his head. "Dammit, I'm telling you I've got to do something in criminal law."

Herb's good unhappy eyes came up. "You'd take Anglin's job?"

"Yes. If you'd hang in there as the boss."

Awkwardly, aware of how alike they were in youth and need and in yearning toward a clean niche in the affairs of the law, they disposed of the cups and climbed, unspeaking, up the stairs. At the courtroom door, they paused. Paulk held out his hand.

"Make a good speech, Herb," he said. "Tear me apart."

They grinned embarrassedly as they moved, beckoned by the Judge, to join Tigart under the bench. Herb would argue first, then Paulk, and Ike would close. Due to the complexity of the case, the Judge said, he would permit the broader interpretation of the rule that confined the lawyers to "reasonable latitude" in their remarks. "However," he warned, "the moment one of you causes me to regret my leniency, I'll reverse myself." The Judge hauled out a fat old-fashioned watch, its gold cover mounted with a tintype of a young Mrs. Sharman, and while he propped it up atop his *National Geographic,* Paulk agreed that forty-five minutes per man would be enough.

XLII

The District Attorney's detractors complained that whenever he stood to address a jury, he looked ill and, at the same time, too boyishly spright. If ever this had been true, Paulk observed, it wasn't today. Herb approached the jury rail calmly. He rustled a few notes from his pocket, stared Ancil Andricks in the eye and began. His preliminary remarks were brief, with no attempt at humor.

"Ladies and gentlemen, you are this moment's guardians of our common right to peace and order in our affairs. As jurors you are responsible to all communities as much as this one, to all points in time as much as to this hour. You represent a system of justice seven centuries old, one proven by the ages and by the default of every other system ever devised. I grant that for the just, judgement is never easy. But I urge you not to be overwhelmed by the seriousness of your task. You need only to exercise reason and conscience. And in this case, I believe, you'll not find that difficult. The logic is clear and your duty becomes obvious when you behold this deed and this man."

Herb tied into Priest without any visible malice. Baby Ray, he said, was an admitted killer and hijacker, a wanderer, pimp, wife-beater, man of no destination and jack-of-all-evil. "My rearing taught me to search for a spark of good in every human being. But as I regard Ray Priest, his past and his crime, I find nothing that moves me to thoughts of mercy. If we are told he was heroic in war, we are told also that he was a malingerer, recalcitrant and deserter. We are dealing with a man useless at everything except combat, and we must conclude, therefore, that if he excels at anything, it is the bloody business of killing."

Cameron was reclaiming his office. His feet were planted, his voice ringing. Paulk scurried to revamp notes which had taken into account only Ike Tigart.

"But, while sketching this red, white and blue portrait of his client, Mr. Paulk did provide us with the illumination of comparison. Millions of other men returned from our wars have not presented their military records as licenses for depravity. I know of none who would sell his wife in a brothel rather than go to work for a living, none who has chosen a life on the filthy underside of things out of pure love for it, none whose ambition is to pass his years drifting around the country like a bubble of scum. Most, thank God, have declined to exempt themselves from law and morals. . . ."

Closely following the State's testimony, Herb reconstructed the highway meeting—"to which this man brought only two dollars, a wife, and a cold and scheming heart"; then the scene at Cabin 4 the following morning.

"Did he continue to drive that pistol into Mr. Hutcherson's brain after he was dead, did he tie that shirt around his neck, not intending to kill? Did he mutilate the body in defense of himself, or of his wife? Did he not spend Hutch's money in beer halls and flophouses and wherever else such men go to squander the profits of crime? It seems indisputable to me that Ray intended everything that happened, with one exception. That is, he never planned to appear here, to answer to us through this jury."

Singer leaned to Paulk's ear. "Hellfire," he whispered, "when did Herb learn how?"

"The murder of Jess Hutcherson was no small tragedy. But I tell you that during the past seven days, a worse disaster has occurred right here in this courtroom. 'At every word,' the quotation goes, 'a reputation dies.' None of us can say what Mr. Hutcherson's immortality was to have been. But whatever it was, we've seen it slaughtered. As vilely as he assaulted the corpse he now assaults the intangible remains; he dismembers even the memory of Jess Hutcherson like the flesh-merchant he is, because he would have you pass your judgement upon the murdered instead of the murderer. I cannot believe you'll be deceived. I cannot think that by lies and a foul, nefarious cunning this man will elude the end the State of Texas has provided for all of his kind."

Still in even tones, Herb took up his copy of the charge and began correlating the law and the facts to the "reasonable deductions" to which the jury was enjoined. The brutality, the post-mortem orgy of violence and blood, he said, was shown and from it, implied malice was an inescapable deduction. Otherwise, the extra blows, the strangling, must go forever unexplained. On the jury's back row, Mrs. Chesterson looked at Mrs. Billingsley and they nodded.

"Secondly," said Herb, "the State has shown you why he killed. Naturally, this perennial habitué of back streets and dirty shadows did not cooperate by declaring his motive to someone who could appear here as a witness. He wasn't that inept; his long fraternity with punks and cons all across the nation had taught him better than that. But he couldn't help cutting a trail that left us all the signs we need."

Applying common sense to the testimony of Browning and Handy Preston, he built the money incidents into the inadvertent temptation of a penniless road bum. "This defendant, by his own admissions, tells you this temptation was not resisted. He admits that when he and his wife left that cabin, every item that was of value to anyone but Hutch left right along with them. We could offer stronger proof only if Mr. Hutcherson could appear here, only if he could tell you how Priest got the gun and said 'Stick 'em up,' or whatever it is robbers say to their victims."

The jury waited, grim and motionless, as Herb dried his face on his handkerchief. He was holding them, giving form and logic to their disordered conclusions. Paulk fought off the persistent fear that Ray was without a prayer.

"Since this is a trial for murder," Herb continued, "the rules forbid me any argument of all the crimes of that night. Yet I can't help thinking how felony begat felony as this plot unfolded, how each wolf bore its pups, how the evils pyramided until we can never hope to sort them all out. But when we brush aside the smutty fictions rendered up by this cold and remorseless man, we see a chain of dark and unspeakable offenses—"

"I'll object," Paulk said, "to argument of any other—"

"Sustain."

With an apology that won him jury friends, Herb advanced to a recounting of events following the homicide. The discarded trousers, the washing of the blood off his hands, the strangely absent fingerprints, the direction telling the porter to stay away from the cabin, the theft of the gun.

"Why do you suppose Baby Ray wanted the pistol? As a memento, a souvenir of his visit to our city? Whatever you think about this, I am thankful some unwarned highway-patrol officer didn't attempt to apprehend him that night. One good man is enough to mourn. But, out of this high-speed flight, there are two more important considerations. One, Priest ran because he knew he had done wrong and would be pursued; no man flees from a justified act, from the exercise of any privilege that is legally his. Two, every decision he made that night was a shrewd one, the output of a rational mind making its choices on the impulse of guilty knowledge. When you come to estimating this man's intent, when defense counsel tries to convince you this was just a 'heat of sudden passion' killing, remember the undisputed facts of that flight and know, beyond any reasonable doubt, that a guilty knowledge existed."

Resting his thigh against Mr. Funderburg's desk, Herb ran through a comparison of Priest's confession and his later claims from the witness stand. "This confession is a distressing document, chilling to read. But you must read it. This is the defendant's story as given *before* he began searching for a defense. No mention of adultery, of self-defense. Back in March, when these claims, if true, could have spared Ray Priest from prosecution, he said nothing about them. Why, back then, didn't we hear of these scandalous events? The only plausible answer is that he hadn't had time to conceive these fables, his imagination hadn't cranked up to its full potential. Now, which will you believe? The statement I hold in my hand, or the sickening lies he dished up in your faces after weeks of frightened reflection in a jail cell?"

It was deft craftsmanship, a disposal of Paulk's argument before he could make it, so that the State's principal weakness sounded like a strong point. Paulk saw the knowing looks; the jury was eating it with spoons.

After a pause, the District Attorney sailed into an attack on Paulk's plan of defense. He described it as freakish and plural and overdone to the degree that it had become a positive factor for the State. "This isn't to say Mr. Paulk has done too little for his client. To the contrary, he's done about three times too much. Instead of a defense, he has tried to peddle us an array of defenses. He claims the benefit of every excuse for homicide found in the Criminal Code. Any of these—insanity, self-defense, adultery—would be sufficient, if proved, to free Ray Priest. But lo, Mr. Paulk tells you his man is innocent three times over, that if Ray could have killed Jess Hutcherson three times he'd have been excusable in every instance!

"This is new in my experience. Never before have I seen a defender so utterly regardless of right as to claim simultaneously every evasion the law affords. He is saying to you, 'If you can't swallow this self-defense capsule, then try the adultery pill and see if it'll go down. And if this sticks in your throat too, be good sports and try our third pill; see if you can gag down the idea that my poor noble Air Force deserter is insane'!"

Herb turned to look at Priest and shook his head. "As much as I deplore the anguish that has been inflicted on innocents by this defense, I must concede that it was bold. When at last we cornered our killer, he came out fighting. The trouble was, he couldn't foresee the result. There was no precedent for this three-barrelled shotgun, so he had no way of knowing it would misfire, would defeat itself by its own ridiculousness.

"Still, fantastic as it is, the defendant's claims ought to be studied, and I would urge you to do so, and to believe them if you can." He dispensed with the self-defense plea quickly, pointing out that Ray was entirely uncorroborated in it, although he had been free to call his wife, an eyewitness, to support the claim if it had any basis in fact. He described the insanity claim as equally unimpressive.

"The defendant tells you he has headaches, that he was injured in the war. Of course, he was wounded in the legs, not the head, but we weren't supposed to notice that. Together with this, we have allowed Ray to be his own diagnostician. *He* tells you he is insane. Then, to support this brilliant self-analysis, comes Ray's old Air Force buddy who, even though he is a top-kick, hardly convinced me he is competent in psychoanalysis, and from him we hear that Ray has moods.

"Ladies and gentlemen, none of us here can be thought expert on the full-blown pimp personality. But if the self-degraded man was other than moody, I would be surprised. I belong to the school of thought which believes that sunny dispositions shine out only from sunny souls."

Herb did not, however, think Sergeant Blossom's testimony entirely worthless. Blossom had revealed that the Air Force could find no madness in Ray and, unintentionally, had shown the jury the necessity of the death penalty.

"The Sergeant—and bless him for his *esprit de corps*—told us how for a year he tried everything possible to correct Ray Priest, to reform him, to coax him into good citizenship. If this veteran noncom wise in the ways of discipline, this loyal and caring friend, failed the job of rehabilitation and in the end was compelled to surrender Priest to a higher authority, then just what are we going to do with him? Isn't this a man beyond correction, a man who robbed and murdered *after* the Air Force had tried everything it could to reclaim him?

"The pivotal question for you is whether we can excuse a killer as insane merely because he, like the rest of us, sometimes needs an aspirin!" Someone at the rear applauded, halting before officers could locate him. The Judge, white with fury, took it out on Andy Grosscup, then on everyone, before signaling Herb to resume.

"We come now to the ugliest face of this defense. Frankly, when defense counsel began injecting these defamations, I was stunned, but I thought he must have a few shreds of proof in support of them. But I was mistaken. No proof ever came, so that at this moment I'm more shocked than when I heard the first atrocious insinuation.

"How does one reply to a fish story? I think of those who will suffer the rest of their lives because of its telling, who cannot be spared its aftermath, no matter how harshly you may by your verdict rebuke it, and I am ashamed—ashamed to have stood by while such a havoc of slander held sway in a court dedicated to truth and fair play. Still, it has happened, and we must deal with it.

"If you can believe Jess Hutcherson capable of seducing a teen-age girl, can you then imagine him taking her to bed with her husband only a few yards away? Can you accept that, stripped naked and with a naked girl, he would enter the carnal embrace with his door ajar, the lights on? Few men could approach their own wives under such conditions!

"If somehow we assume these things occurred, then we can be sure it wasn't a rape. No struggle, no screams to a husband within easy earshot. If there was a sex relationship, it had to result from an agreement of the parties—and there were three parties present. Under the law, if Ray Priest sold his wife, or if he lent her, or if he gave consent by no means other than inaction, he connived the union and thereby waived his rights under the statute of justifiable homicide."

Returning to Priest's record as a procurer, citing Lily Black's testimony saying Ray wanted his wife to support him with her body, Herb made a complete case for connivance. His voice had risen and was quavering as he said, "There was no indignation in this degenerate. Does Ray Priest respect the sanctity of wedlock? Do you think this man could wander into a bedroom and see his wife working at a trade he taught her and be overcome by the uncontrollable rage contemplated by the statutes?"

Little remained but odds and ends. From his notes, Herb discussed Angie gently, dismissed the small defense point about Ray's lost poundage as "gratifying proof that criminals aren't getting fat in our jail," then dispatched the suspended-sentence application, perhaps more effectively than he realized.

"I doubt this is a case in which you'd simply wag the finger of justice, would vote only a mild admonition. Ought we to say to Ray Priest, 'Naughty-naughty, Baby; it's all right this once, but you mustn't do it again'?"

Suddenly Herb looked tired, and sounded it. "To a District Attorney," he said, "the offense he is prosecuting is always the most terrible he has known. Often, this exaggerates. But I can say it to you about this case and feel certain you agree. Jess Hutcherson is dead because he extended a generous, charitable hand.

"All the TNT Hutch handled in his lifetime was never so dangerous as this man. Hutch survived his high explosives, but he did not survive this defendant. Ray Priest wasn't wearing a red label, nothing warned

Hutch that here was someone capable of repaying kindness with death; death under secret conditions that would afterwards be spun into the sordid fabric of disgrace.

"On *voir dire,* each of you swore to uphold the law as given you by the Court. You said on your oath that you could vote the death penalty if the facts justified it. The time has come for you to remember these pledges. If you would shrink from the thought of the deliberate extinction of a life, then shudder as you reflect upon the death of Jess Hutcherson.

"It is easy, even popular, to say that extreme punishment is cruel. But I tell you that if justice is cruel, it's in the same way that God is cruel when He permits a Hell.

"I've learned that seldom does the man guilty of injustice seek justice for himself. Instead, he comes to court asking his jury to collaborate with him in a second injustice, one that will absolve him of the first. So it is that he pours out perjury, injures the helpless, maligns the unanswering deceased. He cries out for Christian forgiveness, for the mercy he refused another; he rails about the preciousness of life just as if he, himself, had not wantonly destroyed it."

"Two minutes, Mr. Cameron," the Judge said.

"One further word," Herb nodded. He hadn't lost the jury for a second. Had it been Ike or Anglin, Paulk might have been on his feet, meandering about, distracting the listeners through the planned discourtesy routine to trial practice. As it was, he sat amazed. For Herb, the hard fall seemed to have become the cure.

"Ladies and gentlemen, our Penal Code aims at the prevention of crime. Punishment is its first essential. We do not decree that there shall be an eye for an eye, nor do we punish just to maintain some natural or theoretical balance. Legal punishment looks ahead to deter others, to put off all the other Ray Priests who otherwise would prey without fear upon our lives and property. Justice requires that while you forgive in your hearts, you judge by your intellect. When we fail to punish, we shall fail at justice, at law, and at survival. You must understand that the just punishment is the one commensurate with the crime; that only the ultimate penalty can deter the ultimate offense.

"Will you, agreeing with these truths, as you must, dilute the penalty in this case? Can you write a verdict announcing to the world that heartless, cowardly, schematic murder isn't a fatal transgression in Bonita County? I ask you to have the courage of necessity. Ray Priest must not outlive his crime; you and I need not be splashed with the blood of the next good man who is murdered. This man has spurned all decency. By his own free choice, he has condemned himself. Vote death, knowing his condemnation is not yours. And together, when your duty is done, we'll pray for the peace of his soul."

Under his breath Old Jack was swearing. Angie wept into her hands. Priest gazed out over the gallery. Paulk turned away as from the horror of the execution.

It was 2:25 P.M.

XLIII

The defendant bent near him as he started to rise. The slack face was bloodless, but the uninhabited eyes remained set, unafraid. "Sir, while you're talking, reckon you could say something nice, so's they wouldn't think too hard of Patty Sue?" Unable to answer, Paulk looked at Singer. The old man stopped grinning. He was resting his crippled hand on Ray's sleeve as Paulk turned to the jury.

"May it please the Court, members of the jury." He avoided the spot where Herb Cameron had stood. He was nervous, suddenly mistrustful of his notes, wishing that a jury argument, like a speech to the Rotary, could be rehearsed. "I cannot approach the eloquence of the District Attorney, and I'm not equipped for the showmanship soon to be exhibited to you by Mr. Tigart. If I am of any importance here, it is because my voice will be the last one raised on behalf of Ray Priest, a man who wants to live.

"As Mr. Cameron told you, the State of Texas maintains a place of death down at Huntsville; the Legislature says we need it. There's an ugly wooden throne set up in front of a black curtain and facing a small amphitheater. To me the curiosity about this chamber is how disclaimed it seems. It appears to exist unowned, disassociated from everything. There's no symbol to identify it with law or justice, with religion or with ourselves, the people. But, just how would you go about relieving the starkness of such a room? What would be the appropriate adornment? Should an electric chair be engraved with the scales of justice—the great seal of this state—the cross of Christianity —the fork of Satan? Should we paint murals on those blank walls, recreating there a panorama of the wine jugs and cheap women and the passions for gold which have led men to this last hideous rendezvous?

"We hear of last meals and last words and the last mile, of shaved heads and new white shirts and blinking lights, of chaplains praying on through the stench of burning flesh. Our skins crawl, but we do not object. We are only fascinated by the lore of the Chair, because we can credit its horrors to a vague somebody else. I cite you to these grim considerations because, again and again, the State has taken pains to inflame you with the gruesome aspects of this killing. I would have you see that death is always brutal. Do you think the State of Texas can kill Raymond Priest nonbrutally? Can you, as a jury, send him to an electrocution that will be performed innocuously, graciously, politely?"

Partly, he knew, he lectured himself; indicted his own soul for the lapses that now, in the dusk of retrospect, pulsed on his conscience like the countdown of a man's life. The words hurt, yet helped. He steadied while he described the trial as a mismatch pitting a lonely nobody, forsaken even by his wife, against all the resources and might of the State. Priest was himself the stake; winning, he could gain only what he already had. Only the State could lose and still live.

He listed next the special measures that had worsened the odds against Ray Priest—the slush fund, the volunteer officers, the reward, the special police bureau. "It seems to me that the big, mailed fist of Texas, as wielded through the standard procedures, is powerful enough to enforce justice. Why, then, if the State wants simple justice, have we seen all these extra, nonstatutory pressures brought against this one small friendless man?

"There, on the State's side of the table, we see another extra, a special prosecutor. No one has briefed me on why the famous Mr. Tigart is among us. Although he promised to give me some lessons in trial work, and has done so, I don't flatter myself that this was his mission. Whatever the special interest he represents, I've no doubt he has served it well. We've seen him oppose every fact relating to the conduct of Jess Hutcherson that day, and we see him now, standing with both feet on Ray Priest. While this does increase Mr. Tigart's stature by the breadth of one hapless pauper, it scarcely explains why he was needed here. Forgive me if I am inclined to look for something less obvious."

So much for Ike.

"Personally, I have numerous regrets as we close this case. But I do not believe you'd have wanted to decide the life or death of this man on a part-knowledge, on edited facts, on a set of circumstances made false by being left incomplete. The aim of the law is certainty, beyond a reasonable doubt. As jurors you were, and are, entitled to the whole story.

"They accuse me of defaming the deceased, but have I? It does not diminish my respect for Mr. Hutcherson's memory to discover that he was human—a man, not a god. Hutch wasn't the first good man to have a bad day. If, that day, he drank intemperately, if he was suffering the frantic upheavals normal to middle age; if, as a robust man, he was troubled by a new realization of what time had so surreptitiously taken away, shall we feel constrained to revise his epitaph? I think not. We need to judge Jess Hutcherson only to the extent that is essential to the *fair* judgement of this other man who is still alive."

As among his regrets he pointed out the pertinent facts that would go forever unknown. Why wasn't there an autopsy; what might it have shown? Who was the 'Texas stranger'; why had Patty turned against her husband, what had she worn that day, why had she been freed under evidence identical to that prosecuted against Ray? Why had Lily Black brought just one of her letters?

"These matters, and others, show you how deficient our preparation has been. But, thank heaven, our mistakes need not be mortal if you, the jury, can avoid error. This isn't said to frighten you. Rather, I want you to grasp that such facts as we do have are critical; that not one, however unpleasant, can safely be discarded from your deliberations."

He met Andricks' eyes, then Gay's, trying to decide which, if either, could be relied on as a weathervane.

Slowly, making his points stretch across the gaps, he summarized the testimony inconsistent with the State's robbery theory. Hadn't the Priests exhibited themselves freely, signed their correct name? "Would a bandit have brought his victim into the city to rob him when, out there on the highway, he could have undertaken his heist at leisure and in privacy? Do you believe this young man and his tough young wife had to murder a tired, intoxicated elder in order to relieve him of his money?

"The State blusters right past these matters, insisting on its hijacking. I'm unwilling to accuse them of fabrication, of perfidy, of glossing over the truth. But I'm tempted to these terms when they lambaste me for offering three defenses for this man. Let me declare that, against *per*secution under the guise of *pro*secution, I would raise a dozen defenses if I could find them!"

Moderately cheered by Juror Gay's nodded amen, Paulk burrowed through the meagre self-defense evidence, then into the question of insanity. He amassed the testimony, law, and all the Psychology II he could remember into what he hoped was a preponderant showing of mental irresponsibility, capping it off with speculations on Ray's attempted suicide. "When a man's horror of life overwhelms his terror of death, I, for one, am convinced he is insane.

"You cannot weigh this issue merely on the fact of the defendant's headaches, his compulsion to run, his war wounds and intolerance of noises. Consider that he was welcome nowhere, that he was poor, that he was burdened by the enmity of his in-laws and the taunts of a wife constantly threatening to leave him and become a 'hustling woman.' Could you, or I, have endured this boy's lot and retained a hygienic, undeviating mind?

"To offset these reasonable conclusions, the State gives us nothing except the opinion of the sheriff, who never laid eyes on Ray Priest until weeks after the homicide in Cabin 4."

Pausing to drink, he glimpsed Laura, still perched in the window, and he could think of no signal to tell her the sun was making her transparent.

"Ladies and gentlemen, most of the thunder and smoke of this past week has revolved around another issue, one that underlies everything. 'She was my wife,' the defendant tells you, 'not his!' When the first implications of the true motive began to pop up through the State's own witnesses, Mr. Tigart sprang into action. You saw him stamping about as if to tromp out a grass fire, heard him scorching the air with objections. When he could no longer shout it down, he tried ignoring it to see if it would go away. Finally he decided to throw a rug over it, to hide these primary facts under gory repetitions on the unprettiness of death. I think he erred in his estimate of your intelligence.

"It was Robert Browning who wrote, 'Call in law when a neighbor breaks your fence, cribs from your field . . . but woos your wife? No, take the old way trod when men were men.' The verse, like the law, grants the inevitable. Both hold that under the circumstances of a faithless wife and an exploiting interloper, no man can be expected *not* to kill.

"It's remarkable how many quandaries of this case are dissolved once we accept the fact of the adultery. It clarifies for us why Hutch drove right past his own home and continued on six miles to a tourist court, why Patty Priest asked for a two-room cabin, why the deceased allowed the car engine to be shut off there although he knew it wouldn't start again, why he went to bed in the back room, why his body was without clothing."

To illustrate Hutch's sex hunger of that day, Paulk reviewed the second-thought U-turn leading to the presence of a pretty girl in the car, the directive to Ray to drive, the roaming hands, the drinking, the sudden promise to give them lodging and a job. Patty's seductive dance, her kitten sounds and air kisses, then again the lifted skirt and the fondling, the back-seat quarrel, the post-office stop. "You cannot disregard these as the inventions of the defendant. The State's own witnesses told you about them before he did.

"Perhaps you wondered at the start of this trial, as I did, why Ray didn't put an end to these afternoon-long preliminary overtures to his wife. But are you puzzled by it now? Here was an armed man, representing himself to be an officer, firing a pistol out the window of the car, boasting of his marksmanship. If we say this boy ought to have put up a battle the first time Hutch touched his wife, then we are saying he should have dared to match his fists against a .45 automatic. Would you have done so?"

He seemed to be nearing an ordeal, something he had dreaded long before Ray Priest. Although he groped, he could not identify it. He sensed it like a ghost in his breast, begging to be heard yet foreign, unknown, to his thoughts. He struggled to understand. In the momentum of his speech, he ached to communicate a thing familiar to his heart yet never admitted to his mind. There was an eerieness, an inevitability. He grew clammy with it, and hastened on.

". . . a lot of motion that night. Patty Sue, up and down with her comic books, strolling back and forth between the rooms. Ray watching TV, tinkering with the car. Only one of the party stayed put." He continued to the moment when Priest awakened from his nap and saw his wife emerging from the bathroom. He paused, trying to swallow the tremor impressing itself on his voice. "Ray saw his wife, naked as the day she was born, disappear into Hutch's bedroom. He got up, followed her."

Suddenly Paulk heard himself shouting, telling them how it felt

because he knew. He knew it all, if his mind did not. The instant, icy
contraction inside; the disintegrating memory, the trust, the unkissed
kisses, the saved-up dreams and kept confidences, the whole love world
consumed and gone in fire that licked in through his eyes. The shriek-
ing nerves, the man drained out of himself, the poisoned soul screaming
in the emptiness.

"Kill him? Yes, he did kill him, he had to kill him, he *ought* to have
killed him!"

The pain as his fist smashed down on the jury rail might have
brought the groan. He stopped, trembling, staring about—coming
awake from a nightmare. Whatever he'd said, the faces were white
and rapt, the courtroom silent. He seemed to stand before them a great
while, hearing the quiet, before his notes regained their meaning, before he remembered to go on. Somehow it was better now. Easier and
better.

"Members of the jury, there has always been high peril in the bed
of the adulterer, as surely as there is sanctity in the marriage bed, and
who would find fault with a doctrine of law that acknowledges them
both?

"I'm not surprised that Ray couldn't account perfectly for what took
place in those few terrible seconds, that his mind has blotted out as
much of that scene as it could. Nor is it strange to me that a husband
would flee from such a scene, or that this boy who has lived on the
road, who has known the road as a refuge, should fly to the highway
when hurt. Ray is no lawyer, not a man to call the police. But whatever
you may have concluded about these things, I ask you to remember
that we're not trying Ray Priest for flight or for stealing an automobile.
The charge is murder."

He turned to the hazardous connivance question, first raking Tigart
for his ring and pencil exhibition, then granting that the evidence confirmed Patty's voluntary surrender to the deceased. "But how does her
connivance bear on whether this defendant connived that coition? Will
you believe that Ray leased out his wife, as the State will contend
through Mr. Tigart, then changed his mind at the last moment and
killed to nullify the bargain? Oh, I'll stipulate right now that this case
is shot through with connivance, but it's of an altogether different
breed. The connivance is against this man's life."

He charged State's connivance in obtaining the first confession and
in the omissions apparent in the statement that replaced it. He alleged

connivance to bury the adultery, to arrange the Lily Black surprise, to recompense the witnesses, to bypass the autopsy that could have established whether Hutch had had a recent sex experience. "Everything Ray told them in his own favor, even the harmless fact of his medals, fell to the cutting-room floor, and there was no one around to warn him, to tell him they were electrocuting him with a typewriter. We live in a slaughterhouse world, infected with every genre of immorality. But, to my mind, no overt criminal act ranks in degree of evil with the deeds done here; the secret yet official tampering with the truth in order to snuff out a human life."

He mauled them with the Sunday attempt to smuggle a psychiatrist into Ray's cell, then dug at the connivances involving Patty Priest.

"Which of us doubts that Patty has been the State's unseen fount of all knowledge, the hidden spirit and, yes, the chief beneficiary of this prosecution? The record doesn't reconstruct all the terms connived between her and the State. But we know she was indicted on the same evidence presented against her husband, that if this was a robbery murder as they say it was, she is as guilty as he. Nevertheless, she is excused without trial. By affidavit the District Attorney swears the evidence against her is insufficient, and in the next breath he tells you this same evidence is enough to send Ray to the Chair.

"We can't reconcile these opposite positions, but we can see through them. They dismissed the indictment against Patty Priest midway in this trial because they wanted to force me to call this faithless, hostile girl to retell for you the lies by which she had already purchased her escape. Can you fail to recognize this defendant as the scapegoat of a traitorous wife, the whipping boy of Jess Hutcherson's prominence? Who is guilty of connivance?"

It was here that he remembered Priest's entreaty: *say something nice about Patty.*

"I'd not defend Ray Priest by laying off all the seaminess of that night upon his wife, whom he loved then, and loves now. I believe there is always some justification for anyone in any situation, and a childish mentality is hers. We know that she remains addicted to comic books and jukeboxes and sodas, yet has a cynical artisanship when it comes to the appetites of men. At fourteen, we are told, she was physically mature, loitering in bars, available as a common pickup, probably through little fault of her own.

"She was reared in a home where the parents intermittently separated, where the father's idea of constructive correction was simply to lock her out. As to her mother? Well, you've seen Lily Black, a woman who wouldn't drive across town to visit her daughter in the Detention Home but who has travelled a thousand miles to be at Patty's side when the reward is about to be dealt out. When have such parents, or any unfit parents, reared a fit child?

"I must admit to you that I doubt Mrs. Black has been as worthless a mother as her own testimony indicated she was. Sitting there with dollar signs in her eyes, Lily told you she permitted her teen-age daughter to leave home with a man who had announced his intention to make her a prostitute. I don't believe that, and I don't worry that you believed it. No mother alive, not even Lily Black's sort, was ever that uncaring. But this does help us picture Patty's home, it reveals a little of why this child became a booby trap for everyone who happened to meet her.

"When we see a good man, we credit also his wife. But seldom, while beholding the man who has stumbled, do we think to peer behind his failure at his wife. There is nothing rare about the destruction of a man by a capricious woman; it is, indeed, the oldest story. In this defendant we have another of those who have loved unwisely. Maybe Ray should have abandoned her to go her own ruinous way. But it has always been the foible of men that while they may forsake the virtuous woman, they cling to the treacherous one, and Ray is no exception. We can pity him for his marriage, but we cannot censure him for it. If blame must be placed, let's condemn the flame as more vicious than the moth."

He noticed, for whatever it portended, that Judge Sharman had not stayed awake.

"Ray never got much from life. Maybe he got very little when he got Patty Sue. But, out there beside some desolate road, sleeping in a ditch with Patty in his arms, he did at least possess something. Whatever she was, she was his. She belonged to him, not to Jess Hutcherson or anybody else!"

He was throbbing with tiredness, eager to be through.

"Law, it's said, is a magic mirror in which we see the reflection of all lives, including our own. Certainly in this case we can't avoid looking upon our own errors. To some unknown extent, each of us is responsible for the scrounging, unanchored life this boy has lived up to now. As I study this whole affair, I have to wonder if we haven't accidentally established a social wasteland, if we haven't sentenced a few unwanted people to inhabit it. Then I am forced to speculate on just what day in what year this pillar-to-post waif ceased being society's unlucky oversight and became, instead, its wastrel; someone accountable to us for what we, by our neglect, made of him. How do you isolate the particular hour in which a hollow heritage, a mean and unchosen environment, stops being a misfortune and turns into a punishable sin? I fear we can never pinpoint that hour in this man's life, just as we cannot cast back through our own lives and single out that first day on which we were responsible for ourselves and knew it.

"It seems to disturb the prosecution that Ray, a stranger confronting a jury of strangers, isn't kowtowing, hasn't snivelled for mercy. He knows his jeopardy, and God knows he has learned to expect the short end of everything. But he hasn't come fawning at the foot of the bench since he knows, also, that his salvation preceded him here, that it stands inherent in the facts. We've not introduced any emotional apparatus because we're willing to settle for plain dry-eyed justice, strictly by the numbers.

"As citizens we thought Ray Priest was wonderful, back there when he was shooting down Communists for us. Is he changed, suddenly an ogre, because he acted under a legal and moral tenet dearer to every husband than any contention ever raised at war? In his place, would you not have killed?"

He looked at the clock, then along the double row of faces. He wondered if he dared quit. The eyes told him nothing.

"Mr. Tigart will rise shortly to demand that you end this boy's life. He will say a great deal. It isn't likely, however, that he will remind you that if you vote death mistakenly, you'll be unable to restore what you've taken. As you weather him out, do not be browbeaten into believing the execution of Ray Priest would prevent the next killing. I beg you to reject every suggestion that the defendant is a nonentity, so inconsequential that he can be sent to his death to appease public grief or as a sympathy offering to a sorrowing family.

"Jess Hutcherson is dead because of a woman. If you heed the angry voices, a second man will die out of this same act of infidelity. Please— let your verdict strike down this and every other conspiratorial prosecution; do not let it say that the protections of the law exist only for the mighty. Ray Priest's rights must be preserved if we are to save the rights we cherish for ourselves. His right, irrespective of how lowly, or lonely, he is, is to live."

Paulk staggered back to his chair. Too long, he thought. Too preachy, too loud, too trite, too thin. Although Jack Singer was holding up his hand, neither of them smiled.

XLIV

He could not bear the prospect of sitting Ike out. As the special prosecutor, his shirttail blousing dissolutely, moved up to the rail, Paulk turned to Jack Singer. "Will you muzzle him for me, if he needs it?"

"Sure," the old man nodded. "Go on, buy yourself a couple of tall cool ones."

Too bushed to excuse himself with Priest or Angie, he walked out. Looking at no one, he went across to the Little Star. Without thought he turned left, toward the booth that had been his and Jerry's. Laura was there, her tranquil gray eyes watching him as she lighted a cigarette. He sat down, and the red-haired waitress brought them coffee without being told.

"Were you expecting me?"

"I don't know," Laura said. "Maybe." She handed him her cigarette, fished out another for herself. "What did Dad think of your argument?"

"I didn't ask him."

"I thought you were marvelous." Her eyes held his. "Especially that one part, where you—well, when you told them how Ray must have felt at what he saw."

He said nothing.

"You feel very close to Priest, don't you?"

"I guess," he said. "Poor guy needs somebody."

She turned aside to gaze out at the street, quite as Jerry once had when it was feared a client might slip away. With the sun on her face, her Mexico tan lightened and was golden. She said, "Wen, have you thought how many people in this case have gone through exactly what you described? Besides Ray, there's Martha Hutcherson, and others."

He said, "Like Anglin's wife, if she knows."

"Also me," Laura said. "Yes, me. It's the reason I divorced Buddy. Then, there's—"

"Me," he said.

Her lips trembled. "I don't think many people noticed it. But right at the height of it, when you meant to say Patty, you said something else."

"All right," he said, conscious of nothing except his weariness, "is this when we talk about Jerry?"

"If you want."

"No, it's you that wants it. Very well. Yes, I know Jerry didn't go to your party that night, that she was out on the highway to meet someone. I knew about it the night she died, and it came back to me again today. I haven't known it in between. I am aware, now, that you and Jack have known it all along." He saw her tears, but wasn't softened. "There, does that satisfy you?"

"No. I keep thinking, so many of us, hurt just the same way. What does it mean?"

"I don't give a damn what it means."

They sat unspeaking, stalemated. Whatever had begun ebbing from him with the start of the case was all gone; nothing had seeped back to replace it. He seemed to have purged himself too finally. There wasn't even a curiosity about Jerry's man, whoever he was. He waited while Laura set off a fresh cigarette. Then, his voice husky, frayed by the long summation, he sought to break the moment into smaller pieces. He said, "I don't think the Hutchersons were there today."

"They weren't. They're very busy."

"I was afraid I'd have to talk before all four of them."

She shook her head. "They've a bigger problem now. I didn't think you needed to hear of it until you were finished. Valle is lost."

"Laura, say what you mean."

"She has disappeared. Sometime yesterday, it seems."

"Are the police helping?"

"They've broadcast a description, but mostly, I think, they're leaving it up to the family. Charles left for East Texas to see if she turns up there, where they have some relatives. Jess Junior got a man from a detective agency and they took off someplace together, I'm not sure where. Not many people know this. They're trying not to have any more publicity."

"I did this."

"No, Wen, Mr. Hutcherson did it. Valle almost said so, in her note. She wrote it the night before—Saturday night. It was odd and, from what Martha felt able to tell me, I think it was—well, partly obscene. There was something about being the kind of girl 'the boss' admired; other irrational things, all in such a jumble that they're worried she's lost her mind. Since she had no money, they're afraid she hitchhiked out of town, might have fallen in with anybody—"

His fingertips were numb, senseless to the heat of his cup. Two for two, he thought. First a crippled gas-station attendant, now a shy, big-eyed child.

"Pay for the coffee, will you?"

He hurried out, past the rundown fronts of Houston Street, on past the Federal Building and along the broken sidewalks to the dead end that was the Rock Island depot. He suppressed the absurd notion to buy a ticket on any train to anyplace, and sat on one of the hard benches of the waiting room, glaring at people who somehow helped by not staring back. A half-hour passed before he went back to the courthouse.

Tigart seemed to have come to the tail end of his argument. The reverberant boom of his big voice filled the rotunda as Paulk crossed it and climbed the stairs. On the court floor, the sound was a deafening barrage. Paulk waited for a comparative lull, then slipped into the courtroom. "How is he doing?" he asked Jack Singer.

"Brimstone," the old man shrugged.

Ike cocked a fist above his head. "This 'boy,' as he is so charitably alluded to by his hired rationalizer, is a pimp, thief, plunderer of corpses; not a tender sprout too young for pruning. Was this crime a prank, the petty mischief of a misunderstood child? Consider him as he sits here, the butcherer of his benefactor, still bold, still fish-eyed and defiant. I've never seen such arrogance in a killer. It's as if he expects you to reward him with a medal, to say by your verdict that Jess Hutcherson, the greatest spirit and heart ever known in our town, was a faker, was in fact a lecher and drunkard who got only what was coming to him!"

The fist circled, then cracked down on the reporter's desk. "Listen, members of the jury! Can you hesitate to vote death? Oh, our idealistic Mr. Paulk—who, I see, has just deigned to rejoin us—pleads that the Chair is no deterrent to murder. I've no conception of how he came by this all-encompassing knowledge, how he has become competent to fathom just how many murders we'd be having in our state if the Death House wasn't there. Maybe, despite his youth and inexperience, he knows. But I'm surer of what I know, and that is that electrocution will keep this murderer from murdering again!

"Put angel's wings on this defendant if you think he can wear them. Turn him loose if you think this trial has rehabilitated him, if you think that while dissecting the memory of Jess Hutcherson to save himself, he has shown that he is too high-minded to rob and kill somebody else. No, you ain't swallering such hogwash any more than I am. You can't forget the death penalty that was meted out by this man. Unilaterally, barbarically, he tried and judged and executed Hutch right there on the spot. He didn't pause to hear Hutch's plea, to hunt out mitigation from Hutch's childhood, to see if he had any medals or if he wanted to call his lawyer. No, this 'unfortunate waif' just wiped process aside and cleaned up Hutch's case in seconds, in the time it took to bash in his head.

"Beware, ladies and gentlemen. This killer is, himself, the harbinger of the kind of law we'll live by if juries weaken, if verdicts become squeamish and milksopped. Unless you punish, we'll get the kind of justice Ray Priest gave Jess Hutcherson. We'll surrender to rule by anarchy, by vendetta, and we can all return to our breechclouts and spears and launch the new age of blood and terror and atrocity.

"We aren't here to squeeze the sponge of pity over this man's head just because he has holes in his socks or a ribbon on his chest. We're here sworn to the safekeeping of each other, to the law's due course and purposes. We've held our noses for a week while we listened to every foul libel he cared to utter. Now it's time to let go and breathe deep, to track down the source of the rot; it's time to send this debauched black soul on to Hell! Yes, to Hell, where it can keep company with its own corrupt kind. Do it, my friends, and be remembered as true men and true women unshirking of your duty."

In the post-concussion still, Judge Sharman's last instruction sounded wan. "Be sure to take all the exhibits with you. All right, Mr. Bailiff, you may take the jury out."

Because he, like everyone, attached a vague significance to the time a jury used, Paulk marked the hour on his watch. It was nineteen minutes before five.

XLV

The deputies hustled Priest away to wait in jail. Some of the Possemen and shop girls trailed away in pairs, but others lingered on the
off chance of a quick verdict. Paulk saw the Singers to the elevator
and off for home. About him he overheard whispered estimates, of-
fers to wager. The old lady with the bulging knitting bag cornered him
to exhibit her work. Since the case had dragged on so long, she said,
her doily for the winner had grown until it was now one-half of an
afghan. If he won, would he want her to complete it? Would he buy
the rest of the yarn, and did he think it fair for her to ask five dollars
a day to compensate her for fingers made plumb sore by the needles?

He edged clear, toward the district attorney's end of the corridor.
Herb and Tigart stood there, the big man still rocking a little in the
rhythm of his speech. "Good boy, Wen," Ike put out his hand. "You
made it rough." Paulk took the grip, liking it. After the fight friendship
returned, and it was good to slip into it as if drawing on a comfortable
old garment.

For a time he stood with the prosecutors, gazing as they did at the
stairs up to the jury room. They shared a temptation and each of them
knew it. For years, trial lawyers had been eavesdropping on Bonita
County juries. It was simply done. Nathan Hart's office was inset into
the main jury room and partitioned off with thin sheetrock. The jury
voices carried clearly into him. To keep matters in perspective, the
lawyers would take turns at dropping in on Nathan, would stay just
long enough for one game of checkers. Presently the three of them
waited on each other to suggest who should go up first. Before there
was a nomination, they saw Uncle Nathan hurrying down the stairs.
He trotted to the nearest elevator. Then, seeing the anxiety of them,
he turned and came back, smiling.

Ike said, "Have you got them settled already?"

Hart's eyes twinkled. "Truth is," he glanced furtively at the crowd,
"I'm going out to get them a cake."

"A cake?" Herb said.

"Yep, and some candles. Thirty candles!"

"Oh my God," Tigart groaned. "Willie Studer's birthday, isn't it?"

The bailiff grinned. "One of the ladies said it wouldn't be right to

319

start work before Willie had a party. I've got to shag—" He sped away, leaving them to stare stupidly at each other. All the hard evidence, the gleaming points of law, the ferocity of the arguments, a man sitting up in jail sweating out seconds, his life up for grabs. And the jury was tuning up to sing Happy Birthday!

"Thirty candles," Tigart muttered. "That does it. In honor of the occasion, they're apt to let him off with thirty years."

At dusk, long after Nathan carried a large white bakery box upstairs, the courthouse quieted. A majority of the hangers-on relinquished the idea of an immediate verdict and went home to supper. Mrs. Tigart telephoned and shortly thereafter, Ike departed, grouching that he wasn't in the mood to barbecue, swearing against the new world and togetherness. (As a boy, he said, he had eaten in the house and gone to the yard when he needed the biffy. Now, thanks to Mrs. Tigart, this logical arrangement was exactly reversed.) After going upstairs for one game with Uncle Nathan, Herb decided to pick up a sandwich and go on to his Naval Reserve meeting. Left alone, Paulk wished he hadn't declined Laura's offer to wait with him; at least, not so brusquely.

At seven, Nathan went out for a roll of Tums.

Paulk thought of Valle Hutcherson and strolled the halls.

On the ground floor, standing before Andy Grosscup's office and looking out, he was surprised to see the stars. The evening rush was over, the streets released from police signalmen, and the courthouse lawn lamps were burning. He was quibbling with himself, asking his mind to tell him what verdict he wanted, what verdict he deserved and whether they were the same, when The Shepherd appeared from the sheriff's office with a tall and toothless harlot on his arm.

"Hey, Wen, I want to see you." To the woman, Shep said, "Okay, honey, that's all there is to it and you can go on home. Be sure you get the money to me by Thursday and I'll take care of the fine." He guided her out the door, then clapped Paulk on the back. "Boy, terrific speech you made today. Made me proud of you. Hell, I don't think I'd mind now if they let him off, whatever it cost me. 'Course, they ain't in no shape to do that—"

"How's your client?"

"Patty? Aw, she's got her back up about Hollis. Friction is hard on me, son; I ain't young as I was. Which was sort of on my mind when I called you downtown yesterday. I was thinking, 'Old Wen wouldn't go back to Kelso, not after all this, so maybe he'd like to come in with me.'" The Shepherd grinned. "Don't get spooked. I knew better, the minute you walked in. So I went ahead and got me a partner."

Paulk cued him dully. "Have you?"

"Yeah, and guess who. I hate his guts, but he can work with my clients, and he's available—Hollis Anglin." He laughed, whacking Paulk's back again. "Care for a bite of supper, boy?"

It was five minutes past eight when Nathan Hart dashed down to the sheriff's office to make his phone calls. Judge Sharman arrived at eight-thirty, frowning, looking handsome and august despite a startling white straw hat which was set too square on his head with its brim flipped up jauntily in front. Herb hurried in wearing his lieutenant-commander's uniform; then came Tigart, smelling of hickory smoke, his shirt collar open and disclosing the wiry red and gray hair snarled on his chest. The courtroom was shadowy, yellow under light from the dusty chandeliers which were thought more jurisprudential than the fluorescents. Somehow, word that the jury was knocking had flown through town and the pews were filling. In the pit people paced in slow motion.

Angie came in panting, hesitating at the door, undecided between the gallery and her seat at the counsel table, until Paulk beckoned to her. Mr. Durfee limped in, puffing out gusts of the Little Star's garlic, and he made his rounds with an air of knowing and a kingly compassion for those who did not. The Judge adjusted a fresh collar as two of Grosscup's cowboys brought Ray Priest from the elevator. The Shepherd was last to arrive.

"I think we're all here, Mr. Bailiff. You may bring in the jury."

Paulk crossed and recrossed his legs and listened for the jury's tread on the stairs. He heard Angie whisper his name, but he did not turn to her, or to Ray Priest. There was no assurance to give them. Why not thirty years, he thought, or prayed; let it be that, or no worse.

The jury came single file, led by Uncle Nathan, followed by Mrs. McCormick; they shuffled, not to step on each other's heels, and their shoes squeaked on the undried wax already laid by the night janitors. As they moved into the box, Paulk kept his eye on Ancil Andricks. The homely face was stern, the wild hair doused flat and dripping. Sure enough, he continued on to the end and stopped at the foreman's chair.

A million words ago, Paulk had yearned for this. Now, as it happened, it meant nothing.

The jurors remained standing until each had found his place. Then, as if they'd rehearsed it, they sat down together.

The Judge thumped his docket book. "You in the audience—let me remind you we'll have no demonstration here, not of any sort." He seemed to consider expanding the warning, then swung aside to the jury. "Ladies and gentlemen of the jury, have you reached a verdict?"

Andricks got to his feet. He drew a paper from his breast pocket. "We have, Your Honor."

"Hand it to the bailiff, if you please."

Hart passed the slip of ruled tablet paper up to the bench. Sharman held it before him, in sight of all, and scowled at Theodore Holcomb. The clerk, late, scurried for his desk without having remembered to remove his hat. The Judge winced, but said nothing. Then, with Holcomb at his station, he unfolded Ray Priest's reckoning.

The Judge examined it, looking at both sides. His expression told them nothing. The lines deepened, the mouth twitched with the same sad consternation with which he had received every verdict, good or bad, through all his presiding years.

"Mr. Foreman, this is your verdict, on which you are unanimously agreed?"

"Yes, sir; it is."

"And so say you all?"

The jury heads bobbed in unison.

The Judge passed the paper to Holcomb. "The clerk will read the verdict."

Theodore stood to wring the most from his function. His voice snagged on a falsetto. He cleared his throat rendingly, cocked about to catch the best of the light, and began again.

"We, the jury, find the defendant, Raymond Elliot Priest, not guilty."

Not guilty!

In the first instant, quiet. In the next, pandemonium. Tigart was up, shouting that the jury must be polled. The mass, the trial aficionados, roared up. Gradually Paulk realized they were whistling, cheering, sobbing in relief for the man they might recently have lynched. The Judge pounded furiously, cried out for the sheriff and for order. Angie

Callahan wept and laughed, her arms closed about her brother's head. Suddenly she was being embraced by strangers, smothered with God-bless-you's. Reporters beseiged the counsel table. Photographers broke barrier, streamed in from the hall and shot the room full of lightning. The aisles flowed forward. Paulk heard his name shouted. He could only stare through the milieu at the jury.

Andricks was smiling. J. N. Gay winked; Willie Studer cringed under Tigart's hot glare. The women were wiping tears, laughing with Angie.

How could it have happened? Had Gay actually voted his stunted body against the height of the sheriff and Ike Tigart? What of Studer? Overwhelmed by the cake party, compromised by it? What of the women? Mellowed by do-gooderness, or mother instinct, or female contempt of Patty Priest? Prison instead of the Chair was one thing, acquittal another. Had a juror resented Ike's plug of tobacco, disliked how he gestured with the gun, been offended by some wisecrack during the pit quarrels? Did some one of them nurture a hidden rebelliousness against the general adulation of Jess Hutcherson? Only a quirk, something unplanned, could account for it. Paulk couldn't think that Priest's testimony, uncorroborated, had been so convincing, or that his argument had spilled forth with such power.

He massaged his cramping thighs and wondered why he wasn't up, shouting with the rest.

With the courtroom restored to partial order, the jury poll began. Holcomb read the verdict to each juror, asked him to state if it was his own, and recorded the twelve peculiarly meek affirmations. In five minutes, it was finished. The commotion threatened again, and the Judge rapped it down.

"Mr. Sheriff," he said, "do I understand that you have a federal hold order outstanding on this man?"

"Yes, Judge, we do. The marshal's office wants him on Dyer Act—"

"You needn't favor us with the particulars," Sharman cut him off acidly. "All right, Raymond Priest, you are discharged from the custody of this court." He pulled at his chin, his gaze scouring out every corner of the jury box, before he went on.

"Members of the jury, it's customary for the Court to thank you for your service. I do thank you. However, I feel I should state that no verdict in my experience has shocked me as much as this one. I hope I am mistaken, hope that my apprehensions are ungrounded. Still, I cannot congratulate you because I cannot feel that your finding is in harmony with the law and the evidence. I realize that the more dramatic claims were produced by the defense, but I supposed you would see that the proof was introduced by the State. Whatever you acted upon as the determining factor, I would ask you to reevaluate it at your leisure. Individually, you should second-guess yourself; ought to discover whether you think sentiment is entitled to priority over the law. If you do so, you may hold sterner values the next time you are summoned to service here. You're dismissed."

Without a word to signal adjournment, he left the bench and the courtroom.

Paulk thought, Ray was obliged to stand and receive the verdict, and nobody had remembered to see to it. Over his shoulder he said, "Now, go shake hands with your jurors." Priest marched stoically, lifelessly to the box and held up his hand. Paulk watched, until Angie kissed his cheek.

"Thank you," she said. "Oh, God bless you, Mr. Paulk. We will try to pay you something, honestly."

He said, "Tell Ray I'll see him in jail after a bit."

He pushed out past the *Tribune*'s Mr. Davenport and clusters of people who grinned and reached for him. If winning felt so rotten, what would losing have been? He rounded the elevator corner, bumped into someone, then glimpsed the husky Marine an instant before the blow took him. Hazily he remembered that Charles Hutcherson was supposed to be away, searching for Valle. Then, through a buzzing painless addlement he saw that he was down, encircled by shoes and shins; that Jack Singer's old briefcase was on his stomach, that flashbulbs were exploding. . . .

XLVI

Priest said, "Who clobbered you, Mr. Polk?"

"Never mind, let's finish our business so I can go home."

"To tell you the truth, ain't much I can do. Me and Angie, we figured you wasn't going to press me about the money, not till—"

"I'm not speaking of that. First, I've spoken to the sheriff, and he tells me Patty doesn't want to see you. He also says he wouldn't permit it if she did."

They faced each other across O'Brien's desk. The rest of the jail, shaded blue and orange under the night lights, was tucked in. The runarounds droned with snoring, with the sighs and gasps of prisoners gone free or erotic in their dreams. Overhead, the blades of an exhaust fan rattled. To Paulk, gazing at the blank zero eyes that should have been jubilant, the noise was the sound of his own falling-apart.

"Don't seem right, now that I ain't guilty. Since you're my lawyer, couldn't you rig up a paper or something?"

"That's over, Ray. The federal court will appoint you an attorney to see you the rest of the way. But get it through your head, no one can help you much over there. We've made a record that convicts you of driving a stolen car across state lines. You'll have to plead guilty or, at least, go in *nolo contendere*. So you better be prepared to take a jolt of about five years, which is what I've been trying to tell you."

Priest popped his knuckles. "Appears to me a man could draw his own personal lawyer, especially when them feds is looking down his throat."

Paulk shook his head. "I'm not your personal property. Further, I'm not as good as you think. You might as well know that I could have put you in the Chair when I let Mrs. Hutcherson go, not to mention a few other softheaded blunders. You were lucky; the jury called all the close ones in your favor."

"It don't make no difference to me, about that stuff. They turned me aloose, that's all I know." Priest blinked, just once, and licked his lips. He was threshing about with his gratitude, hunting a course to its expression. After a minute he said, "I think you done real good. I'd as leave not do no federal time, but it beats riding Ole Sparky over a few lousy bucks."

Perhaps he was too battered, too spent, to react. It seemed so until he discovered he had hauled Priest halfway across the desk and was shaking him.

"Well, goddam, Mr. Polk—"

"Did you rob him?"

"I was trying to tell you, some things sort of keep coming back to me—if you'd get your hands off...."

Paulk sat listening, swimming with nausea. The office sweltered, the jail smells stung his vision. Priest spoke ramblingly, and tufts of foam formed in the corners of his mouth. As he finished, Paulk could see nothing except the wide moronic eyes.

"Then you—you did plan to rob him?"

"Well, not exactly plan. What I said was, I was thinking it over, the shape we was in, that's all. I didn't know what Patty was doing, since we wasn't speaking, not after that dance she done, we wasn't."

"I want this straight," Paulk said. "Patty had agreed to go to bed with Hutch for fifty dollars, and you didn't know it. And you were thinking of 'rolling' him when he was drunk enough, and she didn't know that?"

"Yes, sir, that's about it."

"When did you find out about her deal?"

"When we was high-tailing it, in the Cadillac."

"Would you have robbed him, if Patty's bargain hadn't gotten in the way?"

"To tell you the truth, I don't know; I never stole nothing in my life—"

"You did take his money, afterwards."

"Well, it was Patty Sue gathered it up. I didn't say nothing about it, since he was dead. He didn't need it no more."

"I suppose, now, you remember about that shirt?"

Priest swallowed. "My wife put that on him. They was so much blood, she figured maybe that would stop it, not leave such a mess. She told me about it, after we was in the car."

"Maybe you knew what Patty was up to, during all that wrestling with Hutch before you got to town?"

"Well, I dunno. She never carried on like that before, not in front of me, leastaways. I didn't know what she aimed to do, not till I walked in on 'em."

Paulk's fists were locked shut; it seemed he'd have to bang them open. He said, "All right, Ray—I want the truth. If you had known in advance what Patty intended to do, would you have consented?"

"No, sir! I'd 've argued with her. I'd done told her that feller in Los Angeles was the last one, that we wasn't going to operate that way anymore!"

Paulk groaned, got up, fled. By the time he reached his car, he was anesthetized, feelingless. The initiation was complete. There was only the problem of cauterizing the wounds. Suddenly, he laughed. Not at himself, but at the striking simplicity of the answers he'd never expected to have. For instance, the long enigma about what Patty had been wearing that day.

"One of them California play dresses," Priest had said. "You know, where there's shorts, with a skirt that goes on over them?"

XLVII

Drive fussily, he lectured himself. With kid gloves, on tiptoe, and stop-look-and-listen. No need to wind up a shackled DWI answering to old Judge Grubbs. Not when every drop he could hold left him un-phased, sharp minded, with the bolts of thought zipping about like shooting stars. The "boss," "hustling woman"—how easily it added up. A job to do, and an impetuous glee toward doing it. Which meant the truce was unmade because he hadn't made it; never would be, be-cause he never could.

He parked inaccurately, raced up to the apartment, stripped and beat himself through a cold shower. He shaved, then packed a suitcase unused since college. He shivered, enjoying the night breeze on his skin as he dialed the Singers'.

"Wen!" Laura said. "Where have you been; it's two o'clock. Dad was about to call the police."

"I'm fine, except for a knot on the jaw. Listen, I think Valle Hutch-erson is in Denver. I'm leaving now. Will you go with me?"

"To Denver? Now, tonight?"

"Yes."

"Let me check with Jack. He just gave up and went to bed."

Waiting, he wondered if Laura could have hit upon the meaning of Valle's note; if she, or her father, remembered the Saturday testi-mony and, from it, understood. The child wanted to be Hutch's kind of girl. Thank God, Valle, unlike Patty Sue, could never pass for a woman.

"Wen?"

"What took you so long?"

"Oh, instructions, instructions; you know Pop. He wanted to know who else was going, said he hoped no one, which would increase my chances of being compromised."

He said, "No one else. Jerry won't be along."

"Good," her voice was low, serious. "Are you hungover, Wen?"

"No. I've just had a difficult withdrawal."

"I'll be ready in ten minutes. Oh, wait, Jack is yelling at me . . . all right. Wen, he says tell you there aren't any supermen practicing law. Just good lawyers."

ABOUT THE AUTHOR

Al Dewlen was born in Memphis, Texas, and except for a forty-five-month stint in the Marine Corps and three years spent at the University of Oklahoma, in Norman, has lived all his life in his native state. In 1945, when he left the Marine Corps, he returned to his home town and became a reporter for the local newspaper. Thereafter, he worked on the Amarillo *News* and *Times,* and for the United Press in Dallas. But in 1952 he decided to devote himself full time to free-lance writing and enrolled in the Professional Writing School at Norman, Oklahoma.

His first writing success, the sale of a short story to *The Saturday Evening Post,* was soon followed by the publication of other stories and articles and by two novels, *The Night of the Tiger* in 1956, and *The Bone Pickers* in 1958.

Mr. Dewlen lives with his wife Jean and their son Mike in Amarillo, Texas.